## "I have never

He was dismayed,
difficult than he h
by your originality
it. "But others mig

"Are you trying to be amusing?" She was incredulous. "Do you know how many fine ladies in Kingston sneer at me on the public roads? In church, they refuse to share my pew. One fancy sort actually crossed the road so my person would not offend her. And they talk about me – loudly – so I know exactly what they are thinking. I am trash. No one in my mother's house is going to think anything else – or in your home, either."

He just stared, aching for her. "You are not trash. You are a hundred times stronger, braver and more beautiful than all of your detractors. But you are right about one thing. No one at Belford House will be enchanted by your candour or your skill with a sword. We need to plan your introduction to your mother with great care, Amanda. You must learn the basic social graces – how to walk, how to speak, how to dine. And of course, you must know how to dance."

**Praise for *New York Times* bestselling author BRENDA JOYCE**

"There are no limits to the passion and power of a Brenda Joyce novel. With her full-blooded characters, her page-turning prose and her remarkable creativity, Brenda Joyce is a force of nature. Her books are so intensely satisfying, you never want them to end."
—*New York Times* bestselling author Lisa Kleypas

"…dances on slippered felt, belying its heft with spellbinding dips, spins and twists. Jane Austen aficionados will delve happily into heroine Elizabeth 'Lizzie' Fitzgerald's family…Joyce's tale of the dangers and delights of passion fulfilled will enchant those who like their reads long and rich."
—*Publisher's Weekly* on *The Masquerade*

**A Lady at Last**

"The latest from Joyce offers readers a passionate, swashbuckling voyage in her newest addition to the de Warenne dynasty series. Joyce brings her keen sense of humour and storytelling prowess to bear on her witty, fully formed characters."
—*Publishers Weekly*

"The latest in the de Warenne series is a warm, wonderfully sensual feast about the joys and pains following in love. Joyce breathes life into extraordinary characters – from her sprightly Cinderella heroine and roguish hero to everyone in between – then sets them in the glittering Regency, where anything can happen."
—*Romantic Times BOOKreviews*

# A LADY AT LAST

## Brenda Joyce

MILLS & BOON®
*Pure reading pleasure*

*First published in Great Britain 2008*
*by Harlequin Mills & Boon Limited,*
*Eton House, 18-24 Paradise Road, Richmond, Surrey TW9 1SR*



*ISBN: 978 0 263 86563 9*

*037-0408*

*Harlequin Mills & Boon policy is to use papers that are natural, renewable and recyclable products and made from wood grown in sustainable forests. The logging and manufacturing processes conform to the legal environmental regulations of the country of origin.*

*Printed and bound in Spain*
*by Litografia Rosés S.A., Barcelona*

**Brenda Joyce** is the bestselling author of more than thirty novels and novellas. She wrote her first novella when she was sixteen years old and her first novel when she was twenty-five – and was published shortly thereafter. She has won many awards and her first novel, *Innocent Fire*, won the Best Western Romance Award. She has also won the highly coveted Best Historical Romance award for *Splendor* and the Lifetime Achievement Award from *Romantic Times*. She is the author of the critically acclaimed DEADLY series, which is set in turn-of-the-century New York and features amateur sleuth Francesca Cahill. There are over eleven million copies of her novels in print and she is published in over a dozen countries. A native New Yorker, she now lives in southern Arizona with her husband, son, dogs, cat and numerous Arabian and half-Arabian reining horses. For more information about Brenda and her upcoming novels, please visit her website at www.brendajoyce.com

*Also available from Mills & Boon® and*
***BRENDA JOYCE***

DEADLY ILLUSIONS
DEADLY KISSES
THE MASQUERADE

To my sister, Jamie, without whom this story would not have been possible. Her life inspired the life of Amanda. If only she'd had a hero to rescue her! But I know she's laughing at me now, incredulous that her older sister is such a foolish romantic still. I guess it is silly…
Jamie, this one belongs to you.

# *CHAPTER ONE*

*King's House; June 20, 1820*

HE WAS renowned as the greatest gentleman privateer of his era, an accolade that amused him no end. *Gentleman* and *privateer* were two words that should never be uttered in the same sentence, even if he was an exception to that rule. Cliff de Warenne, third and youngest son of the earl of Adare, stared at the newly constructed hanging block, unsmiling. While it was true that he had yet to lose a battle or his quarry, he did not take death lightly. He estimated that he had already used up at least six lives, and hoped he had at least three left.

A hanging always brought out the biggest crowd. Every rogue and planter, every lady and whore, were flocking into the city to watch the pirate hang. Tomorrow they would be breathless with anticipation and excitement. There would be applause when the pirate's neck was broken with a loud, jarring snap. There would be cheers.

A tall, towering man with tawny, too-long, sun-streaked hair and a bronze complexion, Cliff had the brilliant blue eyes the de Warenne men were famous for. He was clad casually in high boots, pale white doeskin breeches and a fine linen shirt, but he was heavily armed. Even in polite society he kept a dagger in his belt, a stiletto in his boot, for he had gained his fortune the hard way, and he had made his share of enemies. Besides, in the islands, he had no time for fashion.

Cliff realized that he was late for his appointment with the colonial governor. But several fashionably dressed ladies were just entering the square, one a gorgeous beauty. They glanced his way, whispering excitedly. He saw that they were on their way to the scaffolding to inspect the site of tomorrow's hanging. Under usual circumstances, he would mark one for his bed, but he could scent their bloodlust and he was frankly disgusted by it.

The imposing entrance of King's House was directly behind him as he watched the three women stroll to the hanging block. The incessant fascination of the elegant ladies of the ton and island society was convenient; like all the de Warenne men, he was very virile. He recognized the blond, the wife of a gentleman planter he knew well, but the dark beauty was undoubtedly new to the island. She smiled at him, clearly aware of who and what he was, and as clearly offering him her services, should he wish to accept them.

He did not. He nodded politely at her and she held his gaze before turning away. He was a nobleman and a legitimate merchantman, when he was not accepting letters of marque, but, the whispers of "rogue" and "rover" wafted after him anyway. He had even been called a pirate by one particularly passionate lover. The truth was, even having been raised a gentleman, he was more at home in Spanishtown than Dublin, in Kingston than London, and he made no secret of it. When he was on the deck of his ship in the midst of the hunt, no man could possibly be a gentleman. Gentility meant death.

But he had never cared about the whispers. He had made his life into exactly what he wished, without his father's helping hand, and he had earned his reputation as one of the greatest masters of the sea. Although he always yearned for Ireland, the loveliest place in the world, it was on the main that he was free. Even at the earl's estate, surrounded by the family he cherished, he was aware that he was not at all like his two brothers—the heir and the spare. Compared to his land-and-duty-bound brothers, he was very much a buccaneer. Society accused him of being different, an eccentric and an outsider, and they were right.

Just before Cliff turned to enter King's House, two more ladies met with the trio, the crowd in the square growing. A gentleman whom he recognized as a successful Kingston merchant had joined the ladies, as had a few sailors.

"Hope he's enjoyin' his last meal," one of the sailors laughed.

"Is it true he slit the throat of an English naval officer?" one of the women gasped. "And painted his cabin with the blood?"

"It's an old pirate tradition," the sailor replied, grinning.

Cliff rolled his eyes at the absurd accusation.

"Do they hang many pirates here?" the beauty asked breathlessly.

Cliff turned away. The hanging was going to be a circus, he thought grimly.

And the irony of it all was that Rodney Carre was one of the least menacing and most unsuccessful rovers at sea; he would hang because Governor Woods was determined to set an example any way that he could. Carre's crimes were pitiful in comparison to those of the ruthless Cuban rovers now raging in the Caribbean, but Carre was the one inept enough to have been caught.

He knew the man, but not well. Carre was frequently in Kingston Harbor to careen his ship or unload his goods, and Cliff's island home, Windsong, was on the northwest end of Harbor Street. They'd exchanged only a few dozen words in the past dozen years, and usually merely nodded at one another in passing. He had no real reason to be dismayed over Carre's fate.

"And the pirate's daughter?" one of the women asked excitedly. "Will they hang her, too?"

"La Sauvage?" The gentleman spoke. "She hasn't been captured. And beside, I don't think anyone on this island would accuse her of a crime."

Cliff realized why he was so disturbed. Carre was leaving behind a daughter. She was too young to be charged with piracy, even if she had sailed with her father.

It was not really his affair, he thought grimly as he turned back to King's House. Yet he recalled her vividly now, for he had glimpsed her from time to time, riding the waves like a porpoise in nothing but a chemise or standing boldly in the bow of her canoe, recklessly defying the wind and the sea. They had never met, but like everyone else on the island, he knew her instantly upon a single glimpse. She seemed to run wild about the island beaches and on the city streets and was impossible to miss with her long, tangled moon-colored hair. She was wild and free and he had admired her from a distance for years.

Uneasy, he shifted his thoughts. He would not even be in Spanishtown tomorrow when Carre was hanged. Instead, he wondered at Woods's summons. They were friends—they had frequently worked together on island policy and even on legislation, and in Woods's term of office, Cliff had accepted two commissions from him, successfully capturing the foreign brigands. Woods was a resolute politician and governor and Cliff respected him. On one or two occasions, they had caroused together, as well—Woods was fond of the ladies, too, when his wife was not in residence.

Two British soldiers sprang forward as he strode past the six Ionic columns that supported a pediment displaying the British coat of arms to the huge doors of the governor's residence, the gold and ruby spurs he wore jangling. "Captain de Warenne, sir," one said, relaxing. "Governor Woods said you are to go in immediately."

Cliff nodded at him and entered a vast foyer with a crystal chandelier. Standing on the waxed parquet floors of the circular entry, he could glimpse a formal salon done up in red velvets and brocades.

Thomas Woods rose from behind a desk, smiling as he saw him. "Cliff! Come in, my good man, come in!"

Cliff strode into the salon, shaking Woods's hand. The governor was a lean, handsome man in his thirties, with a dark moustache. "Good day, Thomas. I see the hanging will happen as scheduled." The words slipped out, unbidden.

Woods nodded, pleased. "You have been gone for almost three months—you have no idea what this means."

"Of course I do," Cliff said, that odd tension filling him again as he wondered at the pirate's daughter's future. It crossed his mind that maybe he would visit Carre at the garrison in Port Royal. "Does Carre remain at Fort Charles?"

"He has been moved to the courthouse jail," Woods responded. The newly constructed courthouse, completed the previous year, was directly across the square from King's House. Woods went to the bar built into the huge Dutch sideboard on one wall and poured two glasses of wine. He handed Cliff a glass. "To the morrow's hanging, Cliff."

Cliff did not join him in the toast. "Maybe you should attempt to capture the pirates flying the flag of José Artigas," he said, referring to the gaucho general who was at war with both Portugal and Spain. "Rodney Carre has nothing in common with those murdering villains, my friend."

Woods smiled firmly. "Ah, I was hoping you could tackle Artigas's men."

Cliff was interested, as the hunt was in his blood. Woods was offering him a dangerous commission, one he would not usually think twice about accepting. However, he remained on another tack. "Carre has never been foolish enough to attack British interests," he commented, taking a sip of claret.

Woods started. "So he is a decent pirate? A *good* pirate? And what is the point of your defense? He has been tried and found guilty, he hangs tomorrow at noon."

An image came to mind, one he could not chase away. Her hair as pale as a bright star, her shirt and breeches soaking wet, La Sauvage lifted her slim arms overhead and dived off the bow of her father's sloop into the sea below. He had been coming home last year and standing on the quarterdeck of his favorite frigate, the *Fair Lady,* when he had spotted her through his spyglass. He had paused to watch her surface, laughing, and had almost wished he could dive into the calm turquoise sea with her.

"What about the child?" he heard himself say. He had no idea of her age, but she was small and slender and he guessed she was somewhere between twelve and fourteen.

Woods seemed startled. "Carre's daughter—La Sauvage?"

"I heard their farm was forfeit to the Crown. What will become of her?"

"Good God, Cliff, I do not know. Rumor has it she has family in England. Maybe she will go there. Or I suppose she could go to the Sisters of St. Anne's in Seville—they have an asylum for the orphaned."

Cliff was shocked. He just could not imagine a spirit like that imprisoned in such a manner. And this was the first he had heard of the child having family in Britain. But then, Carre had once been a British naval officer, so it was certainly possible.

Woods stared. "You are behaving oddly, my friend. I asked you to come here today because I was hoping you would accept a commission from me."

Cliff shoved his thoughts of Carre's daughter aside. He felt himself smile. "May I hope that you seek El Toreador?" he asked, referring to the most vicious of the rovers plaguing the area.

Woods grinned. "You may."

"I am more than pleased to accept the commission," Cliff said, meaning it. The hunt would surely erase his irascible mood and the restlessness gnawing at him. He had been at Windsong for precisely three weeks—usually he stayed a month or two—and his only regret would be leaving his children. He had both a son and a daughter at his island home, and when he was at sea or abroad, he missed them terribly.

"Shall we go in to dine? I have asked my chef to make your favorite dishes," Woods said happily, clasping Cliff's arm. "We can discuss the details of the commission. I am also eager to ask for your opinions on the new venture in the East Indies. Surely you have heard of the Phelps company?"

Cliff was about to affirm that he had, when he heard the soldiers at the governor's front door shouting in alarm. Instantly he drew his saber. "Get back," he ordered Woods.

The governor paled, a small pistol appearing in his hand, but he obeyed, hurrying to the far end of the salon while Cliff strode into the foyer. He heard a soldier gasping in pain, and another fellow shout, "You cannot go inside!"

The front door burst open and a small, slender woman with a mass of pale hair ran through it, waving a pistol.

"Where is the governor?" she demanded wildly, pointing the gun at him.

The most vivid green eyes he had ever beheld locked with his and he forgot that a pistol was pointed at his forehead. He stared, shocked. La Sauvage was not a child: she was a young woman and a very beautiful young woman, at that. Her face was triangular, her cheekbones high, her nose small and straight, her mouth lush and full. But it was her eyes that stunned him—he had never seen such intriguing eyes, as exotic as a jungle cat's.

His gaze swept down her figure. Her moon-colored hair was exactly as he had thought—a wild curly mane that reached her waist. She wore a huge man's shirt, hanging to midthigh, but there was no mistaking the suggestion of a bosom beneath it. Her legs were encased in breeches and a lad's boots, and were unmistakably long and feminine.

How could he have assumed, even from a distance, that she was a child, he wondered inanely.

"Are you a dimwit?" she shouted at him. "Where is Woods?"

He drew a breath and somehow smiled, his composure

returned. "Miss Carre, please do not point the pistol at me. Is it loaded?" he asked very calmly.

She paled as if just recognizing him. "*De Warenne*." She swallowed. The pistol wavered. "Woods. I must see Woods."

So she knew him, somewhat. Then she knew he was not to be toyed with. Did she know that anyone else would die for brandishing a weapon at him in such a manner? Was she that brave, or that foolish—and desperate? His smile intensified, but he was not feeling amused. He had to swiftly end the crisis, before she was hurt or arrested. "Give me the pistol, Miss Carre."

She shook her head. "Where is he?"

He sighed—and moved. Before she knew it, he had her wrist in his hand, and an instant later, he had her pistol.

Tears filled her eyes and he knew they were tears of rage. "Damn you!" She struck at him with both fists, pummeling his chest.

He handed the pistol to one of the wary soldiers and caught her wrists again, more gently, not wanting to hurt her. He was surprised by her strength; she was so slender she appeared frail, but she was not. However, she had no power compared to him. "Please, cease. You will hurt yourself," he said softly.

She was writhing in his grasp like a wildcat, hissing and spitting like one, too, and even attempting to claw at his face.

"Stop," he ordered, becoming annoyed. "You cannot triumph over me."

Suddenly her eyes met his and she stilled, panting heavily. And as their gaze held, he felt a stirring of compassion for her. Even if she was eighteen, he sensed she was a child in many ways, due to her unorthodox upbringing. And now he recognized more than desperation in her eyes; he saw her fear.

Tomorrow, her father would hang. Today, she thought to accost the governor. "Surely you do not think to *murder* my friend Woods?"

"I would if I could," she spat at him. "But no, I will delay his murder for another day!" She began to struggle uselessly again. "I have come to beg him for mercy for my father."

His heart seemed to break. "If I release you, will you be still? I can arrange an audience with the governor."

Hope flared in her eyes. She nodded, wetting her lips. "Yes."

He hesitated, confused by his odd emotions. It wasn't appropriate, but he wondered how old she was. Of course, he was not interested in her, not that way. How could he be? She was too young, and she was a pirate's daughter. His last mistress had been a Hapsburg princess, acclaimed to be the greatest beauty on the Continent. His daughter's mother, who was deceased, had been an exotic and beautiful concubine, enslaved in the harem of a Barbary prince. Rachel had been a Jewess, highly educated and one of the most intelligent women he had ever met. He was very discriminating when it came to the ladies who shared his bed. He could not be interested in a wild-eyed waif brandishing a pistol the way other women carried parasols.

She was regarding him with a very neutral expression now. His instincts sharpened. "You will behave." It wasn't a question.

Her mouth formed a small, unenthusiastic smile.

Now he was alarmed. Was she hiding another weapon, perhaps beneath that voluminous shirt? While she was not a lady, he did not feel comfortable searching her. "Miss Carre, give me your word that you will behave in a courteous and respectful manner while in the governor's house."

She gave him a puzzled look, as if she did not understand a word he had said, but she nodded.

He briefly touched her arm, in the hopes of guiding her toward the salon, but she flinched and he did not attempt to touch her again. "Thomas? Would you mind stepping out? I should like to introduce you to Miss Carre."

Woods strode forward to the threshold of the salon. He was grim, his color now high. "A mere waif got by my guards?" He was disbelieving.

Cliff recognized his rising temper. "She is worried about her father, and rightly so. I promised her you would allow her to speak."

Woods seemed about to refuse. "She assaulted my men! Robards, are you harmed in any manner?"

The British soldier remained alert and stiffly at attention in the foyer, his fellow officer inside the house by the front door. He was flushed. "No, sir. Governor, I apologize for the terrible intrusion."

"How did she manage to get past you?" Woods was incredulous.

Robards's high color increased. "Sir, I don't know—"

"I asked them to help me find my little lost puppy dog," La Sauvage said, her tone absurdly coy, and she batted her lashes at Governor Woods. Then she swung her hips from side to side and shed a tear. "They were *soo* concerned!"

Cliff stared, quickly reassessing La Sauvage. She had known how to use her considerable female allure to entrap the soldiers. She wasn't as innocent, then, as she appeared.

Woods turned a cold regard on her. "Arrest her."

She gasped, and whirled to gaze at Cliff with shock. The surprise became accusation as the soldiers stepped toward her. "You promised!"

He stepped in front of her, blocking the two soldiers and preventing them from seizing her. "Do not," he warned very softly. His tone was one he only used when he intended to follow it up with a very dire consequence.

Both soldiers froze.

"Cliff! She assaulted my men!" Woods objected.

She turned to face the governor. "And you are hanging my father!" she shouted furiously.

Cliff took her arm, intending to restrain her if need be, but also aware of the urge to protect her. "Thomas, you owe me more than one favor, if I recall. I am collecting now. Hear her out."

Woods stared, dismayed. “Damn it, de Warenne,” he said, very low. “Why are you doing this?”

“Hear her out,” Cliff said even more softly. It was a command.

Woods’s expression filled with distaste. He gestured for La Sauvage to precede him into the salon.

She shook her head, her beautiful green eyes narrowing shrewdly. “You first.” She smiled coldly. “I never walk ahead of my enemies.”

Silently, Cliff applauded her. He worried again, however, that she might be concealing more weapons.

Woods sighed. “Robards, you may wait where you are. Johns, please return to your post outside of the front door.” As both soldiers obeyed, he strode grimly into the salon.

La Sauvage was about to follow, but Cliff had seen her hide a smile and he seized her arm. “Hey! What do you think you’re doing?” she demanded.

Very softly, so Woods could not hear, he murmured, “You are unarmed, are you not?”

She stared into his eyes. “Am I a fool? Of course I’m not armed.”

She did not blink, not once. Her cheeks did not color. Her gaze did not waver. Yet he knew, without a doubt, that she was lying.

His grip tightened. She began to protest, trying to pull back, but he restrained her. “I beg your pardon,” he said grimly, aware that he was flushing. With his free hand, over her shirt, he touched her waist, expecting to find another pistol strapped inside her shirt there. Instead, he was stunned at how narrow her waist was, with no flesh to spare. He could probably close both of his hands around her, if he tried.

“Get your paws off me,” she gasped, outraged.

He ignored her, sliding his hand to the small of her back and trying not to think about drifting it lower. She started to struggle. “Lecher!”

"Be still," he growled, feeling the other side of her waist.

"Are you happy now?" she demanded, remaining scarlet but wriggling impossibly.

"You are making this difficult," he said, and then he stopped. Something was strapped beneath her shirt on the left side of her waist.

She started to pull against him.

He gave her a look, slid his hand under her shirt and over the sharp edge of the dagger taped to her ribs.

"Damn you!" she hissed, attempting to twist away.

To his shock, the heavy underside of a full and bare breast bumped into his hand as he seized the knife.

She went still and so did he.

"Bastard!" She pulled free.

He tried to breathe, but he was aroused. Beneath that loose, oversize shirt was an intriguing body, one that belonged to a mature woman. He slid her dagger into his belt. It was a moment before he could speak. "You lied."

She gave him a furious look and marched after Woods into the salon.

He hoped she did not have another dagger taped somewhere else, perhaps on her hip or her thigh. He could not understand his response to her body, so slim in some places and far too soft in others. He'd had hundreds of beautiful, alluring women. He allowed himself desire when the moment was appropriate or when it suited him. He was not a green boy and he could control his lust. He did not want to feel any stirrings, now or ever, for La Sauvage. But his body had betrayed him.

He was very displeased.

He strode into the salon, leaving the door open. The governor had chosen to sit in a huge armchair, so that he appeared more royalty than royally appointed. He indicated that she might speak, the gesture abrupt and somehow disrespectful.

Cliff didn't care for his manner. Clearly, Woods had made

up his mind and nothing La Sauvage could say or do would change it.

But she began to cry, tears running down her breathtaking face. He knew the tears were contrived, born of her fear and desperation.

"Give her a genuine opportunity to speak," he said to Woods.

"I do not need this," Woods groused. He was angry.

"Please," she whispered, the sound soft and feminine, a plea, and she clasped her hands as if in prayer before her chest. The gesture drew her shirt tight, revealing the shape of her surprisingly lush bosom. Cliff stared, instantly distracted, and so did Woods, apparently not oblivious to her allure, either.

"My lord, my father is all I've got. He is a good man, sir, a good father. He's not really a pirate, you know. He's a planter, and you can go to Belle Mer to see for yourself. We have one of our best crops in years!"

"I think we both know he has committed numerous acts of piracy," Woods said sternly.

Tears streaked her lovely face and she sank to her knees. Cliff tensed. Her face was level with the governor's lap. Did she know how provocative her position was? "He has never been a pirate, you are wrong, sir! The jury was wrong! He has been a privateer. He has worked for Britain, hunting pirates—just like Captain de Warenne. If you will pardon him, he will never sail again, ever."

"Miss Carre, please get up. We both know your father has nothing in common with Lord de Warenne."

She didn't move. Her full, lush mouth began to tremble. Even had she been standing, it was so provocative it would have been impossible to ignore. But she was on her knees, as if a skilled whore before a paying client. Woods was staring at her mouth. His face had become taut, his dark eyes turning black.

Cliff did not like what was happening.

"I can't lose him," she whispered throatily. "If you pardon him, he will obey the law like a saint. And I…." she stopped, licking her lips, "I will be so grateful, sir, forever grateful, no matter what…you ask me…to do."

Wood's eyes were wide, but he did not move.

*She would prostitute herself for her father?* Cliff seized her arm, hauling her to her feet. "I believe that's enough."

She turned a murderous glare on him. "No one wants you here! Leave me be! I am talking to the governor! Go mind your own affairs!"

"Propositioning him, is more like it," Cliff said, feeling quite furious himself. He yanked her once. "Be quiet." He faced Woods. "Thomas, why not pardon Carre? If his daughter is being truthful, he will give up his roving. If not, I promise you I will bring him in myself."

Woods slowly stood. He briefly glanced at Cliff but then his gaze returned to La Sauvage. Although she stood straight and tall, she was trembling. "I am going to consider your proposal, Miss Carre."

Her eyes widened. So did Cliff's. "You are?"

"I intend to spend the night doing so." He paused, allowing his words to sink in.

And Cliff was livid, for he understood.

But La Sauvage was not as experienced as either of the men, and it took her a moment. Then she drew herself up straighter. She was red-faced. "Can I wait here, then, for your decision?"

"Of course." He finally smiled at her.

Cliff stepped in front of him. "And to think I have thought of you as a friend," he said tersely.

Woods raised both brows. "I am certain you would avail yourself of such an opportunity, as well. Now you defend her *virtue?*" He was amused.

It seemed that was what he was doing. "May I assume Mrs. Woods remains in London?"

"She is actually in France." He was not perturbed. "Come, Cliff, do calm down. We shall adjourn to our delayed luncheon, while Miss Carre rests and awaits my decision."

"I'm sorry, I have lost my appetite." He turned to La Sauvage. "Let's go."

She was standing there, appearing very young and very grim—and very resolute. She might have been on the way to the gallows. She shook her head. "I am staying."

"Like hell," he said softly and dangerously.

And the tears filled her eyes—real tears. "Go away, de Warenne. Leave me be."

Cliff fought with himself. Why did he care? She seemed young, but she couldn't possibly be innocent, not having lived the kind of life she had. He wasn't her protector.

"You heard the…lady," Woods said softly. "She won't be hurt, Cliff. In fact, she might be pleased."

He was blinded by a kind of rage he hadn't ever experienced. Images danced in his mind. Woods embracing La Sauvage, Woods ruthlessly availing himself of her slender, yet lush body. He fought to breathe, and when he could speak, he looked at the governor. "Don't do this."

"Why? She's a beauty, even if her odor is offensive."

She smelled of the sea and Cliff did not find it offensive at all. "She is expecting a pardon."

"And you are her champion?" Woods was amused.

"I wish to champion no one," he said sharply.

"Stop talking about me as if I am not here," she cried to them both.

Cliff slowly faced her. "Come with me," he said. "You do not need to do this."

She stared at him, as white as a sheet. "I need to free my father."

"Then get a written contract—your services for his pardon." He was terse.

She seemed puzzled. "I can't read."

He made a harsh sound and faced the governor. "Will you be able to live with yourself afterward?"

He shook his head. "Good God, Cliff, she's a pirate's daughter."

Cliff turned back to her but she refused to look at him, her arms folded across her chest. He was furious with her, with Woods, and even with himself. He stalked out, leaving them to their lurid affair.

Outside, the clouds were gathering, a fresh breeze of almost twenty knots coming onshore. Spanishtown was a dozen miles from the coast, and he had come by coach, not the river, but he knew that the waves had swells and it would be a good day for sailing. In fact, just then he wished to race the wind, running full sail before it.

His temples throbbed. Now he wished to run away? He rubbed his forehead grimly. La Sauvage was not his concern.

But she hadn't understood, for she was naive in so many ways. She thought to buy her father's amnesty with her body, but Woods was going to use her and then hang her father anyway.

Jamaica was his home. And although he only spent a few months of the year there, he was one of the island's leading citizens and very little happened on the island without his consent. Had he been present during Carre's capture, he would have made sure his case never came to trial. But it had, and the news had been reported not just in the *Jamaican Royal Times* but on most of the other islands, too. Even the American newspapers had reported the pirate's conviction. It was too late now to stop the hanging.

And Woods was a strong governor. There had been a few better, there had been many worse. Cliff supported his new policy of attempting to quell the Cuban rovers. No matter what happened now, he needed to remain on good terms with him. They had too many interests in common.

*I am begging you, sir, begging you not to take my father from me. He's a good man, a good father, and he's all I have in the world!*

She was not going to save her father, and certainly not in Woods's bed. Cliff turned, staring at the imposing front doors beneath the white temple pediment of King's House. By damn, he had to act.

He strode back to the house. "I'm afraid I have need of the governor again."

Robards was chagrined. "I'm sorry, Captain. The Governor is not to be disturbed this afternoon."

Cliff was in disbelief, but only for a moment. "This cannot wait." Unconsciously his tone had become soft and so very warning.

The young soldier flushed. "Sir, I am sorry…" he began.

Cliff put his hand on the hilt of his scabbard. He gave Robards a look and stepped past him, pushing open the front door. The silence of the house wrapped itself around him and he knew they were together. His heart raced. He knew all the principal rooms were on the ground floor, as was the governor's private suite. As Woods had decided not to allow La Sauvage an afternoon's respite, he doubted they were in a guest room. No, he had taken La Sauvage to his rooms. Cliff was certain.

Robards had followed him to the threshold of the foyer. "Sir! Please!"

Cliff smiled mirthlessly at him and kicked the door closed in his face. Then he locked it. He strode down the hall, the calm of that moment before a fierce battle settling over him. It was a feeling he relished. The lull before the explosion…

The house remained stunningly quiet. As he traversed its depths, he could imagine them naked, hot, entwined, Woods overcome with lust. His silent rage grew.

He had never been to the governor's private rooms, but King's House had been built fifty-odd years earlier and he assumed the suite was in the west wing, as it was in so many Georgian homes.

He tried four doors as he went down the west hall, all opening onto unoccupied guest rooms. And when he came to the door at the end, he heard soft male laughter.

His blood surged and thickened.

He turned the knob and pushed open the door.

Instantly, he saw them.

Woods stood in the center of the bedroom, a massive canopied bed behind him. He had shed his jacket, waistcoat and shirt, revealing a muscular torso. His trousers were open, revealing his manhood.

She stood by the bed, clad in a man's sapphire-blue silk dressing gown, but it was unbelted and open, revealing her lean golden thighs, soft belly and full breasts. Her expression was one of despair, but it was also fierce and determined. She would not stand down.

Cliff prayed he was not too late.

He strode to Woods, who was so preoccupied with his victim that he did not see him until Cliff raised his fist. Woods cried out but Cliff knocked him backward into the wall, the blow so stunning he slid down it into a heap, as if unconscious.

He stepped over him, reaching for his hair, yanking his head back. Dazed eyes met his. "Society would love this bit of gossip, don't you think?" he snarled. The threat was impulsive but ideal; Woods had a reputation to maintain, and his wife would be livid should she ever learn of his scandalous behavior.

"We are…friends!" Woods gasped.

"Not anymore." Cliff had to fight himself not to hit him again. Then he heard her choke.

He whirled, hurrying to her. She was on all fours, fighting for composure. He knelt, sliding his arm around her, terribly aware of her exposed body and also aware that Woods had probably used her in the most despicable and disrespectful manner possible. Slowly she looked up at him, her green cat eyes huge and hurt and beseeching.

He hoped that what he thought had happened hadn't. "I'm taking you out of here," he said softly.

She shook her head, shocking him. "Leave me…be," she whispered brokenly.

He wanted to kill his onetime friend; he cradled her face in his hands. "Listen to me!" he said urgently. "He is not going to pardon your father no matter what you do, or how many times you do it! Do you comprehend me?"

"But it's the only chance I have to save him," she gasped.

He realized her mouth was bruised. He lifted her into his arms and was surprised again, because she clung. Now there was no mistaking the fact that he wanted to protect her, but he was also aware of her open robe and her soft breasts, pressed to his chest. He had glimpsed the wet treasure between her thighs. "There was never a chance," he said roughly, carrying her from the room.

In the hall he paused, suddenly realizing that soldiers were outside the front door, and he had just assaulted the royal governor. They'd have to make a hasty retreat through a window—and he would have quite a bit of political maneuvering to do in the days that followed. Woods might not be a friend anymore, but they needed to work together if he was to remain a viable and influential resident of the island. Suddenly he realized his burden was oddly still.

He looked at her.

She looked up at him, her hands remaining looped around his neck. She was blushing.

His gaze veered to her beautiful breasts, then lower to her slender torso, her rib cage faintly delineated, her small pink navel and the champagne-colored delta below. Buccaneer or not, he was a gentleman, and he jerked his gaze to her face, feeling his own cheeks warm. With one hand, awkwardly, he tugged the wrapper somewhat closed. "How badly did he hurt you?" he asked roughly.

"Can you put me down?" she asked instead of replying.

Instantly he complied.

She smiled at him, and kicked him very hard in the shin. And then she pushed at him and started to run.

Stunned, he reached for her, but she was agile, swift and determined. She ducked his grasp and raced down the hall, her wrapper flowing behind her nude body like a banner. He started after her more slowly, unhappily aware of a terrible turmoil in him. He almost wished he had not gotten involved, for he sensed this was just the beginning. And when he reached the entry, no one was there.

La Sauvage was gone.

## *CHAPTER TWO*

AMANDA RAN THROUGH A pair of terrace doors and across the patio. King's House took up an entire city block and was built around two courtyards; she rushed down a set of white stone steps and into the gardens there. She stumbled, didn't care and fell to her knees. She began retching. But she hadn't been able to eat in days, she was so sick with fear for her father, and her heaves were dry. Then she lay on the thick, damp grass, allowing herself the luxury of tears.

Her terror overcame her. Papa was going to hang tomorrow at noon. Confronting the governor and begging him for a pardon had been their last chance. She hadn't intended to offer him her body, but when he had started to look at her the way sailors and riffraff did, she had instinctively known what she must do. How often had she seen a woman coyly seduce her father in order to win a brooch or a bolt of silk? There was only one way a woman could ever gain anything from a man and Amanda knew what that way was. She had been raised amongst sailors and thieves and the only women she knew well had been camp followers and whores. The world she had been raised in was founded on violence and sex.

But she hadn't given her body over to Woods, because Cliff de Warenne had stopped her from doing so.

She inhaled, her heart lurching. Why had he intervened? He was the greatest privateer of the day, as rich and powerful as a king. No one could outcommand him on the main—even Papa had said so. And he was reputed to be equally dangerous on land…

*Papa.* Her heart was already grieving and she reminded herself that Papa wasn't dead yet. But the grief and the fear had combined, as potent as opium, a drug she had once been given before Papa had realized what was happening. She sat, tugging her robe more securely closed. Rodney had slit the throat of the buccaneer who had thought to drug her and seduce her, right before Amanda's eyes. He had protected her from the men who had wanted her, when he had been present to do so, and he had taught her how to defend herself with a sword, pistol and dagger, so she could protect herself when he was not there. His cruises often lasted months on end, and he'd leave her with enough stores so she would not go hungry, at least not if he returned on time. He was a good father and now she had failed him, when he was the mainstay of her life. This one single time, a time of life or death, she had let her papa down.

Her mind scrambled and raced, looking for another way to save Rodney. She had dismissed the notion of trying to break her father out of prison some time ago. Most of the crew had been killed in battle with the English officer who had captured the *Amanda C,* and the remaining crew was also in prison, awaiting their moments at the gallows.

If she couldn't forcibly free him, should she go back inside to Woods?

She was ready to vomit again. She had impulsively meant to do what all women did in a crisis, but God, she was repulsed and sickened by what had almost happened. While she had witnessed just about every sexual act possible—or so she assumed—she had never been touched sexually. She had never even been kissed. Rodney Carre had made it clear that any man who dared to do so would have his throat slit and his manhood tossed to the sharks in the sea.

*De Warenne had saved her.*

Amanda hugged her knees to her chest, no longer able to avoid where her thoughts really wanted to go. She was stunned by his selfless behavior. Why had he intervened? Everyone she knew behaved sensibly and selfishly—it was the law of survival. Strangers did not help one another. Why would they? The world was too dangerous to dare to reach out. So why had he saved her from Governor Woods?

Her heart wouldn't stay still. She swallowed, remembering. For he had looked at her, too, even more boldly and brightly than any sailor had ever done.

As upset as she was, her heart started to beat with frantic haste. Bewildered, she clasped her cheeks, which were hot. He had looked at her naked body, but he had also looked at her the moment she had come into King's House, when all her clothes were still on. She couldn't ever recall anyone, man or woman, looking at her with such intense and piercing eyes. It was a look which she was never going to forget and she wished she could understand it.

She knew him, of course. Who didn't? He was instantly remarkable, standing upon the quarterdeck of her favorite ship, his thirty-eight gun frigate, the *Fair Lady*. A huge, towering man with that leonine head of hair, he was impossible to miss. And everyone knew he'd captured forty-two pirates in his short, ten-year career as a privateer. In the West Indies, no one had yet to surpass his record.

Amanda's heart continued to beat erratically. She was uneasy and confused. Why had a man like that helped her? He was far more than a privateer. While she'd heard the fancy snooty ladies in town giggling that he was more pirate than gentleman, they couldn't be more wrong. Pirates were foul, with stinking breath and missing teeth and unclean body parts. Pirates gave no quarter in combat, spilling blood and guts everywhere, although when sworn to loyalty, no better friend could be found. Pirates wore dirty clothes, never washing them, and frequented the ugliest hags and whores.

De Warenne smelled like the sea, mixed with spices from some Far Eastern shore and mango from the island. Although he wore a gold earring in one ear like some pirates did, and those huge gold and ruby spurs, his clothes were spotless. Everyone knew the mother of one of his bastards was a real princess. His reputation as a ladies' man was vast, but his lovers weren't whores and hags, oh no, just the opposite. And why not? He was an earl's son. De Warenne was *royalty*.

And even she, who had never looked at a man in any kind of admiration—except for her father, of course—had to admit that he was achingly beautiful.

Amanda knew she blushed. Too well, she could recall being in de Warenne's arms as he had carried her from the governor's rooms. But why was she thinking about that—or him? She had to free her father before he was hanged.

Amanda realized she had no further options. If she couldn't forcibly break her father out of prison and she couldn't seduce Woods into a pardon, then what could she do?

She choked. What had de Warenne said, exactly?

*Why not pardon Carre? If he doesn't give up his pirating, I promise you I will be the one to bring him in.*

Amanda leaped to her feet. He could help her—he had to!

WINDSONG LOOMED over Kingston Harbor, a huge and formal white stone mansion that Cliff had begun building five years earlier and had finally completed last year. Balustraded terraces jutted out over the harbor at the back of the house, while in the front a double staircase led to another terrace and the imposing white marble front entrance. Identical end pavilions were on the other side of the main house, which was a lofty three stories high. He could stand on the north parapet and look up the entire length of King Street, but he preferred to stand on the south terrace, sipping his best Irish whiskey and watching the incoming ships. He stood there now, having requested a drink from his majordomo, but his gaze was directed toward Port Royal, not out to sea. There he could make out the brick walls of Fort Charles. He raised his spyglasses.

The *Amanda C* was at anchor there, her rigging slashed, all masts broken, cannon holes in her deck. She was a small nine-gun sloop, once swift enough to outrun most naval vessels, now damaged beyond repair. She wasn't flying the skull and bones of a pirate's death flag, but the British tricolor.

Cliff lowered the spyglass. He did not want to brood over Carre's fate or his daughter. Carre was in Spanishtown, awaiting his execution on the morrow. He wished he knew where La Sauvage was. She'd fled so quickly she might have been a vanishing ghost.

He could still recall the feel of her firm but soft body in his arms, even though he damned well wished to forget it.

"Papa! Papa!"

Upon hearing the happy cry of his beloved daughter, Cliff turned, beaming, all thoughts of the wild child-woman gone. Ariella was only six years old, with huge and brilliant blue eyes, an olive complexion and surprisingly golden hair. She was as beautiful as her coloring was exotic, and whenever Cliff looked at her he felt no small amount of awe that this stunning child was his. "Come, sweetheart."

But she had already dashed across the terrace and into his arms. He laughed, lifting her high and then hugging her tightly. She was clad like a little English princess in the finest silk gown his money could buy, a strand of perfect pearls around her small throat. He put her down and she asked, "Did you go sailing today, Papa?" She was very grave. "Because you promised me that you would take me when you next set sail."

He had to smile. She could pretend all she wanted, but he knew very well that she did not like sailing. "I haven't forgotten, darling. And no, I did not take a sail. I had affairs in Spanishtown."

"Good affairs?"

His smile faltered. "It was some nasty business, actually." He tugged on a strand of her hair. "It was a good day for sailing. How many knots do we have?"

She hesitated, biting her lip. "Ten?"

He sighed. "Eight, darling, but you were close." He knew she had blindly guessed.

"Do I have to be able to rate the breeze to sail with you?"

"No, you don't, your brother can do that. Besides, I shouldn't be trying to make a sailor out of you." Ariella showed no particular fondness for the sea, although she tolerated it in order to spend time with Cliff. His son was just the opposite. But he wasn't very disappointed, because she had the most inquisitive mind he had ever come across. In fact, she could spend an entire day with her nose buried in a book, and he didn't know whether to be proud or worried about that. "Soon, sweetheart, you will travel the world with your father."

"But only me, not Alexi. He is not coming with us." She pouted.

He shook his head, amused by her jealousy. "He is your brother, darling, of course he will come. He is a natural born seaman. He will help me sail my ship and navigate for us."

Ariella beamed. "I have memorized the four new constellations you taught me, Papa. It will be a good night to view the stars. Can I show you later?"

"Absolutely." His daughter was brilliant. At only six years of age, she could add and subtract faster than he could, was proficient at multiplication and was beginning division. He had begun to teach her the constellations, and her ability to discern the different stars amazed him. In fact, in a matter of minutes, she could memorize just about anything she could see. She was fluent in Latin and would soon be fluent in French. She was several levels ahead of her older brother in reading.

He finally glanced toward the house where her governess

stood, a slender figure so heavily veiled that her face could not be seen, her body entirely wrapped in orange and blue silk. "Has Ariella completed all of her assignments today?" He looked at his daughter and winked. She was so clever she had undoubtedly done a week's worth of studying in one day.

"Yes, my lord. She has done exceedingly well, as always." Anahid spoke flawless English but with a heavy Armenian accent. She had been Ariella's mother's slave. The entire story was a tragic one, except for the miracle that was his daughter. Rachel had been a Jewess traveling with her father to the Promised Land. Corsairs had attacked the ship, killing everyone who had no value, including Rachel's father. She had been enslaved, but a local prince had quickly been struck by her beauty, making her his concubine. Cliff had been struck by her beauty, too, when he had been negotiating the price of a gold cargo with her master, Prince Rohar. Even knowing that to dare such an affair could mean his death, he had done so. Their affair had been brief, but his Hebrew lover had touched him more deeply than any previous mistress with her dignity and grace. He'd had no idea that she had become pregnant with his child.

It was Anahid who had managed to get a letter to him, six months after Ariella's birth. Rachel had been executed for having a blue-eyed child—for clearly, the child was not her master's. Cliff had been prepared to directly assault Rohar's citadel, but that hadn't been necessary. Anahid had used his gold to bribe the guards and smuggle Ariella out of the harem and the palace. She had been in his household ever since. He knew Anahid would die for his daughter, and she had come to love Ariella's half brother, Alexander, in much the same way. He had given her freedom within days of departing the Barbary coast.

He had never once glimpsed her face.

"And Alexi? How has he fared today?"

He felt Anahid smile. "He did not do quite as well as Ariella, my lord. He remains in the classroom, struggling to finish his letters."

"Good." Alexi was very sharp but was not the devout student his daughter was. His interests lay in fencing, equitation and, of course, his father's ships. "Remind him we are fencing tomorrow at seven o'clock—*if* he finishes his lessons."

Anahid bowed, gesturing for Ariella. The little girl pouted at her father, clearly not wanting to leave. "Papa?"

"Go, child," he began, when he saw his butler appear in the doorway. Cliff could not imagine what had caused Fitzwilliam's current expression, which he had always assumed to be set in stone. Was his heartless servant actually flustered? "Fitzwilliam?"

"Sir." Sweat appeared on the butler's brow. The man never perspired, never mind that the air was always thick and humid, even on the most temperate of days.

"What is amiss?" Cliff left the edge of the terrace.

"There is a…." He coughed. "There is a…caller…sir, if you will…downstairs."

Cliff was amused. "It must be the Grim Reaper," he said. "Does he or she have a card?" Suddenly he recalled the beauty from the Spanishtown square. He was almost certain she had come to have her lust assuaged, and in that instant, he imagined La Sauvage in his bed.

What the hell was wrong with him? Never mind that the wild child-woman was far more beautiful than any woman he had thus far beheld. She was eighteen, if he were fortunate, sixteen if not.

"The caller—" Fitzwilliam swallowed, clearly finding something distasteful "—is in the red room, awaiting you, if you wish to see her."

So it was the woman from the square. He was oddly disappointed and annoyed. "I am not receiving today," he decided flatly. "Boot her."

Fitzwilliam blinked, as he had never been so curt or so rude before. Cliff flushed. "I mean, please take her card and send her on her way."

"She has no card, sir."

An inkling began; he turned. All ladies had calling cards. "I beg your pardon?"

Fitzwilliam wet his lips. "She insists upon seeing you, sir, and she has a dagger—which she pointed at me!"

*La Sauvage*. Then he was striding into the house and across the gleaming oak floors, down the wide central staircase with its dark red runner and into the hall below. It was a huge room with high ceilings, a crystal chandelier the size of a grand piano, the floors gray-and-white marble imported from Spain. The red room was at the farthest end.

Carre's daughter stood there, staring toward him.

His heart lurched, unsettling him. He quickly approached, noting that she was very pale, in spite of her golden coloring, and that her eyes were wild, like those of a warhorse in the midst of frenzied battle. He made a mental note to proceed with caution, as he hardly trusted her. He didn't realize his tone was sharp and abrupt until after he had spoken. "Did you go back to King's House?"

She shook her head. "No."

God, he was relieved! He began to recover his composure. "Miss Carre, forgive me. Please, do sit down. Can I offer you refreshment? Tea? Biscuits?"

She was staring at him as if he'd grown a second head. "I'm to forgive *you?*"

He was reminded of how he must appear—demented, actually, to be asking such a wild, untutored child for forgiveness. Did she even understand that his manners had been utterly lacking? He somehow smiled at her. "My greeting was sorely deficient. A gentleman always bows to a lady. He might say, good afternoon or good morning, or inquire after her welfare."

She gaped. "I am not a lady. You are babbling."

He drew up. "Would you like some tea?"

"A spot?" She mimicked the highborn, upper-class British accent perfectly. "I think not," she continued her mime. "I'd take a grog," she drawled like a sailor. "If you got it."

He wondered if she drank, or merely hoped to provoke him. "Your mimicry is very well done," he said idly. He wandered past her, eyeing her as he did so. She hadn't moved or blinked since he entered the room. She stood defensively, yet also aggressively. That dagger was probably in the waistband of her breeches, beneath the tuniclike shirt. Why had she come? He thought he knew, and it wasn't to jump into his bed.

She flushed. "You know I can't read—you heard me say so. I don't know big words, either."

He felt his chest go soft. "I apologize. Mimicry means imitation. You have a very fine ear."

She shrugged. "Like I care."

He had been trying to put her at ease, but it was a ploy that was failing. He could easily assume that she was undone by his home, which was as grand as King's House and far more majestically furnished, except that she had not taken her huge green gaze from his face, not once since he'd entered the great hall. "What may I do for you?"

She stiffened. "Free my father."

*He had been right.* He tried to smile kindly at her. "Please, do sit down."

She shook her head. "I'll stand."

"How can I possibly free your father?"

"Woods is your friend. Make him let him go." Desperation flickered in her overly bright eyes.

He stared at her. "Woods and I are not feeling very friendly toward one another at the moment, and even if we were, this has gone too far. There are laws on this island. A jury has tried your father and found him guilty. I am sorry," he added, meaning it.

Tears welled. "Then help me bust him out."

He had misheard—hadn't he?

"We can do it. *You* can do it—you've got a crew, cannon, guns!"

He was aghast. "You wish for me to assault the courthouse prison?"

She nodded, but even as she did, she started to back away, tears tracking down her cheeks. Clearly she knew her demands were wishful thinking at best.

"Miss Carre, I am sorry your father was convicted. I wish that were not the case. But I am not a pirate. I am not a brigand. Every commission I have accepted has been given by the British authorities—I do not work against them. I only persecute Britain's enemies."

"You are my only hope," she whispered.

In that moment, he wanted nothing more than to help her. But he could not assault the British prison and seize the convicted pirate.

Her shoulders slumped. "Then he will die."

"Miss Carre," he began, wanting to comfort her but having no idea how to go about it. Had she been a lady of any sort, he would have taken her to the couch and kissed her senseless, until she forgot her terrible dilemma. He would have pleasured her time and again, holding reality at bay. But she was not a lady of any kind, much less one of experience. In that moment, she seemed pitifully young.

She shook her head and ran out of the room.

This time, he was prepared. He caught her in two strides, preventing her from entering the hall. "Wait! Where will you go? What will you do?"

She met his gaze. "Then I'll do it alone," she said. The tears fell but she swatted at them, leaving bright red marks on her own cheeks.

He clasped her by both shoulders. "Miss Carre, do you wish to have criminal charges brought against you? Do you wish to hang?"

She was belligerent. "They won't hang me—not if I say I'm carrying."

He froze. "Are you with child?"

She glared. "I don't think it concerns you! Now let me go. *Please.*"

He somehow knew she rarely used that word. He released one of her shoulders. "I have many guest rooms," he began, intending to offer her a suite so she would at least have a roof over her head. He had to somehow navigate her through the horror of the next day, he decided, and afterward, either to the orphanage at St. Anne's or to Britain, if she really had family there. "Why don't you spend the night? As my guest, of course," he added hastily.

She simply gaped, eyes huge, not uttering a word.

She thought he wished to use her as Woods had tried to do, he realized grimly. "You mistake my meaning." He was stiff. "I am offering you a suite of private rooms for your use, solely."

She wet her lips. "You want…to share my bed…too?"

He flushed. "I am trying to explain that I have no such intention!"

"If you help bust my father out, you can toss me anytime you like, anywhere. I don't care." She had turned pink.

He was disbelieving. "You have my word—the word of a de Warenne—I have only the most honorable intentions!"

"I can't understand half of your fancy talk," she cried, "but I get it. If you don't want to fornicate with me, then I don't need your charity." She marched across the hall.

This time, he let her go. Later, when sleep refused to come, he could think of little else.

IT WAS THE MIDDLE of the night, but the moon was almost full and a thousand stars glittered, hot and bright. The air remained thick and heavy, a sweaty caress. Amanda gripped the iron bars of her father's window, standing outside the building, having dug her way beneath the stockade fence—not for the first time. "Papa."

A rustling sounded from within the interior of the night-darkened cell.

"Papa," she begged, choking on her fear. All hope had died that day and she was violently aware of it.

"Amanda, girl!" Rodney Carre appeared at the window, a bear of a man with shaggy, brownish-blond hair and a darker beard.

Amanda began to weep.

"Damn it, girl, don't you cry for me," Rodney cried. On the bars, his fists clenched, the knuckles turning white.

She loved him so. He was her entire world. But he was angry now and she knew it. He hated tears. Still, he couldn't hit her, not with the bars there between them. "I tried, Papa, I tried," she whimpered. "I tried to get Woods to pardon you but he won't do it."

Rodney's face fell.

"I can't do this, Papa. I can't manage if you're gone!"

"Stop it," he roared, undoubtedly waking the other prisoners up. Amanda stopped crying in that instant. "You listen to me, girl. You tried and done your best. I'm proud of you, I am. No father could ask for such a good, loyal girl."

Amanda trembled. Rodney's praise was rare. She knew he loved her fiercely, for she was his entire world, after the ship and his crew, but they never spoke of any feelings whatsoever, much less love. "You're proud of me," she echoed, stunned.

"Of course I am. You're strong, and brave. You never flinched in a battle. You never shed a tear when you got beat. Girl—I'm sorry for those times. I'm sorry you had to live with such a rough temper. I'm sorry I couldn't give you a fancy home and an English rose garden."

Amanda knew then that this was their final moment, otherwise he'd never be talking in such a way. "I don't care that you hit me. How else was I to learn wrong from right? Besides, you missed more often than not, because I'm so quick." She felt more tears sliding down her cheeks. "I never wanted a rose garden," she half lied.

In the dark, his eyes seemed to shine. "All women want roses, girl. Your mama had a garden filled with them when I met her. She may live in London now, but she has a garden there, too. That's how the noble people live."

So now they would speak of her mother? She'd been born in St. Mawes, near Cornwall, and raised there by her mother, Dulcea Straithferne Carre, until she was four years old. Mama had married Rodney when he was a dashing young lieutenant in the royal navy, before he'd ever gone pirating. But after he'd turned rogue, he'd come to Cornwall, begging Mama for her. Her mother had refused, loving her far too much to ever relinquish her. Rodney had stolen her, tearing her from her sobbing mother's arms and taking her to the islands, and she had never gone back.

Her life with Papa was all she knew. He had been afraid to take her to visit Mama, worried that the authorities might imprison him for what he had done. "You understand, girl, don't you? Why I had to do it?"

Of course Amanda had understood. She loved Papa, and couldn't imagine being raised in Cornwall. But she wished she could recall Mama. Papa told her she was elegant and gracious, a true lady, and so beautiful she stole the breath from her gentleman callers. Rodney was usually in his cups when he began talking about the past and Mama, and he always ended up in tears. He never stopped loving his wife, not for a moment, and he wanted Amanda to adore her, too, even if from a distance. He wanted Amanda to know how special Mama was.

Amanda often wondered what her mother was thinking after so many years. Mama did not know where Rodney had taken her and there had been no contact, not even a letter, although Papa had somehow unearthed the information that she now lived in London in a beautiful home called Belford House.

Amanda wondered why Rodney was talking about roses and Mama, all in the same breath. "Roses don't matter to me, Papa. Surely you know that."

He gave her a long look. "You need to go to her, girl. Dulcea will take you in when I'm gone."

"Don't talk like that!" Amanda cried, shocked. "It's not tomorrow yet and it's not noon."

"It is tomorrow, by damn, it'll be dawn soon. She will be overjoyed to see you again. Amanda, girl, you will finally have that fancy home. You can be a real lady, not the spawn of someone like me."

Amanda stared, torn between terror and dismay. She'd had wild fantasies, of course, of one day seeing her mother and being embraced by the most beautiful, ladylike woman imaginable, of being safe and warm and loved. In those fantasies, she had become a lady just like her mother, and they had sipped exotic tea in a fragrant rose garden. But she was a sensible girl. Her home was the island, her life was her father's. Although they had the farm, it was a life of plunder, and their prize possessions were stolen goods. Although they had one dairy cow and Amanda milked her, she was a pirate's daughter. She was never going to England and she was never going to meet her mother. And it had certainly never crossed her mind to attempt to appear to be a lady, much less become one, except in a foolish flight of fancy.

Was her father mad?

"I'm not a lady—I couldn't ever be one. I love the island. This is my home! I love sailing—I love the sea," she protested with real panic.

"In that, you're my own true daughter," Rodney said, proudly and sadly at once. "God, girl, I don't know what I was thinking, to teach you how to sail my sloop and fire the cannon, to fence better than a master, to shoot a pistol and mend sails. You climb the masts better than my best topmen. You're a woman, not a lad! You should have stayed with your mother. I know that now."

"No!" She seized his hand through the bars. "Papa, I love you."

He drew his hand away from hers and was silent.

Amanda fought not to cry again, but it was a losing battle.

"Promise me," he finally said, "that when I'm gone, you will go to her. You got no one here. You need to go to Dulcea, Amanda."

Amanda was terrified. How could she make such a promise? Mama was a great lady. She was a pirate's daughter. While she believed her mother had loved her once, that had been long ago. She was very afraid her mother would not care much for her now.

"I'm your father and a dying man," he cried, furious. "Damn it, you're to obey me!"

She knew that if the bars didn't separate them, he'd whack her one. "You're not dead yet. Maybe a miracle will happen!"

He snorted. "There's no such thing."

"There was a miracle today," Amanda cried. "Cliff de Warenne saved me from—" She stopped abruptly.

Rodney stared, the whites of his eyes showing. "He what?"

"He saved me…I tried to seduce the governor," she whispered.

Through the bars, he hit her on the side of her head, hard. "You're no whore, damn it! If there's one thing I did right, it was to keep you innocent. You're to give that maidenhead to a good man—to your husband!" he shouted, enraged.

She held on tightly to the bars, until the stars spinning in her head dimmed and vanished. Then she inhaled, shaky from the blow. "I was trying to save you, Papa."

But her father didn't seem to hear. "De Warenne's a gentleman, never mind his command. You make him take you to England. He's one you can trust."

Amanda was in despair. Her father was about to hang and if this was his dying wish, she would have to obey it. "He's odd," she heard herself say slowly, musing aloud. "Why would he help me, a stranger? Why would he fight with his own friend to do so?"

"'Cause that's what them blue bloods do—they get all high and mighty and offer charity to poor sots like us. It makes them nobles feel even higher and mightier when they do so. He gives you charity, you take it, girl," Rodney said. "And never mind your damnable pride!" He hesitated, then said strangely, "Did he notice that you're a beauty?"

Amanda was taken aback. In her entire seventeen years, her father had never once mentioned that he thought her beautiful. But now he was talking about her as if she were truly beautiful, like her mother. "Papa? I'm no beauty. I'm skinny with ratty hair. I wear boy's clothes. And I have very odd eyes. Everyone says so."

Rodney was serious. ""Did he look at you like that fucking Turk did in Sicily?"

Amanda hesitated. "It didn't mean anything."

Rodney exhaled. After a long, grim pause, he said seriously, "He's the one to take you to your mother. I mean it, Amanda, I trust him. He's a gentleman." He stopped.

She knew he wanted to say something more. "He is a gentleman, but what is it, Papa? What aren't you saying?"

Rodney stared. "I wouldn't mind if he decided to keep you for a time."

Amanda gaped. "*What*? You mean, as his mistress?"

"He's rich as sin and he's an earl's son!" Carre cried, slamming his fist against the wall. "I always wanted to see you properly wed, but with me gone, I don't know how that is possible. That will be up to your mother, and you haven't seen her in years."

Amanda began to tremble. De Warenne's strong, bronzed face came to mind, his gaze so peculiarly intense, so strangely piercing, as if he could look into her mind, her soul. She recalled his carrying her from Woods's rooms. She tensed, confused. She might not mind giving him her maidenhead, or not very much, anyway. And he had seemed *kind*.

She must be mistaken, she thought, shaken now. While the Queen Street baker's wife gave her stale bread for free, and the boy who swept the apothecary shop was pleasant, no one else in her world was that way. Maybe de Warenne had rescued her in order to seduce her, never mind that she wasn't the kind of noble lady he preferred. After all, hadn't he tried to get her to stay in his Kingston home?

"Papa, he would never want me as a mistress. He has lovers, all prettier than me."

"You just make sure he's the one to sail you to your mother," Rodney said grimly. "I meant to leave you with something, Amanda, and there's nothing, damn it, not a single pound. I am sorry."

She was more ill inside now than ever, because Papa never apologized for anything and this was the second time he was telling her how sorry he was. "Don't apologize," she said fiercely. "You're the best father a girl could have!" She meant it, and unbidden, tears began again.

"I tried, I really tried," he gasped, crying now, too. "Girl, you got to go."

Amanda realized that the sky was turning boldly orange above the rooftop of the courthouse. The sun was rising—it was dawn. "No," she cried.

In a few more moments, she would have to leave. And the next time she saw her father, he would be on the hangman's block.

"You better go, girl, before they catch you here and find out about the tunnel you dug under the fence." Carre was hoarse.

This could not be happening. She had never been quite sure if she believed in God, but now, wildly, she prayed. "Papa, let me stay. I don't care if they find me." She reached through the bars, desperate.

He hesitated, then clasped her hand.

Oh, God. His hand was warm, strong, calloused and scarred. Years ago, a Scot had severed one of his fingers in a brawl, the blade catching the flesh of his palm. But Amanda held on for her life—and his.

Because once she let go, she was never going to be able to take his hand again.

AT THE LAST POSSIBLE moment, he'd leaped onto his finest Thoroughbred and galloped every mile to Spanishtown. Now Cliff scanned the crowd that had gathered beneath the hot midday sun in the square between King's House and the courthouse. Beautifully garbed ladies with white parasols and well-dressed gentlemen with walking sticks ambled about the hanging block beneath the shade of towering palm trees, chatting casually while they waited for the festivities to begin. Roughly dressed sailors sipped grog and pinched their whores; a few sailors were dancing with their trollops to the heady island tune a Negro fiddler was playing. A group of young boys were throwing stones at the scaffolding as if it were a bull's eye target. They were laughing and becoming vicious. He turned away, scanning the other side of the square. A regiment of soldiers stood at attention outside of the courthouse, and more soldiers patrolled the perimeter of the park, in case the prisoner decided to escape. His heart beat hard, fueled by adrenaline. Where was she?

In a matter of minutes, Carre would be escorted from the prison to his fate. Cliff was certain La Sauvage was present.

He hadn't slept a wink all night, obsessed by the fate of her father and her part in the terrible drama. He suspected she would not resign herself to being a spectator that day, but what could she possibly think to do? He knew one thing: he was not going to let her throw her own life away after her father's. If she thought to attempt to save Carre's life, he intended to stop her before the soldiers did.

Suddenly he felt eyes upon his back. He turned, glancing west at King's House. On the upper floor, a huge window was open. Woods stood there, staring at the scene below.

Cliff turned away grimly. From the corner of his eye, he saw one of the boys slam a rock at the base of the hanging block, his laughter cruel. And he thought he heard a soft choked sound—a feminine sob.

His gaze slammed to the legs of the scaffolding. He saw a small, curled-up ball of rags and a mass of moon-colored hair. Furious, Cliff strode through the crowd, rudely pushing past several gentlemen. The crowd parted, the revelers realizing he was determined and enraged. The boys stopped throwing rocks at her as he approached, becoming silent, turning pale. He caught one of the ruffians by his shirt and flung him aside. "You will answer to me before this day is done," he said.

The boy whispered, ashen, "She's just the pirate's daughter."

Cliff whacked him on the shoulder, hard enough to send him flying. The other boys fled; this culprit crawled through the crowd, coward that he was, then found his land legs and ran away, as well.

He turned, kneeling. "Miss Carre?"

She was wedged beneath the deck where her father would stand in the noose, behind one of the deck's thick wood legs, her knees to her chest, her eyes unnaturally bright and wide, as if with fever. She appeared very small and frightened, a tiny creature hiding from the dangerous world. His heart melted.

"Come out." He spoke in a soft whisper, hoping to reassure her, and extended his hand.

She shook her head. A tear fell.

God, maybe it was better that she stay there, beneath the block, because if she did, she would not be able to see her father hang. But on the other hand, he wanted to get her far away from the square and the hanging, because he was afraid that if he did not, at the last moment she would come out of hiding and view a sight no woman should ever have to endure. "Please, come out. I will take you far away from this," he tried, his tone now cajoling.

She stared, unblinking. Another tear fell.

His heart broke. "There is nothing to be gained by remaining here. Let me take you away." An idea occurred to him. "I'll take you to my ship. I have a cruise to make to St. Kitt, and the day is perfect for it."

Her eyes flickered, brightening.

"A good, moderate breeze, the sea is so sweet," he coaxed.

She wet her lips, hesitating.

"I'll let you—" He stopped. His quarterdeck was sacred. "I'll let you come onto my deck. Come, sweetheart."

More tears fell. She suddenly nodded, extending her hand, and he reached for her. Just as their fingertips touched, the crowd roared, an explosion of sound, and then the jeers began. She cried out, jerking backward, away from his grasp. He glanced up and saw the soldiers bringing Carre out of the courthouse.

The jeers grew, accompanied by cruel and vicious taunts.

"The pirate's had his fun—now we can have ours!"

"Let's bleed him when he's dead and paint our decks with *his* blood!"

"Think he'll beg for mercy? Like the coward he's got to be?"

"Let's make him beg—let's use the cat before he hangs!"

Cliff was ill, a rare feeling. He turned his gaze on Carre's daughter. Urgently, he said, "We need to go *now*."

As if she had heard him, she scrambled on all fours toward him. Cliff reached for her, but she was so goddamned agile she dropped down and rolled under his arm. He whirled to seize her again but she had shot to her feet and was running towards Carre, fighting the crowd to do so. "Papa!"

Carre had entered the square with his escort and he stiffened. "Get out of here, Amanda!" he roared.

Cliff seized her from behind, wrapping both of his arms

around her. She didn't even seem to notice. "Papa!" she screamed again.

Carre met his gaze and a silent agreement was reached. "Get her out of here, de Warenne."

Cliff nodded, still holding her from behind as she struggled frantically to get to her father. "Don't make me throw you over my shoulder," he said tersely.

She didn't seem to hear. "Papa, I love you!"

Carre paused, about to step up to the deck. "I love you, too, girl."

Amanda went limp in Cliff's arms. The soldiers prodded Carre with their carbines, forcing him to go up the five steps to the deck. Looking down at her face, he saw Amanda following his every movement, sobbing soundlessly now. Cliff was about to throw her over his shoulder when Carre said, "Girl! Promise me you go to England to your mother."

Amanda nodded. "I promise," she cried. "I promise," she whispered again, choking.

Carre was thrust before the noose and abruptly blindfolded.

Amanda whimpered.

Cliff didn't think; he reacted. He turned her to face him, holding her tightly against his big body, pressing her cheek to his chest. "Don't move," he warned, trying to envelop her small body with his while cradling the back of her head. He felt her tears soaking his shirt and chest.

He looked up. The noose was around Carre's neck. The crowd cheered and roared and the stones began to fly, raining down on the condemned man.

Cliff looked away, sickened. He buried his own cheek against her curly hair, unthinkingly moving his mouth there. She began to shake like a leaf. He started to back away, taking her with him, and the crowd roared.

Amanda shoved at him, trying to twist around to see.

He held her hard, not letting her turn, not even an inch, determined to prevent her from watching her father gasping for his last breaths. Some hangings were swift and merciful; others were not, the victim dangling for endless minutes until the neck broke. He heard the loud snap, and he thanked the Lord that Carre's death had been almost instantaneous.

In his arms, Amanda Carre fainted.

# *CHAPTER THREE*

"SHE'S DEAD."

The speaker seemed to be a man. What was he talking about? Amanda struggled to make sense of his words. A tall, golden-haired man appeared, his expression strained, his blue eyes frightening in their intensity. She knew him but could not place him. Shocked, she realized he was talking about her.

"She's dead."

"She's not dead—she's *sleeping*."

"She's not moving. She's *dead*."

Amanda began to panic. Was she dead? And who were these people arguing about her? She began to awaken, realizing that she was in the throes of a strange dream. She wasn't dead, she was sleeping. She stretched but her body was weak and it felt battered, yet the pallet she was lying on gave deliciously and then sprang back, like the most heavenly cocoon. No pallet was so soft and firm, at once.

Where was she?

"No one sleeps for a whole day. She's *dead*, Ariella, dead. See?"

Amanda jerked as someone roughly seized her foot through a soft, fluffy cover. Bewildered, she opened her eyes, blinking against the brightness of the room. Then she met a pair of blazing blue eyes and a wicked grin. She cried out.

"I told you she's alive," another child said.

Amanda sat up, her sore body protesting, staring at a small boy with dark hair and familiar blue eyes. He looked past the bed. "Of course she's not dead. She's been sleeping ever since Papa brought her home. I knew that! But I had you, didn't I?"

"You did not!"

Amanda took in her surroundings. She was in a huge canopied bed, the ebony wood intricately carved, the bed hangings a misty blue. Terribly confused, she saw a fireplace with a white mantel carved with vines and leaves. She glanced down. The cover was a pale blue silk, the finest kind that came from plunder. Dazed, she took in a huge room with white-and-blue fabric covered walls. Dear God, all the furniture was matching, upholstered in ivory, blue or white, tufted with gold. And the ceilings were gilded. Then her gaze slammed to the wide-eyed little girl standing by her side.

The child smiled. "My name is Ariella. Papa says your name is Miss Carre. Are you his mistress?"

The boy reached over and jerked hard on her hair. Ariella punched him just as hard in the jaw.

*Papa.* And in that stunning moment, Amanda lost everything for the second time in her life. Grief crashed over and she was drowning in it—she could not breathe. The tears began, but she didn't care. Gasping, she doubled over in pain.

Papa had been hanged. Papa was gone. Murdered by Woods and the British.

"She is ill. I'm getting Papa!" the boy said sharply, racing out.

Amanda vaguely heard. Cliff de Warenne had been there at the hanging, preventing her from watching him die. She must be at Windsong. Oh, God, how was she going to survive the loss, the pain?

A small hand stroked over her arm. "Miss Carre? Don't cry. Whatever is making you so sad, my papa can fix it." Pride filled her tone. "He can make you happy. He can do anything."

Amanda blinked at the beautiful child through her streaming tears. She couldn't recall much, just a terrible sound, the breaking of bones in her father's neck. It was a sound she was never going to forget. "My papa's dead," she gasped to the child. And she hugged herself, doubling over again.

Rapid booted steps sounded. Amanda heard de Warenne. "Ariella!" He was stern.

"Papa, I didn't make her cry!"

Slowly, Amanda somehow looked up, keeping her arms wrapped tightly around herself. And now she began to remember how Cliff de Warenne had kept his arms tightly around her at the hanging.

"I know you didn't. Please join your brother in the nursery. *Now.*" De Warenne nodded at the door, his expression rigid.

Clearly knowing when to immediately obey, Ariella flung a worried look at Amanda and quickly left the room.

Amanda found herself staring into Cliff de Warenne's searching blue eyes.

He had paused at the foot of the bed. "I will not be foolish enough to ask how you are feeling. I am sorry, Miss Carre, for your loss."

Amanda broke into tears again. She turned onto her side and wept in grief. She was aware of him approaching, and felt him hovering over her, but the grief was just too much to bear. "Go away," she wept, but she really didn't want him to go. She wanted him to take her in his arms, the way he had a few hours ago, and to hold her until her wounds healed. Except she knew they never would.

His hand clasped her shoulder. Amanda suddenly realized her shoulders were bare. Her naked body was swimming in a very fine, lace-trimmed cotton nightgown. She couldn't imagine what had happened to her clothes or whose garment she was wearing.

"You are in the throes of grief. It is understandable," de Warenne said softly. "I have sent for my ship's surgeon. He'll give you laudanum. It will help."

The terrible flood had ceased. Amanda turned onto her back and stared up at him. He quickly removed his hand from her shoulder. "Laudanum," she said dully. She knew what laudanum did. When she had broken her wrist as a child, she'd been given it and it instantly erased the pain. Would it also erase her grief?

De Warenne's face was strained. His blue eyes, however, were filled with sympathy and compassion. "If it is any consolation, your father died a swift death."

She started to weep again.

"It will get easier. The anguish will ease. I promise you that, Miss Carre."

She shook her head; she didn't know how that could be possible. "Is your father….dead?" she stuttered.

"No. But my mother died when I was a very small child."

She started, her tears drying. "She did?"

He nodded gravely. "She died giving birth to my younger sister, Eleanor."

Amanda struggled to sit up, and he slid his arm behind her to help her do so. Becoming dizzy, Amanda grasped his bulging forearms, but the wave intensified. She leaned toward him, her forehead finding his chest. The bed tilted wildly and she began to spin.

"You need to lie down with your legs elevated," he said sharply.

Amanda couldn't answer—she was trying to claw free of the spinning gray room. But suddenly she was on her back, all the pillows thrown to the floor, except for a large blue velvet neck roll, which was under her knees. The bed slowed, finally becoming level once again. Amanda opened her eyes, only to find de Warenne sitting by her hip, one arm under her knees along with the pillow, staring intently at her.

"You are exhausted," he said flatly. "When was the last time you ate?"

She had no idea. "I'm fine. I never swoon. I don't know why I got so dizzy."

De Warenne jumped abruptly to his feet, tugging her nightgown down over her calves. He whirled. "Instead of hovering outside the door, Alexi, have a servant bring Miss Carre a bowl of soup and white bread."

The boy nodded, wide-eyed, and raced off.

"I'm not hungry," Amanda said, feeling very foolish now. She started to kick the pillow out from under her legs, unable to dismiss the fact that de Warenne had his hand under her nightgown.

He seized her knees, immobilizing her. "I suspect you haven't eaten in days. Unless you wish to follow your father into his grave, you need to nourish your body, Miss Carre."

His gaze was locked with hers. Amanda couldn't look away—she was mesmerized. It was almost as if he had some genuine concern for her, but that was impossible. A flicker of interest began, piercing through the grief. "I don't want to die," she said slowly, and she realized that she meant it.

He smiled very slightly at her. "Good."

WHEN AMANDA AWOKE the next time, bright sunlight was trying to filter through the closed blue-and-white draperies of the room. She blinked up at the ruched blue fabric of the canopy overhead, remembering everything. She was at Windsong; Papa was dead. She was unbearably saddened.

She wondered how long it had been since the hanging. She recalled having soup and bread, not once but several times, a pretty, plump maid with bright red hair hovering over her and helping her with her meal. She recalled the white-whiskered physician, probing her body and taking her pulse. She recalled drinking tea laced with laudanum, and she thought that perhaps she had done so several times.

Amanda glanced carefully around the room, now remembering two small children, a dark-haired boy and a golden-haired girl. But she was alone now. Had they been figments of her imagination or a part of a strange dream? Or had she really met de Warenne's children? One of them was a prince or a princess, *if* the rumors were true.

*De Warenne*. He had been at the hanging, not allowing her to witness her father's gruesome death. Had he really held her in his arms so protectively? Had that been a dream, too? Amanda was confused. Her memory was faded and torn and it was difficult to decide what was real and what was not.

But as sad as she was—whenever she thought about Papa, a wave of grief washed over her—she did feel slightly better. For one, she didn't feel so bruised and battered. And she was having a hunger pang.

To test her theories, Amanda sat up, stretching. Her legs did not protest, her stomach growled and the room remained surprisingly level.

She flung the bedcover aside and paused. Dear Lord, she had been sleeping in a bed fit for a queen. The covers were silk, the comforter down. The draperies matched the wall fabric; in fact, everything matched and was either silk, satin, velvet or brocade.

She had known de Warenne was rich, of course, but she hadn't imagined him living like this. Then, she hadn't ever been in a rich royal person's home before, either.

She got up, aware of how pleasant the fine cotton was on her body. As she went to the draperies, she passed a huge mirror, the guilded frame carved in swirls and rosettes. She glimpsed her reflection and paused.

It was like looking at a stranger.

A pretty and terribly feminine woman stood there in the glass, beautifully dressed in a lace-trimmed nightgown, her pale hair spilling past her shoulders, almost to her waist. The woman's face had bright, wide green eyes with long, thick lashes, strangely dark, like her eyebrows. She was slightly flushed, her skin sun-kissed, and she had full, pink lips. Her shoulders and arms were entirely bare. If there was any criticism, it might be that her shoulders were a bit broad, hinting at unfeminine strength. But that was hard to notice, because of the way the cotton nightgown draped over her breasts. Small lace straps held the bodice up, but it was low-cut, with tiny gathers just below the straps. Amanda realized she was blushing as she regarded herself.

She didn't look like a pirate's daughter; she looked like a well-born woman.

Shaken, she turned away, quickly opening up the draperies. It was well past midday—the sun was high and bright, but moving into the west. Her bedroom overlooked the harbor and the second thing she saw was her favorite ship, the *Fair Lady*. Her hull was painted black and red. Although she was only fifth rate, her standing rigging was a sight to behold and Amanda thrilled at the complexity of it. How many times had she watched de Warenne on his quarterdeck, his men hoisting sail as the frigate began to leave her berth? How many times had she watched the beautiful *Fair Lady* begin to increase her speed, making sail, her canvas filling? Sometimes she had watched the ship from one of the gun towers ringing the harbor, as it streaked away from shore, heading out to sea, until finally she became a dot, vanishing as if into eternity. How many times had she wondered what it would be like to sail on such a ship, running before the freshest wind?

And then Amanda saw her namesake.

Fort Charles was across the harbor and set upon the small peninsula that jutted southeast into the Caribbean Sea. Even flying the British colors, even with her masts broken in half, even from such a distance, Amanda recognized their sloop instantly. The grief rolled over her, heavy and hateful—hurtful.

*Promise me you will go to England, to your mother.*

Rodney's voice was so loud and clear he could have been speaking to her from the very room. She whirled, but he did not stand behind her. For one moment, she stared toward the bedroom's closed door, willing him to appear. He did not.

She swallowed. "I did promise, Papa. Don't you remember?" Suddenly it was hard to speak.

*I remember, girl.*

She could see him now; she really could, even if it was with her imagination. She brushed at the seeping tears. "I promised you at the hanging. I did. You know I always keep my word. I'll go." Fear began, real and raw. She was going to have to leave everything familiar behind. What if Mama didn't love her the way Papa claimed she did?

*I know, girl. I'm so proud of you....* He smiled at her.

Amanda shuddered. "I'm not sure Mama will be pleased with me."

*She loves you, girl.*

Amanda was about to remind him that she was a pirate's daughter, but her papa's image had vanished. Lord, what was she doing? Talking to herself—or to a dead man? Had she just seen Papa's ghost? She was shaking. It didn't matter. She had made that promise and she was going to keep it, no matter what she had to do to get to England. Surely she wasn't really afraid of a place. Surely her mother would welcome her with a warm embrace and tears of joy!

So she had to focus on the voyage. Amanda bit her lip. Rodney had told her to sail with de Warenne. Could she somehow convince him to allow her to travel on one of his ships? She thought of how kind he had been—or at least, how kind he had appeared. Papa had wanted her to sail with de Warenne because he was a gentleman and Amanda could agree with that. But how would she pay for the fare?

She had very few possessions. She had her dagger, her pistol, her sword, a change of clothes and the gold cross and chain that had been her father's. She had no intention of parting with any of those possessions, and de Warenne would have little need for them anyway. There was only one possible way to pay for her passage. She was going to have to offer him her body.

Amanda tensed. She was more than apprehensive; she was

afraid. Every sexual act she had inadvertently witnessed had been ghastly and revolting. Governor Woods had been disgusting. She had never been able to understand why the lovers she had seen had been so lusty. She had never understood what was so exciting about sex that it made men and women lose their ability to reason.

Amanda had never been more nervous as she left the bedroom. De Warenne had stated that his intentions were honorable, and oddly, she had believed him. But surely he would accept the use of her body in exchange for her passage. Every man she knew would accept that kind of offer. She could even sweeten the pot by telling him she was a virgin.

She found herself in a long corridor with white walls; fine, fancy oil paintings; gleaming wood floors and scattered Eastern rugs. At both ends were stairwells with gold brass banisters, each leading to the great hall below. Amanda went to the closest one and started down the stairs.

Her steps slowed. The front hall was the size of their entire house at Belle Mer. For the first time, she looked up at the high ceiling, which held the largest crystal chandelier she had ever seen. Rich tapestries and more oil paintings were on the walls. The furniture—chairs, benches and tables—was all polished mahogany, with claw feet, velvet or damask upholstery and intricate carving. In the middle of one wall was a pair of doors, and Amanda recognized the front entrance of the house. Open arches led to other rooms.

She hesitated, uncertain, and then she saw the butler.

He was entering the hall, an empty silver tray held flat in one hand, as if it still contained refreshments. He saw her at that moment and went pale, halting in his tracks. The tray fell to the floor with a loud clang.

Amanda marched toward him. “Hey. Where is de Warenne?”

He gave her a furious look and picked up the tray. “His lordship is entertaining and is *not* to be disturbed.”

Her eyes narrowed. "Don't put on airs with me," she said flatly. "You're only a servant."

He straightened. "I am the butler, miss, and the most important servant in his lordship's employ."

She rolled her eyes. "I don't think so. The most important one he's got working for him is the ship's carpenter. You want to make a bet?"

Fitzwilliam huffed. "Might I suggest that you retire to your room and properly clothe yourself?"

Amanda glanced down at her new favorite possession. "I don't think *his lordship* will care how I'm dressed," she said. The nightgown was certainly as decent as any dress.

Fitzwilliam flushed. "If you go to your room, I will inform his lordship that you wish to see him."

Amanda snorted at him. "You need to take a cruise, my man. That might get that stick out of your arse." She started toward one of the arches, where she could just barely detect soft conversation. That was where the old fart had come from, too.

"He will not be pleased," Fitzwilliam said softly to her back.

Amanda thought he sounded smugly pleased himself, but she didn't care. Now she could make out de Warenne's drawl—and the soft, coy laughter of a woman.

She paused on the threshold of a large salon with golden walls and more furniture than any one person could possibly use in two lifetimes. Standing at thc far end was her host, clad in his usual white linen shirt and a pair of equally white breeches, his high black boots gleaming in shocking contrast. He often wore a heavily embroidered Moorish vest but not that day, and his dagger wasn't strapped to his belt. He had, however, forgotten to remove his huge gold and ruby spurs.

Looking at him, her mouth became dry.

And then she saw de Warrene's caller and understood why he would not wish to be disturbed. She could not believe her eyes.

A beautiful, perfectly plump, blond lady was patting his arm and giggling at him. She was elegantly dressed, beribboned and bejeweled. No, she was *fat*, Amanda decided, but of course, most sailors preferred a meaty woman. And her skin wasn't porcelain, it was *pasty*. Her hair was clearly yellow, like straw that had been urinated on.

Amanda's fists clenched. Dismay immobilized her.

The woman was laughing at whatever de Warenne had just said. He was smiling, his expression noncommittal. His gaze did dip when she moved, for her pale green gown exposed huge *cowlike* breasts, which were in danger of falling out every time she laughed—something she did all the time. She had a glass of wine or sherry in her other hand. She spoke, tossing her blond, tonged curls. "I am so pleased to find you at home, Captain. It is a long, *hot* carriage ride from Spanishtown. I was so hoping not to be denied."

"Yes, it is a very long drive—all eleven miles of it. Do you not care for our Jamaican weather?" he remarked, his tone idle. The gold earring he wore glinted.

She pressed closer to him. "It is *so* hard to keep one's gown stiff in such soggy weather. And my hair! It has to be done at least twice a day."

"I imagine it is difficult for the ladies, living in such a clime," he said flatly.

"Oh, I am enjoying my visit to the island, Captain. But I should enjoy it so much more if you were to take me aboard your boat."

Amanda strode forward. "It's a ship, not a boat, my fine lady—a frigate, in fact. Fifth rate, with thirty-eight guns, not counting any cannonade."

The lady's jaw dropped, unattractively.

De Warenne's eyes widened, their gazes meeting. Amanda wriggled her hips and thrust out her bosom. "*Ohh,* do take me on your boat, Captain, sir!"

His face broke into a smile and he choked on a laugh. Then

he scowled very fiercely at her. "Miss Carre. You are in your nightgown."

Amanda blinked. *He had been amused by her.* She softened, smiling back. "It's not my nightgown. I don't know whose it is. In fact, I can't even remember how it got on me." Her gaze narrowed and she looked right at him. "Did you undress me?"

He turned red.

The woman gasped. "I can see I have made a terrible mistake! You and…the pirate's daughter?" She was incredulous.

De Warenne gave Amanda an odd, private look. It was filled with warning, but amusement tinged his features, too. Amanda could not comprehend what he was thinking. Then his expression became stern and he faced the woman. "I was just about to introduce you to Miss Carre, Miss Delington. She is my houseguest."

The woman had turned beet-red. She was no longer very pretty. "I see. I see very well." She glanced at de Warenne, nodded. "Good day, then." She left the salon in great haste.

Amanda watched her go, feeling very satisfied.

He said from behind, softly, "Pleased with yourself, are you?"

She whirled and almost jumped into his arms. Instead, she leaped back, strangely nervous now that they were alone. "She's a fat, pasty sow looking to fuck you," she defended herself.

He blanched.

Amanda knew she had made a terrible mistake, but she didn't know just what that mistake was. "I mean, you didn't really want her, did you? She was a fool! She called the *Fair Lady* a boat."

He inhaled, long and deep. Looking shaken, he walked away from her, sliding his large hands into the flat pockets at his narrow hips.

Amanda was very worried. "Are you angry with me?"

It was another moment before he turned to face her. He smiled a little at her. "No, I'm not. I am glad to see you up and about, and apparently feeling better."

Now she felt even better, she realized, because she had been afraid he was angry with her and that he would boot her from his house. "If you want her," she said, very reluctantly, "I could go and drag her back here. I'm not stupid. I know she thinks I'm your lover or some such nonsense. I could tell her the truth."

He stared.

Amanda tensed. Suddenly she was aware of being alone with a huge, powerful and undoubtedly virile man, while clad in a nightgown. She was aware of being absolutely naked behind the single fine layer of cotton.

"I am not interested in Miss Delington."

Amanda smiled in relief.

"Miss Carre," he said carefully.

Amanda hurried toward him, interrupting. "No, wait. We both know I'm not a lady. My name is Amanda. Or girl. Papa used to call me girl. Or Amanda Girl." She stopped, unbearably sad.

Briefly, she had forgotten that he was dead. It all came rushing back to her now.

"He called you 'girl.'"

She sat down in a huge, lush chair with all kinds of odd tufts. "Yes."

He pulled a green-and-gold-striped ottoman forward and sat down next to her. "How are you feeling?"

"I'm not dizzy anymore."

He smiled slightly. "We made sure you ate before every dose of laudanum."

She tried to remember. "Have I been sleeping for long?"

"On and off for three days. I had been wondering when you would wake up." He smiled again, encouragingly.

She found herself smiling back. His eyes met hers and somehow, their gazes locked.

In that moment, something changed. Amanda stared, filled with confusion. He was the most beautiful man she had ever seen and he actually seemed kind, genuinely so. He was one of the greatest masters of the sea, and for her, that was better than being a king. When he accepted her offer, she was going to share his bed.

She had never desired a man. But sometimes at night, in her dreams, a faceless golden lover came to her, kissing her with heat, and when she awoke, she was filled with a tension she barely understood. Sometimes she woke up on the verge of discovering great pleasure, only to realize she had been dreaming and she was alone.

She wondered if she would start dreaming about Cliff de Warenne. Because he was exactly like her dream lover, wasn't he? Big, powerful, golden…

His eyes widened and he leaped to his feet. He paced away from her, pouring himself a drink. His hand trembled.

Amanda didn't move. How could she be thinking of those very private dreams now? They had business to discuss! But why was he trembling? "Why are you shaking?"

He made a harsh sound, not answering.

She sighed, kicking her feet out. "Maybe you are catching the flu. Some of the sailors have it."

"It's not the flu," he said grimly.

She smiled at him. "That's good." She hesitated, because in spite of what she had to do, she was afraid to begin this particular negotiation. Besides, she was enjoying the chair, the room and such noble company. She hedged. "Why do you have so much furniture? And if you didn't want to fornicate with that woman, why was she here?"

He approached, appearing aghast. "I know you have been through a terrible time, and that we come from different worlds. Amanda, I—someone needs to teach you a few things."

She became wary. "Like what? Reading?"

"A tutor can do that. You cannot use certain language in polite company. In fact, you can't speak of…fornication, ever!"

"Why the hell not?" she asked, genuinely puzzled. "It's all men do, most of the time."

He looked at her and finally, he started to smile. "All right," he said, holding up his hand. "We are victims of our male bodies, I grant you that. Let's start over. You cannot wander this house in such attire."

She looked down at the lovely nightgown. He was going to take it back, she realized glumly. She fingered the lace edge of one strap. Then she looked up. She shrugged, so he wouldn't know that she would care if he took it back.

He regarded her closely. "Amanda." He sat once more on the ottoman, although he'd moved it a bit farther away. "We do need to discuss something else."

He was very serious. Was he going to give her an overdue boot after all?

"I hope I was not presumptuous, but I thought you would prefer a burial at sea."

Amanda stiffened. "I hadn't thought about it! Where is Papa?" she cried in alarm.

"He is in the Kingston funeral parlor. We can bury him at sea. I have arranged it."

Amanda nodded, incapable of speech.

"I was thinking tomorrow," he said, his eyes soft with sympathy. "Can you manage? I can say a few words as ship's captain, or I can summon a minister, or even a naval chaplain."

Papa wasn't buried yet, she managed to think. She would be able to attend his funeral. She met his searching gaze. "I'd like you to bless him."

"Then it is as good as done," he said softly.

He was being so kind again, and he was so impossibly handsome that her heart turned over as hard as a dory being flipped in high seas. She looked up into his brilliantly blue eyes and felt impossibly reassured, impossibly safe, as if she had just crept into harbor with all sails shortened after a raging storm. Maybe she didn't have to be afraid of this man, she thought.

He stood up. "Did you wish to see me for a reason? If not, it's my children's bedtime and I need to go upstairs."

She took a breath for courage, refusing to think about what would happen after he accepted her deal. Instead, she saw herself standing on the deck of the *Fair Lady* in heavy seas filled with white horses. She'd be at the bow; he'd be on the quarterdeck with his officers. They'd press on with a mass of canvas that no sensible seaman would ever attempt in such foul weather. He wouldn't care; he'd be laughing, and so would she. She smiled.

"Amanda?"

She came back to her senses, her smile vanishing. She bit her lip, hesitating.

His gaze veered to her mouth and then back to her eyes. "What is it that you wish to ask me?"

There was no choice now but to plunge forward. Amanda stood up. "I'll do anything—*anything*—if you will take me to England."

He simply stared.

Amanda had no idea what that fixed gaze meant. He was very smart, so he had to catch her meaning. Didn't he? She smiled brightly at him. "I can't pay for a passage, not with coin, anyway. But there are other ways I could pay." And she waited.

He began to shake his head. The odd motion seemed to be a "no," and his expression seemed to be tinged with disbelief. "I see."

Amanda stood, starting to panic. She had to get to England! She had promised. "I said I'd do anything. You know what I mean, don't you?"

Now he had that flush on his high cheekbones as he sometimes did, the color of anger. But why would he be mad? Didn't he understand what she was saying? "De Warenne, I am offering you my body. It's the only way I can pay for—"

"Cease!" His tone was a command.

She cringed in disbelief. "I know I'm not fancy enough for you—" she began, about to tell him that she was a virgin.

He grasped her arm and their bodies collided. "Is this what

you do when you need something? Offer your body in exchange for some goods or service?" he demanded. Instantly he released her, stepping away from her. "I may chase pirates, but I am a gentleman, and a de Warenne," he ground out, his eyes blazing.

She was trembling and her heart raced with fear. She couldn't understand his anger. "I have to get to England. Papa said I should go with you. I just want to pay you!"

He held up both hands. "Enough! Is your mother there?"

Amanda nodded, incapable of looking away. Was he refusing her because she wasn't a fancy, fat beauty? And why wasn't she relieved?

He inhaled. "I had already planned to take you to London, assuming you did have family there."

He had? She was stunned. "Why would you do that?"

"Because you need to go to family," he said harshly.

"But how will I pay for my fare? I am not a beggar, to be tossed a crumb!"

"You won't pay!" He was abrupt. "And I have never once indicated that I think you a beggar. The truth is, I was leaving at the end of the month, but considering all that has happened, we'll leave tomorrow."

"Tomorrow?" She started backing up. All dismay was gone—there was only gut-curdling fear. "That's too soon! And what about Papa's burial?" How could they leave tomorrow? "The end of the month is better." She had just lost Papa, she wasn't ready to meet her mother.

"We will bury your father at sea after we set sail. We leave tomorrow," de Warenne snapped. He pointed at her. "And you will not be dressed like that. I prefer you in a boy's clothing."

## *CHAPTER FOUR*

SLEEP ELUDED HIM.

Huge, almond-shaped green eyes held his. Masses of pale, almost silvery hair framed an equally exotic and beautiful face. Long wild strands twirled past her full breasts, clearly visible beneath the fine cotton nightgown. How could she have appeared in the public rooms of his house, clad in such intimate and revealing attire?

He jerked at his loins, which were full. He debated behaving like a schoolboy, but he hadn't done so since the age of twelve, and felt ashamed to even contemplate the act of masturbation. How could he be this attracted to, and this worried about, the pirate's daughter? Even though he knew her name now, he refused to think of her as Amanda. It must be La Sauvage or the pirate's daughter or even Miss Carre, just as he must fight such an insane attraction.

He turned onto his belly, trying to ignore the raging blood in his loins. He must never forget that she was very young, absurdly young…too young. And she wasn't his type of woman! By the time he had run away from home at the age of fourteen, he had been seducing the daughters of his father's friends. He had always looked older than he actually was and there were many beautiful, elegant older noblewomen to choose from. When the choice was between a wildflower or a hothouse rose, he had always turned toward the latter.

But she was entirely different from them all. He had only to think of her barging into King's House with a loaded pistol or riding her canoe in frothing seas to know that. Then his smile vanished and he cringed, recalling her language in the gold salon. But a moment later he almost chuckled, thinking of how she had deliberately chased Miss Delington out of his house. Aruptly his thoughts veered. Cliff lunged from the bed for a drink.

Was she even innocent? She certainly knew what she was offering. Considering the culture she had been raised in, it was unlikely she was inexperienced. Why else would she so readily bargain with her body? Of course, it was an ancient ploy for women without power or means. She had nothing else to barter with. That dismayed him and saddened him immensely.

He was beginning to have a distinct sense of dread about taking her to England.

He knew he could control and hide his lust. It would be unpleasant and difficult, but he was a disciplined man. And she was too young! He need only recollect that. Because he had shortened his time at home, he would bring his children with him. Alexi had already sailed the islands with him and had been demanding a "real" cruise for some time now. Ariella had been dropping hints and he knew she wished to travel abroad and see the sights she had been reading about. He was acutely aware that his children would provide a distraction for him. They would be a buffer zone.

But there was more. Cliff sat down with a cognac in the dark. Rumor had it that Rodney Carre had once been in the Royal navy. Was it true? Because if so, Amanda's mother might be from a genteel background.

And that worried him terribly.

La Sauvage had no sense of modesty, no sense of shame and no manners whatsoever. If her mother was well-bred, their reunion would be a disaster.

Yet he didn't want her to discover that her mother was a

whore or a pockmarked hag, either. The pirate's daughter had had a difficult life, he didn't need to know the details to be certain of that. She deserved some of life's luxuries and that would require a fine family from her mother's side.

In six weeks, she might be able to acquire some airs and a sense of propriety, just enough not to be so shocking. Anahid could teach her. But he wasn't confident. He wasn't even certain La Sauvage wished any instruction in decorum, and he had only agreed to transport her, not to transform her into a young lady. Besides, it wasn't his affair.

Cliff gave up thinking of sleep. It was almost dawn and he had a voyage to make. His children's baggage had been readied last night, and he had decided to bring their language tutor, as well. That decision had been made with Miss Carre in the back of his mind.

He almost felt as if he had acquired another child, but he had only to recall her in her nightgown to know he had not.

Cliff drained the cognac and dressed. The sky was stained fuchsia over indigo seas when he left his suite. He went directly to the children's wing. Alexi's door was open and he was already dressed and standing at the washbasin, brushing his teeth. He turned and grinned at his father, his mouth full of water.

Cliff's heart softened. He tossed a cloth at him. "Is your sister ready, too?"

"I heard her complaining about the hour to Anahid. Papa, we have good winds today."

Cliff winked. "I know. Do not rush. Miss Carre is undoubtedly still asleep."

He left his son spitting out his rinse water and paused at his daughter's door. "Ariella? Anahid?"

A moment passed and the Armenian opened the door. He felt her smile. "My lord?"

He glanced past her and saw that Ariella remained in her nightshirt, bleary eyed. She was clutching a book to her chest.

He had to smile. "Good morning. Don't worry, Anahid packed dozens of books for you. And if you manage to get through all of that, there is always my Bible."

She yawned.

"We will be downstairs in ten minutes, my lord," Anahid said quietly.

He left. Cliff hurried downstairs and strode into the great hall, an age-old excitement upon him now. He was happiest when making sail. All the demons he had been wrestling with in the course of the night were gone. Within two hours, he would have the wind at his back, the open sea ahead of him, and his children would be with him. Life could not be better, he thought.

Wall sconces had been lit by the servants and the hall was partially illuminated, some early-morning shadows playing across the marble floors. Cliff suddenly spied his houseguest sitting in a studded Spanish chair not far from the front doors. He had certainly not expected her to be up. She saw him, too, and leaped to her feet, her eyes wide.

His steps slowed as he approached her. He refused to recall his brooding of just an hour ago. "Good morning. It is barely dawn. Could you not sleep?" Although he had passed by her door once last night and had overheard her weeping, there was no sign on her face of having spent a terrible night. He had ordered her clothing laundered while she grieved, and she was wearing the loose shirt and breeches now, but she had added a thick gold cord as a belt. It looked suspiciously as if it had come from a drapery tieback.

"We set sail this morning," she said, smiling. "Why would I want to stay abed?"

He felt his world still. Surely her excitement had to do with being reunited with her mother. Surely she did not feel the powerful lure of the sea as he did. "It is a six-week voyage. It will be some time before you can renew your relationship with your mother."

"What are you talking about? I know how long the voyage is." She began to fidget. "The winds are fresh. Do we set sail now?"

Was it possible that she was as excited as he was to be embarking?

"You are staring at me as if I am a loon!" she exclaimed. "It's been so long!" She started to hop from foot to foot. "Is there any reason to delay? I saw your men hoisting sail from my window. De Warenne—I mean, Captain—I need to have a rolling deck under my feet and a good wind in my hair."

And staring at her, impossibly surprised, he felt himself stiffen. Shaken, he quickly turned aside so she wouldn't see how he had physically reacted to her excitement. He wasn't sure he had ever been so aroused.

"De Warenne? I mean, Captain, we are ready to go, aren't we?"

He didn't answer. A six-week voyage loomed. His response was simply unacceptable. As ship's captain, his duty was to protect her and see her safely to her destination, not to ravage her in a moment of madness.

Thank God, he had decided to bring his family with him on this voyage, he thought.

"Are you ill?" she demanded, tugging on his vest from behind.

He made sure he was completely composed before turning. Slowly, he faced her. "I am bringing my children on this voyage and they are on their way downstairs. As soon as they are ready, we will depart."

Her eyes sparkled. "I started sailing with Papa from the time I was six," she said. "Isn't that about your daughter's age?"

"Yes."

Her green eyes narrowed. "You are behaving so oddly! Is something wrong?"

He folded his arms across his chest, keeping his eyes trained on her face. "When was the last time you were at sea? And I do not mean paddling your canoe."

"There was a short cruise to Barbados—Papa had affairs there, legitimate ones. That was last spring."

He would die, he thought, to be denied a real cruise for such an interminable length of time. "You seem to be in very good spirits today, Miss Carre."

"You mean Amanda." She sobered a bit. "I haven't forgotten about Papa, if that is what you mean. I spent most of last night thinking about him. I don't have any tears left." Then she brightened. "The *Fair Lady* is my favorite ship. There's just something haunting about her. Everyone knows she's the fastest fifth rate on the high seas—but that's because of you, of course. And you've never lost a battle! I can help with her guns. Your sailmaker is Portuguese, isn't he? Papa said he's one of the greatest in the world."

Cliff's heart thundered in his chest, preventing speech.

"Can I tell you a secret?" she asked with a grin, blushing. "I've dreamed of riding her decks and racing the wind. This is just like one of my dreams!" She laughed, tossing her hair, which she hadn't bothered to tie back.

He had to turn away again, his breeches painfully constricting. *She'd dreamed of his ship. Had she dreamed of him, too?*

"I can't wait," she said.

He thought about giving in to insanity; he thought about turning, crushing her to his chest, opening her mouth with his teeth and kissing her. He thought about thrusting his tongue as far as he could.

He heard his children's footsteps on the stairs and their happy, animated chatter. There was vast relief and bitter disappointment.

He inhaled, smiled in a more genuine manner, and turned away from her. "I see we are all here. To the cutter, then."

AMANDA GRIPPED the railing and closed her eyes, her face turned up high to the sun and the wind. They'd left Kingston far behind and only a faint pale strip of white sand, framed by jungle-green mountains set against the turquoise water, indicated the island behind them. Ahead, the seas swelled gently. De Warenne was using almost all of his canvas, so the great frigate was rating fifteen knots, racing as fast as she could in such a kind breeze. Amanda opened her eyes and laughed in sheer joy.

She'd known it would be like this, hadn't she? She felt a fist in her gut and half turned so she could view her captain on the quarterdeck. He stood at the helm with his son, whom she had learned was eight years old, helping the boy steer the ship. He seemed taller, his shoulders wider, his hair more golden, as they raced the wind. Just looking at him made it hard for her to breathe.

She didn't care. Six weeks lay ahead—the best six weeks of her life.

She wasn't going to think about arriving at her mother's, not yet.

De Warenne glanced over his shoulder at her. He had been smiling, clearly filled with the same exhilaration as she, but his smile vanished when their gazes met. He looked back over the prow, his expression terribly serious.

He'd been behaving strangely ever since yesterday, Amanda thought, when she'd interfered in his amorous plans. Oh well. It didn't matter now. The sun was high, soft cumulous clouds scudded in the sky, and a pair of dolphins were racing the frigate at its larboard side. But unable to stop herself, as if a puppet on someone's string, she turned to stare at him again.

Neither he nor his son was exchanging words, but the boy was clearly engrossed in steering the ship. He seemed so little in the shadow of his father's powerful body. She grew sad reminded of how Papa had helped her at the helm when she was so small she'd had to be in his arms in order to grasp the wheel. Then her gaze veered to his daughter, who was seated not far from them, appearing every inch the princess that she probably was in her fine, lacy white dress, a book open on her lap. Her father had given her a velvet pillow to sit on, so she wouldn't dirty her frilly drawers. She was pretty and pampered and clearly didn't give a hoot about sailing, for she hadn't looked up once.

Amanda couldn't imagine what it must be like to be that rich little girl. But the child could read—and she was only six.

Amanda felt her cheeks warm. She wished she hadn't admitted to de Warenne that she was illiterate. Did he think her stupid? It had taken her one instant to realize that he adored his fairy princess daughter and was absolutely proud of her. They'd all taken a cutter from the docks below Windsong out to the ship. Ariella had sat in her father's lap, clutching a book as they were rowed out to the frigate. Her brother had argued with her, telling her the book should have been packed in her bags. Ariella had shot right back at him that he was an idiot, as he could barely read *Latin*. De Warenne had ended the argument, telling his son that Ariella could bring as many books as she wished and he had better be reading Latin by the time the voyage was done. Through it all, the Armenian servant had been silent.

De Warenne had looked at Amanda, smiling. "My daughter reads better than many grown men." He'd turned to the child. "What are you reading now, darling?"

"The history of the Pharoahs, Papa."

Amanda didn't even know what a fa-ro was.

She was jealous of his daughter, when she owed de Warenne nothing but gratitude. She also wished she had been invited onto the quarterdeck, as his children had, but she had not. She had no reason to speak with de Warenne, so she had no excuse to go over and ask for permission to go up on the deck considered sacred by every sailor and ship's officer. Maybe he'd invite her to join him there before the voyage was out.

Probably not.

Oddly, she thought of the beautiful cotton-and-lace night-gown. He hadn't taken it back. It was in her small sack with her father's cross and chain and her pistol. Her dagger was in her left boot on the inside of her calf and her sword was beneath the pillow on her berth.

"Papa? I don't feel well," Ariella said suddenly.

Amanda turned to see the little girl standing, holding her history book. She had that peculiar look which Amanda instantly recognized. The child was sea sick.

"Can I go below and lie down with Anahid?" she asked.

"That is the worst thing you can do." De Warenne glanced behind him. His gaze slid over Amanda and he seemed to hesitate.

She thought she knew what he wanted, and because she so wanted to repay him for her passage, she jumped forward. Why couldn't she help with the children? She didn't know anything about children, but she owed de Warenne and how hard could it be? "De Warenne? I'll walk her about the deck."

His gaze softened. "Would you mind, Miss Carre? I believe Anahid is belowdecks arranging the children's cabins."

Amanda smiled at him. "Don't worry. I won't let her fall overboard."

He started.

She laughed. "That was a jest, de Warenne!"

"It wasn't amusing," he said, unsmiling.

She bit her lip. He was so serious when it came to his daughter! The little princess probably wept buckets when he hit her. She sighed and held out her hand. "Come with me."

Ariella smiled at her, extending her free hand while clutching the book with her other one. Amanda helped her down the three steps to the main deck. "You'll feel better in a few days, once you get your sea legs," she told her.

"Really?" Ariella smiled, then turned green.

Amanda dragged her over to the railing just in time, for the child threw up. She sat with her until she was through, then realized Ariella was very close to crying. She was disgusted. The child was a milksop.

De Warenne lifted her into his arms, having materialized behind them. "You will feel better in a few days," he said. "That is a promise."

Ariella fought tears. "I'm fine, Papa. Put me down."

"Are you certain?" he asked.

She nodded. "I want to walk with Miss Carre. I'm better now, really." She managed a small smile.

He slid her to the deck and Ariella took Amanda's hand. Amanda felt like an outsider, her jealousy of the little girl escalating until de Warenne turned his gaze upon her. "Thank you for being so kind to my daughter,' he said, his blue eyes sweeping over her face.

It felt like a silken caress. Amanda couldn't smile back and she couldn't move but she knew that if she wanted him to like her, all she had to do was be good to his children. And she wanted him to like her, very badly in fact.

She wet her lips and tried to smile. "She'll get her sea legs soon. After all, she's your daughter."

He gave her a look that said he didn't quite think Ariella would adjust well to the sea and then he returned to the quarterdeck. Amanda stared after him. How did he keep his clothes so clean, she wondered. He smelled more strongly of the sea than ever, but he still smelled of mango and Far Eastern spices.

"You like Papa."

Amanda jerked. She tugged the girl down the deck and out of earshot. "De Warenne has been good to me and he is taking me to my mother."

"I know. He told us. She's in England." Ariella's eyes were searching, and far too curious for a child of six.

"She's a great lady," Amanda bragged. "Terribly beautiful and she lives in a big fancy house with a rose garden."

"Really?" Ariella thought about that. "Was your papa really a pirate?" she asked seriously as they strolled hand in hand down the deck.

Amanda hesitated. Then she decided there was no way she was going to admit to the truth. "He was falsely accused and falsely hanged," she lied. "He was a planter and a real gentleman. But," she added, veering to some of the truth, "a long time ago he was an officer in the British navy."

Ariella was quiet and Amanda knew she was thinking intensely. What a strange girl! Then the child said, "Why aren't you happy to be going to see your mama? Is it because your papa is dead?"

Amanda stopped in her tracks. She was about to cut the child, but then she saw de Warenne watching them from the quarterdeck. She forced a smile. "I am very happy to be going to see my mother. I haven't seen her since I was even younger than you." But her insides curdled as she spoke. If only she could believe that Mama would be overjoyed to see her.

"Really?" Ariella smiled, but then sobered. "My mama is dead. She was murdered when I was born."

Amanda couldn't help being curious. "Was she a princess?"

Ariella's eyes widened and she laughed. "No. There are no Hebrew royals."

"She was a Jew?" Amanda asked, surprised. She'd met Jewish people before, of course—she'd been to Curaçao once and it was mostly a Jewish island. Papa had said the Jews had come long ago from Spain.

"Papa fell in love with her and they had me. But it was forbidden and a Barbary prince ordered her death. Do you know where Barbary is?"

Amanda stared. She couldn't help feeling sorry for the child but she was very dismayed to learn that de Warenne had been in love with her mother. She had been very beautiful, if Ariella took after her.

"Do you?"

"Yes." Amanda tugged on her and they continued down the deck.

"Papa likes you, too," Ariella said abruptly.

Amanda tripped. "What?"

Ariella smiled at her. "He stares at you all the time and he turns red. He never blushes, except when you are in the room."

Amanda was disbelieving. "I doubt anyone or anything could make your father blush."

"You make him blush. I saw him, this morning when we left the house, and he was blushing on the cutter."

"It's hot," Amanda said irritably. She did not want to discuss Cliff de Warenne with his pampered daughter who had fancy airs and could read a grown-up's history book. By now, they had taken an entire turn of the deck, coming up the port side, and they stood not far from the subject of their conversation.

"I feel better. I want to lie down," Ariella said with a yawn. She turned, releasing Amanda's hand, and pushed open the door to the captain's cabin.

Amanda didn't object, because she felt certain Ariella was allowed to come and go there as she pleased. She herself had never been permitted to enter Papa's cabin without knocking, but he'd often had a trollop in there with him. She'd always assumed that all fathers were the same, but she was beginning to think that de Warenne treated his children very differently from the way Papa had treated her. Papa hadn't cared that she couldn't read and he'd never petted and coddled her, the way de Warenne did Ariella.

Ariella rushed into the cabin. Amanda couldn't help herself; she was faint with curiosity now. She took one step inside so she could peek at his private room, all the while pretending that she had to keep an eye on his daughter, as she had promised.

The cabin was red.

The walls were painted a dark Chinese red and three scarlet rugs were on the floor, one Tibetan, one Chinese, one a fine, thin Aubusson. Amanda knew the differences, because the rugs she and her father had plundered over the years were some of their most valuable booty. A huge ebony bed with four thick, carved posters was against one wall. The covers were red-and-gold damask, the sheets striped in red silk. Red-and-gold pillows leaned against the huge headboard with thick, fat tassels and fringe.

A very fine English table, with curved legs and four chairs upholstered in burgundy velvet were in the room's center. Beneath several portholes was a huge desk, covered with maps and charts. The entire room was filled with odd treasures—an Arabian brass chest with lock and key, African masks, intricately designed and colorful Moroccan vases, Waterford crystal, gold candlesticks. And there was a bookcase, crammed with hundreds of books. Amanda shivered.

She had just stepped inside de Warenne's private lair. It reeked of the man's exotic tastes, his erotic nature, his intelligence, power and virility. She shouldn't be there, she somehow thought.

Someone seized her from behind. "What are you doing in here?"

Amanda reacted on instinct but the moment she drew her blade and pressed it against his chest, she realized her mistake. De Warenne's eyes went wide. She froze, her heart hammering madly, as she was in his arms.

"What is that?" he asked very calmly.

His thighs were thick, bulging muscle, she realized inanely as he held her body completely against his. "It's a dagger," she breathed. "I am sorry…I'll put it down, but you must let me go."

Their gazes were locked. As he released her, she felt him stirring and she gasped, her gaze shooting back to his.

He blushed. His daughter was right, she thought, stunned. Or was she now as mad as the child?

He stepped back, grim. "No one enters this cabin without permission." He half turned, striding to the porthole, where he breathed deeply.

It was too late. Amanda could clearly see that he had been aroused. She slipped the dagger slowly into its sheath in her boot.

He wanted her. She wasn't really certain why. Was it the brief act of violence? Every sailor she knew enjoyed sex after a bloody battle.

"Papa? It's my fault. I wanted to come inside," Ariella whispered from the bed.

De Warenne turned and smiled at his daughter. The expression, however, was strained. "Even you must ask my permission to enter here."

The child nodded, eyes wide, looking back and forth between Amanda and her father.

Amanda tried to breathe more naturally. "I'm sorry." She took a careful glance at him and wasn't sure if she was relieved or disappointed that he seemed to be in control of his amorous nature once more.

His jaw flexed. He gestured for them both to precede him out of the door. When they had done so, he barked, "Miss Carre. A moment, please."

She did not like his tone but she nodded, hoping he wasn't going to discipline her for her trespass. That was what Papa would do. He'd deliver a quick cuff to the head, at least. Her stomach churned with some fear. Papa had been a big man, but de Warenne was taller, more muscular and far younger. Well, if he hit her she wouldn't flinch. He'd see that she was strong and brave—she'd make Papa proud.

"Ariella, if you are feeling better, I am pleased. But going below is still not a good idea. I have summoned Anahid. The two of you can read together on that bench."

"Yes, Papa," she whispered.

"Go." But he smiled now and stooped to kiss her cheek.

Ariella beamed at him and rushed off to Anahid, who was waiting a discreet distance away.

Amanda tensed in anticipation of her punishment, watching his shoulders stiffen before he turned. He gestured. "Would you care—"

Amanda ducked.

He froze, his hand in the air, poised between them. "What are you doing?"

She flushed. She had broken his rules, and she should stand firm. "Nothing. I mean, I won't dodge the blow."

His eyes popped. "*What*?"

"Go ahead, just do it. I disobeyed your orders."

"You think I mean to strike you?" He dropped his hand.

She became wary. "That's what a hand is for, isn't it?"

He took a step toward her and she forgot her resolve, backing up. He halted, and so did she. "Miss Carre! I do not strike women," he said, aghast. "I have never struck a woman in my life, and I never will."

She wasn't sure she should believe him. "Is this a trick?"

He was incredulous, so much so that it was a moment before he spoke. When he did, she saw pity in his eyes. "I am trying to invite you to dine with me tonight," he said.

"You want to sup with me?" This had to be trickery, didn't it?

He nodded. "I thought we might converse."

Amanda was suspicious. Men had one use for women—and it wasn't for conversation. Her heart slammed hard. He had changed his mind. He had decided to take her to his bed after all.

"Will you accept my invitation?"

She didn't know what to think. Was he now going to allow her to pay for her passage in his bed? Her mind filled with hazy but heated images of her golden dream lover, and suddenly, that lover wasn't faceless anymore. Instead it was de Warenne stroking her body, causing her skin to tingle and throb. Maybe she wouldn't mind being in his bed. Everyone said he was a superb lover. She'd heard the island ladies talking about him more times than she could remember. Some of them, the ones who'd shared his bed, had bragged about it to their friends. Somehow, she knew the rumors were true.

Her skin was tingling now, as if she was in one of her secret dreams, but this time, the aching was more intense. She breathed and nodded. “We can sup…and converse.”

His gaze narrowed. “My intentions are honorable.”

She didn’t believe him, not for a moment.

## *CHAPTER FIVE*

AMANDA STAYED by the railing at the ship's stern, standing tall and proud, trying to remain utterly composed. It was very hard to do. Six seamen had carried the teakwood coffin with her father's corpse to the deck, where it now sat, gleaming in the Caribbean sun. The *Fair Lady* had a crew of close to three hundred men, and every available sailor stood on deck, respectfully silent. De Warenne was speaking. He held a Bible in his hands and she knew he was reading from it, but Amanda couldn't comprehend a word he was saying.

The grief had risen out of nowhere, paralyzing her. A few hours ago, when they had made sail, she had been filled with joy. She had forgotten Papa's terrible fate. Now she fought to hold the pain of his loss at bay. It seemed a monumental, impossible task. She was overcome by wave after wave of grief.

She did not want to lose her composure in front of de Warenne, his family and his crew.

*I can't do this*, she thought, the tears finally spilling down her cheeks. *I can't live without Papa. It hurts too much.*

He had been her life. Her mother was a complete stranger and she was never going to take her papa's place.

Her knees were weak, her body was trembling, and the tears kept crawling down her face.

*Please make this dream end*, she thought in anguish. *Please!*

Then she realized that the ship was silent. All that could be heard was the groaning of the masts, the flap of sails, the lapping of water, the sea spray. De Warenne had stopped speaking.

She didn't dare look at him. If she did, she'd start shrieking in pain and rage.

He appeared before her. Speaking low, his tone unbearably kind, he said, "Do you wish to say a few words?"

How could she say anything when she couldn't breathe, much less speak? The silence on the ship was simply awful.

"Do you wish to say goodbye, at least?" he asked softly, clasping her shoulder.

She had to look up. She felt herself drown in both the grief and the compassion in his blue eyes. She nodded, choking on a huge sob.

He put his arm around her and led her toward the gleaming coffin.

Amanda fell to her knees. She hugged the waxed wood, laying her cheek on the cold surface. *Papa*, she thought, *I love you. I always have, I always will.*

*Be strong, girl. Always be strong. You're in good hands now.*

Amanda stiffened, because once again it was as if Rodney was right there, speaking to her. "I'm not strong," she whispered. "It's a lie. I can't go on alone."

*You're not alone, girl, and you are strong. Strong and brave and don't you be forgetting it.*

"No, I'm not," she wept.

Someone clasped her shoulder.

*I got to be going, girl. Let me go.*

Panic consumed her. "Don't leave me!" she cried. "Papa!"

Strong hands pulled her to her feet; a strong arm held her to a powerful body. "Let him go, Amanda." De Warenne nodded at his men.

Amanda started to weep as the six seamen lifted the coffin and carried it to the stern. "Don't leave me," she gasped.

"God bless," de Warenne said.

"Amen," two hundred men murmured.

The coffin was heaved into the sea.

Amanda screamed.

"You need to lie down," de Warenne said, pulling her firmly away from the stern.

She turned and struck at him with both fists, repeatedly, in a frenzy, as hard as she could, as if *he* had murdered her father.

He lifted her into his arms and started down the deck, but she kept hitting him and hitting him, hating him and Woods and all the British and the whole world until the anger vanished and there was only exhaustion.

AMANDA AWOKE a few hours later. She stared up at the ceiling of the captain's cabin, grimly aware that she was in de Warenne's four-poster, which was where he had placed her after the burial. He'd also given her a drink, but she couldn't recall what liquor it had been. She had sobbed herself to sleep.

The cabin was absolutely dark. She glanced toward the portholes, which were open, a pleasant breeze wafting into the room. Outside, the night was black velvet studded with winking stars.

She sat up on top of the red-and-gold damask covers. She fingered a sensuous leopard skin pillow. Papa was gone. He wasn't coming back and she had to face that fact now.

She slid from the bed, barefoot. He had removed her boots or he'd ordered someone to do it for him. Amanda found them and sat down to tug them on. She was no longer in the throes of grief—she merely felt sad and resigned. But that was as it should be. Papa deserved to be mourned, and she'd had no right to have been happy earlier that day.

She wondered where the ship's captain was, and what he thought of her now. He certainly did not think her brave and strong. She had let Papa down.

"Don't worry," she told her father, hoping he could hear her somehow. "There will be no more female hysteria. I'm sorry, Papa, for being such a dumb girl."

This time, there was no answer.

Amanda sighed. She walked out of the cabin and instantly saw de Warenne.

His first officer, a big Scot named MacIver, was at the helm. De Warenne stood, lightly grasping the railing on the main deck, watching the starlight playing over the gleaming black water, sprinkling it with silver ribbons. The winds had eased and the frigate had dropped her speed. The night remained balmy and pleasant—a perfect night for a cruise.

He turned. Many feet separated them, and although his ship was far better lit than her father's sloop had ever been, it remained shadowy and dark. It didn't matter. Even in the dark, even with a good ten lengths between them, their gazes met and held.

Amanda almost felt hypnotized. She walked over to him.

His gaze slid over her face. "Did you have a good rest?"

She nodded. "Yes, I did. Thank you for the use of your bed."

His mouth softened. "Do not say that too loudly—you might be misunderstood."

She had to smile. "I am not worried. I don't think anyone would ever accuse you of trying to take *me* to bed."

He glanced away.

Instantly she recalled his interest in her that morning and his invitation to dine—which had really been an invitation to tryst. Her cheeks became warm, and an odd hollow feeling began in her lower body. Amanda turned to face the sea, grasping the railing. Too late, she realized they stood mere inches apart.

She gave him a quick, sidelong glance, aware that for the first time in her life, she was having feelings of some kind for a man. Standing this close to him left her breathless and restless. Maybe he'd ask her to supper tomorrow night.

He didn't speak, and she turned away. She watched the starlight dancing over the rippling swells. As far as the human eye could see, there was nothing but the shining blackness of the sea. It seemed infinite, powerful and mighty.

And it was comforting. *He* was comforting. She was terribly aware of his big masculine body and the tension in her own limbs, but far more significant was the feeling of being safe and sheltered just by being close to him.

She smiled just a little. She didn't have to ask to know that he was enjoying the absolute beauty and serenity of the moment, and truth be told, so was she. But the real truth was, she was enjoying being near him, and with him.

More moments passed in a new and strangely companionable silence.

Amanda said, "The night is perfect, isn't it?"

He glanced down at her. "I agree."

She met his gaze, felt a fluttering in her chest, then turned her vision back to the endless stretch of shining water. Papa was really gone, but the night *was* perfect. She should feel like a traitor, but she knew he would want her to enjoy such a night.

Then her stomach growled.

De Warenne smiled at her.

Amanda blushed. "That isn't ladylike, is it?"

"You have told me, once or twice, that being a lady doesn't interest you."

She thought of the ladylike nightgown in her sack. "It doesn't," she said, but she felt as if she wasn't speaking the entire truth. In order to change the subject, she added quickly, "If you really wanted to have supper with me, I ruined it."

A brow lifted. "Actually, you haven't and actually, I really did."

She faced him fully. "What do you mean?"

His gaze slid slowly over every feature of her face. "I haven't eaten. I was hoping you might wake up and share my meal."

He had changed his mind about her, she realized. He had decided to take her to bed, after all. She should be dismayed, but she wasn't. She felt terribly nervous and excited. And now, she would be able to pay for her passage. She slowly lifted her gaze to his, thinking about what was to come and realizing that she wanted to join him in his bed after all. Now, she could only pray that she wouldn't make a fool out of herself while there. But she was smart, so surely once he started up with her, she'd figure out what to do.

"I will have our meal laid out. Excuse me." He strode away.

Amanda inhaled, gripping the rail, aware of her pulse escalating. And suddenly she understood desire, oh yes.

"Miss Carre." He gestured from the threshold of his cabin with a brief smile.

Amanda came forward, biting her lip. Even though he remained informally dressed in his linen shirt, his pale breeches and high boots, she wished she was wearing a dress, not that she owned one.

Then she saw the table. The gold candlesticks had tall ivory candles and had been lit. A white tablecloth had been draped over the table and it was graced with linen napkins, gilded flatware, crystal wineglasses and beautifully enameled red, blue and gold plates with gilt edges. A wine bottle sat on a silver coaster next to steaming silver platters. She had never seen such a sight and she could not move.

"Please." He walked past her, drawing a dark red velvet chair from the table.

"We are really going to eat?" she gasped, wondering if she was in a dream.

"Yes, I invited you to dine."

She couldn't tear her gaze away from the elegant table. She had never seen such a table—a queen should be dining there, not Carre's daughter!

"Miss Carre?"

She vaguely heard him, realizing she had been wrong. He would not set up the table this way if he merely wished to toss her on her backside. Stunned and bewildered, she glanced at him. He continued to hold the chair out.

Somehow she came cautiously forward. Once, her father had

held out a chair for his mistress, but they had both been staggering and foxed, laughing wildly over a gesture they considered absurd, mocking the airs of the gentry. Papa had ruined the mockery anyway, by pulling the woman onto his lap instead of allowing her to sit down, while delving deeply into her bodice.

Amanda stared at de Warenne. How could he be so kind, so generous and so handsome? He had sworn he was a gentleman with no untoward intentions, and she was beginning to believe it. He didn't need to stage a grand seduction for the likes of her.

"Please, do sit," he said softly.

"This isn't a seduction?"

"No, it's not." His gaze held hers.

"Why?"

Even in the dim candlelight, she saw him flush. "Why isn't this a seduction?"

She shook her head. "Why are you doing this? Why do you want to sup with me? I'm not a duke or an admiral. I'm not beautiful or elegant. Why?"

He was still, their gazes holding. It was a moment before he spoke. "It's more pleasant to dine in company than alone. I'd also like to hear about your life."

She blinked. "*My* life?" Her life had no significance and no one had ever been interested in any details of it before.

"It's not every day that I rescue a pirate's daughter," he said, his tone suddenly teasing.

Amanda had to smile. Such a statement could have been offensive, coming from someone else. "My life will bore you," she warned. Then, upon impulse, "But I should like to hear about yours!"

He started. "My life will surely bore you!"

She laughed. "You are royalty!"

He chuckled. "Darling, I am hardly royalty." He gestured at the chair.

Amanda was breathless and light-headed. She finally sat

down. No one had ever called her "darling" before. Of course, he hadn't meant it. He called his daughter "darling." She wasn't his daughter and she certainly didn't want to be thought of as a child. But he had uttered the endearment so seductively, and she had a powerful, deep yearning to have him call her darling again—and this time, to mean it.

He pushed the chair closer to the table, then he took a seat facing her, lifting the wine bottle. He hesitated, his smile fading. Then he put the bottle down. "I must ask. How old are you?"

She didn't hesitate. "Twenty-one." She smiled, her heart continuing to beat wildly. She wanted him to think her more mature and worldly than she was. "How old are you?"

He laughed, shaking his head. "Amanda, we both know you are not even close to twenty-one. I am twenty-eight." He hesitated. "I mean, Miss Carre."

She had thought he was in his late twenties and she had been right. She carefully debated what age to tell him, one he might believe. "I am almost twenty," she lied. "And I told you, I am not a lady. You can call me Amanda."

His regard was frankly assessing. He finally said, "Really."

"Really. And I would like some wine," she added.

He poured her a scant finger, then poured himself a large glass.

"And to think I thought you were so generous," she grumbled, reaching for her glass. Had her ploy succeeded?

"My estimation is that you are sixteen, perhaps seventeen," he said, watching her closely.

Amanda sighed. She was seventeen and she would be eighteen in August. Instead of responding, she cast her eyes down and took a draft of the wine. Immediately she gasped, forgetting all about her deception. The wine she drank with Papa had been thick and sour; she had always preferred grog. "What is this?" she managed, stunned.

He leaned back in his chair, smiling broadly at her. "I take it that was a cry of approval?"

"This is delicious—like berries and velvet."

"There is a strong note of blackberry," he agreed, "and just enough tannin to coat the tongue. It's from Rioja."

Amanda was too busy taking another sip to reply. The wine was heaven.

"You'll get tipsy if you don't slow down," he said, but his tone was light. He hadn't touched his glass; he simply kept staring at her.

She wished she knew what he was really thinking. She smiled widely at him. "I never knew wine could be so delicious. Why are you looking at me so closely?"

He flushed and glanced aside. "I apologize."

"Is it my shirt? Should I have braided my hair?"

"Your shirt is fine." His smile was forced. "I was rude. It won't happen again."

Amanda hesitated. She twisted her hair into a knot, then smiled grimly at him. "I don't have any other clothes, except for that nightgown."

He seemed alarmed. "It's not your hair—your hair is beautiful—and it's not your clothes. I would like you to enjoy this meal. My chef is a good one."

She went still. He liked her hair? Every summer she would chop a foot off with her dagger, but it always grew back by the next season. This summer, she hadn't bothered—as her hair had not been on her mind, not with her father's capture. "It's too long," she managed.

His color heightened. "Never cut it," he said tersely.

"Do you really think my hair is beautiful?" she demanded.

His fingers drummed at the tablecloth, long and strong. Finally, slowly looking up, he said, "Yes, I do."

She stared into his eyes, filled with joy, smiling at him.

He glanced away. "How old did you say you were?"

She was not going to tell him the truth. "I am almost twenty, de Warenne."

He lifted his gaze, which was impenetrable now. "That is impossible. You are clearly at that awkward stage, at once half child, half woman."

"You are babbling nonsense," she said, instantly annoyed. "No one is half woman and half child! This morning you clearly thought me a full-grown woman, not *half* of one."

He sat up straighter in his chair, his gaze locking with hers. Amanda stared challengingly at him, waiting for him to respond.

His lips slowly stretched into an odd smile. "You were raised among rowdy sailors. You know the nature of men. I have tried to be a gentleman with you, but I will admit my shortcomings. My nature is a manly one. It doesn't mean anything, so do not read anything into it."

Amanda stared at him. She could not decipher his meaning.

He sent her a very direct and sensual smile, one which could melt hearts and instantly melted hers. She forgot about decoding his odd words. Her pulse rioted and her thoughts jumbled, all at once.

He took the wine bottle and filled her glass. "Tell me a little bit about yourself."

She could barely comprehend him.

"Amanda? When did you and your father come to live on Jamaica Island?"

She inhaled, unable to forget the way he had just looked at and smiled at her. She was still breathless. "I was four," she exhaled.

"Where did you live prior to that?" he asked, his glass now in hand. From time to time he took a sip, clearly enjoying the red wine.

"St. Mawes. It's in Cornwall. I was born there," she said, her scattered wits finally returning.

"St. Mawes…I believe that's on the eastern coast."

She nodded. "That is where my mother was born."

"How did your parents meet?" he asked, his gaze never leaving her face.

He was really interested in her life, she thought, amazed. "Papa was in the navy. He was a midshipman on a ship of the line. He was on leave in Brighton and Mama was there with her mother and sisters on holiday. It was love at first sight," she added with a smile.

She kept expecting him to evince boredom, but he was leaning toward her now. "I had heard some talk of Carre having been a naval officer. A ship of the line, that is impressive."

Ships of the line were the greatest warships in the British navy, huge triple-deck affairs with more than a hundred guns and crews of up to eight hundred or more. She was proud. "Papa was very dashing then, I think."

"And your mother was swept off her feet." He smiled.

"Yes." Her smile faltered. "And then Papa turned rogue."

"After the marriage?"

She nodded. "And after I was born. Mama gave him the boot."

"I wonder if I know your mother's family," he mused. "My brother Rex has an estate in Cornwall, and I have been there, although infrequently."

"She was a Straithferne," Amanda said with renewed pride. "They are a very old family—Mama could trace her bloodlines back to Anglo-Saxon times."

"So your mother is a very fine lady," he remarked.

"She is a great lady. Papa told me that her airs are perfect and proper, no matter the moment, and that she is a great beauty, too." She smiled, but some unease had arisen. It was so easy to forget that in six weeks she would be standing at her mother's door in London. She glanced at de Warenne and saw him watching her intently and she smiled more firmly, as she did not want him to ever guess that going to England scared her more than any sea battle ever could.

"Does the family still have holdings in St. Mawes?" he asked.

Amanda suddenly sat up. "You are asking a lot of questions

about my mother." Her mind sped. De Warenne was an infamous ladies' man and her mother was a great beauty. Was his interest in Dulcea Carre?

Her heart lurched with sickening force.

"Are you all right?" he asked.

She couldn't smile.

"Amanda?"

"Do you know my mother?" she demanded.

"I'm afraid not, nor am I familiar with the Straithfernes."

She slumped in her chair in abject relief.

"I am very surprised that your mother allowed you to move to the West Indies with your father," he said casually.

Amanda remained so relieved that de Warenne wasn't interested in making her mother his lover that, while she noted his neutral tone, she didn't dwell on it. "She didn't. Papa stole me right out of her arms, breaking her heart." When his brows raised in genuine surprise, she said defensively, "He had not been allowed to visit. If Mama had been kinder, he wouldn't have had to steal me away. But she refused any visitation. He missed me, so he took me."

De Warenne was grim. "I am sorry. That is a terrible tale."

She shrugged. "I don't remember any of it. I don't even remember Mama. I wish I did," she added.

"Maybe it is best that you don't remember being torn from your mother's arms," he remarked, his gaze searching.

She stared at him. "I love Papa. I am glad he took me."

He studied her for a moment. "I know."

But Amanda felt saddened. It was very different from the grief she felt over her father's death. She couldn't help wondering what her life might have been like if Papa hadn't come to take her from St. Mawes. The question had haunted her most of her life.

She looked up and spoke defensively. "Mama is a great lady, I'm not. I will never be a lady, but I don't care. I love the sea. If

I could choose any fate, it would be to stay here like this, on a great ship, riding the waves, forever."

His thick dark lashes lowered, hooding his eyes. He didn't speak, but he was toying with the flatware.

"You probably think me a fool," she said with a heavy sigh. "Sometimes I think I am a fool," she admitted.

He didn't look up. "No. I don't think you're foolish, Amanda." His tone was like the stroke of silk. It flicked over her skin, making that humming begin all over again.

Amanda stared at his downturned face. His beauty made her breath catch, quite audibly. His high cheekbones were slightly tinged pink, undoubtedly from the wine. If, a few days ago, someone had suggested that she might be dining alone with Cliff de Warenne in the captain's cabin on his frigate, she would have laughed, outrageously amused. But she was here with him, very much alone, and he had asked her dozens of intimate questions, clearly genuinely interested in her life.

And he liked her *hair*. He had said it was beautiful.

The woman reflected in the mirror at Windsong, the one in the expensive white lace nightgown, had been strangely alluring. Even she could admit that.

But that wasn't her. She was just Amanda Carre, referred to by most islanders as either La Sauvage or the pirate's daughter, a skinny girl with long wild hair, clad in cast-off boy's clothes.

The nightgown, however, was in her sack on her berth below-decks. And her hair could be brushed and tamed…

Suddenly she imagined herself walking into his cabin with a ribbon in her hair, wearing the nightgown. And she imagined him looking at her the way he'd looked at her that morning in the great hall of Windsong. Amanda flushed, her heart thumping heavily in her breast.

He slowly looked up.

Their gazes locked.

Suddenly every sound in the cabin vanished. The soft

flapping of sail, the softer lapping of water against the hull, the gentle creak of rope, the rap of chain, all disappeared. There was only the magnetic and powerful man seated across from her and her own wild heartbeat.

Amanda wanted to be kissed. There was simply no more denying it. She could think of nothing else now.

He cleared his throat. "We should eat, before the food gets cold."

Amanda couldn't find her voice. She had never wanted any man to touch her before, but she wanted de Warenne to kiss her and touch her, and she even wanted to kiss and touch him back. But he had said his intentions were honorable.

He lifted the cover off the first silver platter and steam hissed, escaping, along with the succulent aroma of roasted guinea hen. As he served her, Amanda barely managed a smile. Should she somehow encourage him now?

"De Warenne?" she said. Her tone sounded odd, husky and deep.

He slowly looked at her, not pleased. He seemed grim. "Let's enjoy our meal, Amanda."

"I'm not hungry." She looked at the bed. Why didn't he simply take her over to it?

Suddenly he lunged to his feet. "Excuse me," he said. "I hear Ariella—she must be having a nightmare. Do not wait for me. Enjoy your supper."

He strode from the cabin.

## *CHAPTER SIX*

THE BREEZE HAD NOT picked up and he'd ordered most sail reefed. The great ship had slowed to a few knots and now the sun was rising and staining the sky over the ocean crimson and pink. One of his officers was at the helm as Cliff ripped off his shirt at the railing. In light winds or a lull, it was not unusual for him to take a predawn swim. His men thought him insane, and maybe he was, because he found the brief plunge into the frigid Atlantic waters exhilarating.

He was preoccupied as he swiftly stripped down. Inviting Amanda to dine with him last night had clearly been a mistake. Her every innocent look, smile and word enticed him. He had never met a woman like her before. Perhaps it was the combination of innocence and courage, naiveté and boldness, ignorance and wisdom that was so powerfully alluring. She was a stunning portrait of beauty and contradictions. Or maybe it was the compassion she aroused in him that was so effective. He wanted to protect her and to make love to her, all at once. Last night he had been afraid that he might throw all propriety to the wind and take her to his bed, as she so clearly wished for him to do. He had not heard his daughter crying; that had been an excuse to leave her company and find some composure—and common sense.

But there wasn't any composure and nothing made any sense. In a few short days, somehow, she had become the focus of his life.

Of course, she needed his protection. That had been clear from the moment they had first met at King's House, when she had come inside, waving a loaded pistol and demanding to see the governor. He had quickly seen that she was her own worst enemy—that had been obvious when she had thought to seduce Woods. Leaving her to her own devices was something he could not do. She was entirely alone in the world and grieving the loss of her father. She had no one to turn to but him. He had enough strength to add her to the roster of his responsibilities and duties; therefore, he would.

Last night he had invited her to dine not because he wished her company, although he had enjoyed it immensely until his own lusty nature interfered, but because he was determined to discover some facts about her life. She had been painfully easy to manipulate and she had revealed all that he needed to know, at least for the moment. The mother she was traveling to meet was well-bred, apparently a gentlewoman. She might even be nobility. He wanted Amanda to have a financially secure family, but he was dismayed.

Mother and daughter had been apart for at least ten years. Common sense and every instinct that he had told him that this reunion was not going to be easy or pleasant. Worse, her story was not quite right. He knew she believed it, but his instincts clamored that there was more to the tale than she had been told. And his instincts were usually right.

But even if her story was as she had told it, Amanda was in for more hurt and even humiliation, he was certain. He hoped, very much, that her mother would be thrilled to be reunited with her, but he had no reason to believe that she would be happy to have her pirate's daughter appear in her life. And even if she was thrilled, her friends and family were going to regard Amanda with far less tolerance. The ladies he knew, while beautiful and elegant and excellent in bed, were all rabid snobs. There was no room for eccentricity. How in God's name would Amanda ever fit into her mother's life?

Even a beautiful gown was not going to disguise her speech, her manners and the deprived background she had come from. While he might find her manner charming at times, she had actually shocked him badly once or twice. And he was not easily shocked.

Society was not going to accept La Sauvage and he was certain of it.

He could not understand or accept his desire for her. The lusting had to cease. Nor could he understand the overwhelming urge to protect her from any more hurt, but that was an inclination he could accept. It was, after all, honorable. He was violently aware, however, that protecting Amanda Carre might enmesh him very deeply in her life. He could only hope that her mother was truly gracious, but not immersed in society. If she was a kind and welcoming woman, he would be able to deposit Amanda at her mother's door and walk away, secure in the knowledge that her future would be a good one. He did not want to dwell on the far more likely possibility that Dulcea Carre might be shocked by her daughter's sudden reappearance into her life and unfavorably disposed toward her.

He suddenly recalled the look on Miss Delington's face when she had thought he was Amanda's lover and winced. The reaction of that "sow" was typical of the prejudice and bigotry rampant in high society and he couldn't help fearing the worst for Amanda. Yes, she was a pirate's daughter and she could be uncouth and crude, but she was clever, witty and resolute. She was also one of the most vulnerable human beings he had ever met. He recalled how he had found her last night, curled up on one of the rugs on the floor of his cabin, soundly asleep and impossibly beautiful, but so desperately lacking an anchor in her life. In that moment, he understood why he needed to protect her. Every ship was adrift without an anchor.

"Cap? You sick or something?"

Cliff jerked. He was standing in the buff at the rail, staring at the horizon, so absorbed in his thoughts he hadn't even been aware of where he was. He didn't bother to respond to the seaman. Instead, he stepped onto the rail and dived into the ocean.

The waters were ice-cold and shock briefly paralyzed him. The ice water closed over him, around him, and he began to sink. His mind came to life first, understanding that he must swim in order to live, and then his heart began to beat again, hard and too fast, fueled by adrenaline. He began to swim. It took every ounce of strength he had to powerfully propel himself through the freezing water. For one moment, he thought he might fail. His muscles screamed at him, as did his mind—why? Then he burst through the ceiling of water to the warmer air above and exhaled loudly, and a line was tossed down. He seized it, laughing.

Cliff quickly climbed up the line, invigorated and exultant, and two men helped him easily over the railing. He shook the water from his hair with more laughter, his heart still racing madly from the fight to beat an icy death.

"Cold enough for you, Cap?" MacIver said from the quarter-deck, his tone sly.

Still grinning, Cliff straightened, allowing the early-morning sun to wash over him. He upturned his face for a moment and spread his arms, feeling powerful and pagan, at one with the sun and the sea. Finally, his heart slowed, his shivering ceased, the euphoria dulled. He glanced towards his mate. "You should try it some time," he said, turning for a cotton towel.

He froze. Amanda stood not far from his cabin. He had no idea how long she had been on deck, but there was no mistaking how she was looking at him. She was staring at him as if she had never seen a naked man before.

No, she was staring at him as if she wished to see more of him, now.

His loins filled, instantly rising to her wish.

It was a moment before he could turn away. In that moment, time ceased and there was no thought, no reason, just desire. Her lips moved. His heart thundered and he turned away, aware of one of his men snickering. He seized the towel, intending to wrap it around his waist, but he remained painfully thick, a reminder of what he really wanted. Instead, he used the cloth to dry his hair. He took his time. Then he tossed it aside and casually stepped into his breeches, as if she weren't there. But he could feel her heat and smell her desire.

She was quivering, too.

As he pulled on each stocking, he reminded himself that she was forbidden. His body protested: why? In that instant, he couldn't remember why he had decided that this particular woman was not allowed to him.

And then, before he'd had a chance to tug on his boots, he knew she was gone. Still bare-chested, he turned and glimpsed her hurrying inside his cabin, where she'd spent the night alone. One seaman said, "Guess we know what she's sniffing for." He snickered again.

Cliff reached for his boot and put the dagger he kept there against the sailor's throat. "You don't know anything," he said, and he sliced through his flesh.

The sailor choked in horror, but the wound was only a scratch. "Lock him up," Cliff said through his teeth.

Two of his officers rushed down from the quarterdeck, seizing the seaman, who started blubbering in protest. Cliff turned his back on him, as nothing could make him change his mind. There was no quarter given to insolence, not on his ship, and the sailor had insulted Amanda. He'd maroon the man off Spain, where there were some rocky islands that no one could survive on for long. The sailor was fortunate he'd be marooned instead of keel-hauled. If he was truly fortunate, another ship would rescue him.

He sat down to put on his boots, incapable of calming the savage in him.

AMANDA LEANED AGAINST the wall, trying to breathe naturally. She wasn't ever going to forget the sight of Cliff de Warenne stripping off his clothes in the dawn light, revealing hard planes, taut angles and bulging muscles. She wasn't ever going to forget him climbing to the railing and diving into the ocean. She'd had to clasp her mouth to stop from crying out in fear. She knew he couldn't have been in the freezing water for more than sixty seconds, but an eternity had passed before she'd seen him break through the surface. He had been laughing, dear Lord, as he'd climbed back up to the deck, and then he'd stood there with his arms held high, his face turned to the sun, reveling in his courage, his power, his manhood.

And when he'd looked at her, he'd grown huge instantly.

Amanda gasped, choking on desire. She had thought she understood desire last night, but she hadn't—she understood it now. He was the most beautiful, virile, heroic man she had ever laid eyes upon and she was so hollow and faint she could not breathe. She could not stand the terrible ache and she hugged herself, hard. A long moment passed, and eventually, the shocking tension in her body eased.

Amanda walked away from the wall and opened the cabin door. De Warenne was on the quarterdeck with his officers, his back to her. An image flashed, pagan and godlike, of de Warenne standing naked, worshipping the sun. Then he'd turned and put his dagger to the sailor's throat, in retribution for his insult to her. Amanda inhaled. She had never met a man like this one before.

"Miss Carre?" Ariella smiled up at her, the Armenian woman standing beside her.

Amanda hadn't seen the child approach. She smiled. Ariella, of course, was clutching a book. "Hello," she said, wondering what de Warenne would have done if his children had seen him swimming in the nude at dawn.

"I am having my lessons now and Papa said we are to study in his cabin."

Amanda stepped aside so the child and her servant could pass. Curiously, she said, "And your brother? Isn't he going to study, too?"

"He's with the sailmaker, below." Ariella screwed up her face. "Papa said he could learn how to mend sails." She shook her head, as if the idea was absurd. She added, "His Latin is terrible—almost as bad as his French."

Amanda followed the child back inside. "If your brother will one day captain this ship, he'll have to know everything there is about sailing, and that includes mending sails."

"If he can't speak French, he won't be able to negotiate with traders in France and Morocco." Ariella shrugged, sitting down at the dining table and opening up her book, instantly engrossed.

Amanda flushed. The child was so intelligent. And de Warenne clearly admired that. "What are you reading?"

Ariella never looked up. "I am reading a guidebook to London."

"Really?" Curious, Amanda went to look over her shoulder. There was a beautiful sketch of a bridge. "Is that the London Bridge?"

"Yes." Ariella smiled at her. "Do you want to read my book? I can get another one."

Amanda flushed.

Ariella waited innocently.

"I can't read," Amanda said, her cheeks on fire.

Ariella started to laugh.

"Ariella!" Anahid chastised.

Instantly Ariella was contrite. "I thought she was in jest, Anahid. Why can't you read?"

Amanda shrugged. "My papa was a pirate, remember?" Too late, she realized she had lied about that yesterday. "He never taught me. He didn't think it was important." She stared longingly at the guidebook.

"Do you want to learn to read? I can teach you—or maybe Monsieur Michelle can."

Amanda met the child's blue eyes, her heart racing with excitement. "I really want to learn to read," she whispered unsteadily. "But I am sure your papa won't allow it. He wants you to learn and your teacher is here to teach you, not me."

Ariella merely grinned, gazing past Amanda.

De Warenne murmured, "You are wrong."

Amanda whirled to see him on the cabin's threshold. Instantly, that potent image assailed her and she saw him standing naked and powerful on the deck, glorying in his body and his life. She flushed. His lashes lowered and he thrust himself off of the door.

"I have no problem with lending you Monsieur Michelle or my daughter, for that matter. Reading is a blessing. I am glad you wish to learn." He finally lifted his lashes and looked directly at her.

She still saw him without his clothes and her cheeks remained hot. But this subject was more important than anything. "I already know most of the letters," she said eagerly. "I learned them myself."

His mouth lifted. "I am certain you will be a capable student, Amanda. Have you ever failed at anything?"

She tried to breathe normally. His look, his tone, even his posture, were potent and seductive, and she felt certain he was as aware of the huge tension that had arisen that morning as she was. It remained now, in the room with them, throbbing and needy, somehow predatory, in spite of his daughter and Anahid. She shook her head.

"We can study together," Ariella said happily.

A slender gentleman hurried into the cabin, his arms filled with books and papers. "*Ah, bonjour, mes amis*," he cried. "*Monsieur le Capitaine, bonjour*."

De Warenne nodded. "*Bonjour,* Jean-Paul," he said, his accent undistinguishable from the Frenchman's. "Have you met my guest, Miss Carre?"

"*Mais non,*" Monsieur Michelle said, beaming. He placed the books and papers on the table and took Amanda's hand before she even knew it. She stiffened as he tried to raise it to his lips, crying, *"Enchanté, mademoiselle, je suis véritablement enchanté."*

Feeling absurd, she glanced helplessly at de Warenne. The heat had finally left his eyes, which were soft with understanding now. He gave her a slight nod. Continuing to feel clumsy, she let the tutor kiss her hand. Then she jammed it in her pocket, grimacing. Michelle seemed bewildered.

De Warenne clasped the tutor's shoulder. "*Monsieur,* I am giving you the task of teaching Miss Carre to read and write—which I am certain you can accomplish by the end of our voyage."

Michelle turned white. "I am to teach mademoiselle in six weeks?" He gasped. *"Capitaine, monsieur, c'est impossible!"*

*"C'est très possible, je suis sûr,"* de Warenne returned swiftly, his tone calm, his smile indicating a sudden good humor. *"D'accord?"*

Monsieur Michelle looked at Amanda. *"Oui,"* he murmured, seeming resigned.

Amanda, having grown up in the islands, could understand Spanish, French, Portuguese, Hebrew and Dutch. She could speak a few words in each language, as well, and could get by when she had to. She had understood their entire conversation. *"Monsieur,"* she said, *"Je veux apprendre à lire et je promets d'étudier beaucoup."*

Michelle's eyes lit up. *"Parlez-vous français?"*

"A little," she said, then glanced at de Warenne to see if he was impressed. When he nodded approvingly, a smile on his face and in his eyes, her heart soared and danced.

IT WAS THE MIDDLE WATCH. Cliff stood on the quarterdeck, the wood of the wheel smooth and sensuous beneath his hands, the decks rocking gently beneath his feet, relishing being one with his ship and God, sailing into what felt like the vast blackness of eternity. The sky was dark and starlit, the breeze gentle and sweet, the ocean a gleam of slick black satin. The hours between midnight and dawn were his favorites. He had taken two hours of rest after his supper and would steal another hour or two before sunrise. Until then, he allowed his mind to drift with his ship, lost in a profound sense of serenity.

"Captain?"

He wasn't alone on the quarterdeck—the officer of the watch was on the larboard rail, and two midshipmen stood below by the mainmast—but it was past midnight, and the last person he expected to see was Amanda. He turned, and she smiled uncertainly at him from the main deck below.

She whispered, "Permission to come up?"

"Granted," he replied softly. The solitude of this hour was what he enjoyed the most about it and his men knew it. Unless there was an emergency or a call to action stations, he was never to be interrupted on the middle watch. But this distraction was welcome and he was surprised to realize it.

She quickly stepped up to stand beside him. Not looking at him, she faced the bowsprit, lifting her face to the soft caress of the night's breeze. He stared, helpless to look away. His heart lurched and then drummed, his body filling with tension and heat. Why was he so insanely attracted to her? Was it because she was as powerfully affected by the siren call of the sea as he was, or was it simply the primitive lure of wanting a beautiful woman?

But there had been so many beautiful women in his life and she was different. He had never felt such an intense desire before—or such a deep need to shield her from danger and heartbreak. He reminded himself to keep a careful and proper distance at such a dark and dangerous hour. "It's a beautiful night," he said quietly.

She sighed and smiled at him. "Yes."

"It's late."

"I couldn't sleep."

In the light from the hanging lanterns, he studied her face. He saw no sign of grief. "I understand that you enjoyed your lessons today." He'd summoned Michelle for a report.

She beamed. "I read three sentences!" Then she flushed. "They were silly, about a cat and a dog and a hat."

"I know," he said, impossibly warmed by her excitement and pleasure. "*Monsieur* told me."

Her smile faltered. She glanced directly ahead. "I owe you so much. I am so grateful."

He tensed, for it was impossible not to recall how she had initially thought to pay him for her passage. "You do not owe me anything, Amanda. It is my pleasure to allow you the use of Michelle. I am pleased you wish to learn to read and that you are already excelling at it."

He saw her flush with more pleasure. Then, barely looking at him, she whispered, "You did not invite me to dine tonight."

His tension knew no bounds. His grasp tightened on the huge wheel. Of course he hadn't, as he had feared a repeat of the previous evening's loss of self-control. He spoke with care. "I am sorry for my behavior last night. It was reprehensible for me to leave you to dine alone. But my daughter had to come first."

Amanda stared across the bow. After a long pause, she said, "Ariella did not recall having a nightmare and being woken up in the middle of the evening by you."

He was incredulous. "You questioned her?"

She shrugged, darting a glance at him.

He would never confess that he had lied, and she could not know the real reason he had left her so rudely at his table. "She was half asleep."

She nodded, clearly not believing him.

He amended, "I thought I heard her cry out."

She slowly faced him, her eyes trained on his. "I am not stupid, de Warenne. I am not polite company."

He was shocked. "I enjoy your company very much. If I did not, you would not be sharing this watch with me."

Her smile flickered, her gaze hopeful and bright. "Really? Because you asked me about my life and I never got to ask you about yours."

He laughed. "Ask away, Amanda. Please, feel free."

She smiled eagerly. "Everyone says you are an earl's son. But you said you are not royalty. Yet your servants call you *his lordship*."

"It's not the same thing." He smiled. "I am the third and youngest son of the earl of Adare, Edward de Warenne. That makes me a nobleman, not a royal. Being addressed as *my lord* is a courtesy, as I have no titles."

Amanda seemed perplexed. "I can hardly see the difference between nobility and royalty—you live like a king! Where is Adare? What is it like?"

He chuckled. "Adare is in the west of Ireland, not far from the sea. It is a land of green hills and green forests, especially in the spring. There is no place where the ocean is as blue. It is often misting and it is often wet." His smile softened. "It is the most beautiful place in the world."

Her eyes were shining. "It is wet on the island in the rainy season."

"Jamaica is a tropical place—Ireland is entirely different. It is somehow wild and untamed, even on a sunny day. Time passes differently there. If the islands are paradise, Ireland is magic and mystery. Perhaps that is due to our history, which is ancient. My people came from France, but they were also Celtic kings on my mother's side. In any case, they were all warrior lords. Ireland is a land with a dark and bloody history. We are also renowned for our ghosts."

"I should love to see it!" she exclaimed. "And your home at Adare? Is it like Windsong?"

"I was born at Adare, but it belongs to my father, the earl, and one day, it will belong to my oldest brother, Tyrell. It is nothing like Windsong," he said, and he saw the disappointment on her face. "It is far grander. It was first built many centuries ago, although it has been renovated several times."

"It is grander than Windsong?" She was incredulous.

"My island home could fit inside the house at Adare about three times over." He chuckled.

She gaped. "So you were raised with servants and riches, living very much as you now do?"

"I lacked for nothing," he admitted. "I know that must be difficult for you to imagine."

She shrugged, glancing away.

He somehow wished she'd had a different life, one of luxury, not mayhem and madness.

"Do you go home often?"

"Once every year or two," he remarked, feeling some guilt. "I go as often as I can. My parents have a residence in London, where I frequently put into port, so it is more likely that I should see some of my family there."

"You have a brother?" Amanda asked, the envy written all over her face.

"I have two brothers, two stepbrothers and a sister," he said softly. "And when we arrive in London, you shall surely meet some of them."

Amanda whispered, "I think you are very lucky to have such a grand family and so many places to call home."

"I am very fortunate," he agreed, and he realized he fervently hoped Amanda was going to find such a pleasant existence in London, too.

"What was it like, growing up at Adare?" she asked wistfully.

Cliff was swept back in time. He smiled, remembering being on the verge of manhood, desires raging. "Ah, we were a rowdy, troublesome lot. We avoided our duties and spent as much time as possible racing across the countryside, pursuing light skirts and doing very much as we pleased." He shook his head. "We would cut out on our lessons, gallop about the hills, swim in the river or the lake. Of course, when we were caught, there was always hell to pay."

"The earl must have beaten you," she remarked.

His eyes widened. "I don't think he ever hit any one of us. He could make us drown in guilt with a look."

"He didn't hit you for skipping your lessons?"

He became disturbed. "No, he did not."

Amanda folded her arms across her chest. "That is so odd," she finally said.

"Not every parent uses corporal punishment. I personally think it barbaric," he said grimly. Surely she had not been punished with the rod?

She held her head high. "Well, that's what you think. Not everyone would agree with you."

"No, they would not," he said slowly. "Did Carre ever hit you?"

She kept her chin up. "Of course he did. How else would I learn right from wrong?"

He had a terrible feeling, answered by a terrible rage. "What did he do? Did he use the rod?"

She shook her head, but his relief was short-lived. "He used his fists," she said. "He had a temper and he hated disobedience. He'd whack me on the side of my head—usually on my jaw."

He was aghast. He realized his mouth was hanging open, and he closed it. "Good God! Amanda, you were a child, a female one at that!"

She was wide-eyed. "But that's what fathers do. They punish—with their fists, a rod, the whip. I didn't mind. I mean, it hurt, and sometimes I saw stars. Like when he hit me at the prison. But usually he missed, because I was faster than he was and could easily duck the blow."

Cliff whirled and said, "Howard, take the helm."

The midshipman rushed to his side, taking the wheel. Cliff took Amanda's arm, trying to remain calm when he was blinded by rage. They moved to the starboard side of the quarterdeck, an area no other sailor or officer would ever dare step upon, as it was, by tradition, reserved exclusively for the ship's master. "His blows were frequent?"

She said stubbornly, "I told you, he usually missed."

"You said he hit you at the prison. Surely—*surely*—you do not mean at the courthouse prison or at Fort Charles. Surely he did not strike you in the past few weeks?"

She stared, refusing to reply.

"He struck you recently? He hit a woman?" Cliff was in more shock than he could manage.

"What do you care?" she said harshly. She was trembling. "Papa loved me. It was his way of making sure I obeyed him. He was furious when I told him I tried to do Governor Woods."

Cliff let her go, rubbing his face with his hands. It was fortunate that Carre was dead, because otherwise he'd kill the man with his own bare hands. Then he looked grimly at her. "So it was not his idea for you to proposition the governor on his behalf?"

She shook her head. "Papa told me when I was twelve that my maidenhead was for my husband and my husband only."

He went still. In spite of his shock and horror, his blood heated, filling him. She had never known another man. His instincts had urged him to believe in her innocence, but reason had told him it was unlikely. Now there was no doubt—and he had another barrier to place safely between them.

She said slowly, "You don't hit or whip your children, do you?"

"No, I do not."

She bit her lip, looking down.

He touched her. "I would never hit a child or a woman.

Amanda, you can choose to believe what you wish, but I cannot accept your father disciplining you with his fists."

"He loved me," she insisted, looking up. Her eyes were shining with unshed tears.

He hated himself. "Yes, he did. It was obvious." He turned slightly away, remaining shaken. He had no idea how she had managed to maintain her innocence or her faith in her father, but he was not going to take either away from her. Yet the urge to do both consumed him. He clamped his lips together so he would not tell her what he really thought of Carre. And he would not pull her against his chest and caress her hair. His loins were stiff and throbbing; he knew where such a gesture would lead.

"Does Ariella ever disobey you?" she asked, her tone uncertain.

They were on safer ground. He exhaled. "Actually, she does not. And I wish she would."

"You do?"

He smiled at her, relieved with the innocent subject. "I worry about her. Even when she disagrees with me, she pretends not to in order to please me. I would love to see her object to something dear to her heart."

"You want her to defy you?" Amanda asked, obviously amazed.

"Alexi defies me all the time."

"And you don't hit him."

"He is punished, but not with a fist or a whip."

She turned away.

He felt deeply for her and he wished, foolishly, that she could have been spared her childhood. He decided to move the subject along. "I am glad to see you and Ariella becoming friends."

She glanced at him. "She helped me with my sentences today. She is very clever."

"I worry that she is too clever for her own good. One day, if she does not present me with a love match that I approve of, I will have to find her a husband. Her intelligence will make it difficult to find a suitable prospect. Most men will run away from such a woman with their tails between their legs."

Amanda laughed. "Men do not like clever women," she agreed.

"Some men do," he murmured. He smiled at her, his mind veering to the fact that she was very clever, too. He quickly redirected his thoughts. "I know this may seem premature, but I have given a great deal of thought to Ariella's future. She will be a great heiress, and that will help. But I will have to discourage the fortune hunters."

"She will be an heiress," Amanda echoed, her soft smile vanishing

He realized his faux pas. Carre had left his daughter with nothing, not a single cent, and he damned the man for it. His insensitivity was astounding, and silently, belatedly, he kicked himself. "I am sorry, Amanda. It is your turn to ask me questions, not my turn to bother you with my worries for Ariella's future."

"She is so lucky," Amanda whispered, distressed, "that you are her father and that she is so rich. Don't worry. You will find a husband for her, I have no doubt."

And what about Amanda? Who was going to find a husband for her?

He had never stumbled upon the subject of her marriage before, and he wished he hadn't done so now. It made him terribly uncomfortable, but Pandora had been released from her box. Carre should have arranged her marriage, but thank God he had not, for the man he would have chosen would have been a pirate or some other socially unacceptable thug. It would be Dulcea Carre's responsibility to marry her off.

He somehow despised the notion, but he worried about it, now, too. After all, if Amanda was to marry well, she was going to have to undergo quite a bit of transformation and he wasn't sure she would even wish to try. Gently, he asked, "And you,

Amanda? Do you dream of marriage and a home of your own?" His smile was encouraging.

Her eyes widened. "Who would marry me?"

He could not bear her words. He cupped her cheek, tilting up her face. "You will have suitors, I am sure of it. And you will break a dozen hearts after you have spent some time with your mother." He meant it, but he was afraid for her, too. She would eventually be transformed into a proper lady while under her mother's care. There was little doubt about that. However, he simply could not imagine Amanda making insipid conversation about the weather or last night's supper party. Worse, he wasn't sure she should be transformed at all. He tried to imagine her fashionably attired with proper airs, and suddenly detested the idea of her losing her originality. He wasn't sure she could do both.

"I am not like Ariella," she said, jerking away and staring at him as if stricken. "I am not a princess with a fortune. Please, do not be so mean."

"I wasn't jesting," he exclaimed. "But your mother will surely provide you with a fine new wardrobe, a dancing master and whatever else you need for your new life. In a very short time after your reunion with her, I am certain there will be suitors lined up outside of your mother's home."

"I don't think so," she cried, aghast.

He felt terrible for her. "What do you wish, Amanda?"

"To be free," she cried. "To be a part of the wind and the sea—that's all I've ever wanted!"

How well he understood. He stared, almost reaching for her.

But she backed fearfully away. "That's what Mama will want, isn't it? To make me a lady, to find me a husband, to marry me off?"

"I would think so," he said, and added, "What other choice is there?"

She just shook her head, backing farther away.

He never let her out of his sights as her back found the rail. "Come off the railing, Amanda." He kept his tone coaxing, but it was an order and he was master of the ship.

"I have made a mistake," she cried, but she stepped away from the railing. "I want you to leave me anywhere but London—maybe on Malta," she said.

"Our demons are always greatest at night," he said softly. "Come, Amanda, you are strong and brave and you can manage a reunion with your mother."

She nodded, wiping at a tear. "I'm sorry for being a nitwit."

"You could never be a nitwit, and I would be stunned if you did not have some trepidation," he said lightly. He held out his hand. She hesitated and approached, taking it. He walked her to the steps.

"While we are on the subject of your mother, I have assumed you have an address for her?"

She nodded, her gaze on his, oddly trusting. "Papa said she lives at a place called Belford House."

He was shocked.

"De Warenne? Do you know it?"

He couldn't speak. He knew Belford House, as he had been invited there several times. He knew Lady Belford—and her first name was Dulcea.

She had platinum hair almost the exact same shade as Amanda's and, if he recalled correctly, astounding green eyes. Now, the resemblance was unmistakable.

But she had been married to Lord Belford for many years.

Dulcea Belford was breathtakingly beautiful, elegant and polished, and socially obsessed. She was also promiscuous—behind Belford's back, she had numerous affairs. She had pursued him, in fact, but he had not cared for her conceit or her manner. But he was the only male he knew who was not smitten with the socialite.

He had no doubt that Amanda's tale about her parents was

very wrong and that her mother was not Dulcea Carre, but Dulcea Bedford.

And if he was right, then Lady Belford was not going to be pleased to see her long-lost daughter, not at all.

## *CHAPTER SEVEN*

AMANDA SAT ON HER BUNK in the narrow cabin where she slept. She was sharing the accommodation with Anahid, who was asleep in the cabin's other berth. Other than the two bunks, there was a small table, two chairs and a washstand. Amanda had taken the upper bunk. De Warenne's children slept in the adjacent cabin, which was larger and more pleasantly furnished. But she did not care about the furnishings at all.

It was almost dawn. De Warenne had retired to the captain's cabin for a few hours of rest and even though she ached with restlessness and had not wanted to part company, she had allowed him to escort her to her cabin. She had pretended to be tired, too. But the past few hours, sailing with him through the night and then into the rising sun, had been the most pleasurable of her life. Although she hated discussing her future in England, de Warenne's company was like opium, sweet, potent and addictive. She could not get enough, it seemed. She wished they were still on deck together.

She fingered her small sack, then pulled out the beautiful lace nightgown and stared at it. De Warenne was so different from all the other men she had ever known. He was beautiful and strong, powerful and educated, generous and kind. Amanda inhaled. *He was so kind*. He knew she was afraid of England, and he had tried to encourage her to think that all would be well when she finally met her mother. She knew that was not going to be the case. Mama had loved her, for Papa had said so, but that had been years ago. And even if her mother remained devoted to her missing daughter, she was going to be terribly disappointed when she saw the woman her daughter had become.

Amanda had passed too many fancy ladies on Queen Street in Kingston, and they had always stared at her, their pointy noses turned up in the air. There had always been whispers behind her back. "Look at the pirate's daughter! She is a savage—just like her name!"

And in that moment, Amanda wished she were a real lady.

Because if she were a lady, she had no doubt Mama would welcome her with open arms.

She sighed. Such wishful thinking was foolish. It was even dangerous. Being with de Warenne had made her briefly forget what was going to happen in another five weeks when she arrived at her mother's door. She was almost certain that when she finally faced her mother, she would see shock, horror and then condescension on her face. She was so afraid that it was better not to think about it—as when she was a child, cowering belowdecks, while the pirates above murdered one another, she must close her eyes and clap her hands over her ears and not think about what might happen.

But de Warenne made her smile; with him, she was firmly in the present, the future so far away, and he made her feel safe. In fact, she had never felt so secure in all of her life. She had never felt quite this way with Papa. Yet there was far more in her heart than feeling so well protected.

She was painfully aware of his masculinity. His beauty and virility had been obvious from the start, but in the beginning, when she had seen him on the deck of a captured Spanish galleon, she had been a child and he might as well have been a god. Since meeting him a week ago, her grief had dulled her natural interest. She would always grieve for Papa, but the sadness was softer and easier now. And the child was truly gone. No child could have this wild, impossible yearning—no child could ache in so many private places—no child could start to dream as she was dreaming. There was a new yet familiar hunger in her and it seemed to be rapidly escalating. Seeing him emerging from the ocean that morning like Poseidon hadn't helped.

"Please don't let me fall in love with him," Amanda whispered, and it was only after she had spoken that she realized she had spoken out loud. She tensed, but Anahid never answered her, and she realized the woman was deeply asleep.

Was she falling in love with the handsome, wealthy, nobly born privateer? His image flashed—his soft smile, his bold stare, his taut, hard body, dripping ice water. How could a woman not fall in love with him, she wondered desperately, even a young woman of seventeen?

She did not try to delude herself. He preferred very elegant ladies and he was never going to return her feelings, although he seemed affectionately inclined toward her. But he did want her; she had two eyes in her head and she could tell whenever his lusty nature overcame him.

She hugged the nightgown to her breasts. Her nipples were hard and tight and her skin tingled. Her body was hot and cold, all at once. The way he looked at her warmed her impossibly, and he had looked at her many times that night the way a man looks at a woman he is about to bed. But he had refused her offer to pay for her passage. She had even hinted that she would still do so, but he had not taken the bait. However, her heart and her body were demanding his attention now. She wanted to go to him—and that made her cold with fear.

Because if she gave him her heart, she was ten times the fool—he would ruthlessly break it. Giving him her body would be easier, except he didn't seem inclined to act on his male needs.

Amanda closed her eyes, wishing she knew what to do. She could imagine de Warenne cupping her cheek as he had done earlier. She could feel his hard, large hand on her skin and she trembled. His behavior was so confusing! But then, she had never known a real gentleman before. And he did prefer real ladies. Maybe that was what was holding him back.

She looked down at the nightgown. In it, the pirate's daughter was gone, and she appeared every bit as much a lady as those elegant women strolling in Kingston.

Amanda realized what she had to do and more cold fear crept over her. But men could be stupid and foolish when it came to fornication. How many times had Papa said a man was led by his cock, not his brain? She owed de Warenne so much—more than a few nights in his bed could ever repay—and he did want her, in some basic way. He might be trying to be a gentleman or he might not want her that much, due to her lack of breeding, but in that nightgown, he might easily be managed by his male parts. Wasn't it worth a try?

Maybe she wasn't even falling in love with him. Maybe she wasn't that different from the trollops and whores who ran with the crew; maybe she was just at that age now where she wished to satisfy her body, as they all so openly would do.

Amanda pulled off her boots and stockings, her cheeks on fire now. She lay down, jerking her breeches off, and then her drawers. Tasseled belt, shirt and chemise followed. Very quietly, she washed herself at the washstand, determined not to awaken the Armenian. Then she slipped on the nightgown, quickly brushing her hair.

Her heart thundered in her breast, deafening her. She glanced at Anahid, who remained asleep on the bunk—or so she thought, until the women looked right at her. Amanda grimaced, turning away before she could say anything. She slipped outside into the ebony-gray light just before dawn.

At his door she paused breathlessly. She was operating mindlessly and determinedly now. If she thought, she might turn and flee. She knocked hesitantly. "De Warenne?" she whispered.

There was no answer and she tried again. Amanda was dismayed, for she was certain his door was locked. Even if it wasn't, entering without an invitation was a grave trespass, indeed. She tried the latch and started, because his door wasn't bolted from inside. Her heart lurched and lunged; she pushed the door open and slipped into his cabin.

No lights were on, but gray light was filtering into the cabin from the portholes. She could see him lying flat out on his back in the huge crimson bed, the thin silk sheets pulled up to his waist. He was clearly sleeping in the nude. He didn't stir, which surprised her—how could he sleep through her illicit entry? She would have thought de Warenne to be a man who slept with one eye open and both ears hearing every sound and whisper.

She tried again. "De Warenne?"

He did not move. His broad, sculpted chest, sprinkled lightly with darker tawny hair, slowly and rhythmically rose and fell. Barely able to believe that he remained asleep, Amanda started forward. He slept on. She lifted an edge of the silk sheet. Amanda glimpsed his lean hip, his long hard thigh, and she slid under the sheet with him.

Her pounding heart made her dizzy enough to faint. Moisture exploded between her thighs.

And suddenly he was on top of her, her wrists in a hard grasp, pinned over her head. She cried out and met furious blue eyes.

"What seduction is this?" he roared.

Amanda couldn't speak because she was so shocked that he had been awake, waiting for her, all this time. He held himself over her but his weight was somehow transferred onto her through the firm pressure of his hands and legs. For, while he clamped her wrists, his thighs were between her own legs, forcing them wide. Her nightgown had been pushed up and his skin was shocking against her bare thighs, sparklike. And she had been right—he was entirely nude, because his manhood leaped between them.

A wave of pleasure began.

He inhaled, shaking. "Answer me!"

She couldn't speak. She began to insistently throb in response to the pressure of his restless stirring and she couldn't control herself. She gasped and then whimpered, her body seeking his. Wet aching warmth met slick heat. More pleasure crested.

He grunted, rubbing his stubbly jaw against her cheek, his lashes drifting closed against her skin. "I am so very close to losing my mind and all control and taking you, Amanda," he said thickly. "Is that what you want? Do you really want me to use you and abuse you, as if you were a worthless pirate's daughter?"

His body jerked in a spasm and she cried out, in both physical pleasure and emotional pain. He lifted his head; their eyes locked.

She could barely think. *Of course I don't want to be a cheap and tawdry pirate's daughter. Not to you....*

And he saw her answer. "I didn't think so." He tossed the sheets aside and leaped from the bed, then turned to rake his gaze directly over her exposed limbs.

Amanda jerked to sit, pulling down the nightgown. Instantly he yanked the sheet from the bed, wrapping it around his waist and hiding his huge, engorged penis. He gave her a dark, still-furious look.

Amanda closed her eyes tightly and willed her body to still, to calm. But she had been very close to a fatal precipice, and in that moment, the task of discovering some sanity seemed impossible.

His cruel words made it easy. "I do not want a liaison with you, Amanda." His tone was scathing.

She blinked, saw the distended sheet, and half giggled hysterically. "Of course you do."

He braced himself a foot from the bed. "That," he cried, pointing at himself, "is the reaction I would have to any female who slips into my bed."

The hysterical laughter vanished. He couldn't be telling her the truth, she thought, a terrible hurt beginning. "You wanted me this morning," she whispered, staring only at his face now.

His laughter was harsh. "I am a man! A virile man! I always want sex," he said tersely.

She cringed against the pillows, the pain of rejection stabbing through her like a cutlass slicing open the jugular of the enemy.

"What my body wants is irrelevant, because I am not a beast. What my mind wishes is an entirely different matter—and I do not *wish* to share my bed with you. Could I be any clearer? Must I elaborate?"

She didn't know what *elaborate* meant, but she could guess. She felt tears rising. "I'm not a fancy lady," she muttered, staring at her nightgown. She could put on the nightgown and wash up and brush her hair, but that wasn't going to change anything. He didn't want her. He wasn't like any man she had ever known before—he was educated, a gentleman, nobility. And when they put into London harbor, he would take up with one of his blue-blooded lovers. She choked.

"No, you are not."

Her gaze flew to his because his tone had changed. The rage was gone, and there was only a hard grim quality to his words now. Their gazes held.

Amanda shook her head. "I knew it couldn't be true," she said. "I knew you couldn't really be kind." She slid from the bed and marched to the door, trying to keep her head high when what she wanted to do was cry. *He had been so cruel.*

He hesitated. "Amanda."

She froze. His tone was almost normal, and she prayed he was going to call her back, take her into his arms and smile softly and tell her it was all right—that they would remain odd companions after all and that what had just happened wouldn't change anything.

His expression was rigid. His eyes were hooded. He said, "If I had wished for your favors, I would have already taken you to bed."

She cried out. Then she whirled and ran from him.

Cliff turned and smashed the wall with his fist.

CLIFF STOOD on the starboard of the quarterdeck, arms folded across his chest. He stared almost unseeingly over the railing, where the ocean was a pale, silvery gray, mirroring the clouded sky overhead. White horses frothed and spray spit from the frigate's bow. He was cruising with only courses and topsails set. Still, in such strong winds, they were traveling at a fast clip, one he usually enjoyed. Instead, he was irritated and annoyed.

He slowly turned to look at his passenger. It was just past noon and his children and Amanda were on a short recess from their studies. Ariella had gone below to read, and Alexi was in the rigging with the fore topmen. He was prouder of the boy with every passing day, as he could not seem to soak up knowledge of the ship and sailing quickly enough. He might be a poor student when it came to academics, but he was brilliant when it came to seamanship. His passenger, however, was another matter.

According to Michelle she was rapidly proceeding in her studies. The Frenchman waxed poetic over his new charge's intelligence and dedication, boasting she would be reading the *London Times* by the day they arrived in town. As far as Cliff was concerned, the man was quickly falling under her spell. But why not? Even now, having just come out of the schoolroom, so to speak, she was an enchantress with her windblown hair, her exotic green eyes, her slim but voluptuous body.

Amanda met his gaze, glaring.

He stared back, unsmiling. She had not spoken to him in five days.

In fact, all she had done was glare rudely or ignore him as if he was not there.

He understood that he was being punished for his cruelty. But had she wished to be seduced and ruined? Did she understand that he would have taken her in an instant, with her in his bed so scantily attired, already in the throes of pleasure and passion? Did she know what control and discipline he had used to walk away? Did she not understand that he wished to be honorable with her?

His cruel words had been deliberate, a calculated device to push her as far away as he possibly could, and to forestall her ever trying to seduce him again.

He knew that should there be a next time, he would cave in to a monstrous and barbaric desire.

But goddamn it, he had had enough. He felt horrible, he was guilty, he was sorry, she was right! He did not wish to renew their previous camaraderie, as it was far too dangerous, but did she have to act as if she despised him?

Giving him a hateful look, she turned her back to him and waved up at Alexi. Alexi was seated on a yardarm and he grinned at her. "Amanda! Come up!"

What nonsense was this? Women did not climb the rigging, even if Cliff had seen her do so once, years ago, on her father's sloop.

Amanda turned and looked right at him, her challenge clear. Then she whirled and ran to the mainmast, where she quickly leaped into the main shrouds. He stalked down from the quarterdeck as she scrambled up to Alexi, as agile as his best sailors.

The fore topmen did not know what to do, so they looked at each other and then down at the decks, as if pretending a beautiful woman was not in their midst.

"You really can climb rigging," Alexi said in surprise. "I thought you were joshing me!"

"I've been climbing rigging since I was younger than you," Amanda boasted. She glanced down, meeting Cliff's gaze, before abruptly looking away.

He snapped. "Amanda, please come down. I wish a word with you."

She smiled at Alexi. "It is such a fine day. If these winds keep up, we will cut a few good days off of our voyage."

"I hope our voyage lasts forever. I don't care about England at all," Alexi declared.

Cliff was incredulous. She was going to ignore him when he gave her a direct command? Perhaps, though, it hadn't really been a command, but a request. "Amanda."

Her jaw set. She gave him a sullen look.

"Come down. Into my cabin," he barked. He turned and strode off. If she did not obey, he'd climb up the rigging himself and carry her down over his shoulder, never mind that commanders did not ascend the shrouds.

But he heard her as she landed, soft and catlike, on the deck. She trailed after him, keeping a safe distance, as if he might turn on her like a dangerous predator and bite. But then, he had bitten her, hadn't he, when he'd told her he had no wish to bed her. But damn it, he had not had a choice!

He paused in the center of his cabin as she entered behind him. He decided he would pretend that nothing was amiss, that they had not spent five days with his hoping for a genuine smile and her staring mutely at him with unabashed hostility. He turned, smiling. "I understand you have progressed to a second level reader," he said.

She stared, mouth firm, eyes hard, absolutely mute.

He sighed. "Are you enjoying your studies?"

She folded her arms across her chest, clearly refusing to speak.

"Well, I believe I have proven my point. You are hardly a grown woman. I have never seen such childish behavior in an adult."

She smiled grimly at him.

He was incredulous. "Do you intend to ignore me for the next four weeks?"

"Am I ignoring you, Captain, sir?"

He was at a loss. She was angry and he couldn't blame her. What was worse, he knew the anger was a facade to hide her hurt. It was so utterly ironic. He had only wished to shield her from heartache; instead, he had caused more grief. Softly and truthfully, he said, "I am sorry I hurt you, Amanda. I obviously misled you with my earlier behavior. At least now we both know where we respectively stand. It will be a very long voyage if you continue to glare and refuse to speak to me."

"The voyage is already too long," she said.

"I am afraid there is nothing I can do about the length of our voyage," he said.

She shrugged. "Just think, when we do get to England you can go to your fancy whores."

It was a rare moment, but he felt her pain and did not know how to respond.

"Is that all? I have lessons to finish."

At least they were speaking, he thought grimly. "Yes, that is all."

AMANDA AWOKE, TENSING.

Outside of her cabin's porthole, she heard sabers clashing.

They were under attack? And she had slept through the assault and boarding? She leaped from her bunk, reaching for her sack. She quickly loaded the pistol then tucked it into her pants. She seized her sword and shoved open her cabin door.

Her cabin opened onto the starboard side of the ship. No enemy was boarding from that side. In fact, nothing but the iron-gray ocean could be seen. Swords rattled and clashed from the main deck and then she heard de Warenne.

"Thrust true," he advised. "Steady and true. Do not bend your wrist."

Beginning to understand, Amanda hurried around the cabin. She halted, seeing de Warenne and Alexi fencing. De Warenne was allowing the small boy to test his skills, she realized, and he was very agile for a boy of eight.

De Warenne was a good teacher, pushing his son but not so much that he would tire and despair. Her heart ached. She remained motionless, watching him now that he was thoroughly occupied and could not remark her interest. She had to ignore the hurt. The anger was so much easier, so much better—it was what he deserved.

He was a bastard, a cad; he was a fancy, snooty gent with snobby airs; he wasn't kind, he was mean and cold and cruel; she *hated* him.

If she told herself often enough, maybe she would eventually believe it.

He saw her and signaled to his son to desist. Alexi put the sword down, breathing hard but grinning. De Warenne's gaze took in the pistol in her waistband and the saber she held. Then his gaze lifted.

*I hate him*, Amanda thought. *He would take a fancy lady to bed, but not me; I'm not good enough for him.* She strolled forward. "Your son will be a good swordsman one day."

His eyes were guarded. "Yes, he will. What is that?"

She slowly raised the saber. "My sword." She smiled at him. She was very adept with a saber—she could beat Papa. Fencing wasn't only about strength; it was about balance, agility and skill.

"Do you wish to fence?"

"I heard the blades, and I thought we were under attack." She took her pistol and laid it aside on the deck.

His eyes widened. "So you came up here to help my men defend the ship?"

"Of course," Amanda said. "I am no weak-kneed gentlewoman to swoon at the sight of battle. But I am rusty—I haven't had a chance to fence in a very long time. Do you care to engage?" she asked. Not giving him a chance to respond, she stepped forward and aggressively thrust her blade.

He reflexively blocked the blow. "Your sword is not blunted, Amanda," he said carefully.

She felt her lips widen. She thrust again—he parried. "I won't draw blood, de Warenne," she said, but she thought maybe she would, just so she could see the look in his eyes. A terrible excitement consumed her. With it was her rage. She thrust and he parried, but took a step back. Elated, Amanda went on the offensive. His eyes widened but he merely blocked each blow, allowing her to drive him ruthlessly and rapidly back into the larboard railing.

She laughed, triumphant. "You can do better than that, de Warenne! Surely you are not afraid of my naked blade?"

"You remain very angry with me. I understand," he began.

She was furious. He knew nothing! She thrust and he parried; she feinted and then slipped through his defenses, instantly cutting a long line into his fine, fancy shirt. She withdrew, heady with the scent of victory. "You understand what?" she asked sweetly.

He glanced at the long tear, very surprised, and then he slowly looked up at her.

"I did not draw blood," she said, exhilarated now. She laughed at him.

"You were fortunate," he said, color flooding his cheeks.

"No, I was careful. I chose *not* to take your blood, de Warenne!" She thrust so swiftly that, before he could defend himself, she had taken the top three buttons off his shirt, causing it to gap open, revealing the two thick muscles of his chest.

Above them, someone laughed.

De Warenne was disbelieving.

"Fight, de Warenne," she said fiercely, panting. She was determined to savagely exchange blows—she would ruthlessly engage, there would be no quarter! "Or show your men that you can be outplayed and outfought by a *child*."

He suddenly thrust.

Amanda blocked the blow, but barely. He thrust again and again, driving her back across the ship before she even knew what was happening. In mere seconds, she had her back at the rail and sweat was pouring down her body, pooling between her breasts and legs. She was even more furious than before at his display of skill.

He smiled. "Come now, darling. I have no wish to fight with you, especially as your blade is not blunted. Besides, we both know you cannot best me."

But she would try. She would make him sit up and take real notice of her. She was not a fancy lady, but she could match him in every other way. Amanda growled and attacked. She thrust hard and he met her, taking a step back, a step aside, until they were moving rapidly in a vicious circle of hard blow after hard blow. Iron rang. Sweat burned in her eyes. Of course he was master here. She hadn't expected to win. But she wanted to somehow hurt him. There was nothing she wanted more—she wanted him to feel what she had felt, damn him!

Her arm was aching now. She was at her physical limit, but she would not give up. "Damn you!" she gasped, and she halted, pretending to be exhausted and ready to submit to his mercy.

He bought her game, a grin appearing on his handsome face. "Well done," he began.

Amanda feinted, thrust and sliced off the rest of his shirt buttons. He was so surprised he simply stared down at his shirt, now shredded in two. Then, slowly, he looked up at her. His blue eyes were brilliant, hot, and he slowly, boldly smiled.

*He wasn't angry*. She understood the heat, and a savage sense of triumph rose up in her. He might not want her with his fine intellectual mind, but just now, she had provoked him so thoroughly that he wanted her right then. She knew, beyond any doubt, that reason had been conquered by lust.

"What's wrong, de Warenne?" she murmured seductively. "Maybe it isn't a fancy lady that you really want."

Before she had even delivered this last call to arms, he attacked. He had the edge of both shirt and chemise hooked over his blade, and with one flick of his wrist, blunted tip or no, her clothes would be ripped in two.

She stilled, breathing hard, her body pulsing in frenzied excitement. "Go ahead," she managed. "Take my clothes."

His face hardened. He slowly lowered the big blunted tip of his sword between her breasts. "I believe we are done," he said harshly.

She stared at the tip, then lifted her gaze. "I am *not* done."

His brows lifted. "I have my blade against your heart, darling. In actual battle, you would be dead."

"Most men would prefer me warm and alive in their beds," she challenged tauntingly.

His eyes blazed. He removed the sword, tossing it aside and it clattered across the deck. "You have won, Amanda," he said. "I concede defeat."

He was turning to walk away. Amanda thrust, catching the top buttons of his breeches, and cut them free. He froze.

"Maybe," she said softly, "my opponent would be as easily deceived as you have been and throw his sword aside too soon, falsely thinking himself in no further danger. Maybe, in a real battle, skill will have little to do with the victory. Turn around," she ordered.

Incredulous, he faced her.

She could not keep her eyes on his face. His breeches gaped indecently and she had revealed an interesting portion of his anatomy. More interesting was the rigid line so visibly swelling there.

Her blood drummed in her veins and swelled in her own body. Aware of flushing, she pushed her blade against his heart, somehow tearing her gaze away from his manhood and lifting it to his face. "Yes, I win," she said flatly.

He was breathing hard. He was finally furious with her, and she was savagely elated by that, too. "You have defeated me. Now what? Will you skewer my heart for how I have hurt you? When all I have wished to ever do is see you safely to what is left of your family?"

Some of the tension of the battle eased. Dismay warred with guilt.

He turned and began to walk away, then quickly returned to her. Before she could move, he had seized her wrist. "Put down the damned sword. I wish to speak with you privately and it is *not* a request."

In that instant, she understood that she had pushed him too far. Her exhilaration was rapidly fading. She lowered the sword and he released her, gesturing angrily toward the captain's cabin. She started forward with growing trepidation, putting the sword down on the deck. She suddenly became aware of the utter silence of the ship.

Every hand had come on board, almost three hundred men, to witness her insane attack on their captain.

He clasped her shoulder and propelled her into the cabin.

Her insides tightened and then hollowed, the huge hunger returning. What had she done, to provoke him so recklessly and thoughtlessly, on sheer impulse? And just how angry was he? Was he angry enough to give in to his lust?

He kicked the door closed behind them. He tore off his shredded shirt, stalking past her, his attire beyond revealing and beyond indecent. She watched him throw on a shirt, leaving it hanging over his breeches. She exhaled harshly and he whirled.

"What do you expect? You are reckless and fearless, yet a woman. Any man would be aroused by such violent foreplay. I feel certain that was your plan."

She tried to breathe. "There was no plan. I was angry. I wanted to hurt you. I'll buy you a new shirt."

"You are penniless." He stalked away, pouring himself a whiskey. She watched him drain the glass and then pour another one. His hand was shaking.

"We are in close quarters," he said, glancing at her. "We cannot go on this way. I have already apologized for my behavior. It is time for you to accept my apology. I want a truce."

She was trembling, too, she realized. She hugged herself.

Could she accept his apology? The truth was that she hated fighting with him. She didn't hate him, not at all.

"You will agree to a truce?" he demanded.

"Yes, I will," she managed, stunned. *Oh, my God*, she thought, turning away, shaken to her core. *She had fallen in love with Cliff de Warenne.*

*She was doomed.*

He almost smiled but did not approach, as if deliberately keeping a distance between them. He spoke more calmly. "You have given my crew quite a show today, Amanda."

She bit her lip. She didn't know what to say, as she was still reeling from the realization that she had fallen in love with the most unattainable man in the world.

When she did not speak, he said softly, "I have missed our time together."

She jerked, instantly filled with hope, their gazes meeting.

He was the first to look away. "Will you dine with me tonight? We can share a quiet supper and you can regale me with the details of your studies. We can discuss the logistics of your reunion with your mother, too." He smiled at her.

She had missed him, too, terribly, and if all he could offer her was a few hours each night on deck or dining together, so be it. Wasn't that better than nothing at all? In that moment, she would accept crumbs. Because she hadn't just missed him—she needed him, too. "I should like to dine with you tonight." She hesitated. "What does *logistics* mean?"

His soft, warm smile reached his eyes, making him beauty incarnate. "There are logical details to discuss, such as the presentation I will help you make at Belford House."

Amanda did not want to discuss her fate in London. *She was deeply and irreversibly in love*. "That will be fine."

His gaze slid over her face. "You were very bold today, Amanda," he said. "And you are very skilled with a sword. I have never known any woman to wield a blade as you do."

She inhaled, overcome by his praise. There was no mistaking the admiration in his eyes. "Thank you." And she prayed she could settle for his admiration, as there was no chance of ever having his love.

AMANDA WAS LATE.

Cliff paced restlessly in his cabin, the dining table elegantly set for the intimate supper he had arranged. He knew he was treading dangerously—while a truce was requisite for his peace of mind, considering the duration of the voyage, dining tête à tête was testing his character, his honor, his resolve. He had not been able to stop thinking about her magnificent display with a sword earlier that day. She could have been a Celtic warrior princess from an ancient time when women were brave and fearless, fighting alongside their men. And the heat and violence of the battle they had shared had only escalated every primitive male instinct in him, when those instincts were already so greatly endowed in his nature.

He wished he had really answered her call to arms, for he would have shredded her clothing, forced her to her knees and then taken her in his arms and into his cabin and his bed.

He tried to recover some gracious composure, running a hand through his hair. To force aside his recollection of her stunning swordsmanship, all he had to do was brood over her future fate. He had been thinking long and hard about her arrival at Belford House ever since he had discovered the true identity of her mother. Amanda had no idea she was a bastard, as she must be—he could hardly imagine Dulcea Belford having been briefly married to a young naval officer and then obtaining an expensive divorce. He knew Amanda was going to be shocked and hurt by the truth of her birth.

He felt like cursing Carre for his lies, but he understood what the man had been trying to do.

As for Lady Belford, he knew her well enough to know she

would not be overcome with joy to be reunited with her long-lost daughter. No lady of her stature would openly claim a bastard child, as it meant ruin and disgrace. However, bastards were a part of society—every family had them, often living side by side with their legitimate siblings. These illegitimate offspring were usually labeled long-lost godchildren or cousins, and after a brief period of voracious gossip, no one really cared. Dulcea would probably claim her daughter as a distant cousin. That way, she could take Amanda into her family without jeopardizing her own life.

It had become obvious that he would have to meet with her before ever bringing Amanda to call. He would have to make certain the reunion went well and that Dulcea would acknowledge her as her cousin, at least. Once they had come to terms, he would approach Amanda and tell her the truth as gently as he possibly could. He dreaded that particular interview.

And between now and then, he had to encourage her to make every effort to refine her behavior, otherwise she was truly doomed.

Where was she? Had she had a change of heart since they had declared a truce?

He realized she was forty minutes late. He finally strode from his cabin to see what was keeping her. Cliff was about to knock when he heard her speaking so passionately that he froze. Who was with her in her berth?

"What should I do?" she demand, sounding terribly distressed. "I am at a loss, a complete loss!" Her tone dropped, anguished. "Please help me."

Confused and even jealous, Cliff pushed quietly on the door. As he did so, he saw Amanda standing in the center of the small cabin, her back to him. She cried out, "Papa! If you do not advise me now, who will? Dear God, I need you now!"

His sympathy arose, blended with pity. Amanda was speaking to her dead father? Was she seeing his ghost? Did she really think he would answer her? Did she converse with Carre frequently?

He had assumed her to be well on her way to recovery from her loss. Clearly, her grief remained as strong as ever. He felt like a callous cad for not realizing sooner.

He was about to call to her when she said brokenly, "You are probably angry with me. I haven't forgotten that you wanted me to become de Warenne's mistress, but he is really a gentleman, Papa. I did try to entice him, I really did."

He reeled, as if she had just stabbed him in the chest with the plain little dagger she kept in her boot. *She had been playing him to honor some insane request made by her father?* Instantly, he understood why Carre had wanted his penniless daughter to become his mistress, but that comprehension changed nothing.

She wiped at tears. "Papa, please forgive me for failing. At least I am on my way to Mama… Papa? I don't know what to do. I am so in love."

There had been no time to recover from the first shock. There had been no time for any anger. In disbelief, praying he had misunderstood her, he opened the door fully.

She shook her head, as if speechless. "I know," she whispered, as if her father had spoken to her. "I know I am a fool, I know he will break my heart—but I have never met a man like him before. No one is like de Warenne! Oh, God. I am trying to convince myself to settle for his companionship, but it is so hard! I am so deeply in love. If he would have me, I would gladly be his lover, and I wouldn't care if I received nothing else from him!"

A huge fist had struck him in the gut, knocking the wind out of his lungs. How had this happened? How in hell had Amanda Carre, the wild and free La Sauvage, so independent that she didn't need anyone, fallen in love with *him?*

But hadn't he already guessed? The way she looked at him, her eyes alternately shining with hope and admiration or turning sultry with hunger, was so revealing. Had he misled her even more than he had previously thought? He only wanted to protect her.

He attempted to speak, but his voice refused to work.

"At least I am going to England, to Mama, because that is what you really wanted," she suddenly said. She was shaking, fighting tears. "I couldn't deny you that. But Papa? I am afraid." She wiped her face with her sleeve. "I am really a coward. Now I have let you down, because I am so afraid of England, of Mama. I am more afraid of her than I ever was of the cutthroats who would board our ship and try to kill us. I wish you could come back and tell me I didn't have to go."

Cliff backed out of the cabin. He closed his eyes, unbearably overcome with compassion. This circumstance he could manage; her feelings for him were something else.

He silently walked back to his cabin.

## *CHAPTER EIGHT*

HE WATCHED HER SIP her wine. The monologue he had overheard remained firmly etched on his mind, but she showed no sign of her recent bout of tears. She glanced up. Her eyes were so soft and hopeful; now, he knew what that expression meant. He glanced restlessly away, disturbed. But he had an agenda now, a firm agenda, one he intended to enforce at all costs. He was going to move heaven and earth to make Amanda's reunion with Dulcea a success, but that meant cooperation on her part.

"Are you enjoying the *soupe du poisson?*" he asked casually.

She laid down her spoon, smiling at him. "Very much."

"We have made good sailing. I have calculated that we are a third of the way to Britain."

Her expression tensed and her eyes flickered.

"You must be excited, Amanda, terribly excited."

She stared down at her soup. "Yes."

He studied her down-turned face, trying to decide how to get her to confess her fears, for then he could suggest a shortened course in the social graces. There was no other choice now, not if she was to be successfully reunited with Dulcea Belford. But suddenly she looked up. "Will you just drop me on the London docks?"

It was so easy to see her fear now. "Of course not. I intend to escort you to Belford House."

"And there you will leave me, right?"

He spoke with great care. "I wish to aid you in making a good impression, Amanda. We need to find you a suitable gown. I intend to summon a seamstress to Harmon House the moment we make port. When you have the appropriate attire, I will escort you to Belford House."

Her gaze was riveted on his. "Harmon House? Where your father lives with his wife, the countess?"

"I stay at Harmon House when I am in town. I have no idea who will be in residence when we arrive. The entire family could be there, or no one at all."

Two pink spots appeared on her cheeks, making her seem feverish.

"I can see that you are somewhat anxious. My family will welcome you very enthusiastically. And I will stay with you, if you wish, while you meet your mother."

She folded her arms. "But then you will leave. I mean, she will give me a room. I am going to spend the rest of my life at Belford House!"

He sighed, feeling terrible for her. "You are young and she is your mother. Of course she will wish to take you in, as she should. But when you come of age, you will be able to do as you wish—if you have the funds." And he couldn't help thinking about what Carre had wanted his daughter to do. He couldn't completely blame the man; Amanda was beautiful and passionate, the kind of woman a rich gent would wish to keep. But why hadn't Carre had higher aspirations for his daughter? Had Amanda really spent the first four years of her life with her mother? He thought it unlikely. And damn it, why hadn't Carre sent her to some fine ladies' school to gain instruction in etiquette?

"Well, I will be of age shortly," she said.

"Legally, but I am sure your mother will wish to see you properly cared for. She won't cast you out at eighteen, Amanda. Many unwed ladies live at home into their twenties. Some spinsters never leave their parents' homes."

She just shook her head, clearly dismayed.

"I can help you," he dared, leaning forward. He almost reached for her hand and thought better of it.

"What do you mean?" she asked warily.

"There must be more to your introduction than a pretty gown," he said, trying to sound casual.

She understood; she stiffened. "I know. I am not a lady and no dress will make anyone think otherwise." She added, "I have never worn a dress."

He was dismayed, for this would be far more difficult than he had thought. "I am charmed by your originality," he said sharply, meaning it. "But others might not be."

"Are you trying to be amusing?" She was incredulous. "Do you know how many fine ladies in Kingston sneer at me on the public roads? In church, they refuse to share my pew. One fancy sort actually crossed to the other side of the street so my person would not offend her. And they talk about me—loudly—so I know exactly what they are thinking. I am trash. No one in my mother's house is going to think anything else—or in your home, either."

He just stared, aching for her. "You are not trash. You are a hundred times stronger, braver and more beautiful than all of your detractors. And you are wrong about my family—if you are with me, they will be kind and accepting, and they will become fond of you when they get to know you better. But you are right about one thing. No one at Belford House is going to be enchanted by your candor or your skill with a sword. We need to plan your introduction to your mother with care, Amanda. I have given this a great deal of thought. I wish we had more time, but we have a month. You must learn the basic social graces—how to walk, how to speak, how to dine. And of course, you must know how to dance."

She was near tears. "I know how to walk and talk—but the way I walk and talk isn't good enough, is it?" He was silent. "I don't want to sup with gentry, de Warenne. I don't want to go to England. I don't want to meet my mother, not like this, but I promised Papa!" She stood abruptly, her chair flipping over. She paled, turning to right it.

He leaped to his feet and went around the table, taking the fallen chair from her hands. "It's all right," he said, placing it upright.

She shook her head. "It's not all right. I can't even get up from the table properly and you know it."

He took her hand. "Actually, I have heard you mime and you are very talented."

She froze, keenly interested now. "You mean, when I am mocking some fool?"

He almost smiled. "Yes, that is exactly what I mean. You can imitate the upper-crust tone exactly—I have heard you do so more than once. This won't be as hard as you think."

She stared and then pulled away. "I can practice all kinds of fancy airs, but I will never fool anyone. I don't want to be a lady. I just want to sail ships."

He felt his heart melt. He thought about what to say and how to say it. "Unfortunately, Carre is dead. You have no means, which is equally unfortunate. Your mother will be supporting you. You will have to somehow adapt."

"I have you," she whispered, her gaze wet with tears and glued to his.

His heart raced. "*What*?"

She folded her arms tightly to her body. "I could stay here…with you. I think that would please Papa."

He stared in disbelief, but every moment they had passed on his frigate tumbled with shocking clarity through his mind.

"I am a very good sailor!" she cried. "I'll wager there is no lad on this ship who can climb up to the main royal yard as fast as I can."

He turned white. "Like hell you're climbing up there!" It was the highest yard on the ship.

"I can load balls as fast as the best gunners, too. And I am a good shot with the pistol and you saw that I am a very good swordsman. Please," she added desperately. "Let me sail with you!"

"You wish to sail with me," he echoed, his heart pounding in a timeless manner he recognized. She wished to stay on his ship, sailing the high seas with him. Shaken, he turned away, his loins huge and full.

"I will make my way, I swear it! And I don't eat very much. I can sleep below with the idlers," she begged.

He faced her, shaking his head. "No."

"I will fail miserably in England," she whispered. "You must know it, too."

They simply stared at each other, her face filled with fear and anguish, so much so that he had the oddest urge to agree to her request. But it was insane, impossible. "You won't fail. I am going to help you learn some necessary graces, and so will Ariella and Anahid."

She sat down on the bed, staring at him. "What if Mama doesn't want me?"

That was his greatest fear, as well. He softened, walking to her, but he reminded himself not to touch her, not now. He must not comfort her. "I don't blame you for being anxious. However, I am asking you to trust me. I am going to secure your future, Amanda, before I leave England. That is a promise."

Amanda stared, clearly uncertain. She whispered, "I do trust you. But what if Mama looks at me the way that sow at Windsong did? The way they all do?"

He stiffened. *Lady Belford would be very sorry*, he thought grimly, *if she looked down her fine nose at her daughter*. "I cannot predict the future, but we can do everything in our power to put the odds in our favor. You must work very hard for the next four weeks and I will steer you through your reunion with your mother. I think that, together, we can make your reunion a success. I certainly intend to do my part, but you must do yours."

She bit her lip. "I will try. But I do not have your confidence. I wish I did."

He smiled. "Then I will have enough confidence for us both." He became serious. "Amanda, she is your family. I am a trader most of the time and a privateer the rest. I am also a bachelor. You simply cannot sail with me. It just isn't done."

She looked away. "Why not? You do as you please, don't you? Everyone knows you obey no one and nothing."

Unfortunately, she was right. He hesitated. "My life would be very different if I were not an eccentric," he said grimly, meaning it. "It has kept me separate from everyone else. I have no regrets, but in the long haul, it is better to fit in."

"But I am different, too," she whispered, her gaze seeking his.

They were both outsiders, he thought. "Your fate is Belford House, mine is the high seas. We are entirely different." He sat down on the bed besides her, shaken by how much they had in common. "So? Have we agreed on a plan of action?"

She hesitated and nodded. "I will try to improve my manners, but I am not hopeful, as you are."

"I know you will succeed," he vowed. "Amanda, I won't abandon you," he heard himself add.

She seemed surprised, but then, so was he.

AMANDA WAS EXHAUSTED. She had spent five entire days immersed in her new lessons. Now that her course was charted, she had thrown herself into fancy airs and manners with a fierce, single-minded intent. She was almost certain she would fool no one, but an image was in her mind, one she could not shake. In it was a faceless young woman who wore beautiful gowns and walked with elegant grace effortlessly. This woman sipped tea with her mother in a garden filled with blooming roses of every possible color; this woman was escorted around London by a handsome, dashing gentleman admirer—one who appeared oddly like Cliff de Warenne.

She didn't hate etiquette the way she thought she would, although she hated that she was so clumsy and inept, her efforts currently so comical. She could not walk easily in the long skirts of the caftan she had been given without tripping over the hem or her own feet, and when she did not stumble she would soon forget to shorten her strides. Marching about like a boy in skirts made Alexi howl with laughter. She had been left in the company of Anahid, Ariella and Michelle, and they had chased Alexi away; she had later learned de Warenne had punished him for his laughter, ordering him to write two essays in a single day, one in Latin, as well as a letter of apology. She felt so uncomfortable in the gown and she was afraid she would never become accustomed to it. If she couldn't even walk like those ladies in Kingston, how would she ever learn to dance? By the fifth day, Amanda was in despair. Would she ever be graceful enough to fool anyone?

She was so afraid that she was going to humiliate herself in society and in front of de Warenne. On some level, she had known all along that she could not walk in her mother's door like a pirate's daughter. That would have taken more courage than she possessed.

She tore off the hated caftan. She had been wearing it over her skirt and breeches, in a small act of defiance of which no one seemed to be aware, and her dagger remained in her boot. Was she clinging to her old life, just in case the new one never materialized? She threw the heavily embroidered turquoise, purple and gold caftan to the floor, then kicked it away. Today, she had curtsied so low she had fallen over. She had been mortified. And to make matters worse, de Warenne had been watching from the threshold of the cabin. Instead of impressing him, she had embarrassed herself for the hundredth time.

She covered her face with her hands. Why couldn't Mama love her just the way she was?

*Why couldn't de Warenne love her that way, too?*

Her heart lurched. She dared not be stupid and silly, not in regards to de Warenne! He was her protector, and even her friend, or so she hoped. He was never going to want a commoner like Amanda Carre, a wild child like La Sauvage, as his mistress or even a passing lover.

But he might want her, if she became the lady in her secret dreams.

She had hardly seen de Warenne since her new studies had begun. She had thought he would help teach her to walk, to curtsy and to dance, at least somewhat. Obviously she had misunderstood—or he had had second thoughts about his role in her education. When she had tried to join him in the middle watch, late at night when her instruction for the day was complete, he had ordered her to go to her cabin to get some sleep, making it clear he did not wish for her company. Not being allowed to join him had been a terrible blow. Not only did she yearn for his company—and his praise—she missed him, too. She sensed he was keeping his distance from her and she knew why. She had thrown herself at him and he did not wish to suffer such attentions again.

Amanda wished she had never been so foolish.

There was a knock on her door. As Amanda turned to answer it, she noticed the silver seas outside the porthole and the ominously gray skies. Excitement began—they were in for foul weather. It had been years since she had sailed in a wild storm.

She opened her door to find Michelle smiling at her. She brightened. "Are we going to read some more?" She loved reading almost as much as she loved sailing.

He beamed. "*Non, actuellement,* I am going to start your dancing lessons."

Her heart fell. Thus far, her lessons had only been comprised of walking, speech and the ever-so-basic curtsy. Michelle was going to teach her to dance? If she had to learn how to dance, she wanted to learn with de Warenne. But maybe it was better this way. She didn't want to embarrass herself in front of him again.

"I don't feel well," she lied. "Can't we start tomorrow?"

"*Mademoiselle,* there is very little time left! You must learn to waltz, even if we have no music. *Maintenant, allez-vous.*"

"ORDER TOPSAILS and topgallants single reefed."

"Aye, sir," Midshipman Clark said, hurrying to give the orders.

Cliff turned back to stare across the bowsprit, the winds a strong twenty-three knots. The weather was worsening rapidly and he estimated that within two or three hours, he'd have almost all canvas down. His arms folded across his chest, he attuned his senses to the oncoming storm, trying to gauge it. He had a dark feeling, one he did not care for. "Heavy weather lies ahead," he remarked to MacIver.

"Aye, it does, sir."

"There'll be rain, too." He turned and strode to the edge of the quarterdeck, watching as the sails he'd ordered furled came down. "Clark. I'll have double duty now."

"Aye, sir," Clark said, echoing the orders for another watch to take up stations. Cliff was certain he'd have all hands on deck by sunset—not that one could see the sun, as the skies were becoming heavier and darker by the moment.

"My lord." Anahid approached unsteadily, fighting the rolling deck.

He leaped down to the main deck and grasped her arm. "The children?"

"They are fine, my lord. Alexi wishes to be on deck and Ariella has yet to notice the weather, as she is engrossed in her French assignments."

The ship was riding high swells, but not yet bucking; still, the weather was worsening rapidly. "He will not come on deck until we have passed the storm. And that, I think, will be at dawn.

Anahid, your report?" Every day at precisely four o'clock, Anahid would report to him on Amanda's progress. Her words thus far had been somewhat encouraging.

"My lord, she is a determined student. If we had more time, I would not be worried. But we have only three weeks left! She has been allowed to run wild and behave like a boy her entire life. Such engrained behavior cannot change in a matter of weeks."

"She must make a good first impression at Belford House," he insisted.

"You saw her walking like an aggressive tomboy the other day. She needs more time, my lord. May I be candid?"

"Please."

"She is so proud...yet she puts her pride aside every single day. Every small mistake is a great mortification for her. I think you might wish to postpone her entry in society until she has mastered the skills she needs."

"That can certainly be arranged," he said thoughtfully. "But I would like her to be reunited with her mother immediately, which is far different from a coming out in the ton. She need not be perfect to meet her mother. Will she be able to pass as some kind of gentlewoman by the end of this voyage?"

"I am uncertain."

He was both worried and touched. He had seen how determined his charge was. He admired her tenacity, especially as he also knew how proud she was and how her missteps shamed her. However, Lady Belford would want her daughter to be very polished. He had little doubt. "You will proceed to the best of your ability," he told Anahid.

"My lord? You might wish to praise and flatter her. She admires you immensely."

He flushed, having a terrible inkling that Anahid knew that an unacceptable passion had tainted his relationship with Amanda. "I will take you below."

He held her arm and guided her to the children's cabin,

helping her fight the wind. As he went in, Amanda appeared from her cabin, smiling brightly at him.

He instantly saw that her cheeks were flushed with excitement. "I take it you have some good news to impart?" he asked, as she followed him into the children's cabin.

"We are sailing into a storm," she told him excitedly. "I have not been in a good storm in years."

He slowly looked at her. Most women would be nervous at this stage, and in another hour, close to tears; by the time they were at the storm's heart, most women would be sobbing for their lives, expecting a watery death. He felt himself still. "We are in for very rough seas," he said, "and extreme winds. We are already at twenty-three knots. The children will stay below. You will stay below with them, too."

She gave him an incredulous look.

"That is an order." He turned to face an equally disbelieving Alexi. He also saw that his daughter had finally noticed the storm. She had closed her book and was sitting on the lower bunk, pale with fright.

"Papa!" Alexi jumped up and down. "I must help you navigate through the storm. There is a storm, isn't there?"

"We are approaching gale winds," he said. "But you are eight years old and I am giving you an order. You are to stay in this cabin and comfort your sister."

Alexi stared unhappily. "But…"

"There are no buts!" Cliff exclaimed. "I am your captain and you will obey every order I give you. Am I clear?"

Alexi nodded, flushing.

"And I will be clearer," Cliff said. While his son had never openly disobeyed him before, he knew how badly Alexi wanted to go on deck and witness the storm. But he would be blown overboard before Cliff could react. "I will take the rod to you if you disobey me." He had never made such a threat before, but Alexi had to know he must not disobey him now.

Alexi's eyes went wide. He was absolutely silent.

Cliff stared one more moment, to make certain his son understood that this time, he would pay dearly for any transgression. "Good." He softened, walking over to Ariella and sweeping her into his arms. "What are you reading?"

*"The Iliad,"* she whispered.

"Is it a good book?"

She nodded. "Papa? Will we capsize?"

He laughed, hoping to reassure her. "Of course not! When has your papa ever capsized? Has your papa ever been shipwrecked? We have some strong winds, that is all. Later, there will be rain. But you," he said, placing her back on the bunk, "will be sound asleep, as snug as a bug in your bed. You won't even know we have sailed through a storm, because at dawn, the sun will be shining." He tweaked her chin lightly.

She nodded, not quite able to smile. "The ship is rocking so. It will be hard to sleep."

"Anahid will make you tea, and the rocking will help you sleep, actually. I promise."

She finally smiled at him.

He walked over to Anahid and Amanda, aware that Amanda's rapt attention was devoted to his every word and action. "Anahid," he said, lowering his voice so his children could not overhear. "In another hour, put some brandy in Ariella's tea. It will be better if she sleeps through the night."

Anahid nodded.

He returned to his son, clasping his shoulder. "You are to reassure your sister. You can play a game with her or read aloud, whatever, to distract her."

"Yes, Papa," Alexi said, sounding defiant and contrite, at once.

Cliff sighed. In a few more years, his son would be a rogue and difficult to handle, he was certain. He started from the cabin, pausing to look at Amanda. But she had gone over to his son.

"He isn't being mean, Alexi," she said. "The storm is dangerous—you are so small that a good wind could blow you overboard! And if that happened, your papa would dive in to save you and you would both drown in these seas."

He nodded gravely. "Then I will take care of my sister," he said.

Pleased, Cliff nodded at Anahid and left the cabin. Instantly he saw that the winds had heightened; foam was spraying from the waves and being whipped in the wind's direction. He increased his stride, leaping to the deck. "Knots?"

Clark answered. "Twenty-four."

They were in gale winds. "Furl the topgallants," he said. "Double reef topsails and jibs."

"Aye, sir!"

"Permission?"

He whirled in shock at the sound of Amanda's voice. She stood below him on the deck, fighting the winds, but her eyes flashed green with excitement. He didn't think; he reacted. He leaped to her side and seized her tightly. "You are hardly any bigger than my son! Are you mad to come out on deck now?"

"We are hardly in a hurricane," she shouted. "Twenty-four knots—that's gale winds."

"I want you below," he shouted back.

"Please!" she cried, and their gazes locked.

Only a madman would give in. He took her with him to the quarterdeck, seizing a coil of rope and tying it to her waist and then to his. "You may stay on deck for a half an hour. I wish to speak with you anyway," he said, his voice raised in order to fight the winds. "A storm is no place for a lady."

She lowered her lashes, clearly scheming. Then she sent him a sidelong smile. "But I am not a lady," she murmured, but he heard her anyway.

"How perfect—the subject I wish to discuss!"

"What?" she asked, cupping her ear.

He seized her hand, pushing it down. "I know you can hear me," he said, but he lowered his face to hers. "I am very pleased with your progress in learning decorum, Amanda. Anahid speaks in glowing terms of you."

She was wide-eyed with surprise.

"If you continue as you have been, there is every chance that you will not only delight your mother, but you will have suitors lined up around the block, vying for your attention." He sent her a promising smile.

She flushed, incredulous. "How can you think so? I almost fell on my face today!" she cried against the wind and the slapping seas.

"I am saying so because I have faith in you," he said, and he realized he meant it. "But I know you are anxious. So if you are not ready when we get to London, we will delay what we must."

Relief filled her eyes. She nodded, her gaze riveted to his.

Suddenly his mind played a trick on him. He imagined her, not on the deck beside him, but in a ballroom, in a beautiful ball gown. His heart turned over hard, then thundered. Good God, she would be so beautiful.... For a moment, speech failed him. She would have a dozen suitors, he realized, still stunned. "Amanda," he heard himself say, his gaze holding hers, "when you come out, I must insist on the first dance."

"You want the first dance?" she gasped.

He tore his gaze away, shaken by the possessive desire that had arisen. "I do. In fact, I will make certain to be in London for your first ball—if you promise me that dance."

She turned away, incredulous, but the rope between them went taut. "Of course," she said breathlessly. Then she faced him, still surprised. "But why?"

"Are you not my protégée?" he asked, trying to sound casual. But he knew that she would be too beautiful to resist in a ball gown, whirling about the floor in a gentleman's arms. It flashed through his mind that he might not be that pleased when she was introduced into society, because no gentleman would be immune to her beauty. And suddenly he wanted that first dance very badly—suddenly he ached for it.

He glanced at her through his lashes. "Is it not my right to dance with you before all others?" he asked softly, unable to help himself.

He could not control himself. They were standing near the helm in gale winds, the deck rocking heavily beneath their feet, and he was thinking of this woman, her beauty, her allure and his passion, not the storm. He knew he would feel as intensely passionate dancing with her as he would if he allowed himself to take her to his bed.

She began to smile. "I am clumsy," she warned.

He laughed, relieved by her absurd comment. "Impossible! You are light on your feet—we locked swords, remember? I know you will excel at dancing, just as you will excel at all of your current studies."

She suddenly lowered her dark lashes. "Very well. I will allow you the first dance—*if* you allow me to ride the storm here with you."

"Absolutely not!" he shouted, aghast. "I do not need you going overboard, either!"

She pulled on the rope binding them, then gave him a sidelong, seductive look. "I can hardly fall overboard now."

He shook his head, furious with her for daring to use that dance against him, and glanced again at the high, white foam of the seas. The horizon ahead was now pitch-black, a sight he did not care for. He turned back to her. "I will not barter for that dance," he warned. He was going to have it, no matter what she now intended.

She gave him a look—one far too womanly for his comfort—as if she knew she had triumphed, but she suddenly cried out. He whirled to follow her gaze. One of the topmen was dangling from the topsail yardarm. And from the corner of his eye he saw Amanda's dagger flash as she cut the rope binding them together.

Instinctively he moved to seize her, but she adeptly dodged his grasp, ducking beneath his arm and leaping to the deck below. "Amanda!" he shouted, leaping after her.

She jumped up into the main shrouds; his heart stopped. Was she thinking to save the sailor?

He ran forward, intending to seize her before she got too high up in the shrouds. But she was very agile and was rapidly outdistancing him.

She was already close to the topmast shrouds. Amanda was dangerously high up—high enough that a fall would kill her. He was torn. He could try to chase her up the rigging and force her back down, or he could return to the decks to catch her if she fell. Cliff leaped back to the decks.

He was instantly joined by midshipman Clark. "Catch her if she falls," he said tersely.

He watched Amanda fight the winds, which were stronger so far above the deck. The gale could easily blow her from the rigging. She had stepped into the topmast shrouds but the lad was dangling from the main topsail yard above her, twirling like a puppet on a string. Cliff did not think the boy could hold on for much longer.

Amanda had paused, clearly fighting for strength.

The dangling sailor shouted to her.

Then Amanda began to fight the winds, climbing higher. Slowly she approached the sailor, her small body beginning to twist in the shrouds as the wind played her. She extended one hand toward the lad and Cliff froze. He was expecting her slender body to be torn free from the rigging and blown viciously away at any moment.

The sailor refused to let go of the yard.

Amanda was shouting at him, her words lost in the storm.

She had that dagger, Cliff thought fiercely. "Amanda!" He cupped his hands to his mouth. "Cut the line—send him a rope! *Cut the line!*"

Suddenly Amanda went for her dagger and cut one of the shroud lines. She flung it at the sailor. He reached for it, and when he caught it, Cliff knew it was a miracle. The sailor let go of the yard, and holding to the line, he soared toward the deck. Cliff let the men seize his legs and bring him down, his attention intensely riveted to Amanda as she started down the shrouds. When she was finally close enough that a fall might break bones but not kill her, he leaped into the shrouds, climbing quickly up to her. She saw him and smiled, not just triumphant, but smug.

He was beyond amazement. Cliff reached for her, seizing her with one arm. "Let go," he shouted.

She obeyed and he pulled her against his body. And for one moment, they swung together in the shrouds, Amanda securely in his arms. "Jesus." It was the only speech he was capable of.

"Jesus," he said again. He didn't think he would have ever recovered if she had been flung to her death.

With her cheek against his chest, Amanda cried, "The boy?"

"He's fine," he shouted. In that moment, he realized the winds had dangerously increased and they had to get out of the shrouds. "We need to descend," he told her. "Just hold on to me and do not let go."

She shouted, "I can descend by myself!"

*Like hell*, he thought. He started a careful descent, afraid to miss a step and mistakenly hurl her to the decks. His men appeared and he gave her over to their waiting arms. Then he leaped to the deck. "Someone take her below. Triple-reef the topsails," he ordered.

Amanda faced him, seizing his arm. "Let me stay," she said calmly. "I can help. I think I have proven it."

"You are not staying on deck," Cliff had said firmly.

"I saved that sailor's life."

"The act was beyond madness! You will go below with my children."

"De Warenne. I swear to obey your every order. *Please*."

What woman in her right mind, would wish to stand beside him and ride out the oncoming storm? Only the same woman who had risked her life to save a sailor she did not know. He was never going to forget Amanda scrambling up the rigging, risking her own life to rescue the lad. It had been the bravest act he had ever witnessed. She was, without a doubt, the most courageous woman he had ever known.

"You'll be lashed to the foremast and it won't be pleasant."

She smiled widely at him.

THE SKIES HAD TURNED black a few hours after sunset. The winds had begun to rage at fifty-six knots and had not abated since; the frigate was only carrying her storm staysails. The high seas were completely white and there was no visibility; the air was filled with foam and spray. The frigate bucked wildly. MacIver was at the helm, but Cliff stood beside him, and all hands were on deck. It was well into the middle watch.

Amanda stood just ahead of them both, a rope securely tied around her waist and lashed to a bolt below the foremast shrouds so she could not be blown overboard.

A solid eight hours had passed since she had rescued the sailor. It was, he estimated, two or three in the morning. Amanda had stood beside him, riding out the storm as if she were a part of the wind and the sea. His admiration for her knew no bounds.

"Are we sailin' into a hurricane, sir?" the officer shouted at him.

"No," Cliff shouted back. "We are in her center, Mac. Another hour and we will be through the worst."

"Aye, sir."

Cliff fought the wind, moving to the starboard, glancing at her. She met his gaze with a smile, her eyes fierce and bright. He had not bothered to ask her even once if she was tired and wished to go below, for he knew what her answer would be. "We are in the heart of the storm," he told her.

She nodded. "I know. I can feel it." She gestured at the bow. "There's daylight ahead."

He followed her gaze but saw no sign of the dawn.

An hour later, they both saw the shifting light. Cliff remained standing with Amanda. The winds abruptly began to ease. He scanned the white frothing seas and realized he was not mistaken—the cataclysm was ending. He glanced at her and she smiled, saying, "We have just dropped a good ten knots."

Her ability to gauge the wind and the weather amazed him. "Yes, we have." Then he sniffed the air. "But we are in for heavy rain."

She shrugged.

He asked for a rating—the wind had dropped eleven knots. He barked orders to begin making sail. When he returned to her side, it was to lift his spyglass and stare toward the horizon. As he did so, instantly remarking the rising sun, a raindrop splattered on his hands, followed by another one, and then another one. Before he could utter a word, a torrential downpour engulfed them.

She laughed. "May I cut my stays?"

He smiled, as the winds had dropped to no more than twenty knots. His answer was to slice the bonds himself. He gave her a look, and understanding, she followed him to the helm. "Mac, I'll take over. You did a fine job of sailing tonight. Go below and enjoy a good mug."

MacIver grinned. "Aye, Cap." He glanced at Amanda. Then he tipped his cap at her and hurried from the quarterdeck.

The deluge, impossibly, intensified. But Cliff caressed the huge wheel, the frigate now gliding easily through the waves, the seas frothing white over silver bands on gray. "You should go below," he commented, sending her a glance.

"I like the rain," she said.

He did not speak. She should have resembled a bedraggled child, but she appeared like a goddess from the sea. Her wet shirt clung to her, revealing her full breasts, tight nipples and small, narrow waist. Her clothing seemed to be opaque, indicating that she wore cheap material beneath, but he was not relieved. He told himself not to stare and pulled his gaze away. But the damage had been done. The crisis was over, and he had never wanted any woman as much as he wanted Amanda Carre.

The downpour ended a few moments later. The sky continued to fade and the winds dropped precipitously. And suddenly, the sun was rising before them, crimson streaking the sky and the sea, wisps of blue fighting the gray. The moment was powerful and he shared a glance with Amanda. They exchanged quiet, understanding smiles.

She stared at him, no longer smiling. He felt her heat then, her hunger. Whatever child he had rescued weeks ago in Spanishtown was long gone. A seductive woman remained. His tension thickened.

Cliff turned to order more sail hoisted. As he did so, Amanda muttered something and suddenly crossed to the deck below. The quarterdeck felt strangely empty with her gone. But it was better this way and he exhaled, trying to relax, fighting the blood in his loins. Amanda was right. There was no other experience in the world quite like riding out a raging storm, other than to ride it out with such a woman—or to ride that woman now.

An image flashed recklessly in his mind. He tensed again, seeing Amanda in his bed, beneath him, her face turned up to his, as frenzied and as passionate as the seas had so recently been. He saw himself ripping off her wet shirt and whatever lay beneath it, revealing her breasts, lowering his mouth there and going lower still….

It was better that she had left him, he thought. By now, she was probably in her berth, exhausted and asleep.

And suddenly she was there saying softly, "Permission, Captain?"

He started, then realized that she carried two of his crystal glasses. He began to smile with a different anticipation. "Granted."

She returned his smile, hers far too soft, and hurried up. "Papa always liked a stiff drink after a storm," she murmured.

"Ah," he said, overcome with appreciation. "Thank you, Amanda." He realized his voice was rough.

She handed him the glass, their eyes dancing together. She had recognized his tone, too. He turned away from her and drained the liquid, its warmth instantly filling him. He had thought the second glass was for her, but she switched his empty glass for her full one. As she did so, their gazes locked.

He had to look. Her shirt remained indecently molded to her breasts, her nipples were hard and tight, and her breeches revealed every plump curve between her thighs. He felt his cheeks flame. "Go below, Amanda," he whispered. "Get some rest. You are a brave and fine sailor." He almost choked on the word *sailor*.

"You are soaking wet, and I know you are exhausted, too." Her stare was intense, brilliant. "I'll go below when you retire." But even as she spoke, she leaned against the helm, and her fatigue became terribly evident.

Exhaustion was claiming her. He was hardly surprised, and he realized she was right, he was terribly tired, too. "It has been a long night." He glanced behind them. It was time for the morning watch anyway, and a midshipman was awaiting his turn at the helm. He signaled the officer.

"Very well," he said.

As the officer took the helm, Amanda turned to go down to the main deck below. She stumbled, not with artifice, but with exhaustion, and he caught her. Instantly, he was concerned. "You will catch your death!" he exclaimed, suddenly afraid for her.

She sent him a soft, tired smile, clearly too worn-out now to speak. He had his arm around her, allowing her to lean even more heavily against him. He tried to ignore the feel of her soft breasts against his side as he guided her down to the main deck. It was fortunate, he thought, that she was falling asleep while on her feet. But knowing that changed nothing for him.

Instead of stumbling past his cabin, she pulled away from him, entering it.

He faltered, surprised, but he did not protest—he could not protest. Not when his manhood was raging, numbing his mind.

He followed her inside, staring after her like an idiot while she staggered to his bed, climbed onto it and fell back against the pillows. In spite of her exhaustion, she sent him the most seductive look he had ever received. He did not turn but kicked the door behind him closed, thinking, "Don't."

Her eyes were heavy-lidded. "A very good night," she breathed, reaching for her wet shirt.

"Very," he said, unsmiling. His loins had never been so full. "You need to get out of those clothes," he said thickly, debating what he would do. Honor won. "I'll go behind the screen and you may sleep here. I'll sleep in my children's cabin."

"I do not want to ruin your fine sheets," she murmured, sending him another glance through her lashes. She gripped the hem of her shirt and he tensed. She clearly intended to shrug off her shirt and he knew he must protest. But he didn't move and he didn't speak. He simply waited, wanting her to undress, wanting to see her in all of her naked beauty.

Lowering her eyes, she pulled shirt and chemise up her torso, over her breasts and over her head. Half-naked, she sent him another seductive smile, leaning back into the many red-and-gold velvet pillows against the headboard of the bed. Cliff did not move as she lay there, a Venus in repose, a Venus waiting for him.

*No siren could be as fatal*, he thought. He had wanted her for far too long and perhaps her courage was what had pushed him to this moment. Her long, curly platinum hair streamed over and around her breasts, framing each full globe, taut nipples jutting. He felt himself move forward. He sat slowly at her hip; he lifted her breasts in his hands. A still but savage excitement consumed him.

She gasped in pleasure.

Her weight was undoing his control. "You are more than brave and so terribly beautiful," he said harshly. "How can I refuse this magnificent offer? I am only a man," he said, but his mind was shrieking at him in protest. Some sanity, therefore, remained.

She laid her hand on his arm. "Please."

And he struggled, conscience and honor battling his body, but it was too late. Her simple touch had a profound effect. Lust exploded, unleashed. He hadn't wanted to kiss her, for it was far too intimate, but he caught her face in his hands and did just that, filling her with his tongue. He had wanted to taste her for so long, but his greed demanded instant gratification now. He forced his tongue deeper. When she began to weep in pleasure, he found her breasts, stroking them frantically, tearing his mouth from hers. He pulled her nipples into tighter, harder points and she gasped wildly. He began kissing her breasts, rubbing his face there, and finally he found her nipple with his tongue. Amanda moaned. His other hand crept between her thighs.

Palming her, he felt her spasm through her breeches.

He gulped in air. The pressure in his loins became impossibly painful, too, and the fabric there had become a vice, choking him.

And there was no more thought, no more reason; only lust, desire and emotions he dared not comprehend. Already he had her breeches open and his hand was stroking over hot, wet, throbbing flesh. Amanda cried out, spreading wide for him, arching for his touch, his taste, his manhood. He did as she demanded, stroking her until she sobbed in pleasure.

He was her first lover, he thought, somehow knowing it, and the savage excitement became a maelstrom of possession and need.

He tugged off her breeches, her drawers. She lay panting in the pillows, hardly recovered from her climax, but he could no longer wait. Cliff bent over her, sending his tongue against her distended flesh.

And as he licked her turgid body, his entire being filled with blood. It roared not just in his loins but in his head. She wept wildly, in more pleasure, in more ecstasy, and he reached between them to grip himself. As her cries eased he fought his need, bucking against her.

And then he gave in. He leaped from the bed, strode behind the screen and jerked on his breeches. They opened. He leaned his forehead against the wall and flicked his wrist. Release was instantaneous.

When he was done, he did not move, his wits returning rapidly. He was grim and disbelieving.

*What had he done?*

He inhaled harshly and pushed off the wall, fixing his clothing. He wiped sweat from his face, his eyes. Unfortunately, he could think of nothing he wished to do more than to leap into his bed with her and continue what they had begun.

But he hadn't ruined her—not yet.

He tore off his wet shirt and stepped out from behind the screen. Amanda lay where he had left her. She was soundly asleep.

He stared. She hadn't had the strength to move; she remained on top of the covers, stark naked, her cheeks flushed, but breathing deeply and evenly. Very slowly, he approached.

He could tell himself she was a child until hell froze over, but she was not a child and he knew that now. She was so hauntingly beautiful that his heart began to ache. And she was as passionate as he had dreamed—and they had barely begun.

Instantly he stiffened. They had begun nothing! There was nothing to begin! His intention was to be her protector, not her lover, not a conscienceless cad.

He knew that even if she awoke, she was so exhausted she would fall asleep instantly again. He lifted her so he could slide her under all of the covers. She sighed, her lashes barely fluttering. He went to his chest and withdrew one of his shirts.

When he had slipped it over her head, he pulled the covers up to her chin. She smiled very softly in her sleep. Briefly, he wondered if she were half-awake.

He paced away and sat, tugging off his boots. He then stripped off his soaking breeches, unfortunately aroused. After he had donned dry attire, he poured himself another scotch. As he drank, he sat in one of the high Spanish chairs at his table, staring at her.

What was he going to say to her on the morrow?

He was a clever and honest man, but in that moment, he could not come up with a single explanation for what he had done.

If he were very fortunate, she might not remember what had happened, he thought. But his ego was rather large and he wasn't sure he would really like that, either.

How, in God's name, would he manage the rest of the cruise, now that they had been so intimate? If they remained on course, a full two weeks lay ahead of them. No answer came to mind.

And as the sun rose, he sat there staring and he wrenched at his loins again.

## *CHAPTER NINE*

AMANDA AWOKE IN de Warenne's bed. She did not move, surprised, the silk sheets stunningly sensual against her bare skin. What was she doing in his bed, she wondered, yawning. And then she recalled a golden lover kissing her, touching her and using his tongue upon her.

She sat up, her heart racing wildly. And she recalled the storm.

Amanda glanced at the open portholes to get her bearings. The skies were brilliantly blue with just a few puffy white clouds and she realized it was late afternoon. She glanced down and saw that she was not in her lace nightgown, but in a man's fine linen shirt. She swallowed, knowing it belonged to de Warenne.

She tried to recall the entire evening. Just before dawn, soaking wet and exhausted, they had gone into his cabin. She vaguely recalled lying in his bed and conversing with him as he stood not far from its foot. She could not really grasp what had happened next, because all the images in her head were a blur of heated kisses, silken caresses and an explosion of ecstasy. But those images all contained de Warenne.

Had he made love to her last night? Or had she been dreaming?

She was in his bed, she was clad in his shirt, she was naked otherwise—which led her to one conclusion. Excitement began.

However, she was not bruised or sore. She felt certain she would be aching if they had made love.

She slipped from the bed. Someone had laid out that awful caftan for her, her boots beside it. There was no sign of her clothes, but they were probably still damp and hanging out to dry. She went straight to the washstand and using a soft cloth, cleansed herself. There was no blood.

Disappointment began. She sat down, realizing that if she hadn't bled he hadn't made love to her and she was still a virgin. She must have been dreaming, only this time the dream had been so very different from any other one, for she had never dreamed of such carnally explicit behavior before. The parts of the dream that she remembered were terribly vivid, enough so to make her breathless.

She shook her head to clear it. She might be in love, but de Warenne was not for her. He had spent the past month proving that. He had also shown her genuine honor, when she had never met anyone capable of any kind of nobility before.

Well, it was late and it had only been a dream. She finished washing, combed her hair, braided it and donned the hateful caftan over his shirt. She wondered if she might, somehow, assume possession of the latter.

The moment she stepped from the cabin, she saw him. He and Alexi were on the quarterdeck, focused on the compass there. She assumed he was giving his son a lesson in navigation.

She stared, admiring the way the sun glinted on his sun-streaked hair, admiring the vast breadth of his shoulders, the strong lines of his thighs. She began to recall the night they had shared, battling the storm together, and her yearning increased. He was a great and powerful commander, and while she had already known that, she had witnessed it firsthand. She wanted him so much it almost hurt.

"Mademoiselle Carre!" Michelle cried, pleased to see her.

Amanda turned, dismayed. She felt certain that she knew what was coming, but she wanted to joined de Warenne and his son. *"Bonjour,"* she said reluctantly.

"Good day," he replied with a bow. He waited.

Amanda sighed. After last night, she had no wish to ever attempt a lady's genteel manners again; she wanted to go up on the quarterdeck and join de Warenne and his son. She pinched herself. She was on her way to London and the clock was ticking. Her behavior was hardly that of a lady and she had very little time left to improve it.

"*Mademoiselle?* Your curtsy? Monsieur le Capitaine has been most explicit. I am to expedite your lessons and you are to succeed. The storm blew us days ahead of schedule, for we stayed on course. A miracle, I think." He smiled. "*Mademoiselle?*"

She curtsied and said, "*Monsieur*, I must speak with de Warenne."

He nodded. "If you insist, Miss Carre. But please hurry."

"Thank you," she said. And because she was so happy, she curtsied again. Then she rushed away from him, lifting the skirt of her caftan to do so.

"Walk, do not run!" Michelle exclaimed. "Ladies do not run!"

"This one does!" Amanda laughed over her shoulder. Before she had even reached the steps leading up to the quarterdeck, de Warenne turned. He smiled briefly at her, an odd smile, for it did not seem to reach his blue eyes. He nodded at her. "Hello, Amanda."

She became confused. His greeting seemed wary and cautious, almost distant, and she did not understand. "Permission?"

He glanced past her shoulder. "Denied."

She gaped. He would not allow her to join him? But last night in the storm, they had shared more than most people ever shared in a lifetime. Something had changed between them last night; she was certain they had become true shipmates. "I cannot come up?"

"You have lessons to complete today, Amanda, and as it is almost sunset, you will hardly be finished by midnight if you do not begin now." He sent her another strained smile. Then he turned his brilliant blue eyes on her, and his gaze was searching.

"Can they not wait until tomorrow?" she tried, her heart hammering with confusion and hurt.

"Why?" he asked mildly. "You do not seem ill. You appear to have weathered the storm very well. How are you feeling?" he added.

His question had an innuendo she could not decipher. "I feel fine." She smiled at him, wanting him to smile warmly at her, the way he so often did.

He kept staring. "Did you sleep well?"

How odd his questions were! "I slept very well," she said. She thought about waking up in his shirt. "Thank you for lending me some dry clothing." She hesitated. "I can't remember putting it on or falling asleep, or anything really, other than the storm and the rain." And her vivid dream, she thought, but she would never mention it, especially not to him.

He continued to stare; and then shrugged.

She bit her lip. "Are you angry that I overslept?"

"No." He didn't smile. "However, we stayed on course and I reckon we are two or three days ahead of schedule. Unless, of course, we become becalmed. In any case, I am giving Alexi some instruction now."

*She was being dismissed.* Dismayed, Amanda felt as if a cool and distant stranger had taken over his hard body and his beautiful face. "You are angry with me," she whispered. "But I do not know why."

"Why would I be angry with you?" His eyes flashed with impatience now, and he had never been impatient with her before. "We have an agreement, you and I, or have you forgotten? You are to dedicate yourself to self-improvement while I dedicate myself to securing your reunion with your mother. And we are running out of time."

She felt crushed. She tried to tell herself that he had not become a cold, uncaring stranger, that their friendship remained. Maybe he was still tired after the long night. She slowly nodded, never taking her gaze away from his face. "All right. I understand. And you are right. If I am to make a good impression on Mama and your family and anyone else, I have much to do and only ten days left." Fear tightened her stomach. How could she become a lady in ten mere days?

He hesitated and softened. "I have faith in you, Amanda."

She closed her eyes in relief, for here was the man she loved and so desperately needed. Then she met his gaze. "When I have completed all of my lessons, can I join you on the middle watch?" She could not help being eager.

His face tightened. In disbelief, she realized he was going to refuse her. "Ladies don't share the middle watch."

She was becoming incredulous. "Why are you doing this?"

"Because I have begun to think that I have encouraged your more wayward manners. It is best if you throw yourself entirely into ladylike behavior."

"But I have!" she gasped. "De Warenne, please! I live for moments like those last night. I love sailing beneath the stars, and you know it. Tonight we will have clear skies and moderate winds. It will be a fine night for a cruise."

He held up his hand to silence her. "How will you study all day and share the watch with me through half the night?"

"I can do it," she cried frantically. "And if you deny me the middle watch, then damn it, I don't want to be a lady!"

His face was rigid. "You will only sabotage yourself if you think to withdraw from your lessons now."

She folded her arms across her chest. "If you let me join you, I will apply myself doubly, de Warenne, I swear. If you think my schoolroom efforts lacking because of the watch, I will quietly give it up. But until then, don't punish me when I have been trying so hard to do as you have asked." She swiped at sudden tears. "We are mates! I know you know it, too."

He was pale and he inhaled. "I am not trying to punish you. Very well. As long as you keep up every effort, as long as you do not become too tired to excel at your lessons, you may join me."

Amanda clutched the railing for support, overcome with relief. "I am going to be the best student you have ever seen!"

His expression finally gentled. "Then I suggest you delay no more."

She smiled, almost kissed him, thought the better of it and leaped to the deck, shouting for Michelle.

AMANDA HURRIED to the quarterdeck where de Warenne stood alone at the helm, a towering man bathed in starlight. She had never applied herself with more energy and she was exhausted, but she refused to go to bed. She wanted to spend another night sailing the great ship, at one with him and the sea. All day, anticipation of the watch she would share had filled her.

Oddly nervous, she paused below the quarterdeck. "De Warenne?"

It was a moment before he glanced at her. Before she could catch his eye, his gaze slid away. "Granted."

His behavior was strange, she thought, hurrying up the three steps to pause breathlessly beside him. His powerful presence wrapped itself around her. With it, there was a throbbing heat. Amanda tensed, acutely aware of the man's mesmerizing force.

*I must be mad*, she thought. She inhaled deeply, but the night was scented with him as well as the stars and the sea. He *must* be feeling what she felt. But if he did, wouldn't he turn to her and pull her into his arms? Or was that wishful thinking?

Slowly she faced him, but she couldn't summon up a smile.

He was staring so intently her breath caught. Instantly, he

looked away. Confused and shaken, Amanda faced the bowsprit, hollowed now with raw hunger. Clearly the dream she had had last night had been her undoing.

There was no denying it, his humor was dark and grim. Was he displeased with her? Or had something happened that she did not know about?

"I studied very hard today," she tried. She would do anything to make him smile.

He nodded, not looking at her. "So Anahid said. I am pleased."

She suddenly shivered. He was this cold stranger again, but why? "I thought you would be happy."

He seemed reluctant to look at her. "I am very pleased with the progress you made today."

Amanda stared at his taut profile. Last night, in her dream, he had kissed her as if he was drinking from the well of her soul. She could almost feel his tongue in her throat. And then he had buried his face between her breasts, caressing them until she found pleasure. The urge to lean toward him and demand his touch, his kiss, was unbearable.

He suddenly said, clearing his throat, "Michelle says tomorrow you will be choosing a book from my library."

She nodded, hoping he would be pleased enough to smile at her. "He says it will be a struggle for me, but we will do one paragraph and sound out the words together."

He turned to stare. "What do you wish to read?"

She wet her lips, her heartbeat accelerating. "I want to read about Ireland."

Their gazes were locked. "Why?"

"I know all about the islands and sailing," she said, unable to contain her excitement. She smiled. "I can name all the continents, all the oceans, all the seas. Papa taught me. Now, I want to know about the world."

His glance slid over her. "Ireland is not the world."

"I know. But I will start with Ireland, with its history and culture, and then I will move on to England and then France." She smiled. "What do you think?"

His gaze slid to hers and then past. "I think it is an admirable goal. But why start with Ireland?"

*Because I love you*, she thought, *and you are an Irishman who loves his home. You said it is the most beautiful place on the earth!* She thought about how to reply. "You've told me a little bit about what it was like to grow up at Adare. It sounded so wonderful…I will probably never have a chance to visit there, but at least I can read about it."

He stroked the huge wheel. Spray danced lightly off the hull and the mass of canvas filling the night moaned in the wind above them. "You could start your studies with England, the home of your parents," he finally said.

"I am interested in Ireland," she said stubbornly.

He looked at her and she saw the faintest trace of a smile beginning. "I am sure that one day, you will have the opportunity to visit Ireland, and if you are in the vicinity of Adare, you will always be welcome there."

She thrilled, grasping his forearm. The moment she did so, she thought about every detail of her dream and jerked away. "Will you take me?" she somehow managed, her tone husky.

"I doubt it."

She knew her disappointment showed.

"Your husband is not going to allow you to lark about the world with me, Amanda."

She stared, stunned. "What husband?"

He sighed. "We both know you will one day wed. It is what women do."

"You mean my mother is going to force me to wed, don't you?"

Now he turned to face her, the distant mask gone. "No one will force you to do anything. I said I won't abandon you and I will not. I said I would secure your future and I mean it. If you wish to remain a spinster, so be it," he said harshly. "But we both know your place is at Belford House!"

She found it hard to breathe. "If you took me pirating, I could have a share of the prize and then I would not have to go to Belford House!"

"First of all," he said, after a moment in which he could not speak, "I do not pirate and I do not plunder. Second, if you mean, would I take you on a pirate hunt, the answer is no—and it is not negotiable. Thirdly, you belong with your mother."

"I heard," Amanda said slowly, 'that you ran away from home when you were fourteen."

He stiffened. "Where did you hear that?"

"It is gossip. They all gossip about you on the streets—the ladies you have taken to bed in Kingston, in Spanishtown, in Barbados! I have heard so many rumors, and that is one of them, but I had forgotten it until now. Did you run away from your home at fourteen?"

"Yes, I did. But it wasn't *running away*. I *left* home to make my way in the world."

"You were younger than I am." She was fascinated now.

"I was a boy—you are a young woman!"

"Why would anyone run away from a home like Adare?"

He sighed. "It was time, Amanda, that is all. I finally understood that I had no real future there. I told you, my oldest brother, Tyrell, is heir. My middle brother, Rex, was predestined by the order of his birth to go into the army. I had no certain future to aspire to. My stepbrother, Devlin, was already sailing in the royal navy, and the sea was calling me, as well. But I do not care to answer to authority, so I decided to go it alone."

She nodded eagerly. "And?"

"I packed a small sack and rode to Limerick. I sold my hunter there for a nice piece of change, and worked my way to Boston. We were still at war and the Americans were ignoring the British blockade, so it wasn't easy to do. But once there, I joined an American merchant ship as a topman."

Amanda grinned. "I cannot imagine you as a young lad hoisting sails!"

He smiled back. "It was a long time ago, and the work was dangerous and difficult. But because I started at the bottom, or nearly so, I am very appreciative of every hand on my decks."

She nodded seriously. "Yes, I can see that. But didn't your parents object to your leaving?"

He hesitated. "My father understood. I discussed it with him first. He is a great man, whom I admire and respect, and as his son, I owed him that. He gave me his permission, although he asked me to wait until I was sixteen to leave. I refused."

"And he let you go anyway?"

"He understood I had to go, Amanda. He is that kind of man."

"Papa would have beaten me if I ever tried anything like that. He would have never given me that kind of choice."

De Warenne said tersely, "Your father was too quick with his fists. There is no reason to beat anyone, most of the time."

She stared, suddenly thinking that he was right. All of those times that Papa had hit her, well, he had been in a temper and she hadn't really needed the punishment. Amanda became uncomfortable. She had never questioned her father's actions before. "And your stepmother, the countess?"

"She was very upset. She wept when she thought I would not see her crying. I felt badly hurting her, but I have no regrets. I had to start somewhere, sooner rather than later. As it was, I did not have my own ship until I was eighteen, and she was only a twelve-gun schooner."

"You were master of your own ship at eighteen," Amanda whispered, filled with admiration for him. "I am almost eighteen."

"You are a woman," he said as if reminding her.

"There have been women pirates."

He was clearly aghast. "Don't even think it!"

She began to smile, pleased that he remained so concerned

for her. "Why not? You can see that I am a skilled seaman and a skilled swordsman. Why couldn't I have my own ship? Then I could give up this farce of trying to be a lady." She didn't mean a single word.

"You are trying to provoke me," he said, flushed in the starlight. "I am onto your game! You could not control a crew and we both know it."

"I *was* trying to provoke you," she admitted, "and it was very easy to do." She glanced at him through her lashes. It had been ridiculously easy, in fact. Just as it had been so easy to get him to lust after her with a little bit of swordplay. "I do not want to control a crew. A captain cannot control his ship if he will not commit murder if he has to. Papa has murdered more than his share of mates. I am not inclined to violence and I have never murdered anyone."

"Thank God," de Warenne said, his tone choked.

"Have you ever murdered a mate?"

His jaw was hard. "I have never had to murder one of my own crew. I have, upon occasion, and especially earlier in my career, used harsh discipline. But I have never keelhauled anyone, either. However, I am the exception, not the rule."

Amanda could not agree more. "Tell me about how you came to command the *Fair Lady*," she said, smiling.

He hesitated. "It is late. You have a full day of studies tomorrow—"

"I will be studying at dawn! Please," she said. "I have been wondering about it for some time."

He sighed in surrender. "It is a boring story."

Amanda knew that was simply impossible.

DE WARENNE HAD BEEN RIGHT. Exactly ten days later, Amanda stood staring at the stunning sight of London as the frigate approached. She had been to Lisbon once, when she was eight years old, but she could not recall the adventure. She had been to New Orleans several times, and Charleston, too, but she had never seen a city like this one in her life. She had never seen such a crowded harbor, such a high, jumbled skyline, so many buildings, churches, spires. London was *huge*.

She clung to the railing, enthralled. The past ten days had passed in a whirlwind of study. She had been immersed in her lessons from dawn to dusk, with almost no respite, the frantic schedule given upon de Warenne's direct orders. At sunset, too exhausted to even eat, she would collapse into her berth, instantly falling asleep. However, at midnight she would awaken with no one's help, gulp down a meal of bread and cheese and rush to join de Warenne at the helm. She simply could not miss spending the middle watch with him.

Each and every night began almost exactly the same—he would not quite look at her, his face mask-like, yet she could feel him pulling her inexorably closer, somehow. But he never tried to take her in his arms and eventually they would converse. He always knew what she had studied that day and he never failed to ask her about the specific lessons and if she had liked them.

And Amanda had asked him every question she could think of, wanting to know everything there was to know about Adare, Ireland and his life. He had answered her every question, and by the time each dawn broke, they were usually smiling. But every sunrise, when he left her alone at her cabin, she was so disappointed that the aching was not just in her loins, but in her heart.

Amanda had been dreading the end of their voyage. Although she had applied herself with all the diligence she could muster to her studies, she knew she wasn't going to fool anyone for very long as to who and what she really was. And once they reached London, she knew she would never share the middle watch with Cliff de Warenne again. Last night, realizing that, she had been moved to tears.

But she had never expected London to be such an amazing, grand and thrilling sight.

They had passed towers, ruins and castles as they came up the coast, and the city seemed to be filled with cathedrals and palaces, too.

She felt him before she heard him; his presence had become so familiar now, a huge enveloping power, a cloak of manhood and heat. De Warenne appeared at her side. "Amanda? What do you think?" He smiled at her, but his gaze was searching.

She seized his hand. "I have never seen anything as incredible!"

He laughed, but he pulled his palm from hers. "London is an alluring sight, is she not? The truth is, I am somewhat fond of this city, far more so than Paris. She is a great lady with a complicated character, a study in contradictions—rich and poor, opulence and poverty, grace and lust, devotion and sin."

Amanda looked up at him. She could not smile and her eyes felt huge.

"Shall I show you the sights?" he asked softly.

Her heart leaped wildly. "That would be wonderful," she cried. "Will you show me the sights today?"

He laughed. "I am afraid it is too late, but we have perhaps three-quarters of an hour's ride before we reach Harmon House, depending on the traffic. You will see plenty then, but I am afraid the West End is a facade of opulence and grace."

"I had no idea," she gasped, staring out at the city again. She pointed at a tall, gray castle appearing on the starboard side. "Cliff, what is that?"

He didn't reply.

She suddenly realized she had called him by his given name. She felt her cheeks heat. "I mean, Captain," she floundered.

"It's all right. But we should not be too familiar. No one will understand the camaraderie one can develop on a ship." He finally smiled. "That is the Tower of London, and we are almost at the Tower Bridge."

"And we cannot go past the London Bridge, can we?" she asked eagerly.

His smile reached his eyes. "Have you read Ariella's entire guidebook?"

"As much as possible," she admitted, returning his smile. "If you are taking me sightseeing, then I must make a list of all that I wish to see."

"I don't mind," he said. "I am happy to show you everything that you wish to see."

"Then you may not leave London for years," she teased.

He laughed. "I have never stayed in town for more than a month or so. I would die for lack of good clean air."

Amanda sobered, hating the fact that eventually he would leave London, and she would be staying behind. "How long will you stay this time?" she whispered.

His gaze was sharp. "I haven't decided." His regard wandered over her face. "But my stay will have to be more than a month. You've never been to the opera, have you? Or the theater?"

"I've seen plays, but in the street," she said, her heart racing with excitement. "Are you thinking of taking me to the theater, a real theater, and to an opera?" She was amazed.

"If you are to become a lady, you will be asked to attend many such events. It would be my pleasure to escort you. In fact, if the expression on your face is anything like what it has been since we have reached London, I must insist." His eyes had softened, searching hers.

"And I accept," she cried happily. She felt as if she was in a fairy tale with her very own Prince Charming. She had to pinch herself to remind her that he was hardly her prince. But somehow, he had become her champion.

"We are going to make berth. We'll be disembarking in an hour."

Amanda nodded, briefly watching him stride away, bellowing for shortened sails. Then she turned back to the railing, staring at the passing yachts and the horses and carriages on the wharves and the huge buildings beyond.

THE COACH CLIFF HAD HIRED turned between high, imposing iron gates set in equally high, imposing brick walls. Amanda tensed, gripping the sill of the carriage window. The West End had been more opulent than she could have ever imagined, and they had passed so many mansions that she had lost count, each one somehow more stunning and stately than the rest. Windsong had been a palace in her mind, but it had stood alone on Harbor Street, with no more than half a dozen equally splendid homes scattered about Kingston. She knew all about society, or at least, she had thought she did, but she had been wrong. How could there be so much wealth in one place? London society made that of her island home seem pitiful in comparison.

Immaculate green lawns filled with fanciful flowering gardens bordered the long shell driveway. Ahead, she saw a huge gray stone house set between two taller towers. She felt ill. An hour ago she had wanted to be in London, but she didn't want to take this, her first step, into its fancy society. She wasn't ready, dear Lord.

"We are here," Cliff said softly.

She could barely tear her gaze from the house to look at him. He sat casually beside her, taking up half of the rear seat with his big body, dressed as he had been for the entire voyage, with the exception that he had donned his spurs. He must be planning to go riding, she thought dazedly, for she had seen a huge brick stable with roses creeping up the walls to the left of the house. "Is Belford House in the West End?" she somehow choked.

"Yes."

She could not do this, she thought. "Is it like this?"

He wet his lips. "It is grand, but not quite this grand—Belford isn't as well off."

"Is he also an earl?"

"No. He is a baron."

Mama was living in the home of a baron, Amanda thought,

beyond bewilderment. She had thought her mother would be living in a modest but genteel home; not a castle, not a mansion, and not with a nobleman. "Could she be a servant?"

He hesitated. "I don't know."

The carriage had stopped. Amanda looked outside. Two liveried doormen hurried from the front door where they had been stationed, their uniforms red jackets with gold braid and white breeches, white stockings and black buckled shoes. Amanda did not move. "Please tell me that the earl and countess are in Ireland," she whispered.

His eyes flickered. "Amanda, I do not know where they are. But they will welcome you with open arms. Please, trust me. I have never lied to you and I never intend to."

She stiffened. "But this is their home."

"They prefer Adare. If anyone is in residence, it might be Ty, taking care of estate affairs."

She knew all about his entire family now. "But he would be with his wife. You said they remain besotted and are rarely apart."

Cliff smiled. "A fool's paradise, but I am very happy for them. No one may be here, Amanda. Come. If a hurricane can not frighten you, then surely you can walk into my family home when you are an invited guest."

Amanda wished she were wearing a proper dress. But there was no avoiding leaving the coach now. She had never felt so sick.

The postilion extended his hand. Amanda just stared. Obviously he wished to help her down, but they had forgotten to teach her that bit of decorum, hadn't they? She heard an odd, hysterical giggle. It had come from herself.

Did Mama have liveried doormen, too?

"Take his hand, Amanda," Cliff murmured.

Amanda gave the servant her hand and found herself stepping down from the coach. Cliff leaped down beside her, turning to face the carriage containing his children, Anahid and Michelle. He swiftly opened the door, and Alexi leaped out with a wild war whoop. "Alexi," he objected, "you will spook the horses."

He ignored his father, racing over to Amanda. "What do you think? The city smells!" He wrinkled his nose. "It's not so bad here, but it was stinking at the docks. Did you see how dirty the streets are? And it's so gray and so cold!" he added.

Amanda realized it was very damp, with none of the warmth of the island. "It's cold," she somehow agreed.

Cliff came to stand beside her, Ariella's hand in his. "You will be pleasantly surprised," he said. "Come."

But before they could move the front door opened, revealing a tall, dark man. For one moment, Amanda assumed it was the earl and she wanted to disappear. But Cliff was shouting, "Rex," and even as he did so, she realized the man leaned on a crutch and he had lost half of his right leg.

Smiling, the darkly handsome man swung himself down the front steps. Cliff met him halfway and they embraced.

"What is this? A circus troop or a band of gypsies?" Rex said, his eyes dancing. He quickly left his brother to tower over a wide-eyed Alexi. "A gypsy prince, I think. Hmm, gypsies are outlawed in Mayfair."

"I'm not a gypsy or a prince. But my mother *is* a princess and you know who I am. You're my uncle, the knight, Sir Rex." Alexi was very serious.

"And you must be Tom?"

Alexi shook his head, appearing annoyed and arrogantly so. "I am Alexander de Warenne."

Rex clasped his shoulder. "I know exactly who you are, my boy, and welcome to Harmon House." His gaze settled on Ariella, who was shyly staring at him.

Cliff gestured. "Ariella, your uncle, Rex. If you are ever in need, and I am not present, you can turn to him as you would turn to me."

Ariella nodded, uncharacteristically speechless, moving closer to Anahid. Amanda wanted to move toward them, too.

But it was too late. Rex had espied her, and his gaze widened, moving from the top of her head to the tips of her boots. Cliff was saying, "The children's governess, Anahid, and their tutor, Monsieur Michelle."

Rex smiled vaguely, and as he stared again, Amanda felt herself turn red.

"Anahid, please take the children inside. Alexi, you may explore the house and property but you may not take one step outside of the front gates." As the group began to disperse, Cliff faced her, his eyes filled with such softness her breath caught. "I'd like you to meet my brother."

Amanda went forward, dragging her feet.

"Rex, this is Miss Amanda Carre. She is from the islands and I have escorted her to London, as she was in dire need of transport."

Rex looked at Cliff, both dark brows raised. "Really." Then he turned and bowed slightly, managing the gesture very adroitly and elegantly in spite of his crutch. "It is a pleasure, Miss Carre, and, as I take it you are a houseguest, welcome."

Amanda bit her lip. It crossed her mind that she should curtsy, but she wasn't going to do so in a pair of pants. "Thank you," she mumbled. She stepped closer to Cliff. She felt him touch her arm; Rex's dark eyes veered directly to her elbow and his hand.

"A servant will show you to your room, Amanda," Cliff said, speaking to her as if they were alone. "I know you are indefatigable, but perhaps you wish an hour or so to rest?"

She inhaled, wishing she were anywhere but there. "I am *very* tired," she lied. "Exhausted, in fact." She glanced at Rex to see if he might believe her. His gaze was too scrutinizing for comfort. "And I have such a pounding in my head. My stomach hurts, too."

"Perhaps you should call the physician," Rex murmured, apparently to Cliff.

Cliff took her arm and led her past Rex, their hips bumping. He leaned close. "Have no fear. If you wish to remain in your room tonight, you need not come down to dine. I'll make your excuses."

Once again he was saving her from a fate worse than death. Amanda had never been more relieved or more grateful. She gazed up at him, seeking and finding the reassurance she needed in his eyes. "I think I should stay in my room tonight."

"That's fine." He touched the small of her back and she turned toward the house. A very dignified manservant stood there. "This is the butler, Harrison. He will see you upstairs. He will see to all of your needs, as well."

Amanda nodded.

Cliff watched her go, wishing he could somehow take away her anxiety. He turned to smile at his brother. Rex was two years his senior and although as different as night and day, they were close. But he had not seen him in well over a year and a half. He was about to ask him if he was ready for a drink, but Rex was staring so intently that he felt his smile vanish. "What does that look mean?"

Rex hopped over. "Oh, I don't know. You appear here with a ragged, young waif in breeches who is in *dire* need and stand here in front of the house *embracing* her, very publicly. I must wonder, are you mad?"

He stiffened. "I was not embracing her."

Rex blinked. "I beg your pardon. The two of you share looks as if you are lovers, you walk so closely you appear affixed to one another and just now, while you were whispering and staring into her eyes, she was very much in your arms. Are you my brother or are you an impostor? And if so, where the hell is my brother and what has happened to him?"

## *CHAPTER TEN*

CLIFF WAS FURIOUS. "Your brother isn't mad, he is standing right here, and he is not sharing a bed with a seventeen-year-old *child*." He stormed into the house, absolutely disbelieving, but then, Rex's morality had always been excessive and annoying.

In spite of his crutch, his brother followed him inside, just as swiftly. Cliff went into the library and poured himself a drink. Only then did he face his brother. "I have always preferred women a bit older than my own age, as you damn well know," he added harshly. He slammed down the drink.

"Then you had better think about how you behave with your waif, as anyone with eyes will think as I have," Rex said calmly, although he seemed very curious.

"*You* are mad!" Cliff exclaimed. "I am her protector, as she has no one else. And she is not *my* waif." He hesitated. "She is my protégée—for the moment."

Rex began to smile. "You are her protector? She is your protégée? What, exactly, does that mean? And since when have you had a relationship with any woman outside of a bedroom?"

Cliff slammed his glass down on the marble top of the sideboard. "I rescued her from a jeering, bloodthirsty mob. Her father was about to be hanged and a group of boys were throwing stones at her. Had you been there, you would have rescued her, too."

Rex stared, brows high. "I see you have quite the story to tell. I have all night."

Cliff began to calm. Besides, he undoubtedly needed his brother's advice. "There is a hell of a story. Her father was a pirate and she has spent half of her life on the main, cruising for prizes with him."

Rex was shocked. "Good God! She doesn't look like a pirate's murderous wench!"

"She isn't. She is oddly naive—he never let her witness a battle, and he grounded her when she turned twelve. However, she was raised amongst rowdy rovers and thieves. She was allowed to run freely about Jamaica Island. Before I rescued her at the hanging, I had seen her about, sometimes swimming in a cove, or on a raft, surfing the waves. Everyone knew her as La Sauvage." He smiled grimly. "She was wild. Now—" He stopped. "Now she is caged up."

Rex folded his arms, staring. "What does that mean?"

"In a way, I hate what I have done—and it isn't taking her to bed." But as he paced, he thought of the dawn after the storm, when he had done everything but take her innocence.

"Really? So you are not flushed with guilt?" Rex asked.

Cliff whirled. "She is a *virgin,*" he said, stressing the noun.

"And you would know that because…?"

Cliff felt like smashing his brother, just once. "She told me."

"I see. A suitable subject for a protector and his protégée. By the way, the countess, Lizzie and Eleanor are here. "

Cliff tensed. "Amanda is afraid of society." He shook his head. "She spent all night beside me in near-hurricane winds, smiling, by God, as if a sea goddess, but she is afraid of the ton's mockery and scorn. I have brought her to town so she might meet her only living relative. On board my ship, she has been tutored in the social graces. I have never seen anyone more determined to master a subject they have no care for!" He sighed. "I am glad the countess, Lizzie and Eleanor are in residence. If anyone can help Amanda make a successful transformation, it is those three."

Rex was gaping. "You are trying to transform a pirate's child into a lady?"

"It seemed the obvious course of action."

"Of course it did."

"Knowing she is innocent," Cliff said sharply, "it is my duty to protect her, especially now, when the rakes in town will swarm after her, thinking her an easy mark."

"Of course it is your duty. My charming, rakehell, conscienceless brother, infamous for his seductions of courtesans and countesses, is now the champion of a pirate's daughter. This will be a very interesting Season, I think. You do plan to stay on?" Rex was now laughing.

"I promised her I would secure her future," he said gruffly. "I see I am entertaining you!"

Rex widened his eyes, feigning innocence. "I am hardly amused…I am in shock, frankly. You are going to secure her future, too?"

"That is correct. She has no one else." Annoyed again, Cliff went to the door and closed it. "Actually, her mother is here in London, Rex. She has come to town to be reunited with the woman she believes is married to her father. Amanda has been told her mother is Dulcea Straithferne Carre and that she resides at Belford House. Do you know Lady Dulcea Belford?"

Rex was surprised. He limped to the sofa and sat. "I am sorry. I know of her and I see where you go. You think her mother is Lady Belford…which makes Amanda her illegitimate daughter."

"Amanda has been devastated by the loss off her father," Cliff said, joining him on the sofa. "Now she will learn her parents were not wed. I fear for her reception, knowing Dulcea even as little as I do. But I am determined to make this reunion work. Amanda has suffered enough. She deserves some of life's good fortune."

Rex shook his head. "You must be smitten. Cliff, society is unkind and you probably know it better than anyone. You may be able to ignore the gossip behind your back but she seems quite young and fresh to me. Whatever you think you have done on your ship, Miss Carre does not look ready to enter the ton—and not because she dresses like a boy. Of course you must attempt this reunion with Lady Belford, but I would think twice about casting her into society."

"As for her dress, she has no gowns. I sent a Regent Street seamstress a missive from the docks and I expect a reply before this evening is out. Amanda will not be ridiculed when she enters society, because I am going to be with her and we will wait until everyone agrees she is ready." He stared. "And I am not smitten. I am being honorable, that is all."

Rex patted his shoulder. "It is about time." He chuckled. "Very well. We will call your feelings those of honor. When will you attempt to introduce mother and daughter?"

"I don't know. I am eager to have the help of our ladies now. And I do not mind deferring to their advice, either. In fact, I welcome it." Rex laughed again, and Cliff ignored him. "I will call on Lady Belford tonight, alone. The sooner I make certain she is amenable to the reunion, the better."

Rex shook his head, his smile gone. "I am very aware that, like Devlin, you are a master of the seas. London society is not the main. Your power is finite here. I hardly recall you being at the pinnacle of society. There are whispers behind your back—whispers you seem to encourage and covet. You can do your best to shield Miss Carre from any unpleasantness, but you cannot force Lady Belford to take her in, nor can you make society accepting of her rather unique ways. In fact, society might have some of the very same questions about this odd pairing that I have had."

Cliff stood. "You are wrong. I can and will shield Amanda. I have tolerated those whispers because they amused me. Now, I will throw my wealth around town so blatantly it will be obscene, and the whispers will cease. I never fail. I do not intend for this to be the first time." He started across the room.

"Where are you going?" Rex asked softly.

"I am going to check on Amanda and see if she is pleased with her accommodations. She is not used to servants and I doubt she has asked for a single thing."

"Cliff." Rex stood. "She may be in breeches, but she is a young and very beautiful woman. You're not on your ship. You can't meander into her private rooms so casually. It will be below stairs and then upstairs and all about the ton before dawn. Will you ruin her reputation before you have even launched her? You alone are fodder for gossip, but now you add La Sauvage into the equation. I want you to succeed, but you must proceed with caution."

Cliff felt an unwelcome frustration, for Rex was right. "I am going to check on her—but briefly." He hesitated. "We will speak in the hall."

Rex simply stared after him, his thoughts clear. This was not going to be a mission so easily accomplished.

AMANDA LEAPED TO HER FEET at the sound of Cliff's steps outside of her door. Before he had even knocked, she threw it open, terribly relieved to see him. He stood there, appearing somewhat surprised by her manner, and she had to remind herself not to fling her arms around him. "You did not forget me!"

He smiled. "That would be impossible."

She bit her lip. "You are flirting."

"Am I?" He glanced past her into her room. "Are you comfortable in these quarters, Amanda?"

"Am *I* comfortable?" She had thought the furnishings at Windsong to be luxurious, but this was so very different. The bedroom reeked of past centuries, of a family heritage and tradition she could barely understand. There were faded portraits in old gilt frames in the hall, and the secretary in the bedroom looked as if it belonged in another place and time. Harmon House was so obviously a part of the de Warenne family's history that she could actually feel their ancestors lurking in the shadows of the corridor.

"I take it you approve?"

She nodded. "Why are you standing in the hall? Can't you sit down and talk to me for a moment?" She gave in to what she really wanted to know. "What did your brother say when I left? And what did you tell him about me?"

He hesitated. "I can't come in. I am a notorious bachelor, and if I cross that threshold and a housemaid sees us, your reputation is over before we have ever introduced you to anyone."

She felt her anxiety heighten. In a way, she had already entered society. She was queasy. "I don't really care." Yet that was a lie.

"But I do." He smiled at her again. "I will have a supper tray sent up."

She stared. "You didn't answer me."

"Rex thinks you are very young and very beautiful and he is surprised that I am your protector." Cliff shrugged.

"That is all?"

"That is all. However, I do have news. It is really good news, so you must take it as such."

Amanda was instantly uneasy. "What is it? Is it about my mother?"

"No. My stepmother, my sister-in-law and my sister are in residence. They are out taking tea."

Amanda turned and walked over to a beautiful love seat striped in pale blue, ivory and gold, where she sat. A small fire burned beneath an ornate and carved wood mantel, but she did not see it. Everything was happening too quickly! She wasn't ready to meet the countess, his sister or the woman who would one day become the next countess of Adare. Her stomach heaved.

Cliff walked into the room. "Amanda. They are not like the ladies you have met in Kingston. I swear it. They are kind and generous and they will be delighted to meet you."

Amanda shook her head. "I am doomed, before ever meeting my mother."

"I thought you trusted me."

She looked up. "I do. But they can't possibly be kind. They may pretend to tolerate me, but they will look down on me."

He clasped her shoulder. "I won't try to tell you again that you are wrong. I'll introduce you tonight if you wish, so you don't worry yourself all evening."

Amanda stood, facing him. "I'll wait until the morning." She couldn't form a smile.

Amanda heard footsteps. Cliff turned. A beautiful and elegant young woman was passing by her open door. The tall woman halted, staring in disbelief. "Cliff?"

He dropped his hand. "Speak of the devil," he teased.

The lady glanced at Amanda, her eyes growing wide, and a gleam came into them as she walked in. "I see you have brought home a guest?" she asked too sweetly.

He snaked his arm around her and pulled her very hard to his side. "Yes, I have, a guest I hope you will befriend."

She shrieked in protest and pulled free, punching him in the chest. Then she smiled at Amanda, her topaz eyes filled with interest.

Amanda flushed uneasily.

"Ow. Come back here." Cliff caught her by her ear and this time, pressed a kiss to her cheek.

She hugged him hard. "Who is the devil in this room?" she laughed, releasing him. Then she faced Amanda again. "Hello! I am Mrs. Sean O'Neill and this cad is my brother. Sometimes I love him very much and sometimes I dream of ways to throttle him. He can be hugely annoying."

"Do not listen to her. I am charming and pleasant—unless provoked." Cliff laughed. "Eleanor is the little sister I have told you about, except she is really an Amazon," Cliff said by way of introduction. "Mrs. O'Neill, do meet Miss Amanda Carre."

Amanda trembled, uncertain of what to think. Clearly brother and sister adored one another. She had never thought to see a real lady punch anyone, not even her brother, and this woman *was* a lady—she was beautiful and elegant and the daughter of an earl. Mrs. O'Neill had definitely remarked her breeches and boots. "Hello," Amanda began, almost hoping that the sister would vanish. She waited for the inevitable sneer.

But Eleanor smiled. "Call me Eleanor, everyone does! How do you know my rakehell brother? How is it you are his *guest?* Have you been riding in the rain? And how old are you?"

"Eleanor!" Cliff objected, but he laughed.

"He has kindly brought me to London to meet my mother," Amanda said breathlessly. "And I am not much of a horsewoman. We just arrived—I am from the islands." She waited for his sister to laugh, but she didn't; she continued to smile, as if they were already friends.

"How interesting. My brother is many things—handsome, wealthy, brave, selfish, a boor—but he is not kind."

Amanda stiffened. "He is very kind! He brought me here from the West Indies when I had no way to pay for my passage."

Eleanor gave Cliff a disbelieving look.

Cliff scowled at her. "Amanda's father recently died. She had no one else to turn to."

"Oh, so you have rescued a damsel in distress," Eleanor said slowly. She seemed perplexed.

"Actually, that is exactly what I have done. And by the by, I have brought Ariella and Alexi here."

Eleanor cried out in delight. "And I have brought Michael and Rogan—they are in the nursery with Lizzie's three hellions."

"Then the cousins may have already met," Cliff said, appearing pleased.

Amanda took the moment to sit down hard on the closest chair. Was his sister actually going to accept her presence in their home as if it was a usual occurrence? Didn't she care that Amanda was scandalously attired? Did she know that her father had been a pirate, his fate death by hanging?

Cliff turned toward her. "I have to go out. Before I do so, is there anything you need?"

Amanda hated the idea of his leaving her alone in the house with his family. "I am fine," she lied, feeling ill all over again. Where was he going? It was almost suppertime. She couldn't help wondering if he was visiting one of his lovers, but that thought was too painful to contemplate.

He hesitated and sat down beside her. "I won't be gone for long. Do you want to meet the countess and Lizzie before I go?"

"I think I am going to rest," Amanda said warily. "I can meet them tomorrow."

Cliff stared closely, his gaze searching. Amanda gazed back, wishing they were on the deck of his ship. "We'll do some sight-seeing tomorrow," he finally said.

Instantly she smiled. "That would be wonderful."

Cliff smiled back and stood. He gestured at his sister, who pretended not to understand. "Amanda is tired from the voyage."

"But I was going to ask for some tea and sandwiches, so we might become better acquainted." Eleanor grinned, appearing a bit mischievous.

Amanda was alarmed.

Cliff clasped her shoulder. "You will have plenty of time to become acquainted with Amanda," he said.

She snickered. "You do mean Miss Carre, don't you, Cliff?"

He pushed her out the door. "You remain as impertinent as always," he said.

"And I wonder if you remain as impossibly roguish as always?" She returned sweetly. "Naughty Cliff, to be alone in a lady's room at this hour!"

Cliff turned to Amanda. "Ignore her. I will check on you later."

Amanda had an idea of what his sister had been implying, but she hoped she was wrong. Or did his sister think they were having a lover's affair, right under the countess's roof?

But Eleanor waved at her and disappeared, as if she did not mind the notion at all.

"She is a very bold woman," Cliff said, shaking his head. "And outspoken—perhaps more so than you. She also wears breeches, by the way. I will see you later."

Amanda gaped as he closed her door.

IT TOOK HIM A SCANT ten minutes to reach Belford House, and by the time he arrived, it had begun to rain. Four handsome coaches lined the street, so he knew he was interrupting a supper party, but as it was only seven, the guests had probably just arrived. It was not fashionable to call as he was doing, but he did not care, and no one in society expected him to behave in a proper manner, anyway. He rang the knocker. Everyone except for Belford would assume he was sniffing after his wife. Belford seemed oblivious to his wife's escapades.

A butler ushered him in, ogling his gold earring and the spurs he wore in spite of his tan trousers. He had also donned a beautiful shirt, tie and navy-blue jacket—his concession to fashion. Cliff smiled. "Is Belford at home?"

"His lordship is in Scotland," the servant returned, more interested now in the sheathed dagger at his hip than at the transparent question.

"Then I am in luck," Cliff returned, handing the man his business card. "Please inform Lady Belford that I have an urgent matter to discuss with her." He said.

The man vanished.

Cliff paced the round foyer beneath a crystal chandelier, overhearing male conversation sprinkled with feminine laughter. The entry was sparsely furnished. A beautiful but very worn Oriental rug was underfoot and two ruby-red chairs were at the hall's end, the seats faded. A lampshade that should have been ivory was the color of parchment. Looking around, he realized that the Belfords were in an economic pinch.

As he had guessed, Lady Belford did not mind the interruption. She appeared within minutes of her butler's exit with his card.

He stared as she came into the entry. Now, he could not mistake the resemblance between mother and daughter. They could have been sisters, although Dulcea was a far less striking version of Amanda, and most strangers would think them related.

Considering the scheme at hand, he wasn't all that pleased.

Dulcea was obviously happy to see him. She wore a sleeveless burgundy gown with a faint gold floral pattern, a ruby pendant at her throat and she was smiling as she approached. "My lord de Warenne!" she cried. "This is the most welcome surprise. But I should have so wished for advance notice—I would have set an extra place at the table." Her hand fluttered up and down his sleeve.

Her desire to bed him hadn't changed, he thought, repulsed, but he smiled slightly and bowed. "Thank you for receiving me, Lady Belford. I am aware the hour is an inopportune one."

"It is never an inopportune hour for you, my lord," she said, her lashes lowering as she curtsied.

She was socially far superior to him, and he found her use of a courtesy title obsequious. "Then I am very fortunate."

"Have you just arrived in town? Would you care to join us for supper? We have only just sat down." She smiled, touching his arm.

"I am afraid I cannot stay long," he said. "And I do not wish to keep you from your guests. But there is an extremely urgent matter that we must discuss. I beg you for a private word."

She smiled, giving him a sidelong look, and took his arm. Cliff fought not to pull away and she led him into a small salon with green fabric walls, gilded furniture and green-and-gold upholstery. The upholstery was very worn and faded, increasing his belief that the Belfords were in some financial straits. She released him to close the door. Then she leaned on it, smiling at him. "Then you must come for supper another time, before Belford returns," she murmured.

Cliff stepped back, hesitating. There was no easy way to break such news. "Why don't you sit down, Lady Belford. I have news I wish to impart."

She smiled, taking the chair he offered her. "Good news, I hope?" Her brown lashes fluttered again.

"I believe so," he said, but even as he spoke, he had very little doubt that she would not be pleased. "I have brought your daughter to London, madam."

She smiled still, clearly not comprehending him. "What?"

"Your maiden name is Straithferne, is it not?"

Her smile faded and she paled. "What is this?"

"Your daughter, Amanda Carre, is currently my guest here in London, at Harmon House," he said, watching her closely for her reaction.

Her eyes bulged with shock. She just sat there, staring at him, stunned.

In a way, he did feel sorry for her. He glanced around, found the sideboard with the decanters and poured her a sherry. He handed it to her.

She shook her head, setting the glass down. "I beg your pardon. My daughter is upstairs, with my son, and her name is Margaret. She is thirteen years old."

He felt all sympathy vanish. A cold, hard feeling filled him, similar to that he so often experienced when facing an adversary he did not care for. This woman, however, he had a use for. This woman owed her daughter a proper life. "Lady Belford, let us cease all pretense. It will take a runner no more than a day or two to determine if your maiden name is Straithferne, but I will not even bother, as your daughter resembles you very closely. I am sure you do not know, but Rodney Carre was hanged in June. I have brought Amanda to London so she might be reunited with you, her only living family."

Lady Belford cried out, sagging against the chair. And when she looked up at him, he saw tears filling her green eyes, which were nowhere as exotic or vivid as her daughter's. "You are right," she gasped. "My maiden name is Straithferne." She stood, trembling.

Cliff leaped forward, helping her to stand upright. She leaned against him, shaking, instantly clinging to his shoulders. The moment she did so, he knew she was hoping to soften him with her feminine ways. "You must sit down," he said grimly, attempting to disengage.

But she clung, avoiding his eyes so he could not look into her face too closely. "Oh, God. I am in shock…I cannot believe it… She is here, in London?"

"Very much so. I comprehend your shock. But madam, your long-lost daughter has returned and she is eager to be reunited with you." He set her firmly apart.

Finally she looked up at him. "You must not speak so openly or I will be ruined."

Their gazes met. Hers remained moist, but he saw a hard light there now. "And your daughter?" he asked, despising her intensely.

She produced a kerchief from her bodice and used it on her eyes. "You must *not* speak in such a manner," she said. "Why did you bring her here?"

"So she might reside with you, her only living family!" he exclaimed. "It was that or send her to the Sisters of St. Anne's on the island!"

She stared. "What is she like?" she finally, carefully, asked.

He didn't hesitate. "She is beyond beautiful, with green eyes very much like yours. Her hair is the color of the rising moon and her figure is perfection. She is very clever—she is learning to read and doing well, I might add," he said. Dulcea's eyes widened even further. "And she is brave. I have never met such courage, not even in a man. She risked her life aboard my ship to save a young lad, and she can wield a saber almost as well as I can."

Dulcea cried out.

"What did you expect," he asked coldly, furiously. "You have allowed your daughter to be raised by a pirate, madam, depriving her of a life of gentility, of this!" His arm swept the room.

Dulcea covered her face with her hands, weeping. "How can you blame me?"

Cliff recognized that Dulcea wished to manipulate him, but he was not exactly sure what else she intended now. "Your tears do not move me, madam. However, your daughter's plight moves me very much. What will you do now? She is at Harmon House, expecting a warm reunion."

Her eyes lifted to his and turned to ice. "Surely, surely, you do not expect me to take such a child in!"

"Your daughter needs a home," he said harshly, his worst fears coming true. "She needs a mother. She needs you. I thought it prudent to meet with you first and advise you that she is here, and I can see that I am right. The ton is filled with bastards, Lady Belford. We both know many couples who are raising their illegitimate offspring alongside their heirs. I have brought my own two children here and I shall take them into society with pleasure, not fear."

She shook her head in negation, seizing his arms. "You are not a married woman with two legitimate children! Belford will never understand and he will never forgive me, even if my faux pas occurred before we ever met!"

"*Au contraire*. You lead him about by the nose—and elsewhere—and I feel certain you can convince him of anything you wish."

"Why are you doing this? Why did you determine to bring her here?"

"Why am I behaving like a gentleman?" he asked sarcastically. "Your daughter is an orphan and she is no child. She is seventeen, a woman ready for marriage! Surely you wish to have a hand in her future."

"You are no gentleman!" she said, her pale face so taut it could have been cast from plaster. "Can you not see how distressing this is for me?"

"Your distress it is *nothing* compared to what your daughter has suffered in her short life." He lost all patience now.

She had become still, staring. Finally she said, "You are acting as if you despise me." Her eyes were hard and riveted to his. "But you, of all men, should understand how something like this could happen. You, my lord de Warenne, understand passion as well as anyone."

"We have nothing in common, Lady Belford, except for your daughter!" He laughed coldly. "And I know exactly how you conceived Amanda. You were very young, you were swept off your feet by a dashing naval officer, perhaps while on holiday, and now there is so much regret."

She stiffened. "You are correct. I was very young—I was Amanda's age—and I was swept off my feet and taken advantage of! Carre was a very dashing young naval officer when we met," she said harshly.

Cliff stepped closer and leaned down, their faces almost touching. "You did not raise her, did you, until she was four? Amanda wasn't torn out of your arms by her thieving father, was she?"

Her eyes widened. "Is that what Carre told her?"

"Yes."

She shook her head. "I was sent to a convent to have her, as all unwed young ladies are. My parents intended to give her up to an adoptive family, but one of the sisters there notified Carre and he came and took her some time after she was born. I do not know precisely when." Dulcea took a breath, and touched his arm. "Cliff, even you know that is the way of the world. I could not ruin my future before it even began."

"Did you ever care about your child?" he demanded.

"Of course I did! But I knew her father was caring for her. There was no other choice."

He leaned over her. "There were many other choices, if you had a mother's heart. Tell me. You will not even tell Belford that she is your cousin, will you? You do not wish the inconvenience—or is it a matter of finances? Do not tell me it is Belford you fear. You control him and we both know it."

Her face became hard, almost ugly. "I made a mistake many years ago," she said slowly. "But you would not understand, as you're a de Warenne, born with a silver spoon to dine with and too many estates to count! I made a mistake, but Belford came along and I have a proper life now. Come, de Warenne. Surely you do not expect me to take my long-lost daughter in and suffer the vicious gossip, the attacks on my character, the loss of my reputation?" She paused for breath. "You have pushed me to the wall and I must admit it, our finances are strained. We cannot afford to launch a young woman into society right now. We are living on credit. It will be difficult enough to launch my own daughter when she is of age."

"Then maybe you are taking the wrong lovers," he said softly.

She slapped him.

He deserved it, he decided, but Amanda did not deserve such a mother. She would be miserable in this home. "You have no heart, madam," he said, preparing to leave. "Not only do you refuse to take her in, you offer no solution to her dilemma."

She seized his sleeve. "What will you do?"

"I will not tell the ton the truth, if that is what you are thinking." But what would he tell Amanda?

"Can she not stay at Harmon House? Surely there is room. Perhaps you can employ her, so she might earn her meals and the roof over her head."

He began to shake with rage and knew he must leave before he placed his hands around her pretty little throat and began choking her. "Amanda will become a lady," he managed. "It is her due, her right!"

He saw some of her tension ease. "I am not heartless, Cliff," she finally said. "If you intend to present her, then you mean to find her a husband. But she has no dowry," she said carefully.

He had never been more revolted. "Madam, do not concern yourself with Amanda's prospects. It is the height of hypocrisy. Good day." Incapable of bowing, he strode for the door. He had to leave her presence before he gave in to his rage.

But at the door, he whirled. She stood, as still as a statue in the center of the room. "You have relinquished all maternal rights this night, as far as I am concerned."

She stiffened.

He held up his hand, which was shaking. "I would not send her here, to such an uncaring, unkind person, under any circumstance. Understand this. She has been in my protection since she left Jamaica Island, and she will remain in my protection until she is wed. Good night."

And not giving her a chance to respond, he stormed from the house.

# *CHAPTER ELEVEN*

HE HAD NOT RECOVERED his composure by the time he reached Harmon House. Cliff stormed inside, aware that he was late for supper. But the house was oddly quiet, and he realized the ladies were not in. They must have had supper plans.

Rex limped out of the library, clad in evening clothes. "I thought we were in a hurricane, from the sound of the front door slamming. What is wrong?"

Cliff glanced up the winding staircase, wincing. How was he going to tell Amanda the truth? She was going to be crushed and he did not want her to suffer over her despicable mother. He turned and went into the library. "I just spoke with Lady Belford. She is far more than a whore. She is a bitch."

Rex's eyes went wide. He closed the door behind them. "I have never heard you speak of a woman in such a manner!"

Cliff faced him. "She is the most selfish person I have ever met. She doesn't care at all that her daughter is here—she is far more interested in her own comfort and care and that of her legitimate children. And that was said while she was trying to seduce me to her bed."

After a pause, Rex said, "Are you certain you did not misconstrue her actions and words? I imagine she was shocked by the news you brought."

Cliff laughed. "Trust me, I did not misconstrue anything. It doesn't matter. After spending a half an hour with her, I would not send Amanda to her, not under any circumstance.

Amanda is better off without her mother. The woman is heartless."

Rex was gaping. "Cliff, you can't mean what you have just said."

"Oh, I mean every word." He stomped to the sideboard and poured a double shot of whiskey. Downing it, he downed another one.

"Slow down!" Rex exclaimed. "I see you are very upset, and all this over the fate of a woman you barely know."

That annoyed him even more. "I know Amanda better than I know anyone." He poured another drink, but cradled this one in his hands.

"Really? You have known her for exactly six weeks," Rex said, staring closely.

"I have known her for most of her life," he returned, thinking about all the times he had seen her roaming the island and swimming in the sea. "And we are mates. She has shared the middle watch with me every night. She rode the storm with me. A voyage changes men, Rex. Bonds are forged that can last a lifetime."

"Apparently it has changed you," he murmured.

"You wouldn't understand…I am her protector, but it is more than that." He walked over to the window and stared outside at the night. It continued to rain.

Rex came to stand beside him. "You are going to tell her that her mother is at Belford House? You are going to tell her the truth?"

He slowly turned, feeling dread. "How can I? How can I not?"

"You do not want to hurt her with the sordid truth, yet you do not want to lie," Rex remarked.

"Precisely."

"Cliff, do you care for any advice?"

Cliff sipped. "I should love your advice."

Rex smiled. "Then this is a rare moment, because no one is

as headstrong as you, except for Devlin. If you lie to her, you will regret it. I am certain. She has every right to know who her mother is, and that Dulcea Belford does not care to be responsible for her."

Cliff had already reached that conclusion. "She has suffered so much. She continues to grieve for her father. Amanda is one of the strongest women I have ever met, yet she is also, conversely, so vulnerable, so emotionally fragile. She deserves to be loved. I do not want her hurt another time!" he exclaimed. "I cannot stand the idea that she will shed a single tear over that selfish woman."

"Are you really certain Lady Belford is so black hearted? Perhaps she is really afraid of her husband and the scandal. Perhaps she does care for Amanda, in her own way."

"And what way is that? To put her own welfare over that of her daughter? I am a parent. I would die for my children, Rex. And I would certainly suffer some scandal if that is what I had to do to provide for them."

"Well, you do not have to decide what to say tonight," Rex said. "Will you be all right? I am to join the countess, Lizzie and Eleanor at the McBanes'. I delayed going over only in the hopes of learning what happened at Belford House."

"I am beyond disgust, but I am fine. Go, enjoy yourself, and give Rory and his wife my regards."

Rex smiled. "Proceed with care, Cliff," he said cryptically, and he limped out of the room.

Cliff finished his drink, debating whether to tell Amanda the truth about her mother or not. If he withheld the truth, she would continue to grieve the loss of her father, and in time, she would be better able to withstand another blow. On the other hand, London society was very small and Dulcea Belford lived a few blocks away. It was inevitable that, at some point in time, Amanda would find herself in the same room with her mother, or with someone who knew her. *If only they did not resemble one another so greatly*, he thought. But someone was going to make the connection, and when that happened, Amanda was going to learn that her mother was Dulcea Belford, not Dulcea Carre.

It was better coming from him.

AMANDA HAD FALLEN ASLEEP. She dreamed of the great frigate, the storm and Cliff de Warenne, and in her dreams, she was fantastically free, riding the *Fair Lady*'s decks, soaring over the waves, with Cliff at her side, powerful and beautiful, a force of nature, absolute and relentless. She was thrilled that they were at sea again, but then her dream became confusing….a beautiful lady was there, beckoning to her. But whenever she turned to try to find the lady, the woman disappeared, as if a ghost. Yet Amanda knew she wasn't a ghost. And then she heard her whisper, *"Amanda."*

Amanda turned, becoming frightened, for she was no longer on the deck of the ship but in a grand and empty ballroom, and she was alone. Worse, she was supposed to be in a ball gown, but instead, she was in her ragged breeches and one of Cliff's shirts.

*"Amanda."*

She panicked, turning wildly, looking for the beautiful lady, but the ballroom remained empty.

Where was the lady, she wondered desperately, for she realized the woman had to be her mother.

And suddenly Cliff was there.

She didn't see him, she sensed him, and her terrible anxiety eased.

And in that instant, Amanda was awake, her dreams forgotten. She blinked.

She had fallen asleep with the lights on, as she had been reading, and the fire was crackling in the hearth. Cliff stood on the threshold of the room, staring at her as she slept.

She sat up, tossing hair from her face. "Cliff." She smiled, still half-asleep. He was the man of her dreams and she had never been happier to see anyone.

His gaze slid over her. "It's early. I didn't realize you were asleep," he said stiffly. "We'll speak tomorrow."

Amanda was wearing the beautiful lace nightgown, the one that gave her the appearance of an elegant lady. He thought so, too; she could see it in his eyes. She leaped from the bed, racing to him before he could turn and step through the doorway. "I was reading and I fell asleep. Don't go, please!" She smiled coaxingly at him.

His gaze fell to her bodice and then jerked up. "You must be exhausted. I heard you crying out. Are you all right?"

"Yes. I was having strange dreams." She hugged herself, thinking about calling on her mother as soon as she had the appropriate attire. "Will a seamstress be here tomorrow?"

His eyes flickered. "Yes. Do you have a robe?"

"Your sister brought me some of her things," Amanda said, wondering at his request.

"Why don't you put a robe or a shawl on?" He sent her a tight smile and faced the fireplace.

Amanda stared at him before she went to an old rosewood armoire with paneled doors. Eleanor was a good six inches taller than she was, but she slipped on the cotton wrapper she had been given, one trimmed with pink ribbons and lace. Cliff was uncomfortable and she knew why. His male nature was taking over again and she was acutely aware of it. She could feel it there in the room with them, the hot desire, the huge tension.

But there was more than that. He seemed grim and even upset. "Are you all right?" she asked, approaching.

He turned, glanced at the wrapper, now belted, and nodded. "Of course I am. Come, let's sit down. There's something I wish to discuss."

Amanda was instantly wary. She sat down on the small sofa before the fireplace, and so did he. "What has happened?"

He forced a smile. "Amanda, I have been doing a great deal of thinking. And I don't want you to worry about anything. I said I would secure your future, and I meant it. You do trust me, don't you?"

"You are beating around the bush," she cried, very alarmed now. "I know that is what you said, but I am going to be living with Mama, and in the end she is going to be the one to force me into marriage with some stranger."

His odd smile remained. "By the time you wed, it won't be to a stranger. I am sure you will be very excited about your husband. All brides are in love on their wedding day."

She gave him a look. "You are really worrying me. We both know many brides are terrified of the brutes they are being tossed to."

His smiled became even more fixed. "You are never going to be thrown to any brute, as you have just put it. Amanda, how would you feel about staying here at Harmon House?"

She jerked. "What?"

"How would you feel about it?"

Her mind raced inanely. "What about Mama?"

His smile faltered. He took her hand, tightly. "You have nothing to worry about. You have a place to stay here and I will look after you—as will Rex, my mother, my sister, the entire family, in fact."

Amanda felt cold. She shot to her feet. "What happened?" she heard herself ask, but she somehow knew. He had seen Mama—or Mama was dead.

She began to tremble, but the clawing fear was so awful that she refused to feel it. Mama couldn't be dead, because Papa was dead, and that meant she was alone in the world, except for de Warenne, who was going to sail away sooner rather than later.

But it was as if he had read her mind. "You have me, remember? I swore I would not abandon you, and I won't."

"Is Mama dead?" she managed, fear choking her. She forced it as far away as possible.

"No. But I saw her earlier."

Amanda looked at his handsome face and saw that he was terribly distressed. She had never seen him really upset before, and she understood.

It was as she had thought. Mama didn't want her.

"Your mother is married to Lord Belford, Amanda. Her name is Dulcea Belford now."

Amanda jerked with surprise. This she couldn't understand; this she hadn't expected. "She knew Papa died?" But how had she received word so swiftly?

He took her arm. "She married Belford long ago. They have two children."

Mama was married to Belford? And had been married to him for years? "But that's impossible—she was married to Papa," she gasped in utter confusion. Her heart raced in wild alarm.

He put his arm around her. "I know this is a shock, but she was never married to Carre."

Amanda pulled away, panicking. "You are babbling! I don't understand! Of course they were married, Papa told me so."

He was looking at her so sadly that, in her shrieking heart, she realized he was telling her the truth.

"This doesn't change the brave, beautiful woman that you are," Cliff said softly.

Amanda stared at him, incapable of thinking or feeling. It was too dangerous to do either. He stared back, wetting his lips, but he did not speak again.

She knew, somewhere in the back of her mind, what was happening, but it was better not to really know, not to understand. "So I am staying here."

He took her hand again. "With me." His smile was awful, a parody, strained.

Oddly, she couldn't care that she would stay with him. She

pulled her hand away and stood there, no longer breathing, her heart no longer beating, feeling as frozen as an iceberg. She had never been so cold.

But the whispers began in the back of her mind, no matter how she tried to deafen them, to ignore them.

*Papa lied.*

*They were never married.*

*I'm a bastard.*

*Mama is Lady Belford.*

"Amanda, come sit with me. Let's talk calmly about this. Life can be unfair sometimes—we have all suffered, in one way or another—but there is a bright side. I can launch you far better than she ever could. And we can go sailing," he said, smiling. "Anytime you like."

Amanda didn't hear him now.

*Papa had lied to her for her entire life. They had never married. Had he even stolen her from Mama's arms?*

*Had Mama ever loved her?*

*Mama didn't want her.*

Her heart was beating again. It was bursting through her frozen self-restraint, beating in furious protest against her chest, slam, bam, slam.

He put his arm around her. "You're in shock."

She jerked savagely free and the ice melted, whoosh. "She doesn't want me."

"I didn't say that," he said very carefully.

But she saw the truth in his eyes. "I'm a bastard."

He inhaled. "Many children are born out of wedlock," he began. "Like Alexi and Ariella."

"Good!" she cried, her vision blurring now. "I'm glad, because bastards aren't ladies. And now—" she tore the wrapper off and flung it at him "—now I can be exactly what I want to be!"

He seized her hand. "I'm going to get you a drink," he said.

"And that is not a goddamned lady!" She jerked free, gripping her bodice furiously, wanting to tear the offending garment off. "I want my breeches," she cried, but the material refused to rip.

"Amanda, stop!" Cliff tried, sounding desperate, grasping her hands.

But she was in a profound rage. She was never going to prance about, pretending to be a lady, again! She shoved him away, vaguely aware that his face was white with shock, but it was hard to see now, her vision was so blurred. She hated them both. She hated Papa, the biggest liar on the face of the earth, and she hated Mama, who was a whore, not a lady—who didn't love or want her bastard daughter. She whirled, finding her dagger in her boot. She heard Cliff cry out in alarm, but she had never been more determined. She slashed through the beautiful nightgown, one long perfect line, cutting it in two. She hated it now. She would never wear it again or anything else that any lady might want.

"Don't! You'll hurt yourself!" she thought he said, and he seized her wrist. She screamed, whirling on him and he leaped away, blood dripping from his hand. But she couldn't care, because nothing was real, everything was a lie, and she tore the tattered gown from her body and sliced savagely at the cotton and lace again. She would destroy the gown, her new life, everything.

And she gasped, a stabbing pain trying to cut into her heart the way she had cut into so much cotton. *Mama didn't want her. Papa had lied.* She let go of the dagger. It clattered onto the floor.

Amanda closed her eyes, fighting her comprehension and the pain, but the ugly refrain had become a haunting melody in her mind.

And then, finally, she realized she was not alone.

She looked up at de Warenne.

Tears streaked his beautiful face.

She shook her head, rebelling. "Don't cry," she whispered.

Because she was fine. She hated Mama anyway. And she hated Papa now, too. And as she looked at him she felt a terrible desperation, because she was truly adrift, lost and adrift, with nowhere to go, no destination and no beacon to guide her.

"Come here," he whispered. He went to her, touching her arms. Amanda did not hesitate and he pulled her against his body, wrapping her firmly in his embrace. For one instant, she stood there, in the safest and securest place possible, a harbor that felt like home. For that one instant, she clung. He was her lifeline.

And then she realized she was nude, and that his body was hard, powerful and strong, molded to hers. She realized how much she loved him and how much she needed him. There was so much desire. The cold vanished; heat flared. Amanda looked up, shocked by the throbbing hunger in her. He stiffened with surprise and comprehension, but she didn't care. She felt the hardness coming instantly between them. "Cliff," she whispered, touching his face.

And his eyes turned to flames. He pulled her impossibly closer, springing harder and fuller against her, his mouth covering hers. Amanda gasped, the pain in her chest warring with the heated pleasure throbbing inside her, and then she kissed him back, more desperately and more frantically than he was doing. He gasped, his hands closing on both of her buttocks, molding her to his pulsing loins and carrying her that way to the bed. He pushed her onto the mattress, coming down on top of her, his hard thighs pinning her legs wide. Amanda gasped as his massive manhood pulsed against her sex.

He began licking her lips while rocking against her, and his hand stroked one perfect motion over her breast, down her rib cage, past her navel and into the hot wetness of her delta.

*She loved him so.* Amanda cried out as the pure pleasure begin, a wonderful spiral promising to send her so far away she would never want to come back.

He knew. His thighs pushed hers even wider. He reached between them, grunting, and she felt his phallus spring free. Amanda could not stand it and when he rocked against her, slick, hot and hard, so that she rode his entire length, she wept, exploding into a million pieces.

"Amanda," he gasped against her ear, pushing restlessly against her.

She didn't hear and began to float back into his arms. But then she thought, *Mama*, in so much anguish and so much despair, and the pain that wracked through her was beyond excruciation.

He froze. "Amanda?" Holding her in his arms, he shifted his erection against her thigh.

Oh God. Papa had lied, Mama didn't want her.... She turned toward de Warenne and the pain engulfing her. She wept against his chest.

Cliff pulled her closer, holding her tightly, but it was a long time before her sobs were spent.

AMANDA STARED out of the window of her bedroom as the sun crept upward into the sky, a melody of birdsong filling the damp morning, a cool breeze on her cheek.

She turned to look at the bed, leaving the window open. Cliff was gone, but he had stayed there until dawn, because every time she had awoken, he had held her and stroked her until her tears had subsided. Now, the grief was gone. Papa had betrayed her and she would never think of him again. As for Mama, well, it had been exactly what she had thought. Mama was a snooty lady with airs and she didn't want her pirate's daughter. Amanda didn't care.

But she cared about Cliff de Warenne. And it wasn't de Warenne anymore, it was *Cliff.* She began to smile.

She hugged herself, standing there naked by the window.

He had made love to her last night. He had shown her so much passion and given her so much pleasure, chasing away the pain.

He might not have taken her virginity, because her grief had come between them, but he would, and soon. Everything was going to be different now. They were lovers. There was no going back.

And if they were lovers, didn't that mean she could sail the world with him on his ship? There was no need now to enter society. She had never been more relieved, and she was almost happy.

Amanda began to get dressed.

HE HADN'T SLEPT ALL night. And when Amanda had finally fallen asleep in his arms, he had chosen to stay with her. Although he knew it would be her ruin if a maid found them in bed together, he was even more afraid that she would wake up and suffer in heartache again alone, with no one to comfort her. He had held her until he was satisfied she was so exhausted and emotionally spent that she would sleep until the morning. A few hours before dawn, he had slipped from her room.

He had not gone to his own bed. He was haunted by the sight of Amanda slicing her nightgown into ribbons; by the pain he had witnessed. He could damn her father and mother from now until eternity, but that would not ease her anguish. How much could one small woman bear, he wondered.

Last night, he had lost all reason and he had been about to make love to her. Dulcea Belford didn't want her, but he did. He had been fueled by a fierce and consuming need to make her his own. In the light of day, he was shaken, and he could not comprehend such possessive feelings. If she had not begun to weep, he would have taken her innocence, and then what?

He would have added to her sorrow.

He knew what he had to do. He must keep a firm distance from her. There would be no more visits to her bedroom. He would avoid being alone with her at all costs.

Now, he sat alone in the breakfast room, pretending to read the *London Times*, when he could not focus on a single word. The entire house rose early—Lizzie and Eleanor were up with their children, in spite of the nurses they employed, and the countess enjoyed a walk in her gardens just after sunrise. As Cliff stared at the paper, Rex came inside, followed by Eleanor. He saw them exchange looks.

"What happened to you last night?" Eleanor asked, taking a seat. "Did you go on a bender?" She reached for a pastry.

"When the countess arrives, I have an announcement that I wish to make."

Rex also sat. "Is this in reference to what we discussed last night?"

Cliff toyed with his cup of cold coffee. "Yes." As he spoke, the countess came in, her cheeks flushed from her morning walk.

"Good morning," Mary de Warenne said brightly. She went right to Cliff and kissed his cheek. "We never had a chance to greet each other yesterday. Rather, we passed one another like two ships in the night." Her smile faded as he looked up. "I am so happy you have come home, but now I am worried. What is wrong? Why do you look so grim?"

"I am fine, but Amanda is not." He stood up. "You have yet to meet her, but I take it Rex and Eleanor have filled you in?"

The countess studied him. "Eleanor said she is your guest and that you have brought her to London so she might meet her only living family. Rex has inferred that you are her champion?"

Cliff managed a smile. "Actually, there is more." When he had their attention, he said, "I saw her father before he died. His last dying wish was that I become Amanda's guardian."

Expressions of surprise and disbelief greeted him. Before anyone could object and point out that he had a notorious reputation, one that made him unfit to be the guardian of any young woman, he said, "I was reluctant to agree. No more. It is official and I will have any necessary papers drawn up. As of this moment, Amanda Carre is my ward."

## *CHAPTER TWELVE*

IT WAS ELEANOR WHO began to laugh. Everyone else seemed very surprised. "How can you guard the virtue of any woman?" she said. "I saw you in her room yesterday afternoon. Does she still have her virtue?"

"Eleanor!" the countess protested.

Cliff stood up, his chair scraping back. "We had some matters to discuss, Eleanor, not that it is your concern. And I suggest you think twice about accusing me of stealing Amanda's virtue." But last night, he had almost done just that—and not for the first time. His sister was infamous for her snooping ways. It was fortunate she had not walked in on them last night.

Eleanor was wide-eyed and taken aback. "You must be smitten! You are so touchy! The brother I know is absolutely indifferent to such accusations. Besides, you have never tried to hide an affair."

"We are not having an affair. She is seventeen years old—she is my ward!" he cried. He felt himself flush as he turned his back to her, facing the countess. "I had hoped that her mother would have the honor of a guardianship, but as it turns out, she wants nothing to do with her own daughter. Do you know Lady Belford?"

"I do. That is terrible," Mary cried. "But I understand her predicament. She must be afraid of ruin. Still, to reject one's own daughter is inexcusable! Cliff, have you told Miss Carre?"

He hesitated, exchanging a glance with Rex, the entire terrible evening flashing through his mind. "Yes. She did not take it well." He added, "She is distraught. I am asking all of you to go out of your way to be kind to her. She just lost her father and now there is this."

The countess, Eleanor and Rex exchanged glances. "Of course we will be kind," the countess said softly. "Rex said her background was somewhat dubious, Cliff?"

He sighed. "Her father was hanged for piracy."

Mary started.

"She has had a difficult life. I was hoping to secure a far brighter future for her. If you knew the details of how she was raised, your blood would curdle. No woman should have had to live as she had. Her father was a harsh man."

Eleanor stood and walked over to him. "I had no idea. Cliff, I am sorry for being so insensitive. But when I saw you two together, I assumed you were lovers, even if she is too young for your taste and not the type of woman you prefer."

He smiled at her, relieved. "You assumed wrongly. The two of you have a bit in common," he said. "Even though you are an earl's daughter, you were raised with five boys. She grew up on the deck of a ship amongst sailors. The both of you ran wild. I would especially like your help in this endeavor, Eleanor, if you will give it."

She kissed his cheek. "Of course I shall. I am fascinated now. Have you undertaken to acquire a wardrobe for her? She cannot run about town in her breeches."

"I have and Madame Didier will be here at noon. Eleanor, she has never worn a dress."

Eleanor stared, as did the countess. Then the two women looked at each other. "We will help her make what must be a huge adjustment," the countess said with a smile. "But I must ask, what will you say about her family?"

"Fortunately, her father was a naval officer before he took up piracy. I will twist the truth slightly and maintain that he left the service to become a planter in the islands, as many officers really did. I'll maintain her mother died when she was a small child, and in the hopes of sticking closely to the truth, her mother's family comes from Cornwall, but Amanda is the last of the line."

"That will do, I think, at least for now. And may I assume you are launching her into society in the hopes of procuring a husband for her?" the countess asked.

He tensed. "That is putting the cart before the horse. Amanda is not ready for suitors. She needs six months before she is launched." He looked at everyone. "On the voyage here, she began instruction in decorum and etiquette. She did not know how to read, but she is already reading as well as Alexi. She is very clever and I know she can excel at anything she chooses to do. But I must tell you this—she is terrified of being mocked and ridiculed by the ton. She has suffered such humiliation from the ladies on the island. I will take any and all advice."

"The poor child," the countess said softly. "We will all help, of course we will."

"Cliff, why don't we make certain she is a success from the start?" Eleanor said brightly.

Cliff faced her. "What do you mean?"

"We must begin by calling on our dearest friends, those who will receive Amanda graciously no matter any misstep on her part."

His brows raised; he liked the idea. "And her confidence will begin to grow."

Eleanor grinned at him.

"I have a suggestion," Rex said. "There is no one as gracious as Lady Harrington."

"And I remain good friends with her," Mary added. "I'll speak to her at once. Blanche would be perfect for Amanda's first call."

Cliff knew Lady Harrington very vaguely. Once, his brother Tyrell had been betrothed to her. She was one of the most pleasant and unassuming ladies he knew, as well as one of the greatest heiresses in the realm. "I approve."

"The Carrington ball might be the perfect time for a formal coming-out," the countess said.

He hesitated. "I prefer an informal launch, Mother. But isn't that in a month?"

"It is a wonderful affair," Eleanor said eagerly. "I have always enjoyed their balls! They never have more than a hundred and fifty guests, so for a ball it is rather small. If she is ready, Cliff, it would be the perfect opportunity for her."

Before he could respond, the countess spoke, "You must not wait six months to begin a search for suitors, Cliff. It isn't easy to find an impoverished gentlewoman a good match, much less a gentlewoman with a dubious family background. You must start assessing suitors right away. Unless you are very fortunate, this will take some time. Does she have a dowry?"

He knew Mary was right. It wasn't going to be easy to find Amanda the kind of husband she deserved. He folded his arms across his chest, disturbed. It was as if a snowball had been set in motion, and was about to become an avalanche. But Amanda needed a husband; that was obvious. It was just as obvious that she wasn't polished enough to be courted, despite the progress she'd made. He sighed. "I'll provide the dowry. I'll have my agents find a small but successful estate and we'll put it in Carre's name in trust for her. In fact, I'll get on that right away. We should all begin thinking of possible suitors for her, as you are right. Finding a good match won't be easy."

Mary took his arm. "Darling, Rex said she is a beauty, and that will certainly help. We will all compile a list of suitors. Let me know the moment you have secured her dowry." The countess glanced past him, her smile vanishing.

Everyone turned to face the doorway. Amanda stood there in his shirt, her breeches and boots. She was white with shock.

Cliff hurried to her, noting that her eyes were red from weeping. "Good morning," he said, smiling too brightly. "Would you like to meet my stepmother? We are all having breakfast."

Amanda gave him a hurt, incredulous look. She had clearly heard them discussing her prospects and he winced, wishing he had modified their discussion. He took her arm. "Come, meet my stepmother."

Mary swept forward, smiling warmly. "Welcome to the family, my dear," she cried, taking both of Amanda's hands in hers. "If you are Cliff's ward, we are all entrusted with your care, and delighted at the prospect."

Amanda seemed stunned. She mumbled, "My lady."

"I do not stand on formalities, my dear, not when we are among family." Mary kissed her cheek and released her. "I am so sorry about the losses you have recently suffered. Is there anything I can do?"

Amanda was blushing now. Incapable of speech, she shook her head. "No," she finally whispered. "Thank you."

He was relieved she had shown some polish. He touched her. "Can we have a word after you eat?"

She tore her gaze away from the countess, her eyes huge. "I need to speak to you now," she said hoarsely.

Instantly he recalled kissing her, holding her, his passion beyond control. His heart picked up a far different beat, and he knew she was thinking of that moment of madness, too. He nodded slowly. "Excuse us," he said, guiding her from the room.

In the library, he closed both doors behind them. "How are you feeling, Amanda?" he began. He did not want to discuss last night. He did not know what he could possibly say to justify his reprehensible actions.

"I heard you!" she cried in disbelief. "You were talking about suitors and a dowry!"

"That is what a guardian does for his ward, Amanda. How else could I secure your future?"

She was impossibly pale. "You are not my guardian," she began.

"I have officially declared it. To make certain there is no doubt, I will have some papers drawn up, making it appear that Carre granted your care to me."

It was a moment before she spoke. "If being your ward means I am to be rushed into marriage by *you*, then I do not want to be your ward!"

"I know you are frightened," he began.

"Last night I was in *your* bed!" she accused, her eyes wide with hurt. "Last night you kissed me many times. I thought we were lovers!"

He turned white, shocked. It was hard to speak. "We are not lovers. Last night was a mistake. It will never happen again. You are still a virgin!"

"Barely!" She approached, shaking her head wildly. "You held me and kissed me. Your tongue was in my throat, your hand between my legs! How can you say we are not lovers?"

He knew he was red. "I lost control," he tried.

"And it wasn't the first time!" she exclaimed, trembling. "On the ship, after the storm. I thought I was dreaming, but I wasn't, was I? You made love to me on the *Fair Lady!*"

"I lost control," he repeated stiffly. How stupid he sounded. "You are terribly beautiful and vastly tempting, but it is wrong. You deserve a husband—"

"I don't want a husband. I want you."

He stared. She stared back, pale and trembling.

"I am not making you my lover," he managed, shaken. "One night of foreplay does not make us lovers. I was overcome with lust. But I only wanted to comfort you. I have claimed you as my ward to protect you from rakes like myself."

She started to back away, shaking her head. "Last night changed everything!"

"Last night did change everything. You cannot go to Belford

House, so you have become my ward. Now it is my duty to provide for you." With difficulty, he found some calm. "You need a husband, Amanda. All women do."

She tried to speak and failed. She tried again. "You could be my husband."

He was stunned. All thought vanished, and there was only the slender beautiful woman standing before him, asking him to marry her.

She was shaking, clearly afraid. "I turned eighteen yesterday." She swallowed. "If I have to marry, why not you? I am woman enough to bed down with you and you know it. I could please you greatly—I am certain! And I could give up this pretense. We could sail together! I may not be a fancy lady, but I know you want me. You like me and we are shipmates. I could even give you more children, because I am so young!"

*She was asking him to marry her.*

He had to sit down. *It was terribly intriguing, the thought of her with him on his quarterdeck, riding any oncoming storm together, sailing into eternity. And afterward, falling into his bed, with her, Amanda as wild and passionate as the wind-driven seas.*

She hesitated, coming closer. "You do like me, a little? We are mates, aren't we?"

He opened his mouth to speak, but no words came out. He tried again. "I do like you. Of course I do. But you are a woman and my ward, not my shipmate." He now chose his words with great care.

She was disbelieving. "We have conquered the high seas together!"

He stood abruptly. "I have no intention of ever marrying anyone. Why would I?" He fought for calm, and then spoke more quietly. "Amanda, I have children I adore. I do not need more. I do not need to marry for financial reasons. I couldn't care less about acquiring a title. I do not believe in love. There is no lucid reason for me to ever consider marriage."

Her cheeks became crimson.

"And I like to philander," he pleaded. She was obviously stricken. "I always have and I always will. You already know that. No woman could survive a marriage to me if I did take those vows."

She hugged herself. "Of course you should not marry…not me…I didn't really mean it….I am just confused."

He wanted to rush to her and embrace her. Of course she was confused. She had just learned that she was a bastard, that her mother didn't want her and he had been very intimate with her. "I would break your heart, Amanda—and I believe it has been broken enough for one young life."

She closed her eyes tightly, and he knew she was regretting her rash words.

"Amanda," he said softly. "Last night was my fault entirely. But if you think a bit, you will become pleased that you are my ward. You will be cared for as you never have been, not just by myself but by my family, as well."

"I don't want to be your ward."

He knew he had hurt her and no amount of rationalizing or explaining could change what he had done. "I am sorry," he almost begged. He wished he had never gone to her room last night to tell her the terrible truth. "Amanda, you have no other options."

It was a moment before she spoke. "Your stepmother said it will be hard to find me a husband because I am *dubious*," she said. "Maybe it will be impossible."

He winced. "That is not what she said. She said your family background is rather dubious, which it is. She is eager to help you enter society and succeed there. And it will not be impossible."

Amanda stared at him with hurt, accusing eyes.

"What is it that you really wish to say?" he demanded with dread.

"I want the truth."

He tensed. "In regards to which subject?"

"The subject—" she wet her lips "—of our being lovers."

He slowly nodded, his heart drumming thick and swift. "And what is the question?"

"If I were a lady, nobly born and bred, would we be lovers?"

"That isn't fair," he exclaimed.

"We'd be lovers and you know it! You wouldn't be protecting me, you'd be tossing me!" she cried, batting at tears. "The way you almost did last night!"

He walked over to her, suddenly angry. "That is probably the truth, but not for the reason you are accusing me of. I am not bigoted against you. You are barely eighteen—I am ten years older and more experienced than you!" He was shouting. "You are tempting—I have admitted it! And if you were older and you equaled me in experience, I would gladly do the deed. But you aren't older, you have no experience, and I actually see a glimmer of hope for you. I want you to have a pleasant life, Amanda, and if I *toss* you, as you just put it, no gentleman is going to take a second look at you. How much more succinct do I have to be?"

"I don't know what succinct means and I don't care! I knew it. I'm not good enough for you—like I wasn't good enough for my mother!"

"That's exactly the opposite of what I said."

"Then you are lying," she said, and she struck at him, hard.

He caught her wrist before her palm could connect with his jaw. "I don't blame you for being furious," he said. "I was terribly bold last night. I have said it over and over, that wasn't what I intended, but that is what happened. I am sorry."

"I'm not!" She wrenched free. "I think I hate you now. I wish we had never met, and I certainly wish I was anywhere but here."

He couldn't move or speak. He was absolutely stricken. She ran for the door. Shocked, he chased her. "Wait! You don't mean that—"

She pushed him away. "I mean it. Leave me alone, de

Warenne. Just leave me alone! And do not ever come uninvited into my room again!"

He froze.

She stumbled from the room.

Eleanor was standing outside in the hall, clearly having been eavesdropping on them. Cliff was too distressed to even think of what she had overheard, but when she sent him a cold, cutting look, he began to realize the crisis about to be unleashed.

"Amanda, dear," she said, reaching for Amanda, who was almost in tears. "Madame Didier is here and I would like to help you choose a new wardrobe. It will be a merry time! Let's go up, my dear, and while we do so, I can tell you all about my miserable, dastardly, callous and selfish brother. Oh, did I forget that he is arrogant, high-handed, cruel and a complete cad, as well? But don't worry. He will never have entry to your private room again!"

Amanda sniffed. "He is a bastard, but he isn't cruel or a cad."

Eleanor gave him a dire look and she and Amanda started up the stairs, arm in arm.

"Well done," Rex said, stepping out of the dining room. "Can you not, for once in your life, keep your trousers on?" In disgust, he shook his head.

Cliff scowled, but could not reply. The countess came into the hall. She gave him a worried look and followed Eleanor and Amanda up the stairs.

Cliff leaned against the library doors, his heart aching so oddly. It seemed that no matter what he did, he hurt Amanda, and he suddenly hated himself. She did not deserve his abuse. He had made her several promises, and providing her with a certain future was one of them.

But he was not that future. Of course, he was not.

AMANDA WENT to the bedroom window while the couturier began unpacking her valise. How could she have asked Cliff de Warenne to marry her? Her cheeks burned with mortification.

"Amanda?" Eleanor said softly, from behind.

Amanda didn't hear her. After last night, she had thought they would be lovers, not husband and wife. Being his wife had never been even a part of her wildest dreams. She knew she wasn't good enough for him. But she had gone downstairs to find him discussing a dowry and suitors and she had realized he meant to find her a husband. Amanda had been stunned and frantic. Sheer impulse had caused her to blurt out that terrible suggestion. Now, she was numb.

She had traveled halfway across the world to be reunited with her mother, but her mother did not want her. After last night, she had thought that De Warenne wanted her as a lover, but he didn't. In fact, he was now claiming to be her guardian and he was going to marry her off to someone else.

Amanda just stood there at the window, hurt and bewildered and trying to make sense of her life.

She'd had a plan for all of these past weeks, a plan with de Warenne. She would learn to be a lady with his help so she could enter society and live with her mother. As clumsy as her efforts had been, she had been determined to accomplish the impossible. She had wanted to become a lady, at least in appearance, and not just so Mama would love her. Her entire life, she had been an outcast and outsider, standing outside of fancy houses, peering through the windows into fancy salons and shops, knowing she was different and wishing she were not.

De Warenne had given her a chance to change all of that.

Amanda trembled. She had pretended not to care about changing herself, but the truth was, she had cared, because otherwise, she wouldn't have tried so hard. She still cared. She cared enough to be crying now.

Her home was gone, taken away from Papa by the authorities. She didn't want to go back to the island, where she would have to lie and steal and beg in order to survive. She didn't want to be that wild child again.

Amanda wiped her eyes.

Of course de Warenne didn't want to marry her; she had never expected him to want her as a wife. She had been stupid enough to fall in love with him and she had yearned to be his lover, even for a while. But he was a man of honor, the kind of man she hadn't really believed existed until she had met him. He was being noble now. He had chosen to become her protector on the island, and now he had chosen to be her guardian, when he owed her nothing at all. He could cast her out; instead, he was providing her with a generous dowry so she could marry well.

It hurt, but she was also grateful. The image she had been entertaining recently filled her mind, somewhat altered. Now, clad in a beautiful dress, she saw herself polished and proper, sitting with Cliff de Warenne in a rose garden, and he was smiling fondly at her. But they were only good friends—because she was someone else's wife.

"Look at this ivory and coral," Eleanor was saying, holding up a sprigged pattern. The coral was a faint vein in the sprigs. "With your hair and eyes, this will be lovely on you."

Amanda realized the other woman was regarding her with sympathy and concern. She started, for swatches of fabric were piling up on the bed. She blinked. She had never seen so much silk, satin, chiffon and cotton. Cliff had taken her into his home, he was giving her a dowry and he was providing her with a wardrobe fit for a princess. "Surely, these fabrics aren't for me?"

"You will have any and all that you like," Eleanor announced with a smile. "Cliff is well off and we should take him for every penny that we can. He can be such an insensitive lout!"

"He is a great man," Amanda whispered, somehow meeting Eleanor's eyes.

Eleanor handed the ivory and coral sample to the couturier, touching Amanda's hand. "You are terribly in love with him, aren't you?"

Amanda jerked out of her reverie, flushing. "Of course not! I am so grateful to him for all he has done, for allowing me to stay here in your home, for giving me so much opportunity to better myself." She meant it. She couldn't go back now. Even if it meant becoming his ward, marrying someone else and settling for his friendship, she wanted to become a lady, at least in appearances, if she somehow could.

"My brother," Eleanor said slowly, "has a bit of a reputation. He is not the marrying kind—"

"I know!" Amanda managed a wide, bright smile. "I have seen him on the deck of his ships for years, or on the deck of a prize he has taken. I have seen him strolling on the streets of Kingston, and I have watched real ladies making fools of themselves in the hopes of attracting his attention. Everyone in the islands knows Cliff de Warenne." Even as she spoke, she began to realize that she was not the first woman to fall in love with Cliff de Warenne and find herself rejected. He had probably left a trail of broken hearts all around the world. Now, she would have to ignore her own protesting and wayward heart, as well.

"He is very handsome, very charming and very wealthy. I can imagine how easily a woman could fall for him. But do you know, I have never seen him quite so attentive. His affairs are usually very brief and he has never brought a woman home."

Amanda hugged herself. She wasn't certain she wanted to have such an intimate discussion with Eleanor O'Neill. "I am not dimwitted enough to be thinking of marriage to your brother, Mrs. O'Neill. In fact, he is right to be arranging a marriage for me. The other choice would be for me to return to the islands, and while I love the sea and I love sailing, I can't go back."

Eleanor plucked her hand. "You are being so brave!"

They were on safer ground now. "Brave? I am not brave. Bravery is being alone for months on end, uncertain where your next meal is coming from. Bravery is watching your ship come in—and not knowing who is alive and who is dead."

Eleanor's eyes were huge and Amanda turned away, wishing she hadn't spoken so openly. But it was true. More often than not, Papa's cruises had gone on far longer than planned, and now she could face the truth: he hadn't provided very well for her. In those last months before his death, she had had to fish in the cove, gather mangoes and beg and steal to survive. Once, he had been imprisoned in Cyprus, and he had been gone for over a year. She had been thirteen years old at the time. She had been alone, lonely and afraid. And every time the sloop had crept into the harbor, she had been terrified that Papa would not be on her decks.

There was no decision to make. She desperately wanted the life Cliff was offering her. Maybe the estate he was buying would have a rose garden; if not, she could plant one herself. And while she remained afraid of society, maybe it wouldn't be that bad. After all, Cliff's family was of the highest rank and look at how they had received her. No one had looked down on her, at least, not yet. Maybe the London ton wasn't as bad as the island society. Besides, this was going to be different from wandering Kingston's streets. She hadn't really grasped that until now. She was going to be launched on Cliff's arm while in the midst of his elegant and powerful family.

*I can do this*, Amanda thought. *I have to do this!*

"No wonder," Eleanor said softly, "Cliff looks at you the way he does."

Amanda didn't hear her. She walked over to the bed, Eleanor following. "I only need one dress," she said slowly. But she took the coral and ivory silk from the bed and held it to her bosom, trembling. It was so pretty, so feminine. Suddenly she wanted it the way she had wanted the nightgown which she had destroyed last night. "Do you think I will be pretty in this?" she asked slowly.

"You will be the most beautiful woman in the room, and Cliff will have trouble controlling his desires, indeed," Eleanor said with a gleam in her eyes. "And you need a dozen gowns, Amanda. One will never do."

Amanda could barely believe she would need so many dresses, just as she could barely believe the turn her life was taking. Maybe this was better than becoming Cliff de Warenne's lover. After all, she had never had a secure and safe home of her own. They had struggled to make ends meet at Belle Mer, and there had always been the threat of selling it to pay off their debts.

Papa had lied to her, but he would be so happy for her now. He would want this life for her.

As for Mama, one day they would meet. Amanda would make it so, and when they did, Mama would see an elegant lady with a handsome husband and an estate of her own, not a pirate's daughter, and she would never guess at the hurt and pain she had caused. Because Amanda would hold her head high and smile as graciously as the countess would.

And as for Cliff? They would be friends, maybe even dear friends, and while she might love him forever, it would be from afar, the way she had admired him from a distance on the island. Eventually, she hoped, it would not hurt so much.

Eleanor was holding up a pink-striped ivory. Amanda looked at her. "Tell me what you think I should choose."

LADY HARRINGTON, sole heiress to the huge Harrington fortune, was in her drawing room in Greenwich, their spacious London home, with two callers, her old and dear friends, Lady Bess Waverly and Lady Felicia Capshaw. She sat on a gold velvet settee, a small, dignified woman of twenty-five with porcelain skin and striking blue-green eyes. Her pale, nearly platinum-blond hair was pulled tightly back into an unfashionable chignon, but it was the no-nonsense style she preferred. Although she was very wealthy, her dark blue gown was almost severe, and she wore but two small diamond earbobs and one diamond ring with no other jewelry, as she did not like to flaunt her wealth. Her friends, however, wore frilled and flounced gowns. Bess was sporting a huge ruby necklace, the gift from her most recent lover, a visiting Russian count, while Felicia wore more emeralds than any young widow should ever wear. But her recently deceased husband had left her a small fortune and she was flashing it as she could, desperately hoping to attract her third husband.

And it seemed that she had a viable candidate in mind. Felicia had spent the past hour telling her about an elderly earl, also twice widowed, who had called four times in this past week. "What do you think, my dear?" Felicia asked eagerly. She was a voluptuous brunette.

Blanche smiled quietly at her friend. "Do you want me to tell you what you wish to hear, or what I really do think of all of this?"

Felicia sat up straighter.

Bess laughed. "She wants your approval, Blanche. God, if only we could be as indifferent to life's foibles as you!"

Blanche carefully smiled, not offended but not about to share the truth with either friend. If only she could care about life's vagaries. She sighed. When she was six years old, she had witnessed her mother's brutal murder in a rioting mob. She could not remember that event or any day prior to it, and ever since, she had calmly accepted every twist and turn life offered.

"You do not care for Lord Robert," Felicia pouted.

Blanche patted her hand. "I care for you, my dear. Do you really need to jump into wedlock again, so quickly? Can you not carefully choose your third husband?"

Felicia appeared annoyed. "I am not like you, Blanche, with ice in my veins. It is either Lord Robert or a lover, for like Bess, I dearly miss the passion of the marriage bed."

Blanche was not flustered. Her friends knew she was a virgin. They could not understand why she refused to marry and even if she remained unwed, why she hadn't taken a lover. She had given up trying to explain that men held no interest for her. Her life was safe and secure at Harrington Hall, taking care of her father, and she did not need anything more. No man had ever made her heart race. She wasn't inclined toward women, not at all; she was merely dead in her body, as she was dead in her soul.

"I suggest you take a lover, dear, for a while, but be discreet. And choose more wisely this time." Her second husband had been an impetuous, if handsome, young man who had been killed jumping his Thoroughbred over a dangerously high fence.

As Blanche turned toward Bess, who was deliriously in love with her Russian despite Lord Waverly and their two children, her butler appeared, carrying a silver tray. "My lady?"

Gracefully Blanche rose to her feet to take the proffered card. She was delighted to see that the woman who had almost become her mother-in-law was calling. Once, she had been betrothed to Tyrell de Warenne, but neither one of them had wanted to go forward with the union. He had been enamored of his mistress, whom he had subsequently married. Her father had not insisted upon another betrothal, finally realizing that his daughter wished to remain a spinster, much to Blanche's relief. She was warmly inclined toward the countess of Adare, and knew that Mary de Warenne liked her, as well.

"Who is it?" Bess asked, standing. "I am late. Nicholas is waiting for me at the Beverly Hotel."

Blanche was about to tell her when she saw the countess approaching in the hall outside of the salon, a dark gentleman with her. Her heart skipped a beat, surprising her.

"Oh!" Bess cried, grinning. She jabbed Felicia and lowered her voice. "It is the countess Adare and her dashing, albeit brooding, and very unwed son, Sir Rex of Land's End. There's the perfect lover for you, Felicia—I have heard he has great stamina in bed, never mind his missing leg."

Felicia flushed. "He never smiles."

"The serious ones make the best lovers, darling. I must be off!" Bess kissed Blanche's cheek, greeted the countess and Rex, and hurried out.

Blanche made sure she was smiling as she went forward to greet the countess, trying not to look at Rex de Warenne and refusing to heed Bess's words. She knew him, of course. They had exchanged a dozen words in the course of her brief engagement to his brother. It had always been awkward and forced. In fact, he had made her vaguely uncomfortable, which was odd, as no one really had the ability to cause her any tension. "Countess, what a delightful surprise." She curtsied, deferring to the other woman's superior rank.

Then she glanced at Rex, her smile feeling quite fixed. As she greeted him she avoided his eyes. "Sir Rex, I am so pleased you have called." It was impossible to avoid him entirely, as he was such a big, solid man. From the corner of her eyes, she glimpsed a muscular thigh. "Do you recall my dear friend, Lady Capshaw? She joined me all those years ago at Adare, but she was Lady Greene then."

Introductions were made all around, while Blanche signaled to her butler for refreshments. Organizing the call made her recover the composure she had briefly lost. The countess's visit was not really a surprise, but she was caught off guard that her son had escorted her.

He was never in town. She doubted she had seen him in two years, if not more. Did he spend all of his time at his Cornish estate, she wondered. He had been awarded the estate and his title for his heroism in the war. He had not changed. He remained too big, too dark, with the shadow of some terrible burden in his eyes. But even she could admit her friends were right—he was very handsome, if one preferred the dark, brooding type.

"Sir Rex, it is a pleasure to see you again," Felicia was saying coyly. "I certainly recall our introduction in Ireland."

He nodded at her, unsmiling. "I take it you are well." His dark gaze slid to Blanche and then away again.

Blanche realized Felicia was going to try to get into his bed. She reminded herself that she did not care and quickly turned to the countess. "How long have you been in town?" she asked, smiling.

"A mere two days," the countess said. "Can we stroll on the terrace, dear?"

Blanche realized the countess had a matter she wished to discuss with her privately. Felicia was now asking Rex how long he had been in town, and although answering, he seemed impatient and annoyed. She caught him glancing at her friend's overexposed and lush bosom, but then, all men seemed inclined toward her two very socially active friends.

Blanche didn't really care to leave them together, but she looped her arm in Mary's and they strolled outside. "How considerate of Sir Rex to escort you today," she heard herself say. One of her eyes seemed to be permanently trained on the couple inside her salon. Felicia was being amusing, because Rex was smiling, finally, albeit reluctantly.

"I was very surprised," Mary admitted. "Of all my sons, he can be such a recluse. He is never in town, so I must make the most of it. As you surely know, he avoids society at all cost but he insists he is very occupied at Land's End. How are you, Blanche? And how is Lord Harrington?"

"Papa is well. He is in Stockholm, taking care of some business affairs. I do miss him when he travels," she said truthfully. In fact, she had been terribly lonely until Bess and Felicia had called. Then she amended her thought. She had callers every single day and she was too gracious to refuse anyone, but no amount of conversation could ease the sense of being so utterly alone. With the passage of time, her sense of isolation was becoming worse. Sometimes she would look across her salon at the merry crowd and feel as if she stood outside of herself, watching everyone and knowing no one, not even herself. Even when Harrington returned, as happy as she would be to see him, it didn't change that feeling of being an island unto herself.

But hadn't she wanted her life to be that way? She had only to say the word and her father would arrange a marriage for her. Blanche shivered. She could think of nothing worse than having to wed a total stranger and spending a lifetime with him in pretense.

"I am glad he is well," the countess said. "Have you heard the news? My son Cliff is in town, and he has a ward."

Blanche started. "Cliff has a ward? How did this happen?" He was too handsome and too much of a rake to have a ward, although she would never say so.

"He knew her father, a gentleman planter in the islands, who has recently passed on. Amanda's mother died at birth and he brought her here, hoping to reunite her with her mother's family, but there is no one to reunite her with, it seems."

"Oh, how terrible!" Blanche said, meaning it. "How can I help?"

Mary clasped her arm. "You are such a dear. We were hoping you might receive us. It will be Amanda's first call."

Blanche did not understand.

"We are hoping to bring her out at the Carrington ball, but her father was more ruffian than gentleman, and she was raised in a very unorthodox manner. She is a sweet, beautiful young lady, but her social education has been somewhat lacking."

Instantly Blanche comprehended. "Mary, I should love for you to bring Amanda to my home and I will make certain all goes well, no matter what. I will help launch her, too, if you would like my help."

"Thank you," Mary said fervently. "This is very important to Cliff, and to Miss Carre, of course. We so appreciate your help."

"It is my pleasure," Blanche said. She glanced into the salon again and she was surprised to see Rex standing stiffly by himself, watching them through the window. Felicia sat on the settee by herself, looking bored. Apparently Rex de Warenne was not interested in her friend as a paramour.

It wasn't her affair, yet she was somehow relieved.

## *CHAPTER THIRTEEN*

CLIFF CONTROLLED HIMSELF, when what he wished to do was pace. The entire family was assembled in the salon, prior to going into supper, except for Amanda and his sister. He could not imagine what was keeping them, but knowing Eleanor—and Amanda—he began to worry over such a bold pairing. He had been haunted by their earlier conversation all day, and he still felt ill, deep in his chest.

*I think I hate you now. I wish we had never met.*

He did not know what he would do if Amanda really despised him. He couldn't stand the notion that she wished they had never met. She had become so important to him. But she hadn't meant her words, had she? She had been speaking in hurt and anger, and he didn't blame her.

The children were with them, having already taken their meals in the nursery and preparing for a quiet evening upstairs. Michael, who was Sean's stepson from a previous marriage, and Ned, Lizzie and Tyrell's eldest child, were at the terrace doors with Alexi, having a very serious and excited discussion. As Alexi was holding a slingshot, Cliff knew they needed supervision, but Anahid was nowhere to be seen. Ariella sat on the floor, reading aloud to Eleanor's son Rogan, a year-old boy with bright blond hair and the O'Neill gray eyes. Lizzie's redheaded daughter, Margery, now four, was with them. Both children were rapt, as the tale was one of dragons. Lizzie was seated with them on the floor, as casually as a housemaid, smiling happily at the group, her cheeks flushed from a day spent playing nanny to her three children. As she was with child again, she had never been prettier.

The countess was chasing after Tyrell and Lizzie's other son, Charles, fondly known as Chaz. At two, he was intent on pulling every possible item and artifact off each end table and desktop. Vaguely, Cliff saw Rex seize Chaz before he could destroy a priceless plate. The boys outside vanished, and it was almost dark. Cliff started after them when he heard his sister's breathless chatter in the hall. From the corner of his eye, as he seized the terrace doorknob, he saw a vision in pink.

He turned, shocked, one word in his mind: *Amanda.* And he tripped over his own feet, but somehow caught himself before falling.

She stood with Eleanor on the threshold in a pink silk gown, her hair pinned up, and she was so beautiful he was stunned senseless.

All he could do was stare, smitten by her beauty and her innocence, wanting her insanely.

He somehow sat down in a chair.

She was blushing, smiling shyly.

*My God*, he finally thought, his heart thundering in his chest. She was so beautiful, it hurt—but hadn't he known from the start that she would be a great beauty?

La Sauvage was gone, but he couldn't seem to care, not when faced with the woman she was becoming.

He could not take his eyes off her.

"Cliff!" Eleanor shouted. She had her fists on her hips. She gave him a stern look.

He leaped to his feet and rushed forward, tripping again on the damned rug as he did so. Then he skidded to a halt before her, terribly breathless. Their eyes locked. Oddly, he couldn't think of a thing to say, when he wanted to tell her she was the most beautiful woman in all of Britain.

"Do I look foolish?" she whispered.

His heart turned over, impossibly, dangerously. "You look," he managed, taking her hand, "beautiful…beyond words."

Her color increased. "You don't have to be kind."

He brought her hand to his lips, but did not kiss it. He remained too shaken. "Amanda—" he swallowed, then gave in "—there is no one as lovely as you."

Pleasure filled her eyes and she smiled up at him with more confidence.

He raised her hand to his mouth and kissed it, lingering over her flesh. He was so terribly aware of her. Worse, he had such a yearning inside, and it wasn't just physical. In fact, he could not identify or recognize it—or was afraid to do so. But he couldn't quite release her hand. He wanted to hold on to it forever. "Did you cut your hair?" he asked softly.

She shook her head. "No."

He was relieved. "I'm glad," he whispered. As he looked at every single perfect feature on her face, he realized nothing had changed—but then he looked at the pink silk caressing her bosom, her waist, and he inhaled, because somehow, *everything* had changed.

"Lizzie pinned my hair up. She keeps her hair long, too."

Cliff had a stunning image of Amanda standing starkly naked, her long pale tresses spilling down her back, over her shoulders, over her full, high breasts. Last night, she had been naked, her hair down, but she had been in the throes of grief and despair, slicing her gown to ribbons with a knife. Now, he saw her smiling softly at him, her cheeks pink with desire, waiting for him to come forward and take her to his bed.

He didn't think he had ever wanted anything more. Cliff let her palm go. He cleared his throat. "I take it Madam Didier had a dress a client did not want?"

Amanda nodded. "She was kind enough to make some alterations…how could anyone reject this beautiful gown?"

"You are happy," he breathed. "I will buy you a hundred more."

She smiled into his eyes. "I don't need a hundred dresses. Cliff, I have come to my senses," she said softly.

His smile faded. What the hell did that mean?

"I was hoping," she hesitated, biting her lip, "I could ask you something, after supper."

*You could be my husband.* He was filled with tension, recalling her wish to be his wife. It had been a question, huge and poignant, one he would never forget. "You can ask me anything," he said as softly. Their gazes held again.

Then someone coughed.

Cliff started, realizing they were not alone, and he felt his cheeks heat. He glanced around the room at his family, disliking Eleanor's sly grin, Rex's open amusement, and his mother's and Lizzie's wide stares and knowing smiles. Even Ariella was staring at him with open curiosity, as if he had done something terribly inappropriate and odd.

The countess came forward. "Amanda, dear, I agree. You are so lovely. Why don't you and Cliff have a private word now while Rex goes after the two boys? I will take the ladies into the dining room and Anahid can settle the rest of the children upstairs."

"Thank you," Cliff said to his stepmother. He paused to kiss her cheek. Outside, he heard the boys screaming in wicked laughter.

Mary smiled at him. "I am happy for you," she said.

He had no clue as to what she meant. When everyone was gone, he smiled at Amanda. Even looking at her anew caused his heart to race. He began to wonder at his reaction—and to worry about it. Now that he was her official guardian, he had to get a grip on his composure. Guardians did not desire their wards, it was as simple as that. "Should I close the doors?"

She shrugged. "It doesn't matter."

He left the doors open. "Amanda, I am sorry about this morning," he began.

She laid her hand on his chest, making his heart leap wildly.

"You mentioned a dowry—and an estate." She dropped her hand.

Her simple touch had made him recall every moment in her bed last night. Stiff and uncomfortable, he paced for a moment to distract himself. "Yes. I realized you need a dowry, and I will provide it. An estate will be a part of the dowry. I put my agents on it this morning."

Her eyes were huge. "So when I marry, there will be an estate? Will it belong to me? Or to my husband?"

He was oddly disturbed that she was now speaking of her marriage so dispassionately. *You could be my husband!* "The lure to such a dowry is that it would pass from you to your husband upon marriage. However, I prefer the estate to remain in your name, and to be inherited by your eldest son. A suitor would still find the prospect attractive enough, as a husband controls his wife's affairs and your son would be his son, as well."

"You are so generous," she cried, her eyes huge, and he saw that she was excited now.

He was very disturbed. "So you have come to the conclusion that marriage is best?"

She glanced away, blushing. "Cliff…de Warenne. I spoke recklessly this morning. I mean…I wish I hadn't said what I did…it was so silly!"

"Amanda," he began. "You are not silly—"

"No, wait! I know you would never marry me. Of course I know it! I don't know why I said what I did. I mean, I did think we would be lovers after what happened last night, but you did say a hundred times you only wish to protect me." Her color was high. "I understand. I am not angry. I don't….hate you. I could never hate you."

He went to the doors and closed them, relieved no one was lurking in the hall. "I am very glad for that. Amanda, you do understand, don't you? I'm never going to marry anyone."

She grimaced. "One day you will marry a great lady. She will probably be a princess—I am sure of it."

He sighed, realizing there would be no convincing her. "Is this what you wanted to say? That you regret your impulsiveness earlier?"

"That, but more importantly, I wanted to understand what this estate means for me."

He reached out unthinkingly, his fingers grazing her cheek, then he jammed his hands in his trouser pockets. "The estate will be yours. In fact, this afternoon one of my agents found an interesting prospect. A manor house on quite a bit of land with three tenant farms." He saw her eyes widen so he continued. "The price is oddly low. The manor is south of town, about a half day's carriage ride from here."

She bit her lip, her eyes filled with excitement.

"What is it, Amanda?"

"You are giving me a home of my own!" she cried. "The British took Belle Mer and the *Amanda C*. I have nothing to my name, but you are giving me an estate—my very own estate. Can't you see what this means to me?"

He hadn't, but now he did. "I begin to understand. Have no fear. The estate will be yours, not your husband's." He hesitated. "And does the prospect of marriage now excite you, as well?"

Her smile faltered. "I know you will find a suitable match. I know you will never force me into a union with someone despicable."

"Of course not," he said slowly.

"It is a small price to pay for such a life, don't you think so?"

He was very uncomfortable now, and awed by her stoicism. "It is what women must do. They must find husbands to provide for them. Even if they are great heiresses, they still must marry for security and heirs."

"I know." She walked away, wringing her hands. His breath caught as he watched her without her being aware of it. How difficult would it really be to find Amanda a husband? He no longer considered the modest but necessary dowry; some gent was going to take one look at her and fall head over heels in love. And he was almost jealous at the thought.

Amanda faced him, a great distance separating them. "What kind of husband," she asked slowly, "do you plan to find me? Will he be someone like my father? Not a pirate, of course, but someone strong and fearless?"

He felt his eyes widen in horror. There was no way to respond truthfully, as the last thing he would ever do was foist a savage brute like Carre on her. But he began to suspect that Amanda felt a brute like Carre was her due. "I am going to find you a gentleman, Amanda, someone generous and kind, someone who will never lay a hand on you except in affection."

She started in surprise. "You mean…a gentleman? A real gentleman…like you?"

He felt his cheeks turn red. "That is exactly what I mean." He walked away, her earlier words echoing again, damn it. *You could be my husband.* He whirled. She was staring, brows raised, so he managed a smile. "Would you like to inspect Ashford Hall together?" he asked.

And as he had hoped, she was distracted. She beamed. "You mean, we will go see the estate you plan to provide for my dowry? Together?"

"It isn't far," he mused, very much liking the idea. "We could take the children—they have yet to see the countryside—and Monsieur Michelle, as you must not miss a lesson." He sent her a smile he knew was dazzling. "I had planned to take a look myself at some point in the near future. We can make it a family outing, instead."

Amanda jumped up. Before he could react, she threw her arms around him and hugged him, hard. "I am glad you are my guardian," she whispered, her lips against his cheek.

Absolutely rigid, wanting to kiss her senseless, he took her shoulders, pushed her back, and forced a smile.

Somehow, this was not quite going as planned.

AMANDA STARED out of the carriage, filled with tension as it entered a wide white crushed-stone driveway, passing immaculately trimmed lawns and hedges as it did so. The six-in-hand was the countess's conveyance and the six horses pulling the vehicle were perfectly matched blacks, each with a white star, the bridles and harnesses gilded leather. The de Warenne coat of arms was emblazoned on the lacquered ebony doors—a gold wolf snarling on a black shield, against a field of red set with gold fleur de lis. The seats were sapphire velvet. Amanda sat next to Eleanor in the backward-facing seat. Apparently the front-facing seat was reserved for rank, so the countess sat there with Lizzie.

Ahead, a huge, dark stone palace awaited them, the residence of the viscount Harrington, which he shared with his daughter, one of the greatest heiresses in the land.

The women had been chatting nonstop since they had left Mayfair. Sean was due in town any day, and Eleanor was dying, or so she claimed, as she missed him so. Tyrell had sworn he would attend the Carrington ball. Lizzie was feeling poorly and had almost stayed at Harmon House. Her fourth child was due in February. Having two boys, Lizzie was certain she was having another girl. The countess reminded her to allow the nurses to actually govern the children.

Amanda did not hear any of it.

Her first custom gown had arrived and she was suitably attired in ivory, with a pale green pelisse and a matching hat. Before she had left the house, Cliff had appeared, clasping a small strand of brilliantly glowing pearls about her throat, shocking her.

"A lady requires jewelry," he had murmured softly.

Amanda had been so moved, tears had come to her eyes. She'd had to remind herself that they were just friends and nothing more, not ever.

Now, she could not breathe, much less cry. There were so many dos and don'ts. Do curtsy the moment Lady Harrington enters the hall and do avoid direct, bold eye contact. A demure countenance is always acceptable. If the countess extends her hand, you may kiss the air above it. Speak only when spoken to. Speak quietly and slowly—demurely! Wait to sit when offered a chair and never sit before the countess or anyone else of greater rank—which meant everyone in London. If there is no chair, simply stand and smile demurely. If there was one word to be remembered, it was that one: demure.

There were also several basically safe and acceptable topics of conversation—the weather, the gardens, clothes and shopping, plans for the summer. Amanda had been advised by Michelle to stick to those topics and those only—he had made her memorize them. But after Cliff had given her the pearls, her guardian had leaned close and smiled. "If you are yourself, she will love you."

Amanda doubted that.

"Amanda? You are looking as ill as I was feeling earlier today," Lizzie said, reaching over to pat her knee.

Amanda jerked. The future countess of Adare was very occupied with her children, so they had only really spoken once or twice, but Amanda had never met a more pleasant and less threatening woman. In fact, one of their conversations had occurred with the future countess's dress spotted with flour and a dab of chocolate on her nose. Apparently she enjoyed baking and had made treats for the children.

Amanda tried to smile and failed. She couldn't even speak. This was her first social call and she was certain she was going to be exposed for the impostor that she was.

"Oh dear," Lizzie said, patting her hand this time. "Do you want to hear a story?"

The last thing Amanda wished was to be told a story, but she couldn't speak, so she could not refuse.

"I was in love with Tyrell for most of my life, even as a young child. But he was heir to the earldom and he hardly knew I existed—or so I thought." She smiled almost wickedly. "In any case, we were quite impoverished, and although I was madly in love, I never dreamed Tyrell would one day make me his wife."

Amanda forgot about being terrified of Lady Harrington. She sat up, leaning forward. "You were poor?"

"And far too plump for fashion." Lizzie laughed. "Well, I am still too plump, but Tyrell seems to prefer it. In any case," she hurried on as Eleanor jabbed her, "I will make a long story short. Tyrell was so far above me in class and economy that I might as well have been a housemaid. And he was betrothed to Lady Harrington."

Amanda's eyes widened. "What happened?"

"True love," Lizzie said with a sly grin, causing Eleanor to chuckle. "It was his duty to marry Blanche but he pursued me. And then Blanche kindly broke off their engagement, as for some reason, she prefers to remain unwed. And the next thing I knew, we were standing at the altar, exchanging vows."

"And it has been happily ever after ever since," Eleanor said. She patted Amanda's hand. "Tyrell fell in love with Lizzie long before she ever knew it. You may as well know one thing about the men—and women—in our family. A de Warenne loves once and forever."

Amanda was smiling. "It is very romantic!"

Lizzie said, "You will be fine. Blanche is a very pleasant lady and we have remained on good terms for all of these years."

Eleanor said, "Just smile and nod and try not to speak at all!" She grinned.

"Eleanor," the countess objected as the coach began to slow.

Eleanor faced Amanda, her expression becoming serious. "I never speak my mind in polite company, Amanda. My opinions are too bold and I know it. But when I am at home, or with Sean, I speak and do exactly as I please. I even swear upon occasion.

And if you must know, I am an avid horsewoman and I do not ride sidesaddle."

Amanda was trying to absorb this as she stole repeated glances at the huge stone face of the three-story house. Lizzie had succeeded in distracting her, but only briefly, and her stomach was aching from her nervous anxiety. The de Warenne postilions were opening the carriage doors. "But you *are* a lady," she objected.

"No one in the ton likes an outspoken woman, but behind closed doors, it is another matter entirely." Eleanor smiled at her.

"Eleanor, please. Dear," the countess said to Amanda, "there is a middle road. Smile politely and choose your words with care. But the ladies are right. You will be fine and Blanche is a dear." The countess was stepping down from the coach as she offered her advice.

Amanda didn't know what to think now, especially as she kept recalling Cliff's last whispered words. She was the last to alight from the coach and she followed the three women up the wide stone staircase, glancing backward at the enormous fountain in the center of the driveway amidst the geometric gardens. Harrington Hall made Harmon House seem small and cozy. Her heart was racing with so much alarm that she felt faint.

They were escorted through a vast hall filled with old paintings and into a huge salon with three crystal chandeliers and too many seating arrangements to count when the countess was announced. Amanda stiffened as an extremely elegant blond woman came into the room.

Blanche Harrington was picture-perfect. She was so beautiful, and without uttering a word, Amanda knew she was the epitome of ladylike behavior. Although conservatively dressed in emerald green, diamonds sparkled at her ears and on one hand. She moved with the grace and confidence of one born to extreme wealth and power. But she was smiling warmly and she and Mary de Warenne exchanged hugs, not curtsies.

"It is so good to see you, Mary," Blanche Harrington said, obviously meaning it.

"And I am delighted to be here, Blanche."

Blanche turned, smiling at Lizzie and Eleanor, her gaze taking in Amanda, as well. "It's been too long, Lizzie! And Eleanor, I have not seen you since your marriage."

The women embraced, Lizzie explaining she was so busy with the children and Eleanor insisting the very same thing.

Amanda trembled, clasping her hands, praying she would not make a stupid mistake. Blanche smiled at her as Mary introduced them. "Blanche, this is my son's ward, Miss Amanda Carre."

Amanda felt as if her cheeks were on fire as she sank into her first official curtsy. Panicking, she wondered if her hair was falling from its pins or if she had somehow stained her beautiful dress. When she straightened, she saw Blanche's pleasant expression had not changed.

"Welcome to Harrington Hall, my dear. So Cliff de Warenne is your guardian! You could not ask for a better champion, I think. Have you been in town long?" she asked in a friendly and interested tone.

Her heart rioting, Amanda tried to smile, but she was still too nervous to do so. "He is a wonderful guardian, my lady. And I have only been in town a week."

"London is a wonderful city. I am sure you will be pleasantly entertained while here," Blanche said.

Amanda nodded, realizing that Lady Harrington wished to converse with her. Was she supposed to say something? Her mind raced. She did not want to discuss the weather, as nothing would make her feel more foolish. "Your home is beautiful, my lady. I thought Harmon House grand, but this is even grander." She was trembling. Had she addressed her correctly? "I mean, Your Grace," Amanda whispered, becoming confused. The moment she spoke, she recalled from her previous lessons that only a duke or duchess was referred to as His or Her Grace. She flushed.

But Blanche did not seem to have heard her faux pas. "Thank you, my dear. Lord Harrington, my father, built this estate many years ago. The gardens are my favorite part of the estate."

Amanda hesitated, amazed she hadn't been ridiculed, then asked breathlessly, "Do you have a rose garden?"

"Yes, of course. Would you like to see it?" She held out her hand.

Amanda was nearly in disbelief. "I love roses. I should love to see it," she managed, overcome.

"Why don't we all stroll outside? It is a lovely day," Blanche said. "Afterward, we can take tea."

Amanda stood there, shaken and stunned, as the women walked toward the terrace doors. She inhaled hard. She didn't have to be told to know that somehow, she had passed her first test in society. She hurried after the group.

"CLIFF?" ELEANOR TRIED to appear innocent, but it was no easy task, as she could not wait to bait her brother now.

He was at one of the two large desks in the library, both of which were at kitty-corner at the far end of the large room. Two vast red rugs covered the floors and bookcases lined two of the four walls. He seemed engrossed in paperwork and she had to come forward, a sheet of paper in her hand, calling his name again.

He jerked, glancing up. Then he stood, smiling. "Eleanor! When did you return from Harrington Hall? How did it go?"

She kept a perfectly innocent expression on her face. God, he deserved this! "Oh, fine. Mother is resting before supper—everyone is, actually. Can I have a word?"

He scowled, coming out from behind the desk. "How is Amanda?" he demanded with vast impatience. "Was the call a success?"

She simply smiled at him.

"Do not test my patience now!"

"You have no patience," she cried. Then she smiled genuinely at him. "It was a very good idea to call on Blanche first. The call was a success. Amanda may not realize it, but she has a calm and grace, even when she is afraid. She did make one faux pas, but we all pretended not to notice and she realized her mistake. She can hold her own in society, Cliff—she is clever and, in truth, good at conversation."

He was smiling. "I am so pleased."

Eleanor plucked his sleeve. "But you know society just as I do. Blanche Harrington is one of the few genuinely nice women in town. There are so many vultures out there! I hated society when I was forced to come out. I can't begin to tell you how many English ladies looked down on me because I am Irish. Worse, even though I am an earl's daughter, the rakes in the ton were conscienceless." She made sure not to grin, although she thought her eyes probably danced.

He scowled. "I will protect Amanda from any rogue who dares give her a single glance," he said tersely. "No one will dare pursue her with any intention other than an honorable one."

Eleanor tried not to laugh. "You do take this guardianship very seriously," she said, maintaining an innocent expression.

"Of course I do," he snapped, appearing vastly annoyed. Then he nodded at the document in her hand. "Is that for me?"

Eleanor simply could not prevent a grin. "It is the list of suitors."

Cliff looked at her as if she had spoken Chinese.

"Don't you want to see who is on it?"

He snatched the sheet from her hand and she tried not to chuckle as his brows lifted. "There are only four names here!"

"It is only the *first* four names I have thought of," she said. "Besides, although you are providing her with a dowry, you are not making her a great heiress. We can claim an ancient Saxon family tree, but we have no proof. I am trying to find Amanda the *perfect* husband. You do want her to be very happy and to live in marital bliss, don't you?"

He gave her a dark look. "John Cunningham? Who is this?"

She became eager, smiling. "He is a widower with a title, a baronet. He has a small estate in Dorset, of little value, but he is young and handsome and apparently virile, as his first wife had two sons. He—"

"No."

She feigned surprise, raising both brows. "I beg your pardon?"

"Who is next?"

"What is wrong with Cunningham? Truthfully, he is openly looking for a wife!"

"He is impoverished," Cliff spat. "And he only wants a mother for his sons. Next?"

"Fine," she said, huffing. "William de Brett. Ah, you will like him! De Brett has a modest income of twelve hundred a year. He comes from a very fine family—they are of Norman descent, as well, but he has no title. However—"

"No. Absolutely not."

Eleanor stared, forcing herself to maintain a straight face. "Amanda can live modestly but well on twelve hundred a year and I know de Brett. The women swoon when he walks into a salon."

His gaze hardened. "The income is barely acceptable, and he has no title. She will marry blue blood."

"Really?"

His smile was dangerous. "Really. Who is Lionel Camden?"

She beamed. "Perhaps the best of the lot! He has a title—he is a baron. He has never been wed but he has several children. His home is quite nice, apparently, it is in Sussex, and he has a pleasing income! I believe it is two thousand a year." She waited.

He stared, appearing close to an apoplexy. "So he is a rake?"

"You have bastards!"

"I am a rake! Next."

She choked. "Next?"

"Amanda is not marrying a rake. Her husband will be loyal to her."

"Then maybe you should consider de Brett? He is very handsome and I am sure that he might fall in love with Amanda!"

"Who is Ralph Sheffeild?" Cliff ignored her.

She had saved the best for last. There was absolutely nothing wrong with Sheffeild. "He was knighted during the war for his valor, he is the youngest son of an earl, the family is very wealthy, and he can marry as he chooses. He is *not* a rake. If he is taken with Amanda, it would be perfect!"

"How do you know he is not a rake?"

"I know his reputation."

"He must be a rake, or he would be wed."

"I feel certain he is not a rake," she said quickly. "If he were a rake, the gossip would be all over the ton."

"Does he have a mistress?"

"Not that I know of."

"Then he must prefer men." Cliff smiled in triumph.

"What a leap to make!" She was aghast.

"He is too perfect. Something is wrong with him. If it isn't that preference, perhaps he gambles!"

"He doesn't gamble." She had to control her laughter now. She had no idea if Sheffeild gamed. "And Cliff, he likes women. I have met him personally, I am certain."

Cliff folded his arms across his chest and stared. "Something is wrong with this one, I can feel it. What aren't you telling me?"

"I have told you everything. He is perfect for Amanda!"

He tore the paper, not in two, but in shreds. Then he smiled, letting the scraps drift to the floor.

"Cliff!" she gasped. "What is wrong with Sheffeild?"

"No one is perfect," he retorted. "He is hiding something."

"You cannot reject everyone!"

"I can and I will, until I find the right suitor. Make me another list," he ordered, walking away.

She couldn't resist. She took a book from the shelf and threw it, so it hit him square in the back.

He turned. "What was that for?"

"Oh, let's just say I am going to enjoy watching you taken down a peg or two. And by the by, we are all rooting for Amanda."

He simply looked at her, clearly clueless as usual.

Someone coughed from the doorway, behind her. Eleanor went rigid, then turned. "Sean!" she cried, her heart leaping wildly.

Tall and handsome, he came forward, taking her into his arms. "Surprise," he said softly, just before claiming her mouth.

# *CHAPTER FOURTEEN*

AMANDA WAS SMILING as she hugged her knees to her chest, dressed for supper in the same beautiful dress she had worn to call upon Blanche Harrington. Her call had been a success! She had actually conversed with the great heiress, she had answered her questions in a manner that seemed to please her, and the highborn lady had not been condescending, not even once. There had not been a single sneer!

How could this be happening, Amanda wondered. And she thought of her protector, her smile softening. Maybe, one day, she could find a way to repay Cliff de Warenne for giving her this opportunity. Because in that moment, she was beginning to genuinely believe that she could become a lady, that she could leave La Sauvage far behind in the past, where she belonged. She thought of Papa, but no tears came. He wouldn't mind, she thought, he would be so proud of her now.

The lady she admired the most of all, the kind of lady she aspired to, was Eleanor O'Neill. She was bold and outspoken, but beautiful and elegant. Amanda hid her face on her knees, continuing to smile. She might still yearn secretly for Cliff de Warenne, but her life was changing, and she was thrilled.

*I can do this*, she thought.

A knock sounded on her door. She leaped to the floor, slipping on her brand-new white, lace-up shoes, and went to answer it. Cliff stood there, a smile on his face. "I thought I would escort you down to supper," he said, his gaze slipping over her.

"Did you hear?" she breathed.

He touched her arm. "I heard. I heard you were a success." His eyes sparkled, impossibly warm.

"Have you been to Harrington Hall?" she asked eagerly.

"Yes, I have," he returned easily.

"Lady Harrington lives like a queen, Cliff! The house is like a palace—I had no idea." She was so happy that she could share her triumph with him. "She asked me so many questions—me! As if she cared about what I would say! And we walked in her gardens—she has beautiful gardens. She is such a great lady!"

He guided her into the hall. "I am very glad. You see, Amanda? Society is not as terrible as you think." But he had sobered as they went downstairs.

"Tomorrow, the countess wishes for us to shop on Bond Street and stroll about Pall Mall. What do you think?" She was so excited, ready now for her next step in society. Everything that was happening was almost too good to be true.

Except for Dulcea *Belford*. Not a day went by that she did not recall her mother's rejection, and then firmly refuse to dwell on it or her. She wasn't going to think about her mother now, because her life was almost perfect. Today she was going to savor her very first success.

Cliff was speaking. "I think you should see the sights of London. In fact, I seem to recall promising you a private tour."

Amanda's heart skipped for an entirely different reason. His gaze was frankly admiring. "I haven't forgotten," she murmured, glancing sidelong at him. She was almost flirting, but she had never felt prettier than she did just then.

"It may have to wait until we return from Ashford," he said softly as they went downstairs, where the voices of his family could be heard. His cheeks had become slightly pink and she felt his attention become terribly male. Then she realized that the boys were howling with laughter and someone—Ariella—was shrieking. Amanda winced and glanced at her benefactor.

Cliff scowled. “Alexi is out of control. He, Ned and Michael are fast becoming terrors in this house.”

“They are enjoying themselves,” she whispered, hoping he would not be too hard on them. But they would never be beaten for their antics. Did they know how lucky they were? “Have you decided when we are going to look at the Ashford estate?”

“I was thinking perhaps the day after tomorrow,” he said.

Amanda could not wait, and she sent him a breathless smile.

In the front hall, Cliff paused. “It seems you are becoming quite close to my sister,” he said.

“I do like her,” Amanda admitted. “She has no airs.”

He laughed. “I agree. Well, I am glad.” As they stood there, Rex appeared, herding Alexi and Ned, both boys snickering. “What have they done?”

“They put a toad down Ariella’s dress. They are going to redo their lessons,” Rex said firmly.

“A capital plan,” Cliff said, staring coolly at his son. “I am debating shipping you off to the islands, my boy, so I would think twice about conspiring with your cousin to torture your sister—or commit any other troublesome crime.”

Alexi turned white. “You would send me back to the island!” he gasped.

“Perhaps tomorrow will suit you?” Cliff returned.

“I swear to behave,” Alexi cried.

Ned stepped forward, as serious and grim. “Sir, it has been my fault entirely, I have egged Alexi on. If anyone is to be punished, it is I. But do not send him back to the islands!”

“I will think on it. Meanwhile, after you have completed a copy of today’s lessons, you may write Ariella a letter of apology.”

The boys nodded, humbly heading up the stairs.

“That is what they most definitely needed.” Rex nodded approvingly. He smiled at Amanda. “May I escort you into supper, Miss Carre? Surely you prefer my attentions to those of my egotistical brother. Besides, you can tell me all about your call on Lady Harrington."

Amanda grinned and did not hesitate. She went to his side. "I am delighted to have your attention, Sir Rex." She glanced back at Cliff, raising her brows to see if he approved of her new airs.

He did, for he nodded at her. "Well done," he murmured, his lashes lowering.

Amanda's heart soared.

AMANDA WAS HUNCHED over the secretary in her room, reading a book on the history of London which Monsieur Michelle had given her the day before. Her progress was slow and painstaking, and she had a dictionary at her elbow, one Cliff had given to her while on his ship. It didn't matter. She loved reading and every day it was a bit easier than the day before.

Her bedroom door slammed open and she jerked, turning to see Lizzie standing there, flushed with excitement. Amanda closed her book, carefully marking the place, bemused. "Lizzie? Is the house on fire?" she asked. Lizzie de Warenne was one of the most composed women she knew.

Lizzie was practically hopping from foot to foot. "You must come downstairs. My sister is here with her husband and a friend!"

Amanda stood, unable to quell some nervous anxiety, yet she was excited, too. She had heard a bit about Lizzie's eccentric sister, Georgina, and her husband, Rory, who was a cartoonist for the *Dublin Times,* and quite infamous for his radical political satire. She was thrilled at having such success so soon, not just with Blanche Harrington but the de Warenne family, but also waiting with some dread for the inevitable condescension to occur. Surely her current course could not be all smooth sailing.

Lizzie knew, because she rushed to her, grabbing both her hands. "You will love Georgie, and Rory, too! They are both very outspoken and very radical! I must warn you, they will try to indoctrinate you to their separate causes—Georgie is for the Union and Rory believes Ireland should be an independent country. Hurry!"

Amanda had to laugh as Lizzie pulled her down the hall and downstairs. "I thought ladies were not allowed to discuss politics?"

"Preferably not, but in this family, everyone has a passionate opinion. They will love you, Amanda, as I do," she promised. "And you can be yourself. There is no need for pretense now."

Amanda doubted that. She recalled being alone on the island while her father cruised, trying to attend to their farm, and she thought about the six-week voyage aboard Cliff's ship. It was becoming hard to visualize that ragged waif in breeches and boots who had lied and stolen to survive. She glanced down at her beautiful dress, recalling the brief conversations she had shared with Blanche Harrington and all the lovely suppers at Harmon House. She thought about strolling down Bond Street with the countess and the drive through the park with Lizzie and Eleanor. She wasn't really sure who she was anymore but she was *not* La Sauvage.

"Here she is," Lizzie cried excitedly, pulling Amanda into the hall with her.

A tall, slender woman with dark blond hair instantly came forward, followed by a handsome blond man. "I have heard so much about you," Georgina McBane said welcomingly. "It is such a pleasure to meet you. How do you like London? Do you need someone to show you around? I would love to do so."

Amanda was surprised by her enthusiasm. No two sisters could look less alike. But Georgina McBane was smiling so warmly that Amanda realized she was genuinely excited to make her acquaintance. She really was very much like her sister—a kind woman without pretense. "The pleasure is mine," she managed, about to curtsy.

"Oh, we do not stand on formalities," Georgina laughed.

"Besides, I am just Mrs. McBane. I do not outrank you, Miss Carre."

Her husband was bowing, however, in a very gallant manner, his green eyes twinkling. He seemed torn between amusement and horror. "So I finally meet Cliff's ward. This is an astonishing development," he said, grinning, "but now that we have finally met, maybe I am not all that surprised. Cliff has always had an eye for the most beautiful ladies!"

Amanda blushed, aware that Rory was handsome and flirting with her. "Cliff has been very kind, as has the entire family," she said. "Had he not taken me in, I fear I might have been sent to an orphanage." Then she realized that was not a proper greeting at all. But before she could correct the omission, Rory and Georgina exchanged glances.

"Well, the Cliff de Warenne we know is honorable, perhaps, but he is hardly renowned for his kindness," Georgina said tartly. "Where is the cad, anyway?"

Rory muttered, "And he is renowned."

Georgie poked him in the ribs.

"Georgie," Lizzie said, "I promise to tell you *everything*." The sisters exchanged smiles.

Briefly, Amanda felt left in the dark. She had been astounded at first by the intimacy in the de Warenne family, and the genuine affection they all shared, and now she could not help but envy the intimacy between the two sisters.

The third member of their party was standing somewhat behind Georgie and Rory, almost in shadow. She turned to face him. And the moment she did so, she met a pair of emerald-green eyes framed by thick black lashes—beautiful eyes that were fixed intently upon her. She curtsied; her heart skipped.

The gentleman was staring at her the way Cliff so often did.

"Our friend, Garret MacLachlan," Rory said, chuckling. "Garret, do meet Miss Carre."

Amanda straightened, flustered, as she had hardly expected

a handsome male caller. For another moment, MacLachlan simply stared at her as if he could not tear his gaze away, his interest shockingly direct. And in that moment, she understood that he was admiring her.

It was almost unbelievable. First her success yesterday, and now this, an admiring caller! She almost had to pinch herself to see if she was dreaming. She reminded herself that he was not, exactly, calling on her.

"A pleasure, sir," she said softly.

"I fear I ha' lost my wits," he said even more softly, his brogue heavy and seductive. "Miss Carre, 'tis an honor. I ken you are from the islands?"

She knew she must avoid any discussion about her real past. "Yes, I am, but my father has recently passed. It is hard for me to talk about my previous life there."

"I dinna ken. I am so sorry!" he exclaimed. "Forgive my faux pas. I could na' help noticin' yer beauty," he added. "No Englishwoman I ha' ever met has such radiance."

Amanda blushed, thinking about her sun-kissed complexion. He would surely look at her differently if he knew the reason for her wholesome appearance. "Englishwomen are very beautiful," she managed. "The ladies here are so well dressed and so very elegant. I hope to be as elegant, one day."

"Why?" he asked with genuine surprise. "I think they must imitate you, lass."

Amanda blinked in surprise. "I hope they do not!" She had to smile. "If you saw my poor dancing, sir, you would never make such a statement."

He laughed. "I ha' nay doubt that yer dancing is as extraordinary as the color of yer eyes. Ye ken that they are the green o' the Irish spring."

He was flirting, she thought, thrilled.

"An' perhaps, one day, when ye be feelin' a wee bit better, ye will tell me about the West Indies? Having never been across that ocean, I be very curious, indeed." He sent her a soft smile.

Amanda felt herself nod, some of her caution vanishing. She had the odd notion that he was genuinely interested in the island—and in her. Of course, she had been advised to never speak of her life there, and she had no wish to reveal too much of herself to him. "One day, perhaps," she finally murmured vaguely.

"Would ye care to stroll in the gardens? I ha' never been to Harmon House, but the Countess de Warenne is famous fer her gardens. An' I can tell ye about my country. Scotland makes London seem tropical," he laughed.

He did like her, she thought, amazed. She had been told that when a gentleman invited a lady to stroll outside, his intentions were serious—if he was not a cad. Amanda glanced quickly at Lizzie. Lizzie was beaming and she said, "Go, dear, enjoy yourself. Garret is a gentleman and he has many interesting anecdotes."

Garret offered her his arm, his unusual green eyes warm. Amanda hesitated. Cliff's handsome image had come to mind and strangely, she felt as if in taking Garret's arm she was betraying Cliff somehow. But that was impossible, as he only wished to stroll and converse. And Cliff had made himself very clear—he was looking for a husband for her. Perhaps he would be pleased if she mentioned Garret MacLachlan as a possible suitor.

She had just placed her hand in the crook of his arm, as Monsieur Michelle had taught her to do, when she heard her guardian stride into the room, his spurs jangling behind them.

"I beg your pardon?" Cliff said in a dangerous tone she instantly recognized.

Amanda's heart leaped uncontrollably. She and Garret turned.

Cliff's face was dark as he strode forward, his eyes flashing. "And you are?" he demanded coldly.

Lizzie hurried between them. "Cliff, this is Garrett MacLachlan, the Earl of Bain's son."

Cliff's face darkened even more, telling Amanda that he was

very displeased. His gaze swept Garret from head to toe, and it was terribly condescending.

Amanda tensed as Garret released her hand, his own eyes turning the dark black-green of wet, sea-swept rocks. "And you are?" he asked as coolly.

"I am Miss Carre's guardian," Cliff snapped. "And I do not recall giving you permission to stroll alone with her outside."

Amanda winced. "Cliff," she began in protest, surprised by his manner.

But neither man seemed to hear her. To his credit, Garret did not seem in the least bit shaken by being confronted in such a hostile manner. His smile was cold and dangerous. "So ye be Miss Carre's guardian?" he asked. He looked Cliff up and down from head to toe. "I am a gentleman, sir, an' I ha' asked yer ward to show me the gardens in the light o' day. I hardly realized I needed yer permission fer a proper stroll."

Cliff was flushed. He glanced at Amanda and she knew he was going to deny her. She was disbelieving. "Now you know that you do," he said to Garret.

But Rory rushed between both men to save the day. He clasped Cliff on the shoulder. "Cliff! I vouch for Garret's integrity. You have nothing to fear, especially as Georgie and Lizzie have decided to take some air, as well." He smiled at everyone present.

Cliff looked ready to draw his dagger from his belt. He gave Amanda an odd look, then gave Garret a threatening one. Abruptly, he turned and strode out.

It was a moment before Garret tore his gaze from his departing back. He looked at Amanda, and she finally saw his expression soften. "Is he always so protective?" he asked her. "I have nay dishonorable intentions!"

Amanda tensed, instantly defending Cliff. "He is very protective," she said firmly. "I don't mind. If it weren't for Cliff, I wouldn't even be here."

He started, his gaze searching hers.

She managed a smile. "He escorted me to London at his own expense, sir. I am very grateful for that, and more. I don't know why he is in such a temper, but I do know it will pass." Then the added shyly, "I would like to show you the countess's gardens, if you still wish to walk outside. I have never been to Scotland, and I am interested in learning all about your country."

His green eyes softened. "I hope ye ha' the entire day," he murmured.

CLIFF STOOD at the windows in the smaller salon, the velvet draperies pushed aside, staring at Amanda and MacLachlan. He despised the other man, and he refused to consider why. Amanda seemed to like her caller—but then, why shouldn't she? He knew a rival when he saw one, and MacLachlan would make a worthy adversary. He wasn't just a pretty face, he was a man who had fought his share of battles with his fists, his wits and his sword. MacLachlan had strength of character, power, a title and arrogance, and Cliff had known it the moment he laid eyes on him.

The Scot and Amanda had been strolling about for over an hour, arm in arm the entire time, and he was ready to go outside and tear them away from one another. Enough was enough. He told himself he was not jealous. But just as he prepared to leave the house and end this absurd flirtation, they separated and stood facing one another, all conversation having ceased.

Cliff was shocked, instantly recognizing the impending kiss. He strode for the terrace doors, reaching for his dagger.

"Whoa, my good friend, whoa," Sean O'Neill said, entering the room with Rex. "Whose throat are you about to slit?"

Cliff paused but did not tear his gaze from the couple, who had not yet embraced. "Who the hell is Garret MacLachlan, other than a Scot?"

Rex chuckled. "He is the son of an earl, Cliff." He swung on his crutch to stand beside him, Sean joining them.

Sean drawled, "Ah, I begin to understand. He is pursuing the beautiful Miss Carre?"

Cliff whirled on them both. "He is impoverished—his clothes are threadbare."

"He is the son of an *earl*," Rex repeated, laughing.

Cliff said tightly, "He undoubtedly steals cattle from his neighbors."

Sean laughed. "He is a Scot, Cliff, not a cattle thief."

"It is one and the same," Cliff growled. "Now, excuse me."

"What's wrong?" Sean taunted. "Afraid there will be a wedding at gunpoint? Perhaps MacLachlan is looking for a wife. Elle tells me you are looking for a husband for Miss Carre, as well. This seems to be a stroke of good fortune."

"She is not marrying the Scot," Cliff ground out, leaving the salon. He descended the stairs three at a time.

Amanda and MacLachlin turned to face him as he approached. He set his face into an expressionless mask. "Amanda, the countess wishes a word with you," he lied.

Amanda's gaze riveted on his and he was fiercely pleased to have her entire attention again. "Of course." She faced MacLachlan, smiling far too prettily, causing Cliff's temper to soar. "Thank you for the lovely stroll, and the information," she exclaimed. "The Highlands sounds like a beautiful place."

"There be nay place on this earth quite like it," MacLachlan returned. "I be sorry our stroll has to end, Miss Carre." He bowed. "I ha' enjoyed the gardens immensely—an' yer company."

She continued smiling. "So have I." She curtsied and hurried away toward the house, not looking back once.

Cliff noticed and was savagely pleased, but he was as displeased that Garret stared after her, clearly lusting for her. "State your intentions, MacLachlan," he said softly, throwing down a verbal gauntlet.

MacLachlan faced him. "It be Lord MacLachlan to ye. An' by the by, yer reputation precedes ye. 'Tis shocking that ye be the lass's guardian."

"I do not care if you are shocked, MacLachlan. I have asked you a question and I demand a response."

Garret made a sound of disgust. "'Tis fortunate fer ye that I admire yer father, Adare, as well as I do."

"Really? And why is that?"

"Ye need a lesson in manners," Garret said.

Cliff laughed, enjoying the impending battle. "How old are you, my boy? Because you do not wish to test your strength against me—or anything else, for that matter."

"I be twenty-four," he shot. "I ken ye rule the main. But be warned, I ha' seen my share of battles on land and sea, an' I am not afraid of ye."

"You should be. You are not welcome here."

Garret started. "I wish to call on yer ward again. She is delightful—a breath of fresh air in this town."

"I suggest you take your fresh air in Scotland," Cliff said coldly.

Garret's hand went to the hilt of the dagger he wore. "My father is Alexander the Ironheart, Earl of Bain, an' I am unwed. Ye canna refuse my suit."

"I can and I am. Amanda is not going to be tossed off to a heathen Scot. Besides, you are clearly a fortune hunter."

He flushed with anger. "I ken that Miss Carre's dowry is a modest one. If I were t' seek a fortune, I wouldna be askin' permission to court yer ward."

"Ah, so now we speak of a courtship? My answer stands," Cliff said harshly. "And I will not be moved."

Garret stared, flushed with rage. He finally said, "Ye be Irish. Damn it, we are brothers."

"My brothers are in that house," Cliff said, gesturing at the mansion behind them. "My word is final. Good day."

Garret turned and strode across the lawns, his every stride filled with heat and anger.

Satisfied, Cliff watched him go.

## *CHAPTER FIFTEEN*

DULCEA BELFORD ARRANGED her face into a pleasant smile as she paused before the front door of Harmon House. She tugged her immodest bodice lower, then lifted the knocker.

Her daughter had been in town for well over a week, but she had not had a single glimpse of her. She had, however, run into Blanche Harrington last night at a soiree and had learned that Amanda had called on her, with the Countess of Adare, upon first arriving in London. Dulcea wasn't really surprised. Everyone knew that the Countess of Adare remained on good terms with the woman who had almost become her daughter-in-law, and if Amanda was as unpolished as Cliff had suggested, of course her first call would be prearranged. How clever of de Warenne.

Thinking of him now infuriated her when previously his mere appearance in the same salon had been enough to make her tingle with delicious lust. She had tried to seduce him last year, but he had politely rejected her overtures. Dulcea had not been able to believe it then and she really couldn't believe his callous behavior toward her now—she had never been denied before, or so abused. How dare he scorn her, as if she owed Amanda Carre something. Carre had raised her and if her current plight was not satisfactory, the blame belonged on her father, not on her!

De Warenne's reputation as a masterly and insatiable lover was well-known, and now he had taken up with her daughter. Dulcea had become wet and hot between her thighs but she remained furious. She had quite a few doubts about the liaison. He was a conscienceless rake and he could not possibly be a fit guardian for any young woman, much less a beautiful one. Blanche had confirmed that Amanda was a great beauty. She had refused to confirm that she was at all rough about the edges, however.

Dulcea had sensed that, for some reason, Blanche Harrington was protecting Amanda. But why on earth would she do that?

Dulcea intended to discover what was truly transpiring. But even if Cliff was in bed with his ward, and even if Blanche had some kind of interest in her, the real and shocking news was that Amanda had a dowry. Apparently Carre had left her a small but lucrative estate near the village of Ashton.

How small was the estate, Dulcea wondered. Were there any tenants and if so, how many? If it was lucrative, just how lucrative was it? What if there was a mine?

Dulcea wet her lips, her pulse pounding. She had carefully reconsidered her position toward Amanda since learning of her dowry. Living on credit was horrid. Dulcea did not know how they would launch her own daughter in a few years. Worse, if Belford passed, as he surely would, as he was so much older than she, how would she ever pay off his debts? Of course, she would have to remarry a fortune. But now, there might be a solution for the moment, and that solution was her bastard daughter.

She did not dare acknowledge Amanda openly. She had debated claiming her as a cousin, but if Belford ever learned the truth, he would boot her at once. But she was Amanda's natural mother. As such, shouldn't she be involved in Amanda's prospects? Dulcea hated the notion of groveling before Cliff de Warenne, but she must convince him of her right to participate in the decisions affecting her daughter's future. Surely, she must be the one to control the estate.

She thought her plan was infallible. If he was in her daughter's bed, she could blackmail him into handing over control of the estate.

A doorman escorted her into a salon, taking her calling card and placing it on a silver tray. Dulcea was calling very early—unfashionably so—in the hopes of catching de Warenne before he went out for the day.

She heard his footfall approaching and fought her anger toward him, rearranging her expression into one that was demure and seductive. Seduction would be her first course of action; blackmail the last.

Cliff strode into the salon, his face set in harsh lines, closing the two doors behind him. He faced her, not bothering with a proper or pleasant greeting. "I will not mince words, Lady Belford. You are not welcome here."

Her smile vanished, as did her pleasure at the sight of such a magnificent man. She controlled her temper. "My lord, good morning to you, as well," she murmured softly.

"Do I have to repeat myself? You are not welcome in this house."

She drew herself up straighter. He was despicable! "My daughter lives in this house, Cliff. I am so sorry about our previous encounter. I have come to apologize to you and to inquire after her welfare."

His beautiful blue eyes flashed. "Really? The daughter you have no wish to acknowledge in any fashion whatsoever?" He was scathing.

"I have reconsidered. I wish to meet her. I have actually considered claiming her as my cousin, but I am afraid of Belford." She laid her ungloved hand on his strong forearm. He flinched and she felt a moment of satisfaction, thinking that he was not immune to her charms. "Cliff, I have so much regret!" she cried. "She is my daughter and I wish to help you launch her. Discreetly, of course." She smiled at him, fluttering her lashes."

He pulled away, scowling. "You broke Amanda's heart. Now you wish to toy with it? I wonder at *your* change of heart, madam."

Dulcea realized that seducing Cliff would not be easy, as he seemed to truly despise her. She wanted to attack, but smiled again, instead. "Come, Cliff. How could I have broken her heart? I don't know her and she doesn't know me."

"Carre made certain she loved you, madam. Your rejection aggrieved her to no end," he said harshly.

*He is very protective of her*, Dulcea suddenly thought with real suspicion and a stabbing jealousy. Was he fucking her? "She must be like her father, then. I broke his heart, but I did not mean to. Carre was weak."

Cliff was disgusted. "Amanda is the strongest woman I have ever met. Let us cut to the chase. What do you really want?"

She widened her eyes, thinking of the estate Carre had left her and praying a few pounds could be squeezed out of it. "I told you, I wish to help you with Amanda. How rough is she?" she asked, not caring at all. "Can she be presented in real society? Otherwise, we will not be able to find her a suitor."

Cliff shook his head. "I do not want you anywhere near Amanda, Lady Belford. There is no *we*. I trust you as much as I do a viper. No, I trust you even less."

She stared at him, hating him, thinking about fucking him until he wept in pleasure and then coldly rejecting him while he begged for her attentions again.

"You are only here because you have heard Amanda has some small fortune. Do you think I am a fool?" He laughed coldly, without mirth.

Dulcea made one final attempt, knowing she would soon unsheathe her claws and wanting to do nothing more than scratch his handsome face. "I have every right to help you launch her, sir. I have every right to make the decisions that affect her future."

"You have no rights!" Cliff exclaimed, his cheeks flushed with anger.

She curled her long nails into her palms. "How long have you been in her bed, de Warenne?"

His eyes widened.

She laughed with savage pleasure. "I know you are bedding her. I have heard she is beautiful and young. You used to prefer women like myself, but suddenly, it is the innocent you pursue. And I am the despicable one?" she purred, her pulse pounding, for she saw that she had fueled his anger and it was explosive.

He raised his hands as if he meant to push her into the wall. "Yes, she is young, very young—all of eighteen. She is my ward, Lady Belford! I am trying to find her a husband!"

Dulcea was surprised, because he seemed truly affronted, but she stepped so close to him that her breasts brushed his chest. He jerked. "If I let it be known that you are having a torrid affair with Miss Carre, she'll be ruined, Cliff."

He seized her arm, causing her to gasp with pain, pushing her against the wall. "Like hell! I am not sharing Amanda's bed."

Dulcea laughed, thrilling now. "Even if you aren't, who will believe *you?*"

"You dare to blackmail me?" he gasped, his gaze glittering with fury. Dulcea was certain there was lust there, too. His grip eased slightly. He smiled coldly. "What do you want, Dulcea?"

She hesitated, then moved her hip against his loins. To her shock, they were not full.

His mirthless smile increased. "You could be the last woman in the land and I would not touch you."

She cried out in rage. "I am her mother!" she spat. "I should control her prospects and her estate."

Cliff laughed, releasing her. "I was right. You are heartless, conniving…and I am too much of a gentleman to continue. You will not spread your nasty lies, Dulcea, because if you do, I will make certain Belford knows the truth about you—all of it."

She froze, suddenly afraid.

"That's right. He will know of every single affair, your affair with Carre—and Amanda. Now get out."

"You bastard," she breathed. "You are no gentleman."

"Get out," he said softly, dangerously, "before I throw you out myself."

She shook with rage, but she believed him, because his eyes were dark with fury. She hurried out of Harmon House, climbing into the carriage.

"Lady Belford?" her driver asked pleasantly.

"Shut up," she cried.

She had to think. She wasn't in Cliff's arms, his huge manhood filling her. He wasn't on his knees, burying his face in her sex. And he did not seem to be in Amanda's bed—but something was going on, she could smell it. It was as if he cared about her damned bastard, while he despised her! Most importantly, he was keeping Amanda's dowry securely under lock and key.

"I will have revenge," she spat, trembling. "Harris! Take me to Lady Ferris," she cried.

The baroness of Lidden-Way was the biggest gossip in town. She didn't dare spread any lies, but after all, the truth had a way of revealing itself and no one would be able to prove that she had revealed it.

The baroness was going to love the fact that de Warenne was launching a pirate's daughter.

Dulcea finally breathed and she finally smiled.

AMANDA WAS LIGHT on her feet, but because she had been told to stretch her body to an impossible height, to keep her spine stiff, and to somehow keep a book on her head while waltzing, she couldn't follow the dance master now.

"One two three, one two three," he kept saying, but before he ever reached the second "three," the book fell from her head to the floor.

He released her. "Miss Carre! The waltz is terribly simple. All you have to do is master three steps and stay erect! How difficult can it be?"

Amanda flushed, retrieving the book. She knew the steps, she just couldn't comprehend how to move her feet and not move her back or her head while doing so. It seemed impossible and she was discouraged, but she would not give up. Ladies had to dance, and they had to dance well. Sooner or later, she was going to master the waltz. However, she knew everyone in Cliff's family was hoping she would be ready to attend the Carrington ball, and that was only weeks away.

Mr. Burns sighed. "Shall we?"

Amanda put the book oh so carefully on her head and placed one hand on his shoulder, the other in his palm. He smiled briefly, his expression strained, and chanted, "One two three."

The book fell, clattering on the floor.

"I am sorry!" Amanda cried, flushing with humiliation again. She had never felt clumsier until she straightened. Clutching the book to her chest, her heart stopped. Dismayed, she saw that Cliff stood on the ballroom's threshold, apparently watching her.

She felt her cheeks flame, but there were so many other reactions, as well. She always thrilled to glimpse him, and her heart told her that now, speeding as their eyes met. "How long have you been standing there?" she managed.

He sent her the most beautiful smile she had ever received. "A few minutes," he said, slowly crossing the room, his gaze never wandering from hers.

Amanda became still. There was something powerful and magnetic about his approach, his long, lazy strides, and the intent way he was looking at her. *She couldn't help wishing he had agreed to become her husband.* The moment the terrible and unbidden thought occurred, she shoved it far away. He was her guardian, her protector and her champion. He was her friend. Nothing more, and she must always remember that.

But he seemed entranced as he approached, and she somehow knew he was coming to take her into his arms. His gaze remaining on hers, he said, "I will show Miss Carre the waltz, Mr. Burns. You may leave us."

Burns nodded, swiftly leaving but hiding a smile Amanda did not comprehend.

Cliff paused before her, reaching toward her. Before she knew it, he had taken the book from her hands. Another heart-wrenching smile came her way. "It is a beautiful dance, an elegant dance," he murmured, walking away. He placed the book on one of the many velvet chairs lining the huge room.

Amanda's heart was racing with intense anticipation now. As he returned to her, she somehow whispered, "You will teach me to waltz?" She had dreamed so many times of the dance they would share at the Carrington ball and it had felt as if she must wait an eternity for that single dance. But finally, she would be in his arms, dancing across the room.

If she managed to keep up with him.

He smiled again, taking her left hand and placing it on his broad shoulder, then taking her right in his palm. "Do you object?" he asked softly.

Her heart leaped wildly. She was in his arms and there was no place she would rather be. "How could I possibly object?" she murmured, aware that no more than a single inch separated their bodies. Hers had heated, yearning for more than he was ever going to give her.

But it was all right. This was better than nothing.

His soft smile played again and his eyes warmed impossibly more. His gaze holding hers, he started to dance with her.

He did not count or chant. He waltzed across the floor and Amanda found herself whirling effortlessly with him, their steps so light and perfect, miraculously synchronized, so that the floor seemed to vanish and they were dancing in clouds.

She laughed as he whirled her about the room and he smiled back, into her eyes. They floated and swirled, back and forth, again and again, the dance effortless, perfect and magical. And

Amanda never missed a step. She did not trip or falter. She felt as if she had been dancing this way with Cliff forever and ever. She could not look away from his beloved, handsome face. He would always take her breath away. He was so beautiful and she had never loved him more.

Amanda did not know how long they danced—it could have been five minutes, it could have been an hour. She knew she could waltz with Cliff forever.

Cliff suddenly glanced past her. He faltered.

She cried out, as he had stepped on her toes. He seized her shoulders, preventing her from falling. "I am sorry!" he exclaimed. "I have hurt you!" He seemed shocked by what he had done.

She clung as he righted her. "I am fine," she said breathlessly, and she turned to look at the threshold of the room to see what had distracted him.

A tall, dark, imposing man stood there, splendidly dressed, as regal as a king. He wasn't smiling. He was watching them closely. She knew it was the Earl of Adare.

Amanda trembled.

The earl came forward, his gaze quickly drifting over her from head to toe before moving to his son. Amanda stood breathlessly besides Cliff, aware of being inspected and praying she would not be found lacking. She stole a glance at Cliff and was surprised. He looked almost as Alexi did when about to be set down. He seemed guilty of some small crime, for he was flushing.

Cliff was a hero—her hero. After all, he was a great privateer and a wealthy and powerful man. She knew he loved, admired and respected his father but now, she saw he was still the son of a great and titled nobleman. But why did he expect to be reprimanded? All he had done was teach her to waltz.

Cliff inclined his head in a show of vast respect and deference. "My lord," he said. "This is Miss Carre. Amanda, my father, Adare."

Instantly Amanda sank into the lowest curtsy she could manage, hoping to touch her nose to the floor.

"Miss Carre, I have heard all about you from my wife, and I am delighted that you have become a member of this family," the earl said pleasantly, smiling.

Cliff had taken her elbow, undoubtedly to prevent her from crashing face-first into the floor, and she stood up. "Thank you, my lord," she stammered. This great man seemed to be speaking as if he really welcomed her into his home!

He smiled at her again, the light reaching his vivid blue eyes. "Mary is very fond of you, my dear, and if that is so, I share in her affections. I hope you have been given all that you need to make your stay a comfortable one?"

She blinked and nodded. "More than enough, sir," she whispered, beginning to realize he looked intimidating but that he might actually be as kind as the rest of his family.

He turned his blue gaze to Cliff, his smile fading a bit. His hand clasped Cliff's shoulder with affection. "I am so pleased to see you. I was certainly surprised when I arrived today to learn that you are here," he added.

Cliff seemed to have recovered his composure. "Duty brought me to town a bit sooner that I had planned, as you surely know." He smiled. "And I have brought Alexi and Ariella with me."

The earl of Adare beamed. "I have already met your children. Alexi reminds me of you, exactly, and Ariella seems to be an angel."

Cliff smiled proudly. "My daughter is an angel—a brilliant one, and yes, I am afraid Alexi might become a bit wayward."

The earl chuckled and turned to Amanda, who was listening raptly to the two men. "I have not seen my son in a year and a half. I have some matters I wish to discuss with him. Would you excuse us?"

Amanda nodded, as she would never defy this man. She curtsied again, this time naturally. "Of course. My lord? Thank you for having me. Your home is wonderful…I do adore your entire family!"

Edward smiled again, and briefly, so did Cliff. "And by the by, you are a beautiful dancer," the earl said with approval.

Amanda flushed with pleasure and stole a glance at Cliff to share her joy with him, then left.

Cliff stared after Amanda, aware of being proud of her most recent achievement. "I was certain she would be a graceful dancer," he said, more to himself than his father.

"I have never seen two people dance so beautifully together," the earl remarked, also watching her leaving the room. "Indeed, the two of you look as if you have been waltzing together for years."

Cliff tensed. "Obviously, we have but known one another for a few months." He hesitated, afraid of what his father might be thinking. Then he said, "You should see her with a sword. She could outfence Ty."

The earl's brows lifted. "You are entranced."

Cliff knew his color increased. "She is my ward, sir. I am launching her into society, as Mother must have told you. I am very pleased with her accomplishments." But he tugged at his shirt collar.

"Miss Carre is beautiful and sweet," the earl remarked. "I cannot imagine her wielding a sword. She also seems entranced by you, Cliff." His tone was firm, even stern.

"We were enjoying the waltz," Cliff said tersely. "She has never waltzed before. The countess has surely told you Amanda's story."

"Then you are a good teacher." The earl clasped his shoulder. "Your mother has told me of the bond of affection you share. How vast is that bond?"

Cliff hesitated. "Father, I am not a boy of fourteen anymore." A warning had slipped into his tone.

"I am aware of that," the earl exclaimed. "Cliff, of all my sons, you were the one always jumping the highest fence on your hack, jumps no boy should have dared! It wasn't Ty or Rex I found in the bed of one of my guest's wives, it was you—or have you forgotten that summer when you came home at sixteen? Ty did not run off and neither did Rex, but you had to leave home at fourteen. Although I understood then and I understand now, I did ask you to wait another year or two. I have always been proud of you, but you have given Mary and I many sleepless nights, too. Of course I must worry about my most willful and independent son!"

"You need not worry now. Amanda is my ward and I have vowed to secure a bright future for her. And while I am fond of Miss Carre, I am her guardian, and I am seeking a marriage for her." He hesitated. "I am sorry I worried you and the countess so often as a boy."

"Have you been in her bed?" the earl asked quietly but abruptly.

Cliff flushed anew, about to say no when he realized he would be lying to the earl. He had never lied to Edward and he never would. He could not, not even when he was younger and his scandalous behavior had merited severe discipline from his father.

Edward's eyes widened with comprehension.

Cliff said quickly, "She is innocent. I would never take her innocence, no matter the temptation."

"But you have been in her bed," Edward stated. "Mary is right."

"I am trying to behave honorably!" Cliff retorted, now worried about what the countess had said. "I rescued her from a mob at her father's hanging. I declared myself her guardian when I did not have to do so—I could have left her a penniless orphan in Jamaica! I had hoped to reunite her with her mother, but her mother is the worst of women, a conniving weasel and Amanda has suffered enough heartbreak. I realize I fall far short of your standards. Yes, I have been in her bed. But she remains innocent and it will not happen again."

Edward sighed. "I know you mean it. Cliff, I am very proud of your taking Miss Carre in and providing for her as you have. You have done the right and noble deed in offering to foster Miss Carre and launch her. But I am hoping to protect Miss Carre from any possible ruin. And frankly, although you seem immune to the gossip whispered behind your back, I should like to protect you, as well."

"I can protect myself," Cliff exclaimed, truly surprised.

"Do not even try to tell me you do not care about the gossip. I know you are wealthy enough to withstand it, but I also know that it gets beneath your skin, which is not as thick as you would like me and everyone else to believe."

He flushed, because every now and then, the whispers more than annoyed him. He might be an island privateer, but he was, by damn, the earl's youngest and wealthiest son. "I do not need your protection," he insisted, meaning it.

"Perhaps not. But I wish to give it, and I always will." His gaze was searching. "I see the way you look at her, Cliff. Considering your penchant for seduction, what should I have thought upon seeing you dancing together?"

"I will not ruin Amanda," he said grimly. "But she is tempting. I admit it. However, if the day ever comes where I am such a cad, that is the day I will make her my wife."

For a long moment, Edward stared, his gaze searching. "So that is how you are thinking?" His face softened.

Cliff became terribly uncomfortable. "I have no intention of marrying anyone. I prefer my life exactly as it is. I am thinking of finding her the proper husband. But she is my ward." He paused. "And we are friends."

The earl stared at him for a moment. Then he clasped Cliff's arm. "It is early, but will you join me for a glass of wine?"

Cliff relaxed. "It *is* very early," he agreed, aware of being let off the hook. "But as you pointed out, it has been some time since I was home."

They crossed the ballroom, heading toward a pair of great doors. "I understand you have given Miss Carre a dowry that includes an estate. You are going to great lengths for your ward," Edward remarked.

"There is no other way to secure her future. In truth, it is my pleasure to provide for her," Cliff said easily.

The earl smiled. "I am beginning to realize that. Have you ever considered the possibility that you are in love with her?"

Cliff jerked, caught upon that hook once more, where he squirmed. "Of course not," he said, aware of his heart speeding. They entered the great hall. "I am not like Tyrell or my stepbrothers, to fall madly in love and never look back. I know the family legend is that the de Warenne men love only once and it is forever." He laughed, but it sounded shaky to his own ears. "I have never been in love and I do not expect to ever fall in love."

"Of course you don't. You have decided that you are different from all of the de Warenne men. If you wish, I can help you arrange a marriage for her," Edward said, casting a sidelong glance at him. "Considering her charms and the uniqueness of this relationship, it might be best to marry her off immediately and end this guardianship—and friendship."

Cliff stiffened. Adare never failed in any objective. If he asked the earl to find Amanda a husband, he would do so, and swiftly. For the first time in his life, he told his father a significant lie. "I have a list of possible suitors, although I have yet to carefully analyze it, or other prospects. I can manage, but thank you."

Edward shrugged. "If you change your mind, you need only ask. I am sure a choice of suitable prospects can be found."

"Thank you, but no," Cliff said. "I have the matter firmly in hand."

The earl merely smiled.

"And Edward? Amanda and I will remain friends after she is wed."

"Of course," the earl said.

## *CHAPTER SIXTEEN*

ASHTON WAS A TYPICAL English village, small and quaint, the shops proudly maintained, freshly painted with flowers in the window boxes. The carriage drive from the village to Ashford Hall was but ten minutes, along a charming country road, high, clipped hedges offering the slightest view into the stately homes of the local gentry. But the moment Cliff's coach turned into the sparsely graveled drive leading to the hall, passing two chipped brick pillars, the engraved plaque so worn it could barely be read, he knew the manor was in dire straits.

The grounds alongside the rutted drive were overgrown in places, bare in others. Ahead, a grim gray stone house awaited them. He glanced at Amanda with a frown, but she was leaning toward her window, her face flushed with excitement. He silently cursed, wishing he'd had the foresight to come and inspect the estate alone, before ever allowing her to see it. He'd sent word, however, and they were expected.

Amanda sat beside him, fidgeting as she had ever since they'd been a few miles from Ashton. Ariella and Anahid followed in another coach, with Michelle, Cliff's valet and Amanda's new maid. Alexi had begged to stay at Harmon House, as he and Ned were now inseparable, and upon swearing fervently to behave and obey his uncles and grandmother without question, he had been allowed to remain behind.

Cliff allowed himself to glance at Amanda again. Every time he looked at her, he thought about the two times he had been in her bed and then he thought about Garret MacLachlan. He was not happy with himself, as he was introspective enough to know that a certain degree of jealousy had caused him to deny MacLachlan his suit. Had the Scot called on any other ward, had he another one, he would have allowed the courtship, dismissing the man's strained finances, for his other attributes far outweighed the lack of economy and wealth. In fact, a man with MacLachlan's obvious character was exactly the kind of suitor he wished for Amanda.

He turned away, staring at the gray stone house, noting the roof needed extreme repairs. As it was about to rain, he would undoubtedly learn whether it leaked or not. He was glad to be distracted from his previous thoughts and the fact that, deep within himself, he was ashamed of his behavior.

"We're here," Amanda whispered, so excited her tone was hoarse.

"The grounds are terribly neglected," he commented as the coach halted.

She met his gaze, her eyes sparkling. He realized she wished to fly out of the coach and into the house. Before he could caution her to prepare herself for the worst—and to tell her he would find her a far better property—their door was opened. Amanda leaped from the coach, forgetting her new manners, and he smiled, his heart turning over hard, as it was so often doing these days. He followed her more slowly as their second carriage also halted, the front door to the house now opening. A servant came out, wearing a shabby, ill-fitting suit.

As Ariella, Anahid and Michelle alighted, he and Amanda walked up to the hall. He already knew it had been built in the previous century and had once been walled, but he saw no sign of the original walls. The house was two stories, mostly rectangular, and as melancholy as a home could be. He hated it—it would not do, even if there were three tenant farmers. Amanda deserved far better.

"My lord." The servant came quickly forward, bowing eagerly. Instantly, Cliff thought him inebriated, and a moment later, he smelled the ale on the man's breath.

"Miss Carre, this is Watkins, I believe."

"Yes, I am Watkins, and I have prepared rooms so you may all stay overnight, rather than go to the village inn. My wife is preparing a small supper. My lord, I hope that meets with your approval?"

"That is fine," Cliff said curtly, aware of Amanda standing breathlessly beside him, almost incapable of restraining herself. "Why are these grounds in such a state of neglect?"

Watkins's face fell. "As you know, the previous owner has passed, sir, and the heir resides in town. He only wishes to sell, not to repair."

Cliff was not impressed; he gestured the servant to precede them inside. As they followed, he took Amanda's hand. "Do not be discouraged," he said softly.

She beamed at him, broke free, and hurried after Watkins.

He realized she was not in the least bit discouraged and he was surprised.

He followed the pair into a moderately sized great hall, a rusting coat of armor beside the front door, a pair of swords over the stone hearth. He scowled, looking up at the cobwebs hanging from the rafters and in the corners of the room. The walls needed cleaning and whitewashing, two of the beams overhead were obviously rotten, and the wood floors were heavily scarred and had not been waxed in years. A single trestle table was in the room, and the six chairs did not match, the various types of upholstery faded and torn. He was furious with his agent and with Watkins. "You have had two days notice that we would be here this afternoon. Why is this room not clean?"

Watkins cringed. "My lord, there are no housemaids. I oversee the property, that is all."

"I see bones in the corner there," he said. It appeared someone had thrown their leftovers on the floor a very long time ago.

"The previous owner left a dog, sir. He comes and goes."

"I will not be requiring your services tonight," Cliff said.

Watkins drew himself up, clearly about to protest.

"You and your wife may take the evening off. I suggest you vacate these premises now," Cliff said softly in a tone that was unmistakably dangerous.

Watkins fled and Ariella skipped into the room, then wrinkled her nose. "Pew! It smells in here, Papa!" She glanced around. "You will buy this for Miss Carre?"

Cliff realized Amanda had already rushed down the hall and was in one of the adjacent rooms. "Of course not," he said. He smiled at his daughter. "Maybe you should play outside while I fetch Amanda. We will be staying at the village inn after all."

Ariella hesitated. "Papa, she was so happy to come here today! She told me so…she will be so unhappy if we leave."

He went to Ariella and hoisted her into his arms. "Darling, I believe she will be thrilled to leave," he said, hugging her.

Ariella shook her head. "This estate means everything to her, Papa. She told me how her home in Jamaica was taken away from her. Papa, she has no real home of her own!"

Cliff stared at his clever daughter. "But she lives with us now," he finally said.

Ariella brightened. "I know that, so why can't she just stay with us? Why can't Harmon House and Windsong be her homes?"

He tensed. "I am certain you are aware of what a dowry is, Ariella. I am providing such a dowry for Amanda."

Ariella's brows knit. "So she can marry someone…I know what a dowry is. Papa, doesn't Miss Carre make you happy?"

Surprised and even uncomfortable, he set her down. "I am very fond of her."

Ariella smiled. "You are always watching her and smiling. You seem very happy."

Cliff became still. Did his own small daughter guess at his

feelings for his ward? "You make me happy, darling," he said, hoping to distract her.

But she tugged his hand. "Do you love Miss Carre?"

He was aghast. "What kind of question is that?"

"Alexi and I were wondering if you should marry her, instead of finding her a husband like the Scot, whom you so hate."

"Have you been eavesdropping?" he asked, stunned.

"I can't help it if everyone in the family talks about you and Miss Carre in front of me," she said with a grin. Then she sobered. "I wouldn't mind."

He tugged at his collar, opening it. "You wouldn't mind what?"

"I wouldn't mind Miss Carre being my mother, and Alexi wouldn't mind, either."

He stared, at a complete loss for words.

Ariella stared back, clearly waiting for a response on his part.

He knelt, so they were eye to eye. "Darling....do you wish to have a mother? Haven't I been a good father? Isn't Anahid exactly like a mother?"

Ariella shook her head. "I love Anahid, and I know she loves me, but she is not my mother. She is my friend—and even so, you *employ* her, Papa."

He touched her cheek. "Am I failing you?" he asked, stricken over the possibility.

She shook her head again. "You are the best papa in the world! But I so like Miss Carre and you seem to love her! I couldn't help thinking how nice it would be if we were a real family."

He stood, thinking about Garret MacLachlan. He couldn't help his next thoughts. *If he would not allow her to marry Garret or a man like him, then he should do the deed. Otherwise he must allow her a man of strength, will and character.*

But he did not want to marry, not ever! He felt real panic at the thought. "I am not planning to marry Amanda or anyone, Ariella," he said firmly, but even as he spoke, his heart leaped in a protest he refused to comprehend.

Her face fell. "Oh."

"Why don't you go outside and wait for us?" he suggested.

When she was gone, he took a moment to compose himself, wishing his daughter had not spoken up as she had. As for MacLachlan, he owed it to Amanda to seriously rethink his position in regards to the Scot's suit.

"Cliff! Come quickly!" she cried.

He raced from the hall, uncertain as to whether she was in distress or greatly excited. He raced into the adjacent room and found her in a library, standing beside the terrace doors. Two walls were lined with shelves and filled with books. A very old, faded Oriental rug was on the floor, a single simple desk in the midst of the room, an elegant carved chair behind it. One wall had a door which opened onto a slate terrace, a gazebo in the distance beyond. A fireplace with a beautifully carved wood mantel was on the other wall.

Amanda whirled, facing him, her eyes wide. "Look at this room!" she cried, and he saw her eyes shining with unshed tears.

He hurried to her. "Dar..." he began. Realizing he had almost called her *darling*, he began anew, in consternation now. "Amanda, have no fear. This house will not do. I was misled, as was my agent. We will find you another estate, one in far better condition."

"But you didn't see the rose garden!" she cried, pointing out of the glass door. "Cliff, look!"

He stared past her and saw an overgrown and neglected garden, one filled with rose bushes, many of which were in bloom.

"Cliff!" she begged, seizing his hands. "I don't want another estate...I want Ashford Hall! I love it!"

AMANDA WAS ONLY VAGUELY aware of Cliff behind her as she went up the stairs, which were covered with a torn and worn red runner. She did not see the holes or tears, she saw the red wool, her favorite color, the wool terribly expensive and fine. She saw the beautifully carved banister, the wood so smooth beneath her hand from a century of use. Her heart had been racing uncontrollably for the past hour, ever since she had arrived at the hall, and she felt faint. The manor was so beautiful! It was the most beautiful home she could imagine. Her favorite part was the library and the rose garden outside.

She prayed Cliff would approve.

She paused on the threshold of the first bedchamber, where a bed with thick ebony posters, beautifully carved, was made up in dusky gold covers and pillows. Darker gold draperies fluttered at the single window, and a single chair in faded bronze brocade was in the corner. Amanda bit her lip, instantly in love with the room, hoping it would be hers.

Cliff walked past her, over a rug so faded it was nondescript beige, and he pushed a velvet drape aside. Dust billowed. A piece of the drapery came apart in his hand.

Amanda knew he hated the house. She hurried to his side and peered out at the back lawns, terribly overgrown but lush and green, and at the charming gazebo, which had probably been white once upon a time and now matched the rug under her feet. "There's a pond," she cried in delight.

Cliff sighed. "Yes, there is, and I have little doubt it is but muck and scum."

She faced him defensively. "It can be filled with fresh water—and fish!"

His face softened. "Of course it can. Amanda, do you really prefer this estate?"

"Yes, I do," she cried.

He studied her. "Don't you think it wise to view a few other choices?"

She folded her arms across her chest. "Cliff, you said it was a good price. And there are three farms. I love it here. It's so quiet, so peaceful…so English." She thought of the rose garden again, and couldn't help it, she thought of her mother.

The hurt roiled and she told herself, *don't*. She wasn't going to let Dulcea Belford ruin this wonderful moment. She was becoming a lady now and this was exactly the kind of home she envisioned for herself.

She stared down at the blooming roses, some pink, some white, others red and yellow. She could not wait to take a chair and go outside to sit there and read a new book.

Cliff touched her arm. "We can sit together before supper and make a list of necessary repairs and the furnishings we will need to buy."

Amanda jerked, her gaze flying to his, and when he smiled at her warmly, she felt herself melt. "Does this mean you will purchase the estate for my dowry?"

"If you still insist, after our discussion, then, yes, I will."

She threw her arms around him and hugged him hard. Instantly, she was acutely aware of his hard male body. Being in his arms still felt dangerous and worse, it still felt so right. She would never forget the waltz they had shared, either. She had replayed it a hundred times in her mind since the other day.

*I love you so much*, she thought, and had to bite her tongue to prevent herself from saying the words aloud. Instead, overcome with emotion, she looked him in the eye. "Cliff, how will I ever repay you?"

He pulled away so that she did not continue to grasp his arms. "The only repayment I wish, is for you to be happy," he said, appearing uncomfortable.

"I am happy. You have taken me into your home, your family has been kind and welcoming, and I was even a success in society. And now, dear Lord, there is this house." She beamed. "A home of my own."

But she felt her smile fade. Yes, Ashford Hall would be hers if she insisted—Cliff had made that clear—but she was going to have to marry one day, probably sooner rather than later. She didn't have to think about it to know that she would miss Cliff terribly after she was wed. But she would have this house—a home of her own. And eventually, there would be wonderful children. She wanted a son just like Alexi and a daughter just like Ariella. And whenever Cliff was in London, she would call on him. London was only a half day's coach ride away.

Cliff slowly walked away from her, appearing as if he had something he wished to say. When he did not speak, she went to the bed and sat down on it, just to test the mattress. It was far too soft and would have to be replaced, she realized, but her dismay had more to do with her marriage than the mattress.

Then she looked up and saw him staring, his blue eyes bright.

Instantly, she felt his virile interest and she was fiercely glad that that had not changed between them. At least she had his friendship and his desire, even if he wouldn't act on it.

"I want to ask you something," he said quietly.

Amanda realized he was uncomfortable, but not because he was grappling with his wayward male nature. "You can ask me anything," she said, bemused. She slipped off of the bed, turning to reshape the pillow she had leaned on.

"Amanda."

His tone was so serious and so odd. She faced him, some concern beginning. "What is it?"

He forced a smile, then it vanished. "Do you wish to see Garret MacLachlan again?"

She was surprised by the subject. "Of course I do," she said, bewildered. "He is very gallant, and like you, he is kind." She thought about his call. She had genuinely enjoyed his company, even if she had felt as if she were somehow betraying Cliff. "And he is handsome," she added.

Cliff was flushing. "I denied him the right to call on you, Amanda," he said tersely, "but he is an eligible bachelor. He is also the son of an earl—the eldest son. He has no real means, but his character is upright and he has that title."

Amanda became afraid. "What are you asking me?" She

hugged herself. "Are you thinking of choosing him as a husband?" Panic began. She couldn't marry yet—it was far too soon!

"He hasn't stated that his intentions are matrimonial ones," Cliff said, his face set in a grimace. "But I suspect he is very taken with you, and his intentions might become such."

She realized she was trembling. Garret MacLachlan was so like Cliff, but he wasn't Cliff! "I don't even know him," she managed, her knees useless now.

Cliff crossed the room and caught her, supporting her weight. "I am trying to be honorable," he ground out. "The man is a Scot, with a title, and he could take care of you. You would have to live very modestly, but you would be safe for the rest of your life. A man like that would always take care of his wife."

She clasped her flaming cheeks. "Scotland is far away, isn't it?"

"It is far away, yes, and MacLachlan lives in the west. By ship, however, I believe you could reach his estate in days."

Amanda began shaking her head. "I don't want to live in Scotland," she whispered. "I want to live here, close to London." And close to Harmon House, she thought, close to Cliff.

Relief appeared in his eyes. "It is a barbarian, backward land," he said. "You are certain?"

"I have never been more sure of anything!" she cried.

He put his arm around her and she leaned against his body, overcome with relief. "Good," he said, sounding as relieved. "It is settled, then."

Amanda closed her eyes, her cheek resting against the very fine blue wool of his jacket. She was breathless from the fear she had been afflicted with, but now, she became aware of being pressed completely against Cliff's hard, powerful body and that he had one arm around her. Slowly, she looked up.

He stared down, his blue eyes far too bright. For one instant, she knew he was going to bend over her and kiss her. He shifted his weight, his eyes flamed and he leaned closer.

But she was wrong.

He released her instead and walked out of the room.

AMANDA HAD BEEN GIVEN the gold bedroom after all. Michelle had found six servants and they had transformed the manor, cleaning every speck of dirt, waxing the furniture, mopping and polishing the floors. The difference was miraculous, making her love Ashford Hall even more. While they had taken their supper at the village inn, they had returned to the Hall to pass the night. Everyone had retired an hour or so ago and the house was now achingly silent.

Amanda could not sleep. Hugging her knees to her chest, she thought about the odd conversation with Cliff earlier in that very room. He had not wanted her to agree to a suit from MacLachlan, she realized, and she was beginning to wonder why.

He had seemed to despise Garret on sight. When they had been strolling in the gardens outside of Harmon House, Amanda had seen him watching them from the terrace, and she had felt his intense interest and his equally intense suspicion. Today he had looked so unhappy and grim when asking her if she wished to marry the other man. She laid her face on her knees, and she couldn't help wondering if he was jealous.

She was aware that he remained terribly attracted to her. So often, when he looked at her, she knew exactly what he was thinking—he wanted to take her to bed, in that moment, not a second later. Not only did their attraction remain, it had become stronger with every passing day, impossibly and achingly so.

And as inexperienced as she was, she also knew he found her very pretty in her new gowns. Cliff was approving and admiring of the changes she was making and she had begun to feel comfortable in her dresses and shoes. Recently, it had required less thought to speak and act like a lady.

*You are beautiful…beyond words.*

Amanda had been thrilled when he had softly praised her, and she was as thrilled now, recalling not just his words, but the way he had been looking at her when he had spoken them. There had been so much admiration in his eyes. He had been gazing at her as if he felt the way she did about him.

Of course, he wasn't in love with her. He was fond of her, that much was clear, and he wanted her, so it was very possible that he was jealous of MacLachlan's interest. Amanda did not have to be terribly experienced to know that men did not need much incitement to consider one another rivals, whether for territory, a prize or a female.

She shivered, smiling, because she would not mind his being a bit jealous.

But was he as aware as she was of the changes in their relationship? She wondered. Somehow, their friendship seemed to be growing by leaps and bounds. There seemed to be so much warmth between them. Amanda could not even begin to count the times their gazes would meet and they would share a silent thought, a mutual comprehension or a knowing smile. A dozen times a day she would suddenly turn to find Cliff there, watching her, and he would smile at her, his eyes filled with warmth or admiration or affection. Amanda knew she loved him—she would never stop—but he certainly seemed to care for her far more than he ever had.

She felt certain she was not imagining it.

Which was why this was so hard, she thought in real confusion. He was her benefactor, her guardian, her friend, but she had never loved him more. And the fact that they shared such affection, and that he was so virile and continued to desire her, only deepened her confusion. She wished she didn't have to marry anyone. She wished she could remain his ward forever, so things would stay like this and never change, even if at times like now, in the chill of midnight, it was so physically challenging.

She hugged her knees more tightly to her chest, finding it impossible not to think about the night he had been in her bed, his hard body probing hers, hot, huge and slick, so close to taking her innocence. And that time on the ship, when she had believed it to be a dream, his mouth on her thighs, his tongue devouring her sex. Amanda bit her lip to keep from crying out, wishing once again that they could be lovers, at least. But he was simply too honorable. Besides, she knew now that being his lover, even if for a time, would be impossibly heartbreaking. Or would it?

Amanda took a pillow into her arms and lay down, hugging it and wishing she could redirect her thoughts, but it was far too late. Every night, it seemed, she fell asleep dreaming of his kisses and his body, her own blood raging. But she was a lady now. Ladies obviously suffered through such bouts of physical desire, at least until they were wed.

Amanda could not imagine herself in a husband's bed. The only man she could imagine herself in bed with was Cliff. But he would never marry her, no matter that she was almost a lady now. It felt as if years had passed since that night when she had learned of Dulcea's rejection and the following day, when he had refused to become her lover.

A simple solution occurred to her, shocking her. What if she tried one more time? She could have Ashford Hall and not get married at all—if Cliff would keep her as a mistress.

The pillow slipped to the floor. He wanted her but was refusing to act on his passion because he thought it better that she wed. He was being noble. It probably was better, from society's point of view, and even she realized that if she became his mistress, she'd have to give up this new dream of being a lady. A part of her didn't want to give up that dream. But the truth was, she didn't want to marry someone else.

And she heard his footsteps in the hall.

Amanda tensed. She had not a doubt that he was going downstairs because he couldn't sleep, too—and she knew why. She hesitated, the lady she was becoming truly protesting what she had to do. If she got up now, if she worked her wiles as she never had before, that dream would end.

But she loved and wanted Cliff, not Garret MacLachlan or anyone else.

Amanda swallowed, shaken. She slid from the bed and started across the room, then she opened the door wide.

Cliff was already past the doorway, clad only in his pale doeskin breeches, his beautifully muscular torso bare, as were his feet. But he stopped, turning toward her.

She couldn't smile or speak. She could only stare, wishing for the impossible, afraid of her choice but determined to go forward. She had only to convince him that her plan was the better one and from the blaze of light in his eyes, it might not be as difficult as she had thought.

He was motionless.

The hall was lit by wax candles dripping in their sconces and glass lanterns. Although shadows danced around them, he was clearly visible.

His brilliant blue eyes slid to her mouth and to the lace detailing at the edge of her new pink nightgown's silk bodice, then lower, to the ruches over her breasts. Amanda dared to breathe, hard. She somehow lifted her hand. Her nipples were so tight and erect the silk was abrasive and hurtful. She forgot about choices. There was only the man she loved and the huge throbbing tension that stood between them. "Cliff…"

He shook his head in negation, eyes wide, staring at the peaks before looking back at her eyes.

She wet her lips, managed to speak. "Come to my bed," she somehow whispered.

He inhaled harshly. She saw a strong arousal form against his pale breeches. "I am your *guardian.*"

She wet her lips again. "I don't want to marry anyone else," she breathed.

"We'll discuss this…tomorrow," he said thickly.

"I could stay here…and I could be your mistress," she whispered. "You could keep me."

He flinched. It was a moment before he spoke, his cheeks dully red. "Go back to bed, Amanda." But he did not move.

She simply stood there. "Do you like my new nightgown?" she asked softly.

His color deepened. He was breathing hard, the two broad slabs of his chest rising and falling, as if he'd just run a great distance.

She realized he could have walked away, but he hadn't. She touched the pink silk at her waist, smoothed it down to her hip. Then she looked up.

He was staring, his eyes so hot she thought the hall might burst into flames. A part of her felt awful for so shamelessly trying to seduce him. One moment stretched into an eternity as she waited to see if she would triumph over him. But his next actions weren't clear. He turned his back to her and leaned his forehead against the wall, panting.

Amanda went to him and put her arms around him and leaned her face against his back, followed by her entire body. He flinched when her breasts flattened there and she thrilled, her hands on his tight stomach. He whirled, taking her in his arms, a look of fury and despair on his face, in his eyes. "Damn it!"

Then he cradled her face in his two large hands, holding her so she could not move, and he began to kiss her.

The kiss was hot, hard, demanding and filled with both passion and anger. He opened her mouth, giving her no choice but complete surrender and an even greater response. Amanda tried to kiss him back, gasping in pleasure, but he was controlling the kiss, devouring her, making any response other than a passive one impossible. His tongue went deep.

He released her face, his tongue still deep inside her, grasping her breasts, the silk between his hands and her flesh exquisitely sensuous. Amanda whimpered, gripping his waist. He shoved his hard thigh right between her legs, forcing her to sit astride him.

She began to sob against his mouth, writhing on his leg, rubbing herself there.

He clasped her buttocks and lifted her even higher; her hip brushed his huge erection.

Amanda threw her arms around him and gasped in an explosion of pleasure.

He turned her, pushing her back against the wall, still kissing her, thrusting his leg up higher. She wept as the convulsions intensified.

And when they softened and slowed, he tore his mouth away and held her in his arms, tightly, his cheek against the top of her head, allowing her feet to drop to the floor. The climax fading, she clung to his broad shoulders, new emotions swiftly arising. Being in his arms was the best place in the world. Cocooned by his entire body, she never wanted to be set free.

He gripped her shoulders and pushed her away.

She was still dizzy and faint, not quite coherent. But she looked at him and saw that he remained furious. "Don't," she begged, terrified now. "I don't mind just this, Cliff, just your lovemaking. Please, do not talk of honor now!"

He backed away. "Haven't I hurt you enough? I am only a man, Amanda, and apparently not honorable enough to resist your charms. Damn it! We are here inspecting your dowry—a dowry for you and your future husband—I am *not* making you my mistress! Why do you wish so little for yourself?" he cried.

She had never seen him so enraged, and he was angry with her. "But if I do not mind, truly," she began.

"I mind," he roared.

She flinched, squaring her shoulders. And she made one final attempt, already knowing it was futile. His will was too strong. "I want you. I will always want you. Why is it so wrong?" she cried. "You want me, too, and you care about me, I know you do. We are friends! Good friends!"

"I'm your guardian!" he shouted. "It's my responsibility to find you a husband, not take you as a lover." He was shaking. He jerked on his breeches for some relief. Then he raised his hand, warding her off, preventing her speech.

"You have become a beautiful lady. Why destroy your future this way?" He shook his head. "My family is already mocking my efforts to be noble with you. This is hardly helping!"

After such ecstasy, she was sinking rapidly into despair. It was hard to wrap herself in dignity, but she did. "I have one defense," she said. "I love you."

He inhaled harshly, trembling. "I care for you. Deeply. And that is why I am not making you my mistress," he ground out. "If I need a mistress, there are a hundred suitable trollops in town. I am trying to provide you with a good future, Amanda. But I will not succeed, obviously, if we continue to spend time together as we have this day."

She was trembling. "What does that mean?"

"We should not be alone together. Not ever," he added harshly.

"No!"

He shook his head, his expression telling her that his mind was made up. "I will no longer delay. You need a husband immediately."

Amanda sagged against the wall. "How can you do this?"

He didn't seem to hear her. "I am taking you back to London tomorrow. I will ask Eleanor and my stepmother to comprise a new list of suitors. In fact," he hesitated, "I will solicit Adare in the endeavor. You will be wed within months."

Amanda cried out, horrified.

But he was set against her now. "In the interim, I have a ship making a short run to Holland. I will be on it."

Amanda gasped. "Cliff, please! What about the Carrington ball? It's in three weeks. You promised me the first dance!"

He was as rigid, as unyielding. "I gave you my word. I will be there for the first waltz."

"Don't go," she heard herself whisper.

Their gazes locked. "This is untenable," he said. "I have no other choice."

## *CHAPTER SEVENTEEN*

AMANDA HAD NEVER missed Cliff more.

She knew now that she had made a terrible mistake. He had been gone for more than a week. They had returned to London in separate vehicles, Cliff traveling not with her but with Ariella and Anahid, refusing to even look at her as Monsieur Michelle helped her into the coach they would share. Upon arriving in London, he had gone to bid Alexi farewell, and Amanda had followed him up to the nursery, aware that he had never worn such a harsh, grim expression. Filled with dread, she had stood in the doorway of Alexi's bedchamber, watching him embrace his son. He'd mussed Ned's hair, as well. A brief lecture had followed, with Alexi begging to go with him to Holland, but Cliff had refused. Although he had spent half a day in a coach with Ariella, he had then gone to her room, casting one hard look at Amanda. "You need not follow me through the house."

"Cliff, please don't leave like this," she cried desperately.

His expression had hardened impossibly and he had increased his stride, leaving her standing at one end of the hall, near tears. It had felt like the end of their relationship.

Alexi had tugged at her hand. "What did you do to make Papa so angry?" he had asked in a whisper, wide-eyed.

Amanda could not remember what pitiful excuse she had made.

She had gone to her bedchamber, refusing to cry and wishing she had never tried to seduce him. She had been mad to think she could cause him to violate his sense of honor, she realized. Standing at the window, she had watched him leaving Harmon House with only a small valise. No matter how many times she told herself that when he returned, he would smile at her once more, as if nothing had ever happened, she had the awful sense that their friendship would never be the same. Cliff wasn't just leaving the country for a few weeks, he was putting a great distance between them. No two acts could be more symbolic than his departure and his decision to see her immediately wed. His mind was made up. Very soon, he was going to be walking her down the aisle and giving her over to another man. When he did that, the distance between them would be inviolable and permanent.

Amanda couldn't do it.

She was acutely aware of her heart now. She was deeply in love with Cliff de Warenne and nothing would ever change that. She could not marry a man she neither knew nor loved, not even for the security of a home like Ashford Hall. She had never been sadder, because she couldn't remain at Harmon House this way, either, heartbroken, dependant upon him and still yearning for what would never be.

She was going home, but not until after the ball.

Amanda went to the armoire and slowly took out the beautiful gown she would wear to the Carrington ball. It was the most exquisite dress she had ever seen, elaborate and elegant enough to be a wedding dress, really, with a low square bodice, small cap sleeves, sheer gold chiffon layered over the white floral silk beneath. She had been eagerly anticipating wearing it; she had been sure Cliff's eyes would blaze when he saw her in it. Now, she felt certain he would barely look at her. She had little doubt that he would not be taking the first waltz with her, if he hadn't given her his word.

But Cliff de Warenne never broke his word.

He would be there, and she could imagine how awkward being in his arms would now be. After the ball, she would profess her gratitude for all he had done for her—and then she would say goodbye.

Her heart screamed in protest. Amanda held the ball gown up to her chest and regarded herself in the mirror. She didn't want to be La Sauvage ever again. She didn't want to roam the island like a boy in breeches. She was going home as a lady; if she was allowed to take her wardrobe with her, she would sell most of it and open up a small shop. Otherwise, she would borrow funds. She knew all about sailing and world trade. She would import a small cargo of the most beautiful fabrics—there had never been enough dress shops in Kingston. She would charge the highest prices possible and start saving the profits. As soon as she could, she would buy her own ship and hire the crew to sail it. Once she had her own ship, she could import anything and she would cruise the world, looking for exotic merchandise. Instead of stealing or begging, she would become a merchant, the first female merchant on the island. Ladies weren't merchants, but she would be the exception to the rule, just as Eleanor O'Neill was an exception. As Eleanor had advised, she would be quiet, polite and well dressed in public, and privately she would do as she willed. Only then would she swim in the cove or dive off the cliffs just west of Belle Mer.

A bit of the wild child still existed, she rued, but it no longer mattered.

There was one problem. Sooner or later Cliff would return to Windsong, and she would be drawn there. She imagined herself calling on him in his island manor, a wealthy, independent and respected lady now, a dozen years older, perhaps, wearing jewels she had bought herself. Her heart leaped wildly. She would always be thrilled to see him.

She had to close her eyes, fighting her most powerful dreams that even a dozen years from now, his eyes would light up with admiration and hunger, and he would smile at her in that promising way he had and then pull her into his arms....

Amanda put the ball gown on the bed. She was always going to be tempted to dream of his love, but she had better recognize it was only that, a wild, fanciful dream.

It would be better to focus on the present. Last night she had gone to her first opera with the earl and countess, Lizzie and her husband, Tyrell. Briefly, she had been enthralled enough to forget about Cliff. She had enjoyed herself and there was no opera in Kingston. She was genuinely going to miss his family, she thought, and she would even miss town. A knock sounded on her door, but Amanda did not hear it. Maybe one day Eleanor would come to visit her with Sean and Rogan.

Eleanor appeared in the looking glass, her eyes soft with sympathy.

Instantly, Amanda rearranged her sorrowful expression into a pleasing countenance.

"I did knock. But you didn't answer and I can see you are absorbed in your thoughts." Eleanor touched her as she turned to face her. "You don't have to pretend, Amanda. We all know how unhappy you are. I personally am plotting various ways to bring my brother to all of his senses when he returns."

Amanda continued to smile. "I love my dress," she said, refusing to discuss Cliff. Then she changed her mind. "Cliff has been wonderful to me. Don't be angry with him."

Eleanor's eyes widened. "You need to stop defending him, Amanda. Do you want to tell me exactly what happened at Ashford Hall to make him run away from you this way?"

Amanda felt her cheeks heat. "He has business abroad," she began, lowering her eyes.

Eleanor scoffed. "He could send his agent! You are so modest. Some vanity would serve you well, Amanda. You are wrong. He is besotted with you and I have my suspicions as to why he left town as he did."

"He is fond of me. He has even admitted it." Amanda went to the bed and took up the dress, returning it carefully to the armoire. She did not want to discuss her feelings for Cliff or their relationship with his sister. "He is hardly besotted."

"You should seduce him. He'll pony up if you do."

Amanda flinched. If Eleanor knew why Cliff had left, she would never be suggesting such a thing.

Eleanor sighed. "You might think about it. In any case, we have callers. And no, it is not your most recent admirer, MacLachlan."

Since her return from Ashton, there had been quite a few callers. Blanche Harrington had visited and Amanda had enjoyed her company. They had strolled together in the gardens, happening upon Rex as he returned from a hack, but Rex had been in his usual dark humor. There had been other callers, too, as the countess was genuinely admired and very well-liked. Eleanor had received several ladies she knew from her own comeout years ago. Amanda had been present during every call. No one seemed to suspect that three months ago she had led a very different life. Conversation had become easy for her; she no longer had to worry and fret about what she should or should not say and do. And no one knew that deep in her heart she was grieving.

There were gentlemen callers, too. And now that she planned to go home very shortly, she felt guilty entertaining them. MacLachlan had returned, in spite of Cliff's edict. His father and Adare were friends and the earl openly approved of him. He had brought some bachelor acquaintances with him. There had been other gentlemen, as well, faces she could not recall, names she did not remember, all invited to the house by Adare and his wife to meet her, all being considered as possible husbands.

She felt dreadful deceiving his family now, but she could not tell anyone her plans. She knew that someone would go directly to Cliff to tell him what she intended. The morning after the ball, she would tell him herself. It would be difficult enough to do so. She knew he would be opposed to her plans, but she had made up her mind, and this one time, she would have her way.

"Who is it?" Amanda asked, rearranging her expression into one that was suitably curious. Entertaining was better than grieving and she had no more plans to make.

"I do not know the ladies, but they have called on Lizzie and they are our age." Eleanor smiled. "You have been such a success, Amanda. Surely you are thrilled."

Amanda smiled at Eleanor as they went downstairs. "It seems like I arrived here in breeches a lifetime ago."

"Yes, it does, but it hasn't been that long."

"I've only been in town six weeks," Amanda remarked, her heart twisting. And she had spent six weeks with Cliff on his ship. She felt as if she had known and loved him forever.

Eleanor's next words were strange. "You do know that you can trust me, don't you? I truly think of you as my sister now."

More guilt assailed her. "You have become such a wonderful friend," she said, meaning it. "Tell me about our callers," she said, to change the subject.

"Lady Jane Cochran is the daughter of the Baroness of Lidden-Way. I have heard of her, as she is quite an heiress. The other two ladies have modest inheritances." Having reached the great hall, they crossed it swiftly, Eleanor adding, "Perhaps we will both make new friends." She was rather wry.

Amanda knew that Eleanor missed Ireland and that she only tolerated London because Harmon House was a gathering place for her family. "Perhaps." She was noncommittal.

Eleanor, as always, minced no words. "Lady Cochran seems a bit vain. I do hope she is not jealous of you."

Amanda almost laughed. "Why on earth would she be jealous of me?"

"She is rather homely, dear, and you are so beautiful. They are all unwed and in the market for husbands. Lady Cochran really need not worry, not with her fortune, but I have met her like before and I think she might see you as competition."

"Eleanor, I do not wish to be competition for anyone."

"I know, and I know why," Eleanor whispered as they entered the salon.

Amanda became uncomfortable. Unfortunately, Eleanor seemed to have guessed at her deep love for Cliff. But she was instantly diverted, remarking the three young ladies who were assembled in the salon, all of whom turned to gaze at her. She saw a tall, thin, rather plain young woman wearing a beautiful dress and pearls. From her somewhat haughty bearing, Amanda knew that this was Lady Cochran. Instinctively, Amanda did not care for her. Her overweight friend was quite pretty, actually, with a pleasant smile. The third caller was a nondescript woman, neither tall nor short, fat nor thin, but her expression was boldly curious.

Lizzie came forward to make introductions. "You have already met my sister-in-law, Mrs. O'Neill. This is my brother-in-law's ward, Miss Amanda Carre. Amanda, this is Lady Jane Cochran, Lady Honora Deere and Lady Anne Sutherland." Lizzie smiled.

Amanda curtsied, while the other three women inclined their heads. She sensed a tension in the salon which she did not care for. All was not well.

"We have heard all about you," Lady Cochran said brightly. "And of course, we all know your guardian somewhat. When he is in town and attends a ball, there is quite a bit of swooning. We thought it prudent to greet you and welcome you to town."

"That is very kind of you," Amanda said carefully. Jane Cochran was smiling, but she was neither friendly nor warm. Amanda hoped the call would be brief and uneventful.

"It is very kind," Lizzie agreed, "as we hardly know one another."

Lady Cochran faced her. "We should become far better friends, don't you agree? You will one day be Countess of Adare, and I, the Baroness of Lidden-Way."

After politely agreeing, Lizzie said, "Let me see what is keeping Masters with our refreshments." She hurried out.

"Is your guardian, Captain de Warenne, in residence?" the plump Lady Deere asked breathlessly, blushing.

Amanda suspected that Honora Deere was infatuated with Cliff. She did not mind, as she could hardly blame her. Cliff would never look twice at Lady Deere, although he would be gallant and charming. She smiled at the women. "Unfortunately he has gone out of town to attend to some business affairs," Amanda said. "He will be back for the Carrington ball."

"Lady de Warenne mentioned that you will come-out there," Jane Cochran said.

Lady Deere's face fell. "He is so handsome," she whispered.

"He is so handsome," Lady Sutherland echoed. "Don't you think so, too?" She exchanged a look with Lady Cochran.

Amanda became tense. "Of course he is handsome. One would have to be blind not to think so."

Lady Cochran laughed. "Which you are not! Is he really a buccaneer?"

Eleanor stepped forward. "A buccaneer is a pirate, Lady Jane. My brother is a merchant for the most part and a privateer when it suits him, which is vastly different." She was clearly annoyed and Amanda touched her hand to restrain her.

"What is it that you really want?" she asked Jane Cochran quietly.

Lady Cochran smiled coolly at Amanda then turned to Eleanor. "Mrs. O'Neill, we didn't come here to insult Captain de Warenne. He is so dashing and so eligible and we are merely disappointed that he is not here. We came here to visit Lady de Warenne and make Miss Carre's acquaintance."

Eleanor smiled tightly. "How gracious of you."

And Amanda knew no good was going to come of this call. She thought, but was not certain, that these women had come to snipe at her.

Lady Cochran turned to Amanda. "I have never thought him to be a buccaneer, in spite of the whispers," she said. "He is far too elegant, even if he does wear a dagger and those spurs at all times."

Amanda smiled, but coolly. "He is the greatest pirate hunter of this time, but of course, you know that. He is accustomed to being armed."

Jane smiled at her. "Did he hunt *your* father, Miss Carre?"

Amanda's heart slammed. This woman knew the truth.

And now, with confusion, she felt her malice and understood why Jane so disliked her. These women had come to sneer at her.

"What does that mean?" Eleanor cried, aghast.

"Surely the horrid rumor is not true? Surely your father was not hanged for piracy?" Lady Cochran continued, smiling widely. "I do mean, why ever would Captain de Warenne foster a pirate's daughter and dare to introduce her into society?"

For one moment, Amanda was incapable of speech.

So many images filled her mind. She saw Cliff, striding through the crowd at the Spanishtown Square, coming to rescue her as she hid under the scaffolding where Papa would hang; she saw him as he stood at the helm beside her, beneath a canopy of yellow canvas and silver stars, and she saw him as she came down the stairs, for the very first time clad in a dress, his gaze filled with admiration.

And she saw him as he waltzed her about the ballroom in the house, her skirts encompassing them both.

La Sauvage was *gone.* She had worked so hard to become the woman she now was. Jane and her friends had no right to their condescension and she would not be their sport.

"How dare you come into this house and spread such vicious gossip!" Eleanor cried. "It is a lie, Lady Cochran; Amanda's father was an island planter who drowned."

"How odd, as I heard that de Warenne rescued her at her father's hanging." Lady Cochran glanced at Amanda as if she were a bug she wished to step on. "I heard her airs are only that, airs, and that she has sailed with pirates, slept with pirates, battled with them! How dare she come to town and pretend to be one of us?"

Amanda trembled, lifted her chin and squared her shoulders. "It's true."

Eleanor seized her arm. "Amanda!"

Amanda shook her head, pulling away, furious now. Jane Cochran was not going to take her achievements away from her. She might be leaving London, but she was going home as Miss Carre, a lady with manners, a lady who could dance. "My father was hanged for piracy, and I learned how to climb the rigging of a ship when I was four. I can wield a sword better than most gentlemen in this town. But I can waltz, Lady Cochran, and I can read and write, and I have made many new friends here in town."

"Do not bother," Jane Cochran began.

Amanda stepped directly in front of her, shaking with her anger. "No. You are the one without manners now. My father was an officer and a gentleman before he turned rogue. Half the pirates in the Caribbean were once naval officers, Lady Cochran."

"How dare you speak to me in such a tone!" she cried.

But Amanda wasn't through. "And my mother was a lady—a Straithferne from Cornwall," she cried in return. "I may not have been raised in a fine house with servants to wait on me, but I should have been raised that way. I have every right to speak to you and I have every right to be here. And not just because I am Cliff de Warenne's ward. Not just because the Earl and Countess of Adare wish for me to be here. It is my right by birth."

Jane gaped.

Eleanor stepped forward. "You had better leave this house now, before I throw you out myself." Being tall, she towered over the other woman.

Jane Cochran made a sound of disgust, gestured impatiently at her friends, and they trooped toward the door. There, she paused. "Whatever dowry your pirate father gave you, whatever airs you have taken on, whatever you may think, it is not enough to make you one of us. I am sorry you must be associated with her, Mrs. O'Neill. This is truly a despicable scandal."

Amanda said softly, "What is despicable is that *you* call yourself a lady. Real ladies do not behave as you have just done."

Jane Cochran gasped.

And Amanda smiled at her.

With a furious glance, Jane left, followed by Lady Sutherland. Honora paused, however, pale with shock. She looked at Eleanor and then at Amanda. "I am so sorry!" she cried. Then she ran after her friends.

Amanda realized she had been holding her breath. Rigid with tension, she somehow exhaled. Someone had learned the truth about her and had spread it about town. Someone was trying to hurt her. It simply didn't make sense. Amanda couldn't begin to imagine who would do such a thing.

"Those witches!" Eleanor gasped. She was shaking with rage. "Oh, I shall find a way to make them pay! And wait until Cliff hears of their viciousness. Amanda, you were wonderful!"

Amanda barely heard. She had come so far and that petty Jane Cochran wished to destroy all she had thus far attained. But she didn't know her, so this was the plot of someone else. She looked at Eleanor. "Even I know that ladies do not act so reprehensibly."

"She is a skinny, ugly hag, with the nature of a shrew! She will never find love or affection, just some poor fortune hunter! We must plan our revenge."

Amanda almost smiled. "You are such a loyal friend!"

Eleanor hugged her. "I meant it when I said you have become a sister to me! Oh, what shall we do to her? Shall we spread some terrible rumor about her?"

Amanda smiled grimly. "It is tempting, but while she was rude and nasty, she only spoke the truth."

"Amanda, she can hurt your prospects. We must squash this rumor at once!"

Amanda sat down. Some of her tension was easing. Cliff

would be furious when he learned of this visit. She was still furious. "But it isn't a rumor, Eleanor." She wished she could tell Eleanor that the gossip didn't matter, because she wouldn't be in town for very long. "When I first came to town, I was so afraid that something like this would happen. I have endured such condescension my entire life. I was a wild child once. I did beg and steal when I was alone on the island during Papa's cruises. But I have changed Eleanor. I can read and write and your father said I am a good dancer. Papa was a gentleman once, and my mother is Lady Belford. I am not hiding, not from Jane Cochran and not from anyone." She knew Cliff would approve of her firm stand.

Eleanor sat down beside her. "I know you dislike discussing your mother, but if she would only step forward, this would be so much easier."

Amanda shot to her feet. "No! I don't need her help."

Eleanor took her arm. "Amanda, this accusation must be put down as a vicious lie."

Amanda stared. "Perhaps you are right. But if I am ever faced again this way, I am not going to deny the truth. I am not going to cower. We have three calls to make tomorrow. I promised the countess I would accompany her and I will."

Eleanor stared. Finally she said, "You do not know society as well as I do. I do not want to see you hurt."

Amanda thought about Cliff, who had broken her heart. "Gossip can't hurt me." She did not add that only Eleanor's brother could achieve that. "I am behind in my reading and Monsieur Michelle is testing me this afternoon. I think I should study. And I don't think we should dwell on Lady Cochran anymore." Then she added, "Eleanor, it really doesn't matter. I am not a pirate's daughter anymore."

Eleanor smiled grimly, hugging her briefly again. "You are so brave."

Amanda had just left the room when Lizzie came in, Chaz in

her arms, struggling to get down. She turned. "Where are the ladies?"

"I take it you do not know them well?" Eleanor asked bitterly.

"I do not know them at all. I was introduced to Lady Cochran once, several years ago, at a supper party. We did not even converse after the introduction. What happened? You seem upset."

"They came here to taunt Amanda. Someone knows the truth and they know it now, too."

Lizzie paled and gave up on Chaz, letting him down. He ran across the room, knocking over a small table as he did so. "Oh dear," Lizzie whispered. "Now what do we do?"

"Amanda has decided to do nothing, as if nothing has happened at all. But I know better. We need Mother, and we need to make certain this rumor dies today."

AMANDA NEVER OPENED her book. Instead, she touched the pearls at her throat, the precious gift Cliff had given to her, missing him so much that it hurt. It was hard to be upset about Jane Cochran and her friends when her heart was so broken, yet she remained angry. She did not deserve their scorn, but she had weathered their plot easily enough. She actually felt sorry for Jane, who was clearly an unhappy shrew. Tomorrow she might be cut and scorned anew, yet she would manage. She was proud of how far she had come and she would never hide from anything or anyone again. An ugly rumor—even one that was true—couldn't bring La Sauvage back.

She thought about Cliff, who was somewhere in Holland, who wouldn't even look at her now. Even as angry as he was, he would have been angrier with those women if he had been present, and he would have instantly come to her defense. She knew it and it pleased her. Maybe, in spite of his terrible resolve, he would still be her champion from a distance, just as she would always love him from a distance. She smiled a little.

Amanda turned as a knock sounded on her door. The

Countess of Adare appeared, and from the solemn expression on her face and the compassion in her eyes, Amanda knew that Eleanor had told her what had happened. "I understand there was a very awkward moment downstairs," she began quietly.

Amanda almost pretended not to comprehend her. Then she sighed and sat down. "I am so sorry that such a distasteful encounter occurred in your home, my lady."

The countess started. "Do not apologize to me, my dear! I am worried about you. Eleanor said you were fine, and you do not seem terribly upset."

Amanda hesitated. Finally she said, "It hurt. Of course it did. I did nothing to provoke such an attack."

Mary sat down in an adjacent chair and reached for her hand. "Amanda, dear, this entire family is behind you. We will never abandon you. You do know that?"

The countess's generous and gracious nature had never been more evident. In that moment, Amanda wanted to become a great lady exactly like her—a lady who was unstintingly kind, generous to a fault and always gracious, no matter the provocation. "I think I do. Countess, I know I have thanked you for your hospitality but your affection means so much to me."

Mary squeezed her hand. "I think of you as a daughter," she said simply. Then, with a gleam in her eyes, "But Eleanor is right. At some point, there must be some retribution."

Amanda's eyes widened. She was stunned.

Mary smiled. "My dear, I am an Irishwoman first and last and my ancestors were great warriors, even the women. A bit of their hot blood still runs in my veins."

"But you are the Countess of Adare!"

"True. And I wasn't thinking of taking that dagger of yours and doing anything with it. I was thinking of a more personal form of vengeance. Jane's mother is great friends with Lady Carrington, and I assure you, she will be there at the ball.

Hmm…shall I lend you my diamonds for the ball? Perhaps with my pearl and diamond tiara? Jane will die of envy."

Amanda bit her lip, then laughed. "She would be pea-green, but I can't borrow such finery, my lady."

"Of course you can," Mary said, patting her hand, another gleam in her eyes. Then she directed her regard to Amanda. "But first things first. I approve of your pride, but there is no point in allowing this rumor to ruin your prospects. Therefore, we will make a fourth call tomorrow."

The countess had a plan. "Who will we call on?" she asked, terribly interested now.

"We will call on my good friend Lady Marsden, a very esteemed and powerful dowager countess, and we will put an end to the absolute nonsense begun by Lady Cochran."

Softly, Amanda said, "But it isn't nonsense."

And Mary de Warenne's eyes turned to steel. "Oh, it is nonsense, my dear, for I shall have it no other way."

THE NEXT AFTERNOON Amanda and Mary de Warenne were shown into an opulent salon. Eleanor, Lizzie and Tyrell de Warenne were with them. The heir to the earldom was a tall, dark man who bore a shocking resemblance to his brother Rex. Amanda found him as imposing as the earl, even though they had conversed pleasantly enough before the opera the other night.

Amanda was nervous in spite of her resolve. She knew the first few calls would be difficult indeed. And Lady Marsden was as dignified as she had imagined. She was a heavyset woman with blue-white hair who dared to wear royal blue velvet and sapphires for day. She was entertaining mixed company; two gentlemen and three young ladies were present. Swallowing, Amanda realized that Garret MacLachlan was one of the callers. She finally felt some dread. It was one thing to face those she did not care about, but another to face a man she genuinely liked.

He saw her and his eyes widened in surprise, and then, as if he had not heard the rumors, he smiled quite disarmingly at her.

As the countess led the way into the salon, Tyrell de Warenne pulled her aside. Amanda was very startled.

He smiled at her. "Miss Carre, you are my brother's ward, which makes me responsible for you, as well."

She nodded, wondering where he would lead.

"You are under my protection, which is the protection of Adare. You must calm your fears. We will navigate our way through this very small but highly unpleasant crisis, and by the time my obtuse brother returns home, we will have forgotten there ever was such an unfortunate event."

"I hope that is the case," Amanda said, not at all at ease with the earl's heir. But she smiled at him. "You have many duties, my lord. You really don't have to add me to them."

He grinned. "Of course I do! My wife would throttle me if I did not care for you." His smile faded. "Lady Marsden's bark is far worse than her bite and she is very fond of my mother. Hold your head high and be true to yourself. You will win her over in no time, just as you have won over my family."

Amanda decided to do as he said. "If I were to be absolutely myself, my lord, I might hold my head high while stepping on Jane Cochran's skirts, as she is moving across a very slippery floor."

He laughed. "You remind me exactly of my sister," he said. "Shall we?" He took her arm.

Amanda realized just how symbolic the gesture was, for she was on the arm of the future Earl of Adare. "Thank you for such chivalry," she murmured.

He sent her a smile.

Lady Marsden approached in a terribly regal manner. Amanda was aware that the rest of her company all gazed fixedly at her as Tyrell escorted her inside. She felt her cheeks heat, but she did not lower her chin or her eyes. Clearly everyone in the room except for Garret knew about her dubious past.

"My dear, dear Countess Adare," Lady Marsden cried, embracing her with a smile. "My dear Mary!"

"It is good to see you, too, Dot," Mary said, smiling as they clasped hands.

Across the room, the three women were whispering to one another while glancing over at her repeatedly. Amanda stiffened her spine and smiled at them all.

Lady Marsden now turned her attention to Eleanor, clearly ignoring Amanda. "You, I know, and well," she said darkly to Eleanor. "So you married a commoner—your stepbrother, no less! Why have you not called on me, Eleanor?" she demanded.

Eleanor curtsied. "Because I knew you would not approve of my having made a love match," she said boldly.

Lady Marsden laughed. "But I do approve. You hardly needed a fortune. Besides, he is a handsome rake, is he not? I expect you to bring your husband with you the next time you call—the end of the week will do."

Eleanor nodded, her eyes dancing, but otherwise, her expression was shockingly demure.

Lady Marsden then went over to Tyrell, still refusing to acknowledge Amanda. He bowed and kissed her hand. "I see you remain as well as ever, Lady Marsden," he said. "As gracious, as hospitable. What a splendid gathering."

"Oh, do cease your flattery. You have changed!" she exclaimed. "You are more handsome than ever, if that is possible. Come here, Lizzie. She is with child again? Tyrell! Have you no shame?"

He just laughed.

"It is my fault, my lady," Lizzie said with a grin, curtsying. "I am the one who insists on having a very large family."

Lady Marsden shook her head. "I never thought to see you two again, as you both seem to wish to hibernate in that heathen land you insist on calling home."

Tyrell and Lizzie chatted briefly with the forbidding dowager, inviting her to Adare. Neither Lizzie nor Tyrell seemed at all intimidated by her harsh and outspoken manner. Awaiting her introduction, Amanda glanced across the salon.

Garret smiled at her immediately and approached. There was no avoiding him now.

"Miss Carre, 'tis a happy surprise to see ye here."

She dared to meet his regard. "My lord, it is a lovely day."

His green gaze was searching. "'Tis a fine day…but I see a shadow in those beautiful eyes."

She flushed. He was shameless when flirting. "I am fine."

He seemed doubtful. "I admire yer courage, Miss Carre," he said softly. "Lass, ye have enough fer a dozen men."

She gaped. Had he heard the gossip after all?

Some sympathy filled his eyes. He pulled her away from the others. "I ha' heard the accusations Jane Cochran has made. The shrew needs a lesson in manners, I think."

Amanda tensed. "It's true."

He stared, their gazes holding, and when he smiled at her, it was the soft, heartbreaking smile Cliff had so often sent her. "I think I knew. A wild rose canna be mistaken fer its hothouse cousin. Lass, it only speaks to yer exceptional character that ye be here now."

Amanda was too stunned to reply.

"Lady Marsden, you have not met my brother's ward, Miss Amanda Carre," Tyrell was saying firmly, causing Amanda to stiffen. But she was ready for the dowager, and she was never going to take Garret MacLachlan for granted again.

Lady Marsden's face hardened as she approached. "I know who she is," she said coldly. She turned to the countess. "Really, Mary, is this your doing?"

Amanda did not flinch, not now.

Tyrell flushed with anger and started to speak. Mary took his arm, forestalling him. She smiled. "Miss Carre has become another daughter to me," Mary said with a soft smile. "Her father, a retired naval officer, drowned on Jamaica Island, where he was a planter. He was a friend of Cliff's, and his dying wish was for Cliff to look after her. We have been slowly introducing her to society, and as she is an exemplary and unusual young woman, I had to bring her to you."

Lady Marsden now faced Amanda fully, her eyes suspicious. "Is it true? Did your father drown? For that is not what I have heard!"

Amanda hesitated. The truth was on the tip of her tongue, but then she saw Mary staring at her, begging her not to reveal herself. She owed the countess so much, and she managed a nod. "Yes, my lady, it is true. My father drowned very recently."

Mary sighed. "Dot, Jane Cochran is enraged because she is enamored of my son and Cliff will not give her any attention. And why should he? She is quite homely, with no gracious manners, and he doesn't need her fortune. It is a true indication of her base character that she would spread such very vicious lies about my new daughter."

Lady Marsden seemed taken aback. "I have never liked that Cochran girl," she said after a pause, "and you are right, she has always lacked the proper airs for her superior breeding. Well, if Miss Carre is a new daughter…." She turned to Amanda. "Come here, Miss Carre," the dowager commanded.

Amanda instantly obeyed, curtsying yet again.

"You have suffered terribly," Lady Marsden said. "I realize that now. You are very bold, however, to dare to put a single foot among the ton again."

Amanda smiled. The old lady really wasn't frightening at all. "The countess wished for me to make your acquaintance and I have no reason to hide." That was the truth. "It is a great honor meeting you, my lady."

"So you were raised in Jamaica?" Lady Marsden asked. "Is that not the West Indies?"

Amanda nodded. "Yes it is."

"Hmm. I am very fond of travel. I wish for you to tell me what the island is like and advise me if I should make a voyage there in my advanced age."

## *CHAPTER EIGHTEEN*

AMANDA WAS BEGINNING to feel very sick inside. Two weeks had passed and it was after six in the evening. At half past seven, they would be leaving Harmon House to go to the Carrington ball. Cliff had not returned.

She stood at the window in disbelief and dismay, clad in a wrapper, her hair pinned up, wearing the countess's stunning pearl and diamond tiara and the necklace Cliff had given her. All she had to do was be helped by a maid into her ball gown and gloves and a diamond bracelet the countess insisted she also wear. Amanda bit her lip.

He would never disappoint her this way. Something terrible had to have happened to have delayed him. Either that, or he was far angrier than she had thought.

If he did not come, she wasn't going to the ball. In spite of all that had happened, the first dance was his. She would not give it to anyone else.

As she stood there, shivering, for the early autumn night was cool, her heart raced uncontrollably. She had been in a nervous, excited and apprehensive state all day. She had been afraid of their first reunion, of what his expression would be, of what he might say. She knew it was foolish, but she prayed he had forgiven her for what she had done at Ashford Hall. She prayed he had changed his mind about putting so many barriers between them. Even if he had not, she had to see him again. She was emotionally exhausted.

And then she saw a hired hansom turn through the two brick pillars at the end of the drive. Amanda cried out, pushing open the window and staring as it approached. The black carriage came up the drive and paused before the house. The door opened, and Cliff alighted.

She held on to the sill tightly, her heart hammering wildly now. He hadn't let her down. She looked at him and was consumed by her feelings of love.

He glanced up.

Although she was two stories above, their gazes instantly locked.

Amanda didn't smile, she could not.

He didn't smile, either, but as he strode toward the house, he stared up at her, until he passed under the portico and out of sight.

Amanda closed the window, shivering. Cliff had come home.

HE STRODE INTO THE HALL, making a conscious effort to appear unhurried when what he wanted to do was run. He never veered, heading directly for the stairs, his pulse pounding with excitement. He would greet his children, and then he would casually say hello to Amanda. He knew he had to keep a distance from her, but he had missed Amanda more than he had ever missed anyone in the past two weeks. She had haunted his mind night and day. In fact, his nights had been sleepless; they had been hell. But he remained convinced that he had done the right thing in leaving, and in soliciting Adare to the cause of her marriage.

And whenever he brooded about that, his insides turned into knots.

He had begun to have some grave doubts about being able to hand her over to someone else at the wedding altar.

"Cliff," Tyrell said from behind him.

Cliff was dismayed but he halted, facing his oldest brother, who had stepped out of the smaller salon where he now saw Rex and Sean seated. Everyone was already attired in their black tailcoats and evening trousers. Not only did he wish to see his children and Amanda, he had to get a leg on.

He had also begun to think about the waltz. He could not help it—he couldn't wait to take her in his arms and dance her around the room.

But he hadn't seen Tyrell in almost a year. He respected and was very fond of his older brother, never mind that he was becoming more and more like Adare every day. He smiled and the two men embraced.

"You are late," Tyrell remarked, a slight smile on his face.

"I am aware of that. What time are we leaving?" He tried to control his impatience. Why hadn't Amanda smiled at him? Perhaps she was angry with him for his behavior when he had left London. It had been churlish, and if she was angry, he wouldn't blame her.

"Half past seven. Are you rushing up the stairs to dress?" Tyrell asked too casually.

Cliff stared at him. "Why else would I be rushing up those stairs?"

Tyrell smiled. "There was some doubt today about your return."

His tension eased very slightly. "Why? I gave Amanda my word I would return for the ball. She has promised me the first dance. How is she?"

"Very well," Tyrell remarked, "in spite of the fact that someone spread a nasty little rumor that she is a pirate's daughter."

Cliff felt himself still. Rage began. *"What?"*

Tyrell briefly told him what had happened.

Cliff trembled with more rage. As Sean and Rex stepped into the hall, he said, "She must have been devastated."

"She wasn't in the least bit devastated, and in any case, the rumor has been laid to rest," Tyrell said.

Cliff didn't believe him. Amanda's worst fear had been the

scorn of society. He turned to rush up the stairs, but Sean stepped in front of him. "If you are on your way up to visit your children or if you are going up to dress, I can allow you to pass." His expression was bland. "But I am under strict orders from my wife *not* to allow you to see Amanda before she finishes dressing."

He was in disbelief. "I wish to speak to her. She is my ward!"

Sean started laughing at him. "You are besotted. Why don't you give in, surrender, confess, admit it?"

Cliff felt like landing a solid blow in his stepbrother's smug face. "You are the besotted one. For God's sake, every time I enter a room, I have to scan the premises to make certain you and Eleanor aren't behaving like adolescent lovers behind the sofa."

Rex approached, also clearly amused. "You are not allowed to visit Amanda until she comes downstairs. Relax, Cliff. It's only been, what, two weeks?"

"It has been eighteen days," he growled, and when everyone chuckled, clearly entertained by him, he turned red.

"I suggest you greet your children and make some haste," Tyrell said evenly. He turned and walked back into the salon. Sean followed.

Cliff looked at Rex, who sobered. "She is fine. She has great courage and even greater dignity, Cliff. She stepped out the next day with the countess and Tyrell and an end was put to the gossip before it began."

"Are you certain?" Cliff asked intensely. "Because you do not know the condescension she suffered while growing up on the island."

"I am very sure. Cliff? The waif you brought home in August is gone."

Instantly, he recalled Amanda standing in the hall at Ashford House, clad in a pale pink silk nightgown, the most desirable woman he had ever beheld. He already knew the waif was gone. "I need a hot bath," he said, a lie, because he needed a cold one. And he turned and ran up the stairs.

IT WAS PRECISELY half past seven when he came down the stairs, clad in his tuxedo and making a final adjustment to his necktie. His heart was thundering and he could not deny why. It felt as if eighteen months had passed since he had been with Amanda, not eighteen days.

His entire family was assembled in the hall, apparently waiting for him. He saw no one, as his steps slowed and he reached for the banister to steady himself.

She stood in their midst, a vision in white and gold.

His thundering heart turned over hard one final time and he stilled.

Amanda smiled hesitantly at him.

He stared, no longer capable of drawing a breath. Her hair was swept up, tendrils framing her beautiful face, and her exotic green eyes were riveted to his. The ball gown was almost Grecian in style, sensually flowing over her curves. She wore his pearls at her throat but the countess's diamond jewelry. She was more than beautiful, and now, there was no more denying how he felt.

He had missed her so badly he had decided to return earlier than planned a dozen times in eighteen days. Now, he knew why.

She had become the center of his life the day he had rescued her from Governor Woods. She was still the center of his life. She meant everything to him. He could never bear such a separation again.

*I am in love*, he thought, incredulous. In his entire life, he had never been more stunned.

He stood there, staring, overwhelmed by the enormity of his emotions.

For this was what love was and he had no more doubts. It was a huge and swelling, all-consuming joy, a sense of completion, exhilaration and need. He needed Amanda the way he needed the wind and the sea to live, to breathe. And it was so much passion, at once raw and emotional. And it was the determination to never see her hurt, abused or scorned again.

He had fought it as hard as he could. Someone had told him earlier to surrender. He was so dazed and overwhelmed he couldn't recall who had done so, but that person was right. It was time to surrender at last.

It was time to surrender to Amanda.

He realized that the hall was silent and he had been standing there staring at her as if a smitten, speechless fool. Well, he decided, stepping down the last steps, finally smiling, that was what he now was—senselessly besotted and smitten, at long last a man in love.

She stared as he approached, her eyes huge, as if she somehow knew.

He didn't think twice. He touched her chin, tilted it up. "You are too lovely, Amanda. So lovely, it is hard to even speak."

Her eyes widened in surprise, then filled with relief. She smiled at him, and her eyes told him she had missed him terribly, too.

He realized he was smiling widely, helplessly, himself.

"You're not angry?" she finally asked.

"No." He touched her cheek, her neck. His body stirred. He thought about kissing her, deeply, and then he thought about finally making love to her, until he heard a cough. He hesitated, controlling the now-consuming urge. "I bought you something."

She nodded, her eyes shining, and he reached into his pocket and brought out a velvet jeweler's box. He opened it, revealing pearl and diamond drop earrings. Amanda wet her lips. "You thought of me," she whispered. "While you were gone."

"Yes." He handed her the box, aware of his having made a huge understatement, and took one earring and fastened it to her ear. As he touched the lobe, his loins engorged more fully and she also stiffened. He knew his tension was also hers. Their gazes met.

She no longer smiled.

Tonight, he thought, he would touch and caress and mold and taste every part of her nude body. Such thoughts were not helpful and he forced them aside. He fastened the other earring and dropped his hands. They had been trembling.

"Thank you," she said softly.

He just smiled, still overcome by the bursting emotions in his chest. He would analyze them later, and later, he would also consider what they really meant for them both. It was still hard to comprehend that he could be feeling this way. He held out his arm. "We have a ball to attend."

She took it, smiling. "Yes, we do."

AMANDA WAS DAZED. She was in a palatial Greenwich home, in a magnificent ballroom the size of Cliff's ship, surrounded by hundreds of elegant ladies and gentlemen from the uppermost crust of society, and she was on Cliff's arm. He had been introducing her left and right to almost everyone they passed as they made their way through the glittering, bejeweled, laughing throng. No one had been condescending, nor had there been any curious stares. Amanda realized that the rumor Jane Cochran had tried to spread had been killed before it had ever had a chance to flourish.

Most important of all, Cliff wasn't angry with her.

In fact, whenever their gazes met, which was repeatedly, he sent her a soft smile and Amanda was instantly breathless.

She wasn't sure what was happening. She only knew that she did not want the night to ever end. But it would, and tomorrow she was going to tell him that she must leave.

"The dancing is about to begin," Cliff murmured. They had paused near the edge of the dance floor. Gentlemen were leading their partners out. Cliff faced her, releasing her arm for the first time in hours, and he bowed.

She curtsied, overwhelmed by his beauty, his masculinity, her love. In fact, she loved him so much her heart ached from the vastness of the emotion. The evening promised to be perfect. And now, they were making a memory she would cherish forever.

Amanda reminded herself not to think about the next day, not until dawn came. She was going to live that night as if it was the only night in time.

He held out his hand and she slipped her palm into his. Smiling, he led her a few steps onto the floor and she moved closer, her palm closing on his shoulder as his fingers touched her waist. The full orchestra began to play, and Cliff began to waltz her across the room.

Amanda gave herself over to the sheer joy of being one with the man she loved. The floor vanished as they floated effortlessly.

Amanda met his gaze, which was suddenly so intent. If she did not know better, she would think him as deeply in love as she was. She warned herself not to read too much into his warmth and affection. He had always been fond of her and he had never been afraid to acknowledge it.

"You seem happy," he said softly.

"I have never been happier," she admitted.

"Then I am glad." His gaze slid over her face briefly, to the edge of her bodice. When it lifted, he smiled again.

Amanda's heart turned over hard.

They did not speak again, and when the music ended, Amanda gazed into his beautiful eyes, wishing for another turn. "Will you give me another dance?" she whispered.

His jaw flexed. "I would love to, but your card is full." He casually glanced away, then back. "I will take the last dance, Amanda."

She smiled, relieved.

But then he spoke, his tone odd. "Have there been many suitors while I was gone?"

She tensed. "Yes. Your father made certain of it."

His glance slid away as he led her from the dance floor. "I must speak with Adare in the morning, then."

She was shocked. In spite of the intimacy they had been sharing, in spite of his warm, lingering glances, his intentions hadn't changed. He would still marry her off to another. Dismay filled her. But she already knew how easily he could hurt her. That was the price of her love.

She pulled her hand from his. Her intentions hadn't changed either, but of course, he did not know what she planned.

"Enjoy the rest of your evening, Amanda. Maybe we can take dessert together, as well," he said, formally bowing.

"I will plan on it," Amanda returned, managing a smile. She stared after him, wishing the dance could have lasted forever, until someone coughed. She turned, realizing a gentleman was awaiting his turn. She somehow curtsied as he bowed, not quite catching his name, and a moment later, she was being escorted back onto the dance floor. As another waltz began, she glanced back at the crowd and saw Cliff staring at her, his gaze hard and bright. She did not know what such a bold and displeased look could signify, other than that he did not care for her current partner. She sighed and gave up trying to comprehend him. It was going to have to be enough that they were friends again.

SEVERAL HOURS LATER, Amanda stood by herself near a large gilded column, exhausted from so much activity and attention, not to mention the state of her emotions. She had gotten through two-thirds of her card, and she wished it were not full. She doubted she could manage another dozen dances but she would, so she could have one last dance with Cliff.

The dance floor remained crowded. She saw Eleanor in Sean's arms, being whirled about, the two of them looking as besotted as newlyweds. She smiled, trying to imagine what such love must be like, but she quickly gave up. That kind of affection was not going to be a part of her life and she must focus on her future as a respectable lady and an island merchant.

A moment later she saw Cliff on the dance floor and her heart leaped wildly. She would always thrill at the sight of him. He was taller than most of the men in the room, his tawny hair glinting under the lights from the three crystal chandeliers, and he was dancing with Honora Deere, who was crimson and starry-eyed. Amanda smiled, understanding the young lady too well. Even though Honora had been with Jane Cochran that awful day, Amanda was happy Cliff was giving her a dance.

"Miss Carre?" Garret MacLachlan appeared, bowing.

She smiled, not having realized he was at the ball. Her eyes widened. He was clad as a Highlander in a bright blue jacket, a blue, black and red kilt, his knees bare, and blue stockings. He wore a beret, as well, and a ceremonial sword. Amanda curtsied, for he had never been more handsome, but to her surprise, he took her gloved elbow and prevented her from sinking deeply, helping her to rise instead. "My lord."

His smile was odd. "I ha' been admirin' ye fer some time now, lass. Ye be the most beautiful woman in the room."

She knew she blushed. "You, sir, are a terrible flirt."

But he did not smile. "I be speakin' the truth. Amanda," he said, startling her as they were not on a first name basis, "I ha' come to say g'bye."

Her eyes widened. "You are leaving?"

"Aye. I ha' been summoned home. Will ye miss me?"

She hesitated. "Of course," she began, but she did not want to lead him on.

His eyes darkened and he studied her. "Ye love yer guardian," he finally said. "I watched ye dancin', Amanda. I watched yer eyes."

Amanda did not know what to say. Then she thought of how Garret had accepted the truth about her life with such steadfast poise and nobility, praising her for her accomplishments instead of scorning her for her past, and she touched his arm. "Yes, I do."

He slowly shook his head. "Then I wish ye the best, lass."

"You don't understand."

"Aye, I ken."

"No, it's not what you think. I love Cliff and I always will, but he doesn't return my feelings. I am going home, Garret, to the island, and I am never marrying anyone."

Garret smiled oddly. "I dinna think ye'll get far," he said.

She started, not certain as to his meaning.

Then he took her hand and kissed it warmly, surprising Amanda. "G'bye, lass." He bowed briefly and strode off.

Amanda stared after him, as did every woman he passed. She sighed, thinking that she would miss him, for he had become a friend. She did not think she had broken his heart, however. He had never declared his love for her, and she did think him a bit of a rake. She fervently hoped he would one day find someone to love him as he deserved.

"Amanda?" a woman asked, from behind her.

Amanda did not recognize the woman's voice. The intimate form of address was very incorrect. Somewhat taken aback, she turned. And instantly she became rigid.

A very elegant and beautiful blond woman stood there, attired in a magnificent rose satin gown, her diamonds sparkling. Amanda inhaled, feeling as if someone had struck her a brutal blow in her chest.

The woman was blond, green-eyed, beautiful and so oddly familiar. It was almost like looking at herself in the mirror in another decade or two.

Amanda stiffened.

"You know who I am," Dulcea said, her tone strained, her regard unwavering.

"I know. You are Dulcea Belford," Amanda said tersely.

Dulcea hesitated. "I am your mother, dear," she said.

# *CHAPTER NINETEEN*

AMANDA STARED, trying to breathe with composure. This was her mother—the woman who had dealt her the ultimate blow. The anguish Dulcea had caused, which Amanda had thought successfully vanquished, surged forth, briefly paralyzing her. She had been anticipating this encounter, but she had never dreamed it would be tonight.

"I am your mother," Dulcea repeated softly. Her regard was intent.

"No," Amanda finally said, firmly. She held her head high, terribly glad she was wearing the jewelry Cliff had given her and the diamonds, which belonged to the countess. She could not think clearly, perhaps because her heart was racing with such alarming speed. But Amanda knew one thing. She must not allow her mother to ever learn that she had caused her so much grief.

"I have no mother. I have never had a mother. I had a father, but he is dead." She fought emotions which seemed determined to arise. "Let us not pretend for a single moment that we are mother and daughter." Amanda pressed back against the wall. "We are not."

Dulcea gasped. "That is unkind!" But her gaze was moving over Amanda from head to toe. She kept looking up at the diamond and pearl tiara.

It was another moment before Amanda could speak. "No, *Lady Belford*, I believe you are the unkind one." Amanda told herself to turn and walk away. There need not be any kind of discussion at all. Not far was a billiards room, where ladies and gentlemen were engaged in conversation and games. She could go there and mingle. But she could not make herself walk away, and she began to shake. "I came here after my father's death to find you. It was Papa's dying wish! Do you think I wanted to leave the island? Do you think I ever once believed you would welcome me? But I could not refuse my father. How dare you accuse me of being unkind?"

Finally, Dulcea's stare was unwavering upon Amanda's face. "I was beyond shocked when de Warenne notified me that you were at Harmon House. Amanda, we must discuss this so that you can understand my side, but privately, please. Let's step outside."

"There is nothing to discuss," Amanda managed, very close to horrific tears. Why would she wish to cry now? Surely she was beyond the hurt her mother's rejection had caused her. But her feet would not respond to the directions given by her mind and she simply stood there, unmoving, staring and finally taking stock of her mother.

This was the woman who had given birth to her and then so carelessly given her up. *She had finally met Mama; Mama, who had refused to accept her.*

"Don't you want to hear my side?" Dulcea cried, reaching for her hand.

Amanda shrugged, pulling away, but she was shaken. Did she want to hear what her mother had to say?

"This has been a wonderful night for you," Dulcea said softly, smiling now. "Clearly, you are a great success. I am proud of you, Amanda. So terribly proud."

Amanda trembled. "No, you're not. This is a pretense! You do not care about me and you never have." Her mother's words hurt.

"That's not true," Dulcea gasped. "Of course I care about you! Don't you want to know the truth—the entire truth?"

Amanda hesitated. As dazed as she was, her instincts screamed at her in alarm, telling her to walk away from this woman. This woman still had the power to hurt her the way almost no one else could. But she was leaving England as soon as possible and she would never see Dulcea Belford again. Shouldn't she discover what had happened two months ago—and eighteen years ago? If she did not do so now, she never would.

"Very well." Amanda gave her a jerky nod, somehow keeping a few shreds of her composure and her dignity about her. They walked down the hall and stepped outside onto a large terrace. A few couples and groups were taking air, but no one paid them any mind.

"When I realized I was with child, Amanda, I was not even seventeen years old. I was terrified," Dulcea said quietly when they had removed themselves from the couples on the terrace.

Amanda's heart accelerated. She could easily imagine how frightened Dulcea must have been. Dulcea had been even younger than she was when she had conceived. "Did you love my father at all?"

Dulcea smiled. "At that time, yes, I did. He was so dashing and handsome in his naval uniform. He had a charisma, Amanda, one that made many young women turn to look at him as he strutted down the street."

"He never stopped loving you," Amanda heard herself say. "But you married Belford." It was an accusation.

"I was beyond fortunate to marry Belford!" Dulcea cried softly. "Amanda, your father and I knew each other for three weeks and then he set sail. When I realized I was carrying, I didn't know what to do! I was so young, and my mother was already introducing me to gentlemen like Belford, men with small fortunes but old lines and significant titles. As far back as I can recall, I knew that was how I would one day wed. Marriage has nothing to do with love. I am fortunate to have become so fond of Belford." She paused. "Amanda, we were both so young.

It wasn't love, it was passion." She hesitated and added, "It was what you are feeling for de Warenne."

Amanda shook her head. "I have never admired anyone the way I admire Cliff. I will freely admit how I feel about him. He is my hero, my champion and I will love him until the day I die."

Dulcea's eyes widened.

"And Papa loved you that way, or almost that way," she cried. "He raised me on stories of your great beauty, your grace, your elegance and your kindness. He had you on a pedestal. He made certain I should look up to your memory, as well. God, I feel sorry for my father!"

"I didn't know Carre felt as he did. How could I?" Dulcea retorted. "He never told me! Amanda, I did not come outside to argue with you."

Amanda blinked in real surprise. Why hadn't Papa said something?

Dulcea sent her a small, rueful smile. "I am not callous or cold, Amanda. I am a flesh-and-blood woman with a heart, a home, a husband and two children. I assumed Carre forgot me. Why would I assume anything else?"

"I don't know," Amanda said slowly. She told herself not to allow herself to soften toward Dulcea, as she could not trust her. She must not trust her. "You said you cared about me, but it's not true." *It couldn't be true*, she thought.

"It is true! How could I not care about my own daughter? But you were taken away from me the moment you were born. I was seventeen and not given any choice."

Amanda refused to believe her. "Don't even try to tell me you would have kept me if you had been given a choice!"

"I wept for days after you were taken away," Dulcea cried, wiping at her own eyes now. "However, my mother had plans for me to marry well, and I had no intention of defying her. But Amanda, I thought about you frequently and I worried so, especially when I heard Carre had turned pirate."

Amanda was becoming confused. Dulcea seemed so sincere. But she hadn't really answered her, either. She hadn't said that yes, she would have given up a future with a title to raise her daughter.

"Papa loved me and I loved him. He was a good father. You hardly needed to worry." She would defend her father always, especially to Dulcea. "If you were so worried, why didn't you write?" she demanded.

"Belford would cast me out if he ever knew about you. I had to keep a safe distance. Surely you understand? My dear, you have had such a difficult life!" Dulcea said. "I am so sorry! I wish it had been different, Amanda. I do."

Amanda was suddenly furious. "You had a chance to make a difference two months ago, when I came to town. But you did not want me. So you can tell me again and again how you cared and worried, but I will never believe it!"

"Captain de Warenne shocked me when he appeared in my home, announcing that you were in town!"

"He is the one who made all the difference. He rescued me, protected me, provided generously for me, all out of a sense of honor, of nobility. He took me into his *home*. He provided my *dowry*. His family has welcomed me with open arms—unlike you," she exclaimed. And it became hard to breathe. Her mother had opened a wound she had thought long since healed.

Dulcea's eyes were wide. "I thought Carre provided the dowry."

"No, Cliff did so, at his own expense." Of all the things her mother could have responded to, she had chosen the subject of her dowry. "Papa never asked him to be my guardian. That is an utter fabrication on his part. When *you* rejected me, *he* claimed me as his ward out of the goodness of his heart. *He* provided my dowry when he did not have to do so, because *he* swore he would secure my future." Dulcea had not done any of those things.

Dulcea's chin lifted. "Is he sleeping with you?"

Amanda backed up, shaking her head in denial, but she felt her cheeks warm. "Our relationship is not your affair," she managed. "I am not your affair." Tears were somehow seeping. "He would never behave so dishonorably!"

"He hasn't tried to seduce you?" Dulcea asked, her regard intent and unwavering.

"No, I tried to seduce him," Amanda said defiantly. But she was uneasy. She sensed some greater purpose on her mother's part now. It was as if lie upon lie was being told.

They stared.

"My poor darling," Dulcea said, taking her hand.

Amanda flinched, wide-eyed. She pulled her hand away. "Don't you dare offer me sympathy now."

"I am your mother! You refuse to believe me and I cannot help that, but I know what it is like to fall hopelessly in love. No one will ever blame you for falling for Cliff de Warenne. Half the women in this room would give almost anything, including their reputations, to be his latest paramour. I understand, darling. I do."

Amanda shook her head. "I have to go." Nothing had been resolved, she realized. She wished she could believe Dulcea, but she did not.

"Wait!" Dulcea's tone cracked like a whip. "I went to Harmon House recently to see you. I begged de Warenne to allow me to claim you as a cousin, to help him find you a husband. I asked that you come live with me. Not only did he refuse my pleas, he would not let me see you!"

Amanda was shocked. She began shaking her head. "No. I don't believe you! Cliff would never do such a thing! And if he turned you away, he did it for a good reason."

"Why on earth would I lie?" she cried. "Ask your doormen. I came to see you, to become a part of your life, and he refused me!"

Amanda knew one thing. Cliff might not love her the way she loved him, but he would move heaven and earth to do what was best for her. "There is no one I trust more than Cliff. If he sent you away, it is because he knows you are a liar. Why? Why are you making such an effort to convince me that you care? What could you possibly want?"

"I am telling you how much I want to be your mother. I am telling you how much I miss you. I want you to come live with me at Belford House."

Amanda had to seize the terrace railing to remain standing. *"What?"*

"We will say you are my cousin, a distant one, and I will find you a husband, Amanda. It is my duty to do so." She smiled.

Amanda was reeling. "I am going home!" she cried. "I am going back to the island and I am not marrying anyone."

Dulcea gasped. "What are you saying? You cannot possibly think to go back to your pirate way. Your life is here now, with me!"

Amanda stiffened. "I am not a pirate, Mother, or didn't you notice? These pearls belong to *me.* This dress is *mine*. My dance card was *full* tonight. In fact, I have been told I am a beautiful *lady*, many times."

"Darling." Dulcea took her hands. "I did not mean to insult you. This will be our chance to get to know one another, to become a family. Once you are wed, I fear it will be too late, and I should like to help you find the right husband."

Amanda began to laugh, as it was absurd. Her mother wished for her to move to Belford House now? She felt certain Dulcea wanted something, but it was not her daughter's happiness. "It's too late. I do not want to know you. I am going back to Jamaica, and I am starting a business there. I am giving Cliff his dowry back."

Dulcea turned white. "That is utterly foolish! I cannot allow you to go to that island at such a tender age. Your future is here, with me and with a husband and home of your own. My God, Amanda, do you not realize how fortunate you are to have a dowry like the one de Warenne has given you? Without it, you have no chance to wed! With it, you will live modestly, but well!"

Amanda pulled away. "Why are you doing this? What do you want? I have told you twice I am not marrying."

Dulcea's gaze was wide and hard. "It's de Warenne, isn't it?"

Cliff's image seared Amanda's mind. What she desperately wanted, she could not ever have. "Yes, you are finally right. This is about Cliff. But it is also about me. I want to become an independent woman," she said quietly, with pride. "And the truth of the matter is that I cannot and will not marry another man."

Dulcea cried out.

"No one can change my mind." Amanda was suddenly exhausted. Worse, she was feeling ill enough to retch. She had to get away from Dulcea; it was also time to leave the ball, as the magical evening had been utterly ruined. Maybe, when she was finally alone in her bedroom, she would curl up and give in to the urge to cry. But she wasn't sure what she was crying for. One fact was clear, however: she was no closer to comprehending the woman who was her mother now than she had been before meeting her. She started to leave.

"I can change your mind," Dulcea said, her tone sharp.

Amanda froze. Then slowly, with dread, she faced her mother. "I don't think so."

Dulcea smiled at her. "What if I help you attain your wildest dreams?" she asked softly.

Amanda's heart thundered. "You do not know me, and therefore you do not know any of my dreams."

"You do not dream of being de Warenne's wife?" Dulcea asked, almost coyly. "Amanda, you can have exactly what you want!"

Amanda began to shake. "Stop."

But Dulcea came close, so that their faces almost touched. "I will help you, darling. I've seen how he looks at you. All you must do is lure him into your bed. You will do so at Belford House, and when he is with you, I will make certain Belford discovers you both." Dulcea smiled, triumphant. "You will be the captain's wife before the year is out."

Amanda was sick. "I will never trap Cliff into marriage!"

"Why not?"

Amanda despised Dulcea then. "I don't think you could ever understand." She hurried away, lifting her gown and breaking into a run.

Her tears finally began.

Dulcea Belford was horrid.

But Dulcea rushed after her. "You fool! This is the answer to all of our problems! To all of our prayers!"

And in that moment, Amanda had to know what her mother really wanted. She whirled. "What does that mean? What problems could you possibly have? What is it that you really want? Why don't you try being honest for once? Maybe, just maybe, I will help you—not because I care, but because, in spite of everything, you are my birth mother."

Dulcea seized her hands, her eyes brilliant, madly so. "I am in desperate straits, Amanda. Belford is so deeply in debt that last week, our credit ran out. We have no more means. I am begging you to help us."

"By marrying for funds," Amanda said slowly, stunned.

"Forget that damned dowry he gave you. He is the one. You are still a virgin, aren't you? Even I know he would do the honorable thing, especially as we could threaten a scandal if he did not."

So this was the plot. Dulcea had wanted her dowry at first, until she had conceived the plan of marrying her daughter to Cliff for his fabulous wealth. Amanda wiped the moisture from her eyes. She had been right to refuse to trust her. "Once, long ago, I foolishly dreamed of being in your arms. That dream is gone. It's late. Good night." She walked away.

"Call on me tomorrow, darling," Dulcea called after her as if she had not heard. "I will introduce you to Belford and the children and we will make our plans!"

Amanda hurried into the house, afraid she might retch now, in public. The room began to spin. She had no stamina left. On the threshold of the ballroom, she paused, grasping the doorway. She did not want to espy Cliff now, as he would take one look at her and demand to know what had transpired. She did not want to ever discuss what had just happened with Dulcea. On the other hand, she had never needed to be in his arms more. But if that happened, she might not have the courage to tell him she was leaving tomorrow—and she might change her mind about leaving, as well.

After a moment, some of the dizziness passed. Amanda inhaled, still trembling, still sick. A terrible aftertaste lingered. Finally, she had met her mother; finally, she knew the truth about her. Amanda gagged, realizing she still had to retch after all. She had to leave the ball, immediately, before she undid her success of the evening.

She scanned the dance floor, hoping to find someone who could take her home—anyone but Cliff. To her relief, Cliff was not there, although she did glimpse the earl and countess dancing, both of them smiling. She was ice-cold, deep in her heart and in the marrow of her bones. At least the nausea was manageable. She glanced across the room.

Then she saw Rex, standing by himself near a gilded column, dark and handsome, but clearly brooding. His gaze was unwavering, directed some distance away.

Amanda made her way over to him. He remained so preoccupied that when she came up to him, he did not even notice her. She became aware of the covertly sensual way he was staring through his lashes, as if to disguise his interest. She followed his gaze and realized he was staring at Blanche Harrington, who was stunningly attired in a green ball gown and surrounded by a group of ladies and gentlemen. She had never seemed more elegant or lovely. Was Rex interested in the great heiress? She was surprised. If he was, it was unfortunate, as even Amanda knew by now that an heiress like Blanche would marry a great title.

Rex started, noting her for the first time. "Are you all right?"

Amanda forgot about the other woman. "I am exhausted." She managed a smile, then a wave of dizziness hit her again. Rex grasped her arm. "I do not feel all that well. Would you mind taking me home? If it is not too much trouble?"

His gaze was far too penetrating. "I'll find Cliff. He will see you home. I think he is having a cigar in the smoking room."

She stiffened. "Please, Rex, I hate putting you out, but I'd prefer not to see Cliff right now."

His eyes widened.

Amanda didn't even try to pretend. "He will see I am upset. This is not the time or the place. I plan to speak with him first thing in the morning. Please," she repeated. "I really feel poorly."

He did not hesitate. "I will gladly take you home. I have had enough of this ball, anyway. These kinds of events don't amuse me at all."

Amanda was terribly relieved. She could not leave the ball quickly enough as he guided her from the great room. But the bitter taste of what had just transpired between her and Dulcea remained. She was certain it would linger for the rest of her life.

## *CHAPTER TWENTY*

CLIFF WAS VERY ALARMED as he strode into Harmon House. It was almost two in the morning, and just when he had realized that he had not seen Amanda anywhere at the ball in a good hour, a servant had come up to him to tell him that Rex had escorted her home. Something was amiss. He was her escort, not Rex. He felt certain someone had cut her, but he could not understand why she hadn't come to him.

And he wasn't happy, either, about the way Dulcea Belford had been regarding him just before he had left. There had been something spiteful and calculating in her expression—and there was an odd glint of triumph. He dearly hoped Amanda had not exchanged words with her mother, but he was almost certain that she had. If so, that would explain her hasty departure, but not why she had gone to Rex instead of him.

The house was silent. Lizzie, Tyrell, the earl and countess had all left the ball shortly after midnight, but Sean and Eleanor remained and would undoubtedly stay for another hour or two. He took the stairs two at a time and paused at Amanda's door. Obviously, it was late, and he should not barge into her bedroom at this hour.

His heart tightened. He had thought of little else that evening than his extraordinary feelings and the woman who had somehow, impossibly, engendered them. He had been looking forward to a very long, very deep good-night kiss, and far more. He had been anticipating having her in his arms, in his bed, and touching her as he wished. He smiled, leaning against the wall.

He was a de Warenne. When the men in his family fell in love, it was once and forever. He could survive this night alone, because once she was his wife, he would never sleep without her again. Knowing Amanda, she would join him on his voyages, at least until she was carrying his child.

*His wife.* He had never dreamed he would ever think such words or want to make such a commitment. But Amanda was going to become his wife, and soon, of that he had no doubt. First thing in the morning, he would buy her a proper ring, so he could propose marriage to her. He would even get down on one knee. Normally, he thought romance nonsense, but God, he wanted to be as romantic as possible with her.

*His child.* He adored his two children, and fatherhood was the greatest joy of his life. Now, he could think of nothing more joyous than Amanda carrying another son or daughter for him. But she had been rudely deprived for most of her life. He wanted to give her everything life had to offer, all of the finer things she had missed, the opera and champagne, rubies and pearls, fine art and gowns designed by Parisian couturiers, safety, security, love. His heart danced. He could wait for a third child. He was getting so ahead of himself.

He glanced at her door, images of Amanda at the ball filling his mind, the most beautiful woman present, the most courageous, the most unique. He had never declared himself before and he felt awkward and even gauche now. He had never dreamed he would one day ask a woman to marry him, either, but he would somehow find the right words, even if she so often made him tongue-tied. He realized he had his hand on the knob. If he went inside now, he thought, he was going to make love to her.

But she deserved a proper proposal first, just as she really deserved a genuine wedding and a wedding night which she would never forget.

He fought his own base instincts, because he wanted to make love to her then and there. Although he had been with many women he had not truly made love to any of them.

He sighed and went back downstairs to the west wing. He banged on Rex's door, hoping he was alone. However, his brother was known to carouse, his amputated leg not hindering his conquests. "Are you asleep, Rex?" he demanded.

His brother grunted. "Not anymore."

Cliff stepped into the bedroom as his brother sat up and lit a lamp. He was alone, fortunately. "What happened? Why didn't you summon me? I was Amanda's escort. I should have brought her home."

Rex appeared annoyed. "Go back to bed, Cliff. Speak with her in the morning. She seemed upset, somewhat." He turned off the light and flopped back down, clearly ending the conversation.

But Cliff didn't go. "Did she say why she was upset?"

"No, she did not. Good night."

"How distressed was she?"

"I do not know! Good night, Cliff!"

Cliff sighed and left. If it had been truly important, Rex would have alerted him. He would speak with Amanda in the morning, before he went to Bond Street for her ring. He would buy her the most magnificent diamond he could find. Just in case he could not find the right words to express his feelings, the grand gesture would.

He smiled to himself.

CLIFF HAD HARDLY SLEPT at all, too overcome with his feelings to do so. It was shortly after eight, and he and Tyrell were the only ones taking breakfast at that hour. His brother was reading both the *Herald* and the *Dublin Times.* Cliff fidgeted, sipping coffee, his stomach twisted into knots. Amanda would probably remain abed for a few more hours, and the Bond Street shops did not open until eleven. He wanted to see her before he went out. Time had never crept by with more infuriating delay.

"What is wrong with you?" Tyrell remarked.

Cliff realized he had been drumming his fingers on the table. "Nothing."

"You appear like a green-broke race horse about to be let out of the starting gate."

That was exactly how he felt, but he did not say so. And then he heard her steps. He jumped to his feet as Amanda appeared in the dining room doorway, fully dressed in a pale ivory-and-gold striped silk. She looked as if she had slept only a few hours, as well. Strain was mirrored on her face and in her eyes.

Something *had* happened last night, he realized grimly, instantly concerned. And damn Rex for making light of it. Cliff rushed forward.

"Good morning." She nodded at Tyrell, her smile forced, and then she turned to Cliff. "I would like a word with you. In private," she added quietly.

In that stunning moment, he felt as if she was the adult, he the child, and he was being summoned for a set-down. "Of course," he said. He glanced at Tyrell. "Excuse us."

Tyrell nodded, returning to his newspaper.

Cliff followed Amanda down the hall and into the library. As he stepped inside, she closed the door behind him. "I am becoming increasingly alarmed," he said, remarking her every feature. "You did not sleep well."

She sent him a wan smile. "Neither, apparently, did you."

"What happened last night? Why did you leave in such haste? Why didn't you summon me? I would have taken you home!" he exclaimed.

She smiled again, more firmly. "It was obvious you were enjoying yourself," she said.

What was she talking about? "I was enjoying watching your incredible success," he said, and he flushed, for that wasn't what he really meant. He added, "I was enjoying watching you."

Her chin lifted. "There is something I wish to discuss."

His alarm escalated dramatically. "Are you upset with me? Have I done something to offend you?"

"Oh, Cliff." She smiled fully now. "How could I be upset with you? I will forever be grateful for all you have done for me, and last night was wonderful." She hesitated, coloring. "I will never forget our waltz."

"You are speaking as if we will never waltz again!" he exclaimed. He stepped closer, intentionally towering over her. He had no intention of losing her now. "You are speaking as if you are going somewhere."

She wet her lips, her gaze on his. "I have made plans," she whispered.

"Plans? What kind of plans?" he demanded, dread uncoiling as swiftly as a serpent.

"While you were away, I realized I have no wish to marry. I am going home."

For one moment, he gaped at her, absolutely shocked. "What?"

"I am going home. I cannot marry. I will not. Please, do not misunderstand. I will forever be grateful for all that you have done for me, but my place is in Jamaica. I am going to open up a shop, with borrowed funds, and eventually, I intend to start a shipping business."

He felt as if someone had dealt him a physical blow and he became so dazed he could hardly think. "You want to go back to the island," he repeated. "But this is your home!"

"Harmon House is *your* home." She smiled firmly at him. "I know you are shocked, as you had other plans for me, but I will not back down."

His mind began to work. "You want to open a shop? What is this about?" His senses returned. "What happened last night?"

"This is not about last night, not precisely. I have taken far too much from you and your family. I made my plans while you were gone, when I had a chance to really think. Cliff, I know you only want what is best for me, and I am so appreciative. But

I don't want to marry a stranger. As much as I love Ashford Hall, Jamaica is my home. If I do not marry here, I must provide for myself, and that is what I will do. I know all about trade and shipping. I have made elaborate plans," she added. "I feel very confident I can become a success."

He fought for calm. It was a long moment before he could speak. "Of course you do not want to marry a stranger," he said. He hesitated, wanting to blurt out his feelings but very unsure of how he would be received. He had never had such a failure in confidence before. "You do not have to marry, Amanda," he said slowly, "until you wish to." He was resolved to win her heart, if he had somehow lost it. "But you can stay here. I will turn all suitors away."

She shook her head. "That is the point, Cliff, I cannot stay here. I want to go home and start my business immediately."

He had to grip the back of a chair as he stared at her, incapable of understanding her now. "Was it Dulcea? Did she say something to you last night? Although you do not seem stricken with hurt..."

Amanda interrupted. "I spoke to her. She wanted me to live with her at Belford House, among other things."

He tensed. "But instead, you are running away to the island?"

She lifted her head. "I am not running away! And I am not leaving because of Dulcea. I did not particularly like her and I don't care if I ever see her again. I am not going to argue with you, although I wish you could understand. You rescued a child in Spanishtown. I am a woman now. You can't take care of me this way indefinitely. It is time I took care of myself." Her gaze was moist.

"Why can't I take care of you," he tried. "It is a pleasant task."

"It defeats the purpose of my becoming independent."

He stared, at a loss. Why did she wish to be independent now, when he was so deeply in love? Women were not independent! "If you really wish to go back to the island, I will take you." This seemed to be a solution for them both. "If you want to open up a shop, I will gladly loan you the funds. As for shipping—"

"No!"

He stopped, shocked. "You do not want my help anymore?"

"You do not understand," she cried softly. "I wish to do this alone! I must do this alone! "

He was now aghast. Was he going to lose her? And he knew he could not. He would do whatever he had to so that he won her heart all over again. "Why? I simply cannot understand what is happening here."

She bit her lip, finally tearing her gaze away from him. She smiled so sadly again. With real dread, he watched her slowly pace toward the fireplace. The transformation, he realized, was complete. He had thought her changed last night, but no, he saw the true difference now, in that moment, with her telling him she had no wish to be dependant on anyone, not even on him. An elegant lady was slowly taking a turn about the room, choosing her words with care, and they were words of rejection. He was realizing that now. She finally faced him. "Do not be so upset."

"I cannot turn my back on you. Please, don't ask me to do so." He was begging, he realized.

"I am not asking you to do so. I am asking you to set me free."

He was horrified. "Is that how you feel?"

She was white, but she somehow nodded.

And finally he understood. Until this season, society had always made him feel like a caged animal, and he would have to leave, rushing to make sail, rushing to be free. Of course she felt that way. She had spent two months in town, and she'd had enough. Beneath the stunning and genteel facade, La Sauvage still lived.

As frightened as he was, he was also fiercely glad. "I will take you home," he said. And he would watch her make over her life from the shadows, because whether she wanted it or not, he would always be her protector and her guardian. For the first time in his life, he would deny his virile interests and he would wait as long as it took to woo her back to him.

He went over to her and clasped her small hands in both of his. "I brought you here to set you free," he whispered roughly, "not to imprison you in society's cell."

"I know."

"Do you regret the wardrobe, the reading lessons, the waltz?"

"Of course not! You don't understand." She touched his face. "I am not going home as La Sauvage, I am going home as Miss Carre. I do miss the wind in my hair, but it isn't society I must escape. I have to go home because I can't be your ward anymore."

She had just stabbed him in the heart. He dropped her hands. "I thought I understood. You wish to run from *me?*"

"I can only tell you again, I must make my own way now, without a husband, without a guardian—without you. But we will always be friends, won't we?"

He turned away. Was she rejecting him? He tried to think, but his heart was screaming at him. Nothing made sense anymore. This couldn't be happening. He could not be losing the only woman he had ever loved. If she had been running from society, he would have let her go and followed and waited for her. But if she was running from him, he could not let her go.

He slowly faced her.

"I have hurt you!" she cried. She clasped her hands to her face, which was starkly pale, in spite of two bright spots of crimson. "Cliff, you have been the best champion a woman could ever have! In my heart, you will always be my champion. And one day, when I am wealthy and respected, I will call on you at Windsong and we will reminisce over these times!"

"Like hell," he said.

"And I am going to pay you back for every cent you have spent on me. Finally, I am making *you* a promise!"

"I don't want to be repaid, not one cent," he cried. "This is about what happened at Ashford Hall!" he accused, pointing at her. His hand was shaking.

She backed up, gasping, and he knew he was right. "I don't know what you mean!"

He stalked her, recalling her attempt at seduction and his brutal rejection of her. How he wished he had taken her then, entirely. "I rejected you."

She flushed. "You are a man of honor. You were right—my advances were wrong!"

"And this is why you run." Triumph began, but it was predatory and savage.

She shook her head. "No!"

He trapped her against the wall. "You said you made these plans while I was in Holland. I went to Holland because my desire for you was beyond all control. I went abroad so I would not take what you were offering. And while I was gone, you decided to leave…me."

She inhaled. "Yes."

Relief began and his emotions, just slightly, eased. The rest of his body, already battle ready and fiercely aroused, escalated its tension. His loins engorged fully. "Now you are being honest with me," he whispered, sliding his hand to her cheek.

She gasped, comprehension filling her eyes, but she cried, "What are you doing?"

He had wanted her insanely that night, and even months ago, on his ship, when she was untutored and naive. His heart thundered. He leaned closer. "You know what I am doing."

For one moment, Amanda stared, realizing he was going to give in to his desires, at last. "Cliff," she breathed, reaching for his shoulders.

He pulled her into his arms, against his massive chest, his mouth covering hers.

He had intended a savage, possessive, demanding kiss. But the moment he felt her lips, he softened, the anger, the fear, the savagery vanishing. This woman he loved. And he needed her now and forever.

He touched her mouth softly with his lips, again and again, coaxing them to open wide and wider still. She gasped and he entered her, thrilling, and she began kissing him back, their passion slowly and surely increasing.

Cliff thrust his tongue deep, pressed her more firmly against the wall, and shifted his loins against her hip, already wanting to explode in his release. Amanda wept, clinging to his arms.

He pulled away, gripping her hand. "Come with me," he said flatly, and before she could speak they were crossing the room.

The hall was empty. He glanced into the dining room, but Tyrell was hidden by his newspaper. He gave Amanda a look, one which spoke of all of his intentions, and he saw her nod, her eyes huge. They ran up the stairs.

The moment they were in her bedroom he released her, slamming the door and locking it. He threw off his jacket, meeting her gaze. She stood near the bed, as still as a doe paralyzed by an oncoming light. But she was breathing hard, almost as hard as he.

He approached, taking her in his arms. "I want to make you happy, Amanda," he said thickly. He stroked her cheek. He wasn't sure how much control he could exercise now.

She nodded. "Cliff…hurry."

He hadn't been sure she wouldn't think to refuse him in the end. He cried out, carrying her to the bed while she flung her arms around him, kissing his neck, his jaw, his cheek. He laughed exultantly, because nothing was more important than taking this woman—his woman—now, and giving her more pleasure than any one woman had a right to.

He laid her down, tearing at the buttons on the back of her dress. They popped and scattered across the rug.

She smiled breathlessly and tore his shirt open, too, more buttons spewing. Then she inhaled, laying her palms on his chest. Her hands were shaking wildly.

He thrilled at her admiration, and flung his shirt aside. She gasped, ogling his chest and arms and he laughed, somehow shrugging her gown off. All laughter died. Sexual tension thrummed in the room. They fell to the bed in a swirl of pillows, sheets, petticoats.

He took her mouth again while fumbling with her chemise and corset, trying not to grind himself between her thighs. He was going to embarrass himself, he realized, as he had no self-control left.

She seized his belt and opened it, and their eyes met while she fumbled with his breeches. Every caress caused his loins to grow. He had to smile. "Darling, I am trying to be a gentleman—"

"Do not bother!" She gasped, setting him free.

He went still, poised above her, as she fumbled with his manhood, stroking it. He gave up, arching into her hand, crying out, shaking but somehow controlling himself.

He flung his arms around her, spread her legs and slid up against slick, wet heat. Amanda writhed against him. "Cliff, I cannot wait," she gasped, nipping his jaw urgently.

"I don't want to hurt you," he managed, pressing into her. "I want to pleasure you."

"Oh!" Her eyes grew wide and startled.

But he was still, as stunned as she was by the intense beginning of their union, her flesh seizing his. "Hold on, darling, my love," he whispered, and slowly, inch by inch, he made his way home.

She shuddered wildly, clinging, and finally he drove past her innocence, unable to repress a cry of savage joy. She gasped once as he did so and then began to weep in pleasure, not pain. He felt her spasms beginning and he exulted again, moving hard and swift, intently, seeking his own climax. And when she wept, sobbing his name, he gave over to her, in the most savage explosion of pleasure he had ever experienced.

When her pleasure finally faded, Amanda simply held on to

Cliff. Her love knew no bounds. She dared not think past the emotions filling her heart, her soul, her entire existence. She ran her hand down his hard, muscular back, awed by the power beneath her palm. She felt him stirring inside of her and she smiled.

He raised his head and smiled back at her, the most heart-wrenching smile she had ever received. "I hope you are well pleased?"

She kissed him, closing her eyes, intending a peck, but it took on a life of its own. When they were both breathless and fully aroused, she managed to open her eyes. "I am very well pleased," she said coyly, wriggling just a bit.

His huge manhood throbbed restlessly inside of her. "That, my darling, was but a brief appetizer," he said, eyes glittering, dimples deep. "There are several courses to come before the main one."

"Really?" she gasped, tears forming, for he was slowly withdrawing his huge length, and as slowly, penetrating again. Her mind began to blacken; he left her, causing real dismay.

"Darling, the first course," he said, bending over her distended lips. He flicked his tongue between them and over her own small turgid flesh, laving her there. Amanda instantly wept his name, exploding fiercely.

When she returned to some small degree of sanity, he was moving inside her, watching her closely, his face strained with lust.

She touched his cheek, her arousal spiking. "I want another course," she managed, incapable of even the smallest smile.

His eyes widened. "Yes," he said, shifting away.

She seized his wrist, managing to give him a very significant look. "Oh, no, a different meal—a very large one."

He went still.

Her heart threatening to make her faint, Amanda pushed him onto his back. He went willingly. His erection stood up, hard and straight. She bent over him and tasted heaven.

He cried out.

AMANDA SAT at her secretary, clad in a nightgown, a small candle giving some light, studying the letter she had written. In her bed, Cliff lay sprawled out, asleep. It was well past dusk. They had made love all day.

She had seen his signed name many times, and now she carefully forged his signature and folded up the instructions she had written, brushing a tear from the parchment. She placed it in an envelope and sealed it. Her heart shattered for the hundredth time since she had left him in her bed alone.

He had taken her by surprise that morning. If she'd had a chance to think about what their passion would really mean, she might have rejected his advances, because being in his arms meant everything to her. A wiser woman would have avoided this, not because she loved him so deeply, but because he didn't love her back.

Amanda felt very certain that when he awoke and came to his senses, he was going to insist they marry, out of his sense of honor and duty.

Nothing had changed. She was foolishly and hopelessly in love with a man who did not love her in return. She wondered how it would feel to be his wife and learn of an extramarital affair. Or worse, to see him with another woman one day. It was time to become an independent woman.

The temptation to remain with him, just for a while, was huge. Being his mistress even temporarily would be so glorious—but he was going to insist on marriage now and she could not accept his terms. Knowing it would eventually end would be a dark cloud spoiling every shared moment. Besides, Amanda wasn't sure she would ever be able to go her separate way if she continued on as his lover for very long.

She got up, the floor creaking. She winced but went to the armoire, the letter in her hand, and slipped on a wrapper. She had just opened the door, as quietly as possible, when he said, "What are you doing?"

She turned, forcing a smile. The moment she faced him she was utterly distracted, as he sat in her bed, starkly nude and in his state of impossible glory. For one moment, she forgot what she was about, but then she recalled the letter hidden by the skirt of her wrapper. "I thought to find a maid and ask for some wine and maybe something to eat."

But what she really planned to do was have her message sent to the docks. If MacIver believed the instructions he was about to receive, he would be taking her home tomorrow, on the very next tide. As Amanda had seen Cliff writing instructions to his various crews, she felt confident that MacIver would never think twice about following his new orders.

Her heart cracked irreparably apart. Tomorrow night she would be at sea. She must not think about how hurt and angry Cliff would be. Sooner or later he would find another lover to comfort him, she thought. The idea made her feel bitter; she was instantly ashamed of herself.

Cliff yawned and stretched, making her heart turn over, causing her body to heat. A gleam came to his eyes. "A very fine idea. Ask for champagne—and then come back to bed." He sent her a soft but seductive smile that caused moisture to explode between her thighs.

*I will never stop loving him*, she thought.

So much sorrow came. She was certain that he would soon lose any affection that he had for her and eventually, he would forget her entirely. But she smiled at him and slipped from the room. "I'll be right back," she said.

"Hurry," he murmured.

And as she found a housemaid, all she could think of was how angry he would be when he learned of her betrayal.

## *CHAPTER TWENTY-ONE*

AMANDA SAT IN THE hired hansom outside of Belford House, her smaller bags at her feet. It was hard to think, much less alight from the coach. She had decided to have one last word with her mother before leaving London. She hadn't said goodbye to Cliff and raw grief consumed her. Of course she couldn't face him this way—it would be too difficult after the night they had just shared. She was aware of being a coward now.

She closed her eyes tightly against the burn of tears, crying for them both. He had left her that morning in an exceptionally cheerful mood, telling her he'd see her before supper, having no idea that by evening, she'd be far out to sea. He'd gone out almost directly, his step a swagger. Amanda had watched him leave from her bedroom window, her heart beating in frantic protest, loving him anew, wanting to call him back. She'd had to remind herself again and again that eventually, sooner, rather than later, their paths would cross on the island. But what difference did that make? She was not going to become his lover, even if he still wished it, as that would solve nothing, just as she wouldn't marry him out of his sense of obligation toward her. She sighed, wiped her eyes, and slipped to the street.

The driver spat chewing tobacco onto the ground.

Amanda went up the walk and rang the bell, seeking some composure. A moment later she was standing in the foyer, trying to prepare herself for a final moment with her mother. It was so odd to think the word *mother,* and to have no real feelings of affection for Dulcea. But one fact remained: Dulcea was her mother by birth and she had two children who were Amanda's half siblings. She was compelled to see her one last time before leaving London forever.

Dulcea hurried into the hall, her eyes wide, smiling. "Amanda! You have changed your mind. I am so pleased you have come." She stopped, evincing surprise. "I do not see your bags. Haven't you come to stay here with me?"

"I have come to say goodbye. I told you, I am going home." And Amanda finally realized that a part of her was hoping for some small sign of affection from this woman, in spite of their previous encounter.

Dulcea paled. "How can you do this? You will give up your new life here, in town, to live on an island infested with pirates, to live among them?"

"I believe I told you, I will open up a shop. I intend to remain a gentlewoman. Eventually I will have a shipping concern."

"You are mad, and you are an ungrateful girl!" Dulcea trembled, her eyes blazing. "I have offered you a home, a real home, and you merely walk away to find adventure? You are exactly like your father."

Amanda stiffened. "You have offered me nothing, Lady Belford. All I ever wanted was some genuine affection from you. All I have seen in your eyes is calculation and greed. I came here hoping that the other night at the ball was not the truth. But it was, wasn't it?"

Dulcea was still, myriad emotions crossing her face. Then she spoke more calmly. "I am angry because you are hurting your prospects. If you see calculation, it is because I want what is best for you! You are—" She stopped, lowering her voice. "You are my daughter, no matter the past. I want a bright future for you."

Amanda did not believe her. "Why do you care so little for me? Is it a defect of character on your part? Or am I at fault?"

Dulcea drew up. "Of course I care for you. I told you so at the ball."

Amanda shook her head. "You do not care for me, you care for whatever wealth I can bring to your home. I am a *lady* now, but somehow, still, I am not good enough to receive your affections. Is it because I am a bastard? So I will pay for your sins? Or is it because you see a pirate's whelp standing here now? I have done all that I could to change myself, but it isn't enough, is it?"

"It is not enough," Dulcea agreed eagerly, "but I could help you become a great and genuine lady. I still plan to see you wed to de Warenne. Amanda, you will become a reigning socialite."

Amanda felt only disgust. "And you will rule the ton with me, while we both live fabulously off Cliff's wealth."

"Why not?" Dulcea said happily.

And finally, she felt the loss of the dream of her mother which her father had instilled in her. Coupled with her grief over losing Cliff, it felt unbearable. Her hands shaking, Amanda took off the pearl earrings Cliff had given her, handing them to Dulcea. She would never part with his first gift, the necklace. "Here. Sell them. Maybe it will help. As soon as I make my first profits, I will send you something, as much as I can, and hopefully it will be enough to tide you and your children over." She could barely believe what she was offering, but she meant it. Dulcea Belford did not care for her, but she was her mother and she was in distress, and her two children were her half brother and half sister.

"How can you do this? I am offering you everything, Amanda!"

She was offering nothing at all. "Goodbye...Mother." Amanda walked out.

HE HAD BEEN SMILING from the moment he had left Amanda in her bed. As it was later in the afternoon, his face was actually beginning to ache. But now, truly, he understood what love was. It was a great swelling of joy and happiness. He could hardly believe he had once thought himself immune to the emotion and had actually referred to it as an affliction.

He entered Harmon House, his gaze veering toward the stairs. The engagement ring he had just purchased was burning a hole in his breast pocket. He had rehearsed a dozen different proposals, and all had seemed deficient and inane. He somehow wanted to convey the depth of his feelings, if he hadn't done so yesterday and last night.

He still wanted her terribly. Last night he had made love to her a hundred different ways, and he simply could not wait to do so again. He dearly hoped she understood what he was expressing when he kissed her and touched her and held her. He felt certain the three words every woman longed to hear might be difficult to enunciate. But after last night, she had to know how deeply in love he was.

About to rush up the stairs, he hesitated. His father had just stepped into the front hall, his expression controlled and difficult to read.

He tensed, feeling fourteen, not twenty-eight, and turned, removing his hand from the banister. "Before you set me down, you should know my intentions are honorable." He reached into his pocket and removed the sapphire-blue velvet box and opened it. The eight carat diamond sparked, catching the light.

The earl smiled. "Cliff, I had no doubt that you were intending marriage. You made yourself clear the day I arrived here. I believe your exact words were that the day you ruined her, you would marry her."

"I was hardly planning the event when we spoke of it."

The earl raised a brow, as if he did not believe him, then said, "The ring is exquisite and it suits her. Congratulations." He clasped his shoulder. "I am thrilled for you both.

Cliff finally relaxed. "You will not berate me for my impatient behavior?"

"No, I will not," the earl laughed. "We are virile men, and when smitten, there is no stopping us." Briefly, a faraway look came into his eyes, and Cliff knew he was thinking of his wife.

Then he came back to the present. "May I say one more thing?"

Cliff had been glancing up the stairs, his impatience now full-blown. He turned back to the earl. "Of course."

"I am very proud of you. If I have been harder on you, and less tolerant of your behavior, it was not because I loved you any less than Tyrell or Rex. Nor was it due to your reckless nature and the many sleepless nights you caused me and my wife. Cliff, no one was more acutely aware of the fact that you are my youngest son than I."

Cliff no longer thought of Amanda. He stared, uncertain as to where his father was going with his monologue. Growing up, he *had* been treated differently than his brothers. However, he had been impossibly wild, which had given the earl cause to be harsher with him. "I don't quite understand."

"I have been harder on you because, as my youngest son, you have needed more character, more strength and more ambition to survive well in this world. Considering the man that stands before me today, I think my stratagem in raising you was correct."

Cliff flushed with pleasure, as the earl's praise was rare. "I know there were many times when you wanted to whip me, but you never did. I am a father now, and Alexi is also a handful. I understand why you had to be tougher with me than my brothers."

"You have made a kingdom from the sand and the sea, an achievement only your stepbrother Devlin can claim, and clearly, your sense of duty and honor is as strong as your brothers. Not only is it apparent in your care of your children, you rescued a damsel in distress and became her champion. I am very pleased with the man you have become."

Cliff smiled. "Thank you, Edward."

Edward smiled back. "Your damsel awaits."

Cliff grinned, his heart racing. "Indeed, she does. There is something I must do, and hopefully, not make a fool of myself in the process."

"She will never see you as a fool, son. Her eyes shine when she looks at you."

Cliff turned toward the stairs when a servant approached. "Captain, sir?" He was carrying an envelope.

Cliff was impatient. "In a moment—"

"Sir, Miss Carre explicitly stated I was to deliver this to you at four in the afternoon. It is four, sir."

Cliff about-faced with genuine surprise and an inkling of dismay. What was this? "Where is Miss Carre?" he asked, taking the envelope and noting that it was formally addressed to him in her scripted hand. Dread began.

"She went out shortly after noon," the servant said.

Cliff tore open the envelope and unfolded a letter.

My dear Cliff,

By the time you receive this letter, I will be well out to sea and on my way home. I hope you understand my need to go back to the islands and that you freely allow me to leave. Cliff, I am so deeply in your debt. I do not have enough words to express my gratitude for all you have done. I remain eternally devoted to you. I will miss our friendship and your children, indeed, I will miss your entire warm, loving, wonderful family. But I must seek my own way in the world. I pray you will soon come to understand.

When you return to Windsong, I would like to call on you, if you will allow it, as I dearly wish to remain dear friends. Until then, my best regards to you, your children and your family.

With Affection, Amanda

Cliff stared at the page, absolutely incapable of comprehending what was written there.

"Cliff? What is it?" the earl demanded.

He slowly reread every word. When he was done, one refrain echoed in his mind. *She had left him.* He looked up.

Edward had seized his shoulder. "Is it Amanda?"

*She had left him.* She had left him after he had made love to her all day and night, expressing with his body what he could not express with words. He was finally, deeply, eternally in love, and the woman he desired had rejected him.

*She was writing about friendship and affection.*

*He carried an engagement ring in his coat pocket.*

"Cliff? May I?"

Cliff shoved the letter at his father, reeling. How was this happening?

She wished to be *friends?*

He began to shake. This was the woman he loved. This woman was going to be his wife. And she was sailing without him across the Atlantic Ocean?

Images assailed him, bloody and murderous, of pirates and rogues attacking innocent merchant ships. He strode for the door. He could not assimilate what she was thinking or what she wanted, and just then, he didn't care. What he did understand was that he, and he alone, would transport her to the West Indies. To do otherwise was to risk her life.

*Didn't she love him?*

"Cliff," the earl tried. "Do not take this literally."

Cliff didn't hear him. It was finally beginning to sink in. "Get me a coach, a hansom, a horse, instantly," he snarled at the doorman.

On the front steps, he paced back and forth, now incredulous. Women fell all over themselves for his favors, but she had left him.

How could Amanda do this?

So much hurt stabbed through him that he halted in his tracks, incapable of another step. He had suffered sword wounds, pistol shots and knife wounds, but he had never felt this kind of hurt. It wasn't physical, it was a thousand times worse.

Hadn't she been in love with him a few weeks ago, before he left for Holland?

And finally, the anger began. Cliff cursed. *Friendship?* Was she insane? He did not want friendship, he wanted a wife…he wanted her love.

"Sir." A groom came running up the drive, leading a horse.

He grabbed the reins and swung into the saddle. He would stop her, if she hadn't set sail yet. As he galloped into the street, almost causing two carriages to collide, he began to realize it was unlikely that she had left. He was at the wharves and shipping offices every day, attending to his own business affairs, and he was fairly certain that not a single ship was scheduled to depart that day for the islands, although two ships had left yesterday. He spurred the gelding on. Coachmen cursed at him as they were forced to the curb.

However, he was not completely certain of the schedules, and he was aware that the tides would have been favorable for a departure that afternoon, beginning at 3:00 p.m. He cursed.

If she had left, he'd ready his ship and chase her down.

This was not ending her way; in fact, this was not ending at all.

He was a de Warenne. Amanda belonged to him, now and forever, and he would pursue her until he found her and won her over. If she had loved him once, he would make her love him again.

But when he got to the wharves, something was wrong. Cliff was halfway to the shipping offices used by his company when he realized, in real disbelief, what that was. He pulled his mount to a sliding halt, whipped it around and gaped in absolute shock at the empty berth where the *Fair Lady* should have been; where she had been at anchor yesterday and last night.

For one moment, he stared, pulse pounding, blood roaring in his veins, in his head.

And his world went still, the vast stillness before great battle. When he spoke, it was so softly, no passerby could hear. "*Where the fuck is my ship.*"

TEN DAYS LATER, Amanda sat at the Portuguese desk in Cliff's cabin, engrossed in a stunning history of Alexander the Great. She was determined not to wallow in grief—or worse, regret—and the only way to do that was to immerse herself in reading. For once in her life, she avoided going on deck. She couldn't even look at Mac or another officer on the quarterdeck without seeing Cliff there, and remembering in perfect detail all the times they had shared at the helm, under the stars, racing the wind—some of the happiest moments of her life. Once she went back to those days, she would be thrown back to the time shared at Harmon House, to the lovely family suppers with Cliff admiring her from across the dining table, to the afternoon when he had taught her to waltz, and the night of the Carrington ball, a night that remained bittersweet. And she could so easily relive, again and again, their final day and night together, spent passionately and tenderly making love. Once the grief began, it was consuming, a flood tide that was impossible to stop.

It was better not to think or sleep. Instead, she had read a dozen books in ten days.

Her eyes hurt and ached, as did her back from being hunched over. She paused for a moment and Cliff's smile came to mind, as did his beautiful face and his brilliant blue eyes, so soft with warmth and affection. Amanda inhaled, jumped to her feet, pacing, trying to force the image aside and if that did not work, to outdistance it. Instead, his smile vanished and his eyes turned dark with desire.

She was hot and cold at once. Once a thought of him began, she would want him desperately, and simultaneously, she would become sick with the burden of such a loss. And there would be damnable regret.

Worse, because she cared so much, she wondered time and

again what he had thought and felt when he had realized she was gone, leaving only a letter behind. She knew him well enough to know he would be furious that she had taken his ship, but she also thought he would be hurt, because no matter what else they might be, they had been good friends. She had betrayed him by leaving and by taking the frigate, after all he had done for her, and she knew he would see it that way, in black and white, not gray.

She wondered if he would even consider her a friend now. She knew she would never be able to stop herself from calling on him at Windsong when he returned to Kingston, but her devastation would be complete if he turned her away.

Of course, it would be better that way. But she couldn't imagine her life without Cliff in it somehow.

A knock sounded on the cabin door. Amanda went to answer it and found a young sailor there. "Miss Carre? Cap asks to speak with you."

Amanda swallowed, envisioning Cliff at the helm in his linen shirt, a Moroccan vest and his starkly white breeches and high boots. But when she nodded and stepped onto the main deck, Mac's lean back faced her. He had not questioned the orders she had forged, although he had admitted that it was unusual to receive written instructions when his captain was in port. Amanda had quickly covered, explaining that Cliff was preoccupied with his children. Mac had accepted that and they had set sail at a few minutes past three in the afternoon.

She slowly approached the quarterdeck. Mac gave the wheel over to Midshipman Clark and came down to stand beside her. He was grim. "Good day, Miss Carre."

"Good afternoon." She inhaled the fresh salted air, the scent of the sea but could not receive any pleasure from the tang and the brine. "What is wrong?"

"We are being hunted," Mac said.

Amanda tensed. She knew all the slang seamen used. Mac

could have said they were being chased or pursued, but each word had different nuances. "Who would be hunting us?" she asked, her heart thundering now.

"I don't know. They were espied at sunrise, but by noon, it became clear this is a hunt. Whoever is hunting us, he is light and swift and closing in rapidly. I give him another hour, at best."

It was Cliff, she thought, and there was a rush of excitement. Dread instantly followed. If it was Cliff, he probably despised her now. As she looked behind them, she could feel his power, his presence, even though the pursuing ship was but the size of her thumb. He was hunting his ship. Or was he?

If he was absolutely enraged, he might be hunting her, seeking retribution. Surely, that was not the case, because if so, their friendship was over.

"No pirate would ever take us on," Mac shook his head, "unless he was insane—or commissioned to do so. Appears to be a schooner. I've taken a good look through the glasses myself, and I am counting fifteen guns. We can't outrun such a small, light ship, but we can fight. We can easily destroy her. I'm calling action stations."

Amanda was shivering now, although she was warmly dressed. "I think I know who it is," she whispered, staring at the horizon. She thought she could actually feel his seething fury, and her fear and dread escalated.

Mac started. "Pray tell!"

Amanda braced herself for Mac's anger now. "I forged de Warenne's orders. I have made a terrible mistake!" she added, realizing in horror it was true.

He simply looked at her. "What?"

She inhaled. "I forged the captain's orders. He did not order you to transport me home. I gave those orders. I forged his signature." She wet her lips as Mac stared in growing disbelief. "He didn't know what I intended."

"Jesus have mercy on us both!" Mac exclaimed. "He will keelhaul me—you are lucky you are a woman!"

She wet her parched lips again. She was genuinely afraid; so much was at stake. Had she destroyed their bond of affection?

"Sweet Mary!" Mac blanched with utter comprehension. "Of course he's hunting us. You stole his *ship!*" Then crimson rushed to his face. "You stole his *best* ship!"

Amanda stared at the racing schooner, its two square sails visible. Mac was wrong. Within a half an hour, Cliff would be boarding and they would be face-to-face. She couldn't breathe adequately. "I *borrowed* the ship."

"That's not what he will think," Mac cried. He turned and started bellowing for the royals to come down.

*Mac was right.* He was looking at what she had done not just as a man, but as a captain. Amanda realized she had crossed a line, one that might not be repairable. Her fear intensified. Papa would kill anyone, man or woman, for doing what she had done. Cliff would never lay a hand on her, but he would be as enraged as any commander.

Oh, God, had she finally destroyed the bond they shared?

Sails were furling in rapid succession. "You had better wait below somewhere," Mac snapped. "Signal the schooner. Make certain it's the captain, and we will give him permission to board." He glared at her and strode back up to the quarterdeck.

Breathing hard, shaking like a leaf, Amanda rushed into the captain's cabin, her pale skirts swirling. She slammed the door and debated bolting it, but what was the point? Cliff had come for his ship, and she had no intention of trying to avoid him or even escape his wrath. As sweat began pouring down her body, she realized that what she wanted to do was not to defend herself or explain. She just wanted to go into his arms and take everything back.

But she had come so far. She had to remain resolved. She couldn't be his lover, and she couldn't marry him to uphold his honor. Then she laughed, aware of being in some hysteria. He wasn't going to think about honor now! He was going to think about punishment and taking his ship back.

She heard the canvas slapping the masts, waves lapping the hull. The frigate had slowed to a few knots. She trembled. She had to weather the impending storm and repair their relationship, somehow. Except, it was going to be a hurricane.

And hurricanes destroyed everything in their path.

*I'll never stop loving him*, she thought, *no matter what happens next.*

Grappling hooks sounded; metal clawing wood.

Amanda bit her lip, hard, her underclothes drenched. She wiped perspiration from her face. She had to salvage their friendship, no matter how furious he was, no matter how long it took.

She heard a cutter butting against the hull, and the men throwing down a rope ladder.

Amanda ran to the porthole to shove it open. She needed more air, but it was already wide.

The cabin door blew in off its hinges.

She cried out as Cliff filled the doorway.

His face was a tight, hard mask of fury, under absolute control. His legs were braced, but the deck did not roll. Amanda breathed hard. She wanted to tell him she was sorry, but no words would come forth.

He pointed at her, his eyes glittering savagely. "I have two things to say to you, madam."

She nodded, heart lurching. He *hated* her now.

"You are coming home with me. And we are getting married."

And with a final stare, he stormed out.

## *CHAPTER TWENTY-TWO*

AMANDA RAN AFTER HIM, shocked. He still wanted to marry her? She should have known that his sense of honor would far outweigh his anger and her betrayal.

He strode to the quarterdeck, snarling, "Get me a bottle of whiskey."

An officer leaped to obey.

Amanda hesitated below him on the main deck. He whirled and pointed. "This is not an opportune time."

She inhaled, rigid now. She needed to explain, if she could. She could not stand seeing him so angry with her. And what should she do about his statement that they were to wed? The terrible truth was, she did not want to fight him, not now and not ever. She could not triumph over him, anyway, if his mind was made up.

And clearly, his mind was made up now.

"Sir!" MacIver was pale.

Cliff smiled coldly at him. "Do explain your participation in Miss Carre's games."

"There was a letter with your orders, sir. It is in my berth. Your signature was affixed to it. I will get it now," Mac said tersely.

For one moment, Cliff stared at him, his expression harsh and uncompromising. Beneath the anger, she realized, he was *hurt*. Amanda summoned up her courage and said, stammering, "I forged the orders and your signature."

He gave her such a chilling look that she decided she was

wrong. She hadn't hurt him—he was furious and he despised her. "How clever." He turned to Mac. "You will bring the orders to me after your watch."

The officer came striding forward, a bottle of Irish whiskey and a glass in hand. Cliff took the bottle, ignoring the glass, tilted his head and drank, long and hard. Amanda shivered, realizing she was hugging herself. She should be terrified of such a man in such a state. If he hated her now—and she thought that he did—how on earth could he even think of marriage?

*Because,* she thought sadly, *he is noble and good.*

He drank again. Finally, she saw some of the terrible tension in his shoulders and back ease. Then, slowly, he turned to look down at her. His grim countenance wasn't as tight or as controlled, nor was it quite as hostile. He gestured with a nod at his cabin.

And Amanda saw the hurt in his eyes.

His anger was a facade. She hated what she had done, but she'd had to leave him, hadn't she? She turned and started across the deck, her heart hammering wildly, her shoulders square, trying to keep some composure wrapped about her like a heavy winter cloak. She heard him land catlike behind her and follow. She entered his cabin, walked to the bed and placed her back at the footboard, although she hardly expected an assault from behind. His attack would be direct and brutal. She had not a single doubt.

He paused in the center of the room, standing as if on a bucking ship. Torn from its hinges, the door lay on the floor, the doorway open.

"You left me," he said tersely, his gaze unwavering on hers.

She exhaled. "I am sorry. I am sorry for borrowing your ship, and I—"

"You left me after the night we shared."

She tried not to think about being in his arms, when he had seemed to love her as much as she loved him. "I told you that morning what I intended. The time we shared didn't change anything." She saw him flinch. "It was wonderful, but I meant it when I said I had to go home. I know you are angry. I know I took the coward's way, and I shouldn't have conned Mac—"

"I don't care about the ship!" he cried, stunning her. "I am glad you took my frigate—at least you would be safe from rovers. Damn it! *I made love to you and you left me!"*

She hugged herself harder, trying to ignore that painful figure of speech. "I knew you would want to marry me, Cliff, for all the wrong reasons. How could I accept that? The night we spent together only fueled my desire to leave."

"For all the wrong reasons? Our passion *fueled* your desire to leave me?"

"You misunderstand me," she cried. "I do not want to hurt you. But you ruined me, you would decide to marry me. Honor is not the right reason, not for me."

He stepped closer, his gaze piercing. "Do you even know my reasons, Amanda?"

"Yes, I do." Somehow she tilted up her chin, yet she felt tears falling. "You are the most honorable man I have ever met. I know my letter hardly stated the depth of my feelings, but after all you have done, and all your family has done, you must surely know that leaving you was very difficult."

"The depth of your feelings," he said. His nostrils flared, his gaze brilliant. "Do you refer to the friendship you wish to maintain—and your affection for me?" He was cold and sarcastic, taking a final step toward her.

He towered over her now. She wanted to step backward, away from him, but she held her ground. "I didn't think you would wish to continue our friendship. But it is so important to me. I will beg you to forgive me so we can remain dear friends."

"I don't want to be a dear friend," he said harshly. "And goddamn it, do not tell me you felt as a friend does when you were in my bed!"

She stiffened. "That's not fair."

"You left me. That's not fair," he shot back, giving no quarter.

"After all you have done, it wasn't fair, I agree completely. But I was desperate."

He shook his head. "I will never believe you are desperate to be a shopkeeper. And what woman is truly independent? Only a spinster or a widow. You are neither."

Slowly, hating her words, she said, "I had planned on the former."

"Like hell," he spat.

She accepted the dread filling her then. "You despise me now."

"Are you truly so ignorant, so oblivious? How on earth could I ever despise you?" he exclaimed, leaning closer. "Would I be standing here demanding marriage if I despised you?"

She started. Her heart skipped wildly; she tried to ignore it. She whispered, "Why did you really pursue me?"

"I am a de Warenne," he said, straightening. "As my father said so recently, there is no stopping us, not if it is a question of love."

She gasped. Had she misheard?

Then he shook his head. "I will never believe you wish to be a shopkeeper! A beautiful lady stands before me, but if I strip away that gown, I know La Sauvage lives."

She trembled, afraid she had misunderstood him completely. "I am never giving up the woman I have become. I like her far too much. But you are right, underneath, I still prefer the wind in my hair to a ball. Cliff! What do you mean, a question of love?"

"It means I must have the truth," he demanded, his gaze glittering. "Damn it, Amanda, do I not deserve the truth? I have been haunted by your words—you do not wish to be my ward. Is that not what you said? You ran away, not to be a shopkeeper, but to leave me! What have I done to cause you to dislike me so?" His wide eyes flickered with anguish. "I thought the bond we shared was something far different."

"Cliff! I do not despise you." She hesitated, her heart pounding madly. She had hurt him and she genuinely hated the choice she had made. Worse, he still didn't understand and while she was afraid to confess her love, she had no choice. He deserved the entire truth. "My feelings haven't changed. They will never change," she whispered, reaching out to touch his cheek.

He caught her hand and gripped it tightly, against his chest. "Then I don't understand. How could you leave me?" he demanded. "Do you still love me? Because I made love to you, Amanda, and I have never made love to a woman before."

Amanda cried out, incredulous.

"It was the most miraculous experience of my life, next to the realization I had in the front hall when I saw you in your ball gown. I believe I have loved you since you were a wild child, roaming the beaches of the island. Or maybe I began falling in love with you at King's House, when you tried to assault the governor." His eyes blazed with emotion. "I tried very hard to deny not just my passion for you, but the feelings in my heart. I have never been in love before! Various members of my family have accused me of being obtuse, and now I agree with them. It took that eighteen-day separation for me to realize that I missed you the way I had never missed anyone before. When you came down those stairs, I realized I was fighting not lust, but love." He took a breath and finally, he smiled. Then the smile vanished. "Honor has nothing to do with my proposal." His gaze was fierce. "If you still love me, I must know *now*."

Amanda was dazed. She went into his arms and allowed the tears to fall freely. "I have never stopped loving you. How could I?" Then she looked up. "Is this a dream? Do you really love me? How can you love *me?*"

"Well," he said, smiling, his eyes going soft and dark at once, "if I exclude the obvious, such as your beauty and courage…" His smile faded and his expression became serious. "I admire you as I have never admired anyone. But there is something more. When you were gone—when you left me—I felt lost and incomplete. I felt confused." He hesitated. "I felt fear and panic."

Amanda embraced him, realizing this man had probably never been afraid in his life. "I never wanted to be a shopkeeper," she whispered against his chest. "I never wanted to leave you and I never want to leave you again."

For one moment, he wrapped her as tightly as he could without crushing her. "Thank God," he whispered back, tilting up her face. "Once, you told me you could think of nothing you would rather do than sail with me."

Her heart leaped wildly, explosively. She reached up so she could clasp his beautiful face in her hands. "There is nothing I would rather do."

His smile returned, beatific. He lifted her into his arms. "Then we are going cruising, my darling." He carried her to the bed. "I have missed you. And I intend to show you just how much."

He bent his head and he kissed her deeply. Amanda kissed him back, her heart exploding with so much love and joy, the emotions were almost unbearable. "I feel like Cinderella," she gasped as he laid her down.

He moved on top of her, his smile tender. "I am no prince."

She laughed. "Cliff, you are Prince Charming in the flesh—and I think you know it!"

He grinned with a dimple and began kissing her in a very leisurely and torturous manner. "I am not taking over command of this ship," he murmured when they both came up for air.

Amanda could guess what that meant—ten days spent in his cabin and in his bed. She could barely wait. "I am very pleased. But my darling, do you wish for an audience?"

He smiled at her. "Actually, I wish to give you something, and I do not mind an audience." He sat up, reaching into the pocket of his pale doeskin breeches. Then he held out a huge diamond ring.

Amanda gasped.

"May I?" he asked.

"When did you get this?" But she held out her hand, stunned and amazed.

"Hmm." He slid it on. "You were probably boarding this ship and about to make sail while I was making this purchase."

Her smile vanished and their gazes locked. "I am so sorry," she said.

"I should have told you that I loved you when we were making love."

She touched his jaw. He turned his head and kissed her hand, then he smiled, his eyes taking on a familiar gleam. "How badly do you wish for a society wedding?"

She became still. "I haven't given a wedding of any kind a single thought."

He leaned close, kissed her for a while, then murmured, "Could I persuade you to allow Mac to marry us?"

She sat bolt upright. "Yes."

"That was easy enough," he said, clearly smug and pleased. "But I had hoped for the opportunity to show off my powers of persuasion."

"You can show them off after we are wed," she breathed, shaking in disbelief. "Do you mean…now?"

He stood and held out his hand. "Yes, I do."

She removed her ring, giving it to him, and then took his hand, their gazes locked. With a soft smile, he led her from the cabin, only pausing to retrieve his Bible from his desk. "Mac. You have a wedding to perform. Hand over the helm to Clark."

Mac grinned. "Aye, sir!" He leaped down to the main deck. "Sir, permission to call all hands?"

Cliff shrugged. "I am not captain here. Do as you will."

Mac turned and nodded at Clark. Amanda faced Cliff, who squeezed her hand as footsteps sounded, the sailors from below-decks racing up, those in the yards lithely dropping down. An eternity stretched out and she realized that her every dream was coming true. She was a lady at last, and she had Cliff's heart.

Images of a beautiful life flashed in her mind. She saw them with Ariella and Alexi at Windsong, spending a cozy summer evening on the balcony overlooking the turquoise sea. She saw herself and Cliff in his ebony four-poster bed, lost in the throes of passion. She saw herself cradling an infant child in her arms, with Cliff leaning over her, smiling at them both. Tears blurred her vision.

"Ready, sir?" Mac asked.

"Yes, I am," Cliff said, clearing his throat. "But I would like to say something first. I must make my own vows."

He took both of her hands in his. "Amanda. I hardly know where to begin." His eyes became moist. "You became the center of my life, of my existence, the day I rescued you at King's House. Shortly after, I vowed to protect you and secure your future. Today, I am making those vows come true."

She started to cry.

He smiled, his nose red. "I give you more vows now, my darling. I vow to honor, cherish, respect and admire you. I vow to forsake all others, and most importantly, I vow to love you, with all of my heart and my entire soul, now and forever. Life is uncertain, but I vow now that I will move heaven and earth to give you a life filled with comfort, luxury, joy and peace—a life you so sorely deserve. And Amanda? I will do my utmost to keep the bad at bay and to bring good fortune to our home. I want you to be utterly happy."

Amanda was crying and she could not stop. Cliff de Warenne was a man of his word, and her future had been secured. She took his face in her hands, trembling. "I love you so. You have been my protector and my friend, my guardian and my champion, my lover and my hero, too. You have been everything to me and you are everything to me—you will always be my life. Cliff, you are my heart!" She paused to wipe her eyes.

He bent to kiss her, his expression serious and intent.

"I am hardly done!" she cried.

He smiled. "Please, then."

She inhaled. "I already love Alexi and Ariella, Cliff. I vow to be a loving, kind, compassionate mother to your children. And—" she became shy "—I would like to bear you more children, if you will let me."

His gaze finally swam with tears.

His eyes blazed. "I should like that, too." He was hoarse.

"I gave you my heart on this ship, many months ago, shortly after we made sail," She smiled tremulously at him. "You are my Prince Charming, and I will never stop loving you, Cliff."

His gaze held hers, searching and moist, and she gazed back, overcome. Then he began to smile and he leaned forward to kiss her.

Mac coughed. "No kissing yet, Captain!"

Cliff straightened in surprise as above them chuckles sounded. "I had forgotten," he murmured. "Please, Mac, do proceed."

"Do you, Captain de Warenne, swear to honor, love and cherish this woman, forsaking all others, until death do you part?"

"I do," Cliff said, now grasping her hands.

"Do you, Amanda Carre, also swear to honor, love and cherish this man, in sickness and in health, in good times and bad, until death do you part?"

"I do," Amanda said tremulously.

Mac said firmly, "By the power invested in me as captain of this vessel, I now pronounce you man and wife."

Cliff slid her beautiful ring back on her finger. Amanda went into his arms, and above them in the rigging, around them on the deck, all hands hurrahed.

And then, suddenly, Amanda stiffened, and glanced over her shoulder.

Papa stood there, smiling at her, and then he gave her a small salute. *I've been waiting for this day, Amanda girl. I'll be going now.*

And he vanished.

"Papa," Amanda breathed.

"Amanda?" Cliff asked with concern.

Still in his arms, she raised her face to his, smiling. "Have I told you lately that I love you?"

He smiled back. "Pray tell me again." He started kissing her. And again." He continued kissing her. "But I believe in *show* and tell."

Amanda closed her eyes as he kissed her, showing her his love. He hadn't just secured her future, he had secured her dreams. He was so wrong—he was most definitely a prince—he was *her* prince and nothing was ever going to change that.

# EPILOGUE

*Windhaven, Ireland*

THE BALL WAS IN full swing. As it was the first ball held by the once very notorious—and still rather notorious—Captain de Warenne in the home he had built for his bride, everyone in the three southern counties had come. Just two hours from Adare, the mansion sat on the cliffs overlooking the sea. From outside, it resembled a French palace more than it did an Irishman's country home. Within, it was almost shocking, as the decor was an eclectic mixture of oriental, Middle Eastern and European influences, the furnishings from every corner of the world. Gossip abounded. After all, no one had ever dreamed the greatest rogue of his era would ever marry, much less for love. The whispers held that he had not only built such a grand estate as a testament of his undying love, but that he had put the entire property in his wife's name.

"They are a magnificent couple," The ancient dowager Baroness O'Connell cackled. "He is the most handsome man in Ireland, and she is so delicate, so graceful and so beautiful!"

"A perfect match!" Her good friend the dowager Countess Marion shook her head in agreement, using her quizzing glass to follow the movements of the waltzing couple. The captain and his wife were alone on the dance floor, as this was the first dance of the evening. "He is a very strong dancer," she pronounced. "But she is a bit more advanced, I think. They do not waltz, my dear Katherine, they float!"

"It is as if they have danced together forever. How romantic they are!" She sighed. For one moment, as the members of his family took to the floor, the earl and Countess of Adare ahead of the others, she watched the newlyweds, who seemed entranced by one another. She sighed again. "They are so in love. He cannot keep his gaze from her."

"Well, that is the fate of the de Warenne men—to find true love, never mind the scandal the finding causes, and to love once and forever."

And recalling several recent scandals, including that of the earl and countess Adare, both cronies laughed. For to them, it was but yesterday.

The baroness leaned close and lowered her voice to a whisper. "I did hear the most absurd and ridiculous rumor."

Eagerly, her friend bent to her. "Oh, do tell, Katherine."

"I heard," her whisper lowered, "that Mrs. de Warenne is a pirate's daughter!"

For one moment, the countess blinked, and then she started to laugh, shaking her head, the baroness joining her. "Look at her! She is the epitome of elegance—all young ladies should aspire to such grace and beauty! It is impossible!"

"I agree," the baroness chuckled. "Simply impossible!"

And the two old women laughed at the sheer absurdity of the notion.

**On sale 2nd May 2008**

## *A RECKLESS BEAUTY*

*by Kasey Michaels*

**A rebellious innocent**

Fanny Beckett has adored her adopted brother forever – where he goes, she follows. But when she pursues him into battle, Fanny finds herself not only in the line of fire but also in the embrace of a handsome stranger!

**A jaded lord**

Valentine Clement, Earl of Brede, has seen enough of fighting to know that there is no adventure to be found at Waterloo. The moment he sees the reckless beauty, he is duty-bound to save her. Although with such a woman, it may well be his lordship who is in need of protection…

*Available at WHSmith, Tesco, ASDA, and all good bookshops*

*www.millsandboon.co.uk*

On sale 2nd May 2008

## *AN UNCONVENTIONAL MISS*

*by Dorothy Elbury*

Miss Jessica Beresford is headstrong, impetuous and poorly dowered. Benedict Ashcroft, Earl of Wyvern, knows he should steer well clear of her, however dazzling her beauty. He cannot dally with such an unconventional miss…can he?

## *THE WARRIOR'S TOUCH*

*by Michelle Willingham*

When Connor MacEgan's hands are crushed, he may never wield a sword – or touch a woman – again. Aileen holds a secret that could break their hearts long after she has mended his hands…

## *THE SCOUNDREL*

*by Lisa Plumley*

Brawny blacksmith Daniel McCabe is not the marrying kind. He likes his freedom just fine, and no lady is going to change *that!* But an unexpected delivery will make the bachelor rethink his roguish ways.

*Available at WHSmith, Tesco, ASDA, and all good bookshops*

*www.millsandboon.co.uk*

0508_11_MB146

# *A delicious addition to the Moreland family novels!*

*Gloucestershire, 1878*

Ever since Anna Holcombe refused his proposal, Reed Moreland has been unable to set foot in the home that was the backdrop to their romance – Winterset.

But when Reed has dreams about Anna being in danger, he heads back to Winterset, determined to protect the woman he still loves. Once again passion flares between them, but the murder of a servant girl draws them deep into deadly legends of Winterset…and a destiny neither Anna nor Reed can escape.

**Available 18th April 2008**

www.millsandboon.co.uk